Critical acclaim for David Baldacci's novels

'It's big, bold and almost impossible to put down . . .
Decker is one of the most unusual detectives any
novelist has dreamed up . . . I called this novel a
master class on the bestseller because of its fast-moving
narrative, the originality of its hero and its irresistible
plot . . . Highly entertaining'
Washington Post

'Skilfully constructed . . . Difficult to put down . . .
Another winner'
Booklist

'Brilliant plotting, heart-grabbing action
and characters to die for'
Daily Mail

'Baldacci inhabits the skin of his creations –
tripping us up with unexpected empathy and
subtle identification'
Sunday Express

'As expertly plotted as all Baldacci's work'
Sunday Times

'Baldacci cuts everyone's grass – Grisham's,
Ludlum's even Patricia Cornwell's – and more
than gets away with it'
People

The Last Mile

David Baldacci is a worldwide bestselling novelist. With his books published in over 45 languages and in more than 80 countries, and with over 110 million copies in print, he is one of the world's favourite storytellers. His works have been adapted for both feature-film and television. David is also the co-founder, along with his wife, of the Wish You Well Foundation®, a non-profit organization dedicated to supporting literacy efforts across America. Still a resident of his native Virginia, he invites you to visit him at DavidBaldacci.com and his foundation at WishYouWellFoundation.org.

DAVID BALDACCI

The Last Mile

PAN BOOKS

First published 2016 by Grand Central Publishing, USA

First published in the UK 2016 by Macmillan

This edition published in the UK in paperback 2016 by Pan Books
an imprint of Pan Macmillan
The Smithson, 6 Briset Street, London EC1M 5NR
Associated companies throughout the world
www.panmacmillan.com

ISBN 978-1-4472-7753-8

13

A CIP catalogue record for this book is available from the British Library.

Typeset by Ellipsis Digital Limited, Glasgow
Printed and bound by CPI Group (UK) Ltd, Croydon, CR0 4YY

To the memories of Alison Parker and Adam Ward,
two brilliant lights taken from us far too soon.

And to Vicki Gardner,
whose courage and grace are inspiring testaments
to the resiliency of the human spirit.

The Last Mile

1

Mars, Melvin.

In here, anywhere, anytime, they called out your name backward, and he would instantly respond when he heard his.

Even on the toilet. Like being in the military, only he'd never joined. He'd been brought here very much against his will.

"Mars, Melvin?"

"Yes, sir. Here, sir. Taking a crap, sir."

Because where else would I be except here, sir?

He didn't know why they did it this way and had never bothered to ask. The answer would not have mattered to him in the least. And it might have led to a guard baton slamming against the side of his head.

He had other things to concern him here at the Texas State Penitentiary at Huntsville. It was called the Walls Unit because of the prison's redbrick walls. Opened in 1849, it was the oldest prison in the Lone Star State.

And it also housed the execution chamber.

Mars was officially Prisoner 7-4-7, like the plane.

The guards at the death row prison from which he'd been brought called him "Jumbo" because of it. And while he wasn't huge, he wasn't small either. Most folks would look up to him, if only because they had to. Six-two, plus three-quarters of an inch tacked on for good measure.

He knew his exact height only because they'd measured him precisely at the NFL combine. They'd measured everything about him at the combine. While going through the process his mind had drawn parallels to slaves on the market square as potential owners methodically poked and prodded the merchandise. Well, unlike his slave ancestors, at least he would have had lots of money to deal with the wreckage of his body after his playing days were over.

He was also still two hundred and thirty pounds. No fat, just rock. No mean feat with the crap they served for food in here, processed in huge factories, loaded with fat and sodium, as well as chemicals they probably used to make everything from concrete to carpets.

Killing me softly with your crappy food.

He'd been in this place almost as long as he'd not been in this place.

And the time had not gone by fast. It didn't feel like twenty years. It felt like two hundred.

But it didn't matter anymore. It would be over soon. This was the day.

His final, final appeal.

Denied.

He was dead.

He had been brought to the Huntsville Prison from the Polunsky Unit's death row in Livingston, Texas, sixty miles to the east, in anticipation that this time the state would get its man after a two-decades-long wait. His lawyer's pale face had held a bleak expression when she'd conveyed this news to him. But she would wake up the next day.

Not me.

Soon he would be listening for the tap-tap of heels heading his way.

The puffing of the burly guards holding the shiny shackles.

The solemn warden who would forget his name the next day.

The pious man of God clutching his Bible and reading aloud his verses because you were supposed to have something spiritual to cling to on your way out of here. Not out of prison. Out of life.

Texas executed more inmates than any other state, over five hundred in just the last thirty years. For nearly a century, starting in 1819, they did it by hanging. Then they used the electric chair called "Old Sparky", and three hundred and sixty-one inmates had been put to death by electrocution over four decades. Now Texas used lethal injection to send you off to the hereafter.

Either way you were still dead.

By law, executions could not begin before 6 p.m. Mars had been told that they would come for him at midnight. Well, nothing like dragging this out, he thought. Made for a really long and really shitty day.

Walking Dead Man, he'd been called.

"Good riddance," he'd heard more times than he could count from the guards.

He didn't want to look back. Not to the epicenter of this whole thing.

But really, how could he not?

So as the final moment neared, he started to think of them.

The murders of Roy and Lucinda Mars, his white father and black mother.

Back then that combination had been weird, different, exotic even, certainly in West Texas. Now it was commonplace. Every kid coming in now looked like bits and pieces of fifty different types of humanity.

One recently incarcerated punk was the product of biracial parents, who in turn were also the children of nontraditional pairings. So the new kid—an idiot who'd blown away a store clerk over a shoplifted bag of Twizzlers—was a mishmash of black, brown, and white, with a dash of Chinese thrown in. And he was also a Muslim, though Mars had never seen the man get on his knees and pray five times a day, as some did in here. His name was Anwar. He was originally from Colorado.

And he had started telling people he really wanted to become Alexis.

Mars sat up on the bunk in his cell and looked at his watch. It was time to do his thing. The last time he would ever do this, in fact.

His jumpsuit was white, and on the back were the letters D and R printed in black. They stood for "death row". Mars had equated it to a snake's rattle, warning folks to stay the hell away.

He dropped to the coolness of the concrete floor and did two hundred push-ups, first on fists and then on fingertips, and finally from the downward dog position, lightly touching the crown of his bald head on the concrete with each pass. Next he performed three hundred deep squats in sets of six, exploding up with every rep—depth charges, he called them. Then followed yoga and Pilates for strength, balance, range of motion, and, most important, flexibility. He could touch his toes to his forehead with his legs ramrod straight, no small feat for a big, ropy-muscled man.

Then came the thousand stomach and core reps that seared his abs like acid. It was the reason he had rock-hard obliques, and an eight-pack, his belly button stretched so tight it looked more like a mole than where his umbilical cord had once attached. Next came flat-out plyomania where he pushed off all four walls and the floor in a series of maneuvers, many of his own devising.

He was like Spider-Man, or Fred Astaire dancing

on ceilings. He had a lot of hours to plan such things in prison. His life was very structured, but it also offered up a load of free time. Most inmates just sat around doing nothing. There were no classes, no rehabilitation of any kind.

The unofficial prison motto was straightforward:

Rehab is for pussies.

Finally, Mars ran in place for so long that he lost track of time, high-kneeing it the whole way. It was crazy that he was doing this today of all days. But he had done it pretty much every day since he'd been in here, and part of him felt this was his last act of defiance. They would not rob him of it. At least he didn't have to refuse the traditional final meal, because Texas no longer offered one. He didn't want their crap inside him at the end. He preferred to die on an empty stomach.

No one had visited him, because he had no one who wanted to visit him. He was alone, as he had been the last twenty years. He wondered what the papers would say the next day. It would be a small story probably. There was nothing new about another black man getting the Lone Star State's lethal spa treatment. Hell, it was hardly worth a photo. But they would recount the crimes of which he'd been convicted. Surely they would. And that would be the only memory of him for many.

Melvin Mars, the murderer.

He cooled down, the sweat pooling off him and

staining the concrete that was already badly scarred with far worse things than perspiration. Condemned men had been known to defecate on the floor before they walked to their deaths.

As his breathing normalized he sat on his bunk and tipped his head back against the wall. In his old cell he had named the walls Reed, Sue, Johnny, and Ben, after the superhero fighting team the Fantastic Four. It was just something do in a place where he had nothing to do. Each day filled with whatever he could think of to fill it.

Mars often fantasized about sexy Sue Storm, but he more closely related to Ben Grimm, the Thing, the freak. As an athlete Mars had been a freak, in a good way.

Yet he could be thoughtful, like the brainy Reed.

He also related to the flame ball Johnny Storm, Sue's kid brother, because he felt like he was on fire every second of every day. Principally because every day was like every other day in here. A living hell, actually, hence the flames.

This was Day 7,342 for him. The last day for him.

He looked at his watch again.

Five ticks till Doomsday.

He had spent a year in solitary shortly after going to prison. The reason was simple. His life was over, his dreams shattered, his hard work for naught, and he was pissed beyond all reckoning.

His punishment for beating the crap out of three

prisoners and then taking on a half-dozen guards and more than holding his own until they Tased and nearly clubbed him to death? Twenty-four hours a day in a sixty-square-foot cell with a slit for a window for a year. No words spoken to him. Never saw another face. Never felt the touch of someone else's skin. The food was shoved through the door slot along with toilet paper and occasionally washcloths and soap and even less occasionally clean prison garb.

He showered in a corner where the water was either ice or scalding. He slept on the floor, and mumbled, screamed, cursed, and finally sobbed. That's when he'd realized that human beings, for better or worse, were undeniably social creatures. Without interaction they went mad.

And Mars *had* nearly gone mad inside that cell. It had been Day 169. He remembered it clearly, had even scratched the numbers out on the wall with bloody fingernails. His mind had nearly gone; there was but one shred left. And he had used that shred like a life vest in a tsunami, his port in the storm. He had focused on an imaginary old girlfriend, Tatiana. In his mind she was married now with six kids, big-hipped and bloated, surly and unhappy, and so missing him. But back then this imagined person had been perfect. Her face, her body, her limitless love for him allowed him to survive Day 169 and then make it through 196 more.

When the door opened the first face he saw was

Tatiana's superimposed over the body of a three-hundred-pound racist nightmare of a young guard named, aptly, Big Dick, who told Mars to get his mulatto butt up or else he'd be eating through a straw for the rest of his life.

And when it was over Melvin Mars was a changed man. He had never done anything that would ever put him back in there. If he did, he knew that he would have killed himself. He wouldn't have waited for the death chamber.

Death chamber.

It was right down the hall. The last mile, they called it. Yet it wasn't a mile. It was actually only thirty feet, which was good because most guys collapsed before they got there. But they had big guards who picked you up and carried you the rest of the way.

Texas killed you dead whether you took it brave or not.

The Supreme Court had debated the cruel and unusual aspects of death by lethal injection because of quite a few instances where the inmate had been in terrible agony before he died. The court had come down on the side of letting it continue, appalling agony be damned. It wasn't like the condemneds' victims hadn't suffered horrific pain and fear. So who could say they were wrong? Mars couldn't. He just hoped they got it right with him.

The death chamber was not large, nine by twelve feet, with cheery turquoise-painted brick walls and metal door, which seemed out of place with the room's purpose. You were being executed, not vacationing in the Caribbean.

The gurney, which came with a comfy pillow and sturdy leather straps, was set near the center of the room. There were two adjacent rooms with glass windows looking into the chamber. One was for families of the victims. The other was for family of the person being executed.

Mars knew that in his case the groups were one and the same. And he also knew that both rooms would be empty.

He sat back on his bunk soaking in the stink of his own sweat, his mind drifting back to the only good memories he had left.

He was hardly a jumbo in the world of college football, but he'd been big for a running back. Most important, he'd been long on talent. The NFL was considered a lock for someone like him. He had been a Heisman Trophy finalist his senior year, the only tailback in the group. The others had all been quarterbacks. He could run over, around, or simply through anyone. He could block, and his soft hands could catch the ball coming out of the backfield. And he nearly always made the first guy miss with an instinctive lateral move—a rare talent the NFL gurus lapped up.

And when he needed the turbos they flared to life and he was gone. The only thing left to do was hand the ball to the ref after scoring and go let coach pat his butt on the sidelines.

His official time in the forty-yard dash at the combine was 4.31 seconds. Twenty years ago that was serious speed even for a corner or a receiver, much less a monster running back with shoulders as wide as the sky who made his living smashing between the tackles. And it would still be considered exceptional wheels even today.

God-given it was. He was the total package. A freak of nature, they called him.

He felt a smile spread across his sweaty face.

Yes, a lock. A lock with a big paycheck. This was long before the salary constraints for rookies had been implemented. He could have scored big bucks from day one, millions and millions of them. A mansion, cars, women, respect.

He was a guaranteed first rounder, everyone said. Probably top five. He would probably go ahead of several of the quarterbacks he had competed against for the Heisman. It was rumored that the New York Giants, coming off a couple crappy years, and the Tampa Bay Bucs, coming off many crappy years, and both armed with a high draft pick, would love to take him and open the bank of their wealthy owners in doing so. Hell, he might even hoist some Super Bowl hardware one day. It was all looking good. He'd worked his ass off for all of it. No one had given him anything. The hurdles had been immense. He had leapt them all.

And then the *jury* had spoken. "We find the defendant *guilty*"—and no one in the world of professional football gave a damn about 4.31 Mars, Melvin anymore.

Jumbo had crashed.

There were no survivors.

And in a few minutes, there would be no more of him. He would be laid to rest in a potter's field because he had no one left to bury him proper.

He would have been forty-two years old in two months. His forty-first had been his very last birthday, as it turned out.

He looked at his watch again. The time was up. His watch told him that, and so did the sound of the footsteps coming down the hall.

He had long since made up his mind. He would die like a man. Back straight, head high.

Suddenly he felt a lump in his throat and his eyes moistened. He tried to breathe normally, trying to keep it all together. This was it. He looked around his cell and saw the walls of his death row cage back at the Polunsky Unit.

See you, Sue, you fine woman. Adios, Johnny. Godspeed, Ben. Take care, Reed.

He stood and put his back against the wall, maybe to stiffen his spine.

The Last Mile

Like going to sleep, man. You just ain't waking up is all. Like going to sleep.

The door to his cell opened and the men were revealed standing there. Three suits and four uniforms. The suits looked terrified, the uniforms ticked off.

Mars noted this, and also that there was no man of the cloth holding his Bible.

Something was definitely off.

The man with slender glasses and a build to match stepped gingerly into the cell as though he expected the door to close, trapping him inside forever.

Mars could seriously relate to the feeling.

The other suits' expressions were now wary, like they knew there was a bomb in here somewhere but they had no idea when it might go off.

Skinny Glasses cleared his throat. He looked at the floor, the wall, the ceiling, the one light high up on the ceiling, everywhere except at Mars. It was as though the big, sweaty biracial dude five feet from him was invisible.

He cleared his throat again. To Mars it sounded like all the muck jostling around in the world's largest sewer.

Staring at the floor now, Skinny Glasses said, "There's been an unexpected development in your case. Your execution has been called off."

Mars, Melvin didn't say anything back.

2

He was still dressed in his white jumpsuit with the warning on the back, but something else was missing. He had been taken from his cell to this room without having to don the chains, a first since his time in prison. Although a half dozen guards lined the wall just in case he became unruly.

Four men sat across from him. He didn't know any of them. They were all white, all dressed in baggy suits. The youngest was about his age. They looked like they would rather be anyplace else on earth.

They stared across at Mars. And he just as resolutely stared back at them.

He wasn't going to say anything. They had brought him to the party. They were going to have to start the music.

The man in the center of the table rustled some papers set in front of him. "I'm sure you're wondering what's going on, Mr. Mars."

Mars inclined his head slightly but still didn't say anything. He hadn't heard a white guy call him "mister" since . . . hell, he couldn't remember a white guy ever calling him that. At the NFL combine they'd just called him "Holy Shit." In prison they called him whatever they wanted to.

The man continued. "The fact is that someone else has confessed to committing the murders that you were convicted of."

Mars blinked a few times and sat up straighter. He put his huge hands that had made soft targets for many a quarterback on the table.

"Who?" His voice felt strangely unfamiliar, as though someone else was speaking on his behalf.

The man glanced down the table at one of his colleagues, who was older and looked more in control than the rest. This man nodded at the younger gent.

The first man said, "His name is Charles Montgomery."

"Where is he?"

"In a state prison in Alabama. He's actually also awaiting execution. For unrelated crimes."

"Do you believe he did it?" asked Mars.

"We're investigating."

"What does he know?" asked Mars. "About the murders?"

The man again looked at the older man. This time the fellow seemed indecisive.

Mars sensed this and swiveled his gaze to him. "Why else would you have stopped my execution? Because some con in 'Bama said he did it? I don't think so. He had to *know* something. That only the real killer would have."

The older man nodded and seemed to view Mars in a new and more favorable light. He said, "He did. Certain things that only the murderer would have known, you're exactly right on that point."

"Okay, that makes sense," said Mars, taking a deep breath. Despite his words, he couldn't seem to process what they were telling him.

"Do you know Mr. Montgomery?" asked the first man.

Mars turned his attention back to him. "Never heard of him until you said his name. Why?"

"Just trying to verify certain facts."

Mars nodded again. He knew exactly what "fact" the guy was getting at. Had Mars hired Montgomery to kill his parents?

"I don't know him," he said flatly. He looked around the room. "So now what?"

"You will remain in prison until certain things can be . . . verified."

"And what if you can't verify them?"

The older man said, "You have been duly convicted of murder, Mr. Mars. That conviction was upheld over many appeals over many years. You were scheduled to be executed tonight. All that cannot be overturned in a few hours. The process has to be given a chance to work."

"So how long before the process works its magic?"

The man shook his head. "I can't give you a reliable timetable now. I wish I could, but it would be impossible. I can tell you that we have folks on the way to Alabama to interview Mr. Montgomery more thoroughly. And on this end the Texas authorities have reopened the investigation. We are doing all we can to see that justice is done, I can assure you."

"Well, if he said he killed my parents and I'm still in prison waiting to die, I'd say that justice *isn't* being done."

"You have to be patient, Mr. Mars."

"Well, I've been patient for twenty years."

"Then a bit more time will not inconvenience you any."

"Does my attorney know?"

"She has been informed and is on her way here as we speak."

"She should be part of this investigation."

"And she will be. We want full and complete transparency here. Nothing less. Again, our goal is the truth."

"I'm nearly forty-two. What about all these years of my life gone? Who's gonna pay for that?"

The man's face turned to granite and his tone became more officious. "We need to deal with one thing at a time in a professional manner. That is how it has to be."

Mars looked away, blinking rapidly. He doubted that if these guys were in his shoes they would be so calm and professional about it. They'd be screaming bloody murder, threatening to sue everyone even remotely involved in all this. But he was just supposed to deal with one thing at a time. Be patient. It shouldn't be an inconvenience.

The hell with you!

He wanted to go back to his cell, the only place he really felt safe. He rose.

The men looked surprised.

Mars said, "Let me know when you get this all figured out, okay? You know where to find me."

"We actually had some more questions for you, Mr. Mars," said the first man.

"You can send them through my attorney," he said. "I'm done talking. Figure the ball's in your court. You know everything about me and the case against me. What you need to do now is do the same on this Montgomery dude. If he did kill my parents, then I want out of here. Sooner the better."

The guards took him back to his cell. Later that morning he was transported via prison van back to death row at the Polunsky Unit.

As he was being escorted to his old cell one of the guards whispered to him, "You think you gettin' outta here, boy? I don't think so. Don't care what them suits say. You a killer, Jumbo. And you goin' to die for your crimes."

Mars kept walking. He didn't even turn his head to look at the man, a reedy-looking punk with a huge

Adam's apple. He was always the one to give Mars a hard jab in the back with his baton for no reason at all. Or spit in his face when no one was looking. Yet if Mars took a swing at him he'd be rotting in here forever, regardless of what happened with this Montgomery guy in Alabama.

The cell door clanged shut and Mars, his legs oddly wobbly, lurched over and fell rather than sat on his bunk.

He immediately hauled himself up and from long habit put his back against the concrete wall and faced the door. No one could attack him through concrete. But the door was another matter.

His mind went over all that had just happened in the last ten hours.

His execution was to take place. He was prepared for that, or as much as anyone could be.

And then it had been called off. But if they weren't convinced by this guy in Alabama, could they still execute him? The answer to that, he knew, was probably hell yes.

Don't mess with Texas.

He closed his eyes. He wasn't sure exactly what emotions he was supposed to have. Happy, nervous, relieved, anxious?

Well, he was feeling all of them. Mostly, he was feeling that somehow, some way, he was never leaving this place. Regardless of what the "investigation" showed.

19

He wasn't being fatalistic. Simply realistic.

He started to sing a tune under his breath, so the guards wouldn't be able to hear. Perhaps it was stupid under the circumstances, but it felt right anyway.

Oh when the saints, oh when the saints, oh when the saints go marching in, oh Lord I want to be in that number, when the saints go marching in.

3

On the very last day of the year, Amos Decker sat in his rental car in the drive-through line at a Burger King near the Ohio-Pennsylvania border pondering what to order.

Most of what he owned was in the backseat and trunk of the car. He still had some things back at a storage unit in Burlington. He could not part with them, but he didn't have the room to bring them with him either.

He was a big man, six-five, and about halfway between three and four hundred pounds—the exact number depended on how much he ate at a particular meal. He was a former college football player with a truncated stint in the NFL, where a vicious blindside hit had altered his mind and given him pretty much a perfect memory. Hyperthymesia, as it was technically known.

It sounded cool.

It wasn't.

But it had been nothing compared to walking into his house one night to find his wife, brother-in-law, and daughter brutally murdered. That killer was no longer among the living. Decker had seen to that. But the conclusion of that case had also led him to move from Burlington, Ohio, to Virginia to take up a unique position with the FBI.

He still didn't know how he felt about it. Thus he ordered two Whoppers, two large fries, and a Coke so big he had difficulty holding it even in his huge hand. When he was anxious, he ate.

When he was really anxious he was a garbage disposal.

He sat in the parking lot and devoured his meal, the salt on the fries sticking to his fingers and sprinkling across his lap. Outside the snow was falling lightly. He had started his journey late and was tired, so he wouldn't finish the drive tonight. He would grab a bed at a motel in the Keystone State and then complete his journey the next day.

Special Agent Ross Bogart, the man he would be working for at the FBI, had told him that all of his traveling expenses, within reason, would be covered. He'd actually offered to fly Decker to Virginia, but Decker had declined. He wanted to drive. He wanted some time to himself. He would be working at the FBI with a woman he'd met in Burlington, a journalist named Alexandra Jamison. She'd shown her smarts during the investigation of his family's murder, and Bogart also wanted her as part of his unusual team.

Bogart had laid out to Decker the details of his vision of this team when they'd both been back in Burlington. It would operate out of the FBI's Quantico platform. It would bring together FBI agents and civilians with special skills to reopen and, one hoped, solve cold cases.

Maybe we'll be a team of misfits, Decker thought.

He didn't know how he actually felt about moving to the East Coast and essentially starting over. But he'd figured he had nothing left in Burlington, so why not? At least that was how he had felt last week. Now he wasn't as confident.

Christmas had come and gone. Today was New Year's Eve. People would be out partying and celebrating the coming new year. Decker would not be among them. He had nothing to celebrate, despite the new job and new life. He had lost his family. Nothing could replace them, thus he would never have anything to celebrate.

He threw the bag of trash into a receptacle in the parking lot, climbed back into his car, and drove off. He turned on the radio. The top of the hour was coming up as he found the local NPR station. The news was coming on. The lead story had to do with a death row inmate whose life had been spared, melodramatically, at the last minute.

It had been a last-second Christmas present, the announcer said.

The man's name was Melvin Mars. And he had

23

been convicted over twenty years ago of killing his parents. Now, all of his appeals had been denied and the state of Texas was ready to take the man's life as punishment for his crimes.

But startling new evidence had emerged, the announcer said.

A prisoner in Alabama had confessed to the crime and had allegedly offered up details that only the real killer could have known. Mars, a former college All-American, Heisman Trophy finalist, and top NFL prospect, was currently still behind bars as he awaited the results of the ensuing investigation. But if that investigation verified the confession, reported the announcer, then Melvin Mars could go free, after two decades behind bars. His NFL dream was over, of course, but perhaps justice would finally be served, if a bit late.

Damn, thought Decker, as he turned off the radio. *Some justice for Melvin Mars.*

Then his mind started whirring, his memories flashing past in neat chronological order, though Decker did not really need his hyperthymesia to remember this one.

Melvin Mars was a star running back at the University of Texas. The Longhorns had played Decker's team, the Buckeyes of Ohio State, on the last week of the regular season in a nationally televised game. Decker had played linebacker on his squad. He was tall for a linebacker and was a good player, but not

24

great. He had the size, strength, and toughness, but didn't have the wheels and pure athleticism of the truly outstanding players.

Mars had made life miserable that afternoon for Decker and the Buckeyes. Texas had ended up winning by a whopping five touchdowns and ruining any chance Ohio State had for a national championship.

Mars himself had scored four times. Three by running and once with a nifty catch-and-run starting at the Buckeyes' thirty-five-yard line. Decker remembered that one well. He had been covering Mars on the play as he came out of the backfield.

He had hit Mars with everything he had as soon as he caught the ball. But Mars had somehow managed to keep on his feet, juked the corner and then the safety, and then run over another safety coming in near the goal line as Decker lay on the field thirty yards back. It had seemed like the fifth time Mars had gotten the better of him that day. As his coaches later pointed out on film day, it was actually the tenth.

Decker had gone to the bench after that hit and miss. The Longhorns were up by twenty-eight points with less than six minutes remaining. They would tack on one more score when they got the ball back after an interception. It was Mars again who hit the Buckeyes' starting middle linebacker—a wall of granite named Eddie Keys, who would go on to play twelve years with the Forty-Niners—so hard that the man had been blown backward into the end zone as Mars made his last score of the day.

Melvin Mars.

Decker had thought the guy would be a shoo-in for the NFL too. It was a big story back then about Mars being arrested. But Decker had been working hard for his own shot at the big leagues and the arrest and conviction of Melvin Mars finally had faded into the past.

Two decades in prison. For a crime he maybe didn't commit.

Another man had confessed. Had details only the real killer would know.

It was so close to the murders of Decker's family that not even his unique mind could grapple with the possible odds of it.

He drove right through Pennsylvania, and then south into Maryland and farther south into Virginia. He didn't stop to sleep. His mind was alert and awake and thinking.

He was thinking about Melvin Mars.

A name from the past.

Decker did not believe in fate, or even its little cousin, serendipity.

Yet something had made him turn on the radio right at that very moment. If he had taken a couple minutes longer to eat his meal, or stopped to take a leak, he might never have heard the story.

But he *had* heard the story.

So what did that mean?

He wasn't sure. And he also wasn't sure that the name Melvin Mars would ever leave him again.

Hours later he reached the address he'd been given. It was at the Marine Corps Base Quantico, one of the largest U.S. Marine bases in the world, and also home to a basketful of federal law enforcement platforms.

The facility was behind high fences with a guard gate where serious men in uniform stood holding automatic weapons.

Amos Decker drove up to the gate, rolled down his window, drew a long breath, and prepared to start his brand-new life.

4

Three rooms.

A bedroom about the size of a prison cell. A bathroom about a quarter the size of that. And a third room for everything else, including the kitchen.

It was far more space than Amos Decker had been accustomed to over the last year and a half.

He set his bags down and looked around his new home. He should grab some sleep, but he wasn't tired.

He could sleep all day sometimes, but other times, like now, his mind would not allow him to rest. His brain was on fire.

There was a small table across from the kitchen area. On the table was a laptop computer with a note stuck to it. The note was from Agent Bogart. The laptop was his to use. There was secure WiFi here. Bogart would be by later.

Decker checked his watch. It was five in the morning. Bogart had expected him to stop on his drive and probably anticipated his arriving here later this afternoon or evening.

Decker made a cup of coffee, black, with a heap of

sugar, and carried it over to the table. He sat down and opened up the laptop. He went online and searched for the name Melvin Mars.

There had been quite a few stories written in the last few days on Mars. Decker read all of them, his perfect memory imprinting each indelibly onto his brain.

But he also wanted to know more about the man's past. And a few minutes later he found it.

Melvin Mars had been on the cusp of the NFL draft held in April of each year. It was projected he would go top five until he'd been arrested and charged in the murders of his parents, Roy and Lucinda Mars.

Decker looked at the grainy pictures of the pair on the screen. Roy was white, with strong features, and even in the blurry photo his penetrating eyes were readily apparent. Lucinda was black and remarkably beautiful, with bountiful hair that fell to her shoulders. Her face was crinkled into an infectious smile.

Clear opposites, at least on the surface. Interesting.

Decker sipped his coffee and kept scrolling.

The murders had taken place on April second. The bodies were found in an upstairs bedroom. Both had been shotgunned, their faces obliterated, and then their bodies set on fire. The house stood by itself well off the road. They lived in rural Texas. There had been no one around to hear them die.

The bodies were found by firemen responding to a

911 call. The fire was put out and the house became a crime scene.

Folks around there knew the Marses. Well, they knew Melvin because of his talents on the gridiron. He had been a high school football legend in Texas, and had continued that fame in college as a Longhorn.

So where was Melvin when his parents died?

He had graduated from college the previous semester, having gone to summer school each of the last three years in order to graduate early. He had plans for his life, it had been reported then. And with the draft coming up he wanted to be free from academic obligations. He was a man who thought ahead, it was said. He was not some people's image of a football player who could run over people but didn't have the means to carry on a conversation. It was said that he didn't have an agent because he was going to negotiate his own contract with an NFL team. He had done research, talked to current and former players.

So, again, where was Melvin?

The police found him sleeping alone at a motel. He had paid by credit card. That was how they located him.

His story had been relatively simple. He had been visiting a friend. He had left the friend's place with the intention of driving home. He had had car trouble, however, and stopped for the night at the only motel on that stretch of road. He had known nothing about his parents' murders until the police knocked on his door.

This was before everyone had cell phones or email addresses, or a Facebook page or Twitter account. You could actually be off the grid with no way for folks to contact you, an unbelievable thought now.

Mars had not initially been a suspect. He had gone into seclusion even as rewards were offered for any information about the crimes. A period of time went by as the police investigated.

Decker focused on one story that detailed how Mars had become a suspect.

The friend he had visited remembered Mars leaving earlier than he had told the police he had. The motel was less than an hour from his house, so why didn't he simply drive the rest of the way that night? Again, Mars said he'd had car trouble and pulled into the motel. He planned to call his father the next morning to come out and check the car.

The only problem with that was when the police asked him to try to start the car, it roared to life immediately. He had no explanation for that other than to say the engine had sputtered and then died right as he reached the motel. He said he'd actually pushed it into the parking lot. The other troublesome fact was that a car resembling his had been seen later that night in the vicinity of his parents' house.

The motel clerk told police that Mars had checked in at 1:15 in the morning. The friend said Mars had left her place at ten. It was only an hour-and-forty-minute drive to his home from there. That left time for him to drive home, kill his parents, and then drive back and check into the motel.

The motel clerk testified that Mars seemed disheveled and upset. He also testified that the clothes Mars had on appeared stained with something. The clothes he described Mars as wearing were not the ones he had on when the police showed up. It was conjectured that Mars had dumped the bloody clothes somewhere and then changed into a fresh set at the motel.

The other troublesome fact was that the shotgun belonged to Mars. He used it for hunting, and had indeed hunted game birds and turkeys with it. Thus his prints were on the weapon.

And the gasoline used to ignite the Marses' bodies had come from their garage. It was fortunate that that house had not burned down. The only damage was in the bedroom where they'd been found.

Lastly, blood matching Lucinda Mars's had been found in the car. It was pretty damning forensically.

Decker rose to pour another cup of coffee. It was growing lighter outside. He was oblivious to this. He sat back down and kept reading.

But what would be the motive for Mars to kill his parents?

After he was arrested and charged with the murders, the police announced their theory. With the NFL draft coming up and Mars expected to sign a huge contract, it had come down to money. His parents wanted more of it than Mars was willing to share. There had been arguments. Mars had felt jammed. He didn't want negative publicity. He had carefully groomed his image in the hope of getting lucrative endorsement deals in addition to his football contract. He had his whole life mapped out. His parents potentially stood in the way of that, at least according to the prosecution.

So to get rid of this problem, Mars had planned and then executed their murders. He had visited the friend to establish an alibi, gone home, killed them, and then driven to the motel. However, like many killers, he had tripped over the small details. But it was really the timeline that had crashed everything for him. No matter how much you plan things out, if you were indeed in one place killing someone while you said you were in another place sleeping, the timeline can never be made foolproof. There will always be cracks, even if only small ones. But if the police focus on them and start digging, those cracks can grow large and bring the whole lie down.

And that apparently was what happened to Melvin Mars.

So the prosecution could show motive and they could show opportunity. And it was Mars's own gun—constituting the necessary means—that had done the deed. Thus they had all three essential elements to prove guilt. And they set about to convincingly prove it all beyond a reasonable doubt.

Witness after witness was paraded before the jury and gave their testimony. The mosaic began to form. The prosecutor, a Tennessee grad and thus no fan of Texas football players, it seemed, did a bang-up job stitching the evidence together.

The defense tried to poke holes but didn't do enough damage. And when Mars did not take the stand the defense rested.

The jury was out barely enough time for the jurors to use the bathroom before they came back with their guilty verdict.

Mars had been given a fair trial. The evidence met the burden of proof.

Roy and Lucinda Mars had been killed by their only child, Melvin.

The punishment of death had been imposed. Mars's NFL career was over before it even started. And so was the rest of his life.

End of story.

He had been scheduled to be executed, when another man had come forward and confessed to the crime.

Charles Montgomery.

Decker studied the photo of the man on the computer screen.

White guy, in his seventies. Muscled, tough and mean-looking. Army vet with a lengthy criminal record. He'd gone from petty crap, to serious stuff, to very serious stuff. He was in a prison in Alabama awaiting his own execution on several other murders committed years ago.

So if Montgomery was telling the truth, how had the case against Melvin Mars gone so badly sideways?

Reports said he had details of the crime that the police had withheld all these years, just as a matter of standard procedure. Montgomery apparently knew some of them. But why come forward at all? Because he was already in prison? Because he felt remorse? Because he was going to die anyway? To Decker, who had lots of experience with hardened criminals, Montgomery simply didn't look like the remorseful type. He just looked like the killer that he was.

Decker finished his coffee and sat back.

Someone knocked on his door. He looked at his watch. Seven-thirty.

He answered the door.

Special Agent Bogart looked back at him. He was carrying a large briefcase. He was well into his forties, tall and fit, with dark hair attractively mingled with silver. He possessed the air of quiet authority that one acquired by commanding people in difficult assignments. Childless, he was also separated from his wife and in the process of divorcing.

Behind him was Alex Jamison. She was tall and pretty, with brown hair, and her expressive eyes lit up when she saw Decker. She was holding a bag of food.

A jubilant Jamison said, "Surprise. Happy New Year!"

A beaming Bogart said, "I got word you had arrived early. Welcome to the FBI."

Amos Decker said, "I have a case I want to investigate."

5

Decker munched on his bacon, egg, and cheese biscuit. Meanwhile, Jamison and Bogart were reading the articles on the laptop about Melvin Mars.

Bogart finally looked up and said, "Fascinating stuff, but that's not really in our jurisdiction, Amos."

Decker finished eating, took a final swallow of coffee, rolled up the wrapper, and made a three-pointer into the trash can next to the kitchen counter.

"What exactly is our *jurisdiction*, then?"

In answer Bogart opened up the briefcase and pulled out a large binder. He handed this to Decker. "I've already given Alex hers. These are the cases we're considering. Read up on them. We'll discuss them later at our meeting."

"We're here now. We're meeting now."

Bogart said, "There are two other members of the team."

Jamison said, "I've met one of them, Amos, you're going to like her."

Decker kept his gaze on Bogart, who said, "So you knew this Melvin Mars?"

"I played against him in college. The only words I can remember saying to him were, 'Sonofabitch, how'd you do that?'"

"He was that good?"

"He was the best I'd ever seen."

Jamison said, "Well, he might be getting out of prison. That's a good thing."

"If he's innocent," amended Decker.

"Well, yes, of course."

"I doubt they'll release him unless they're absolutely sure," pointed out Bogart.

Decker gestured to the laptop. "Did you know that there are hundreds of people released each year from prison because they've been found to be innocent?"

"A small percentage considering the number of people incarcerated," replied Bogart, who was looking a bit impatient.

Decker said, "It's estimated that two and a half to five percent of all prisoners in the U.S. are innocent. That's about twenty thousand people. DNA testing was first used in court cases in 1985. Since that time, three hundred and thirty prisoners have been exonerated by DNA. But DNA testing is possible in only about seven percent of all cases. And in twenty-five percent of the cases where it *was* used, the FBI was able to exclude the suspect, so the percentage of prisoners who are innocent might be higher. Maybe a lot higher."

"I can see that you've done some research on this," said Bogart dryly.

A long silence ensued.

"Decker," said Bogart. "This is not really what we do. We investigate cold cases in order to try to find a killer."

"What if Mars isn't the killer?"

"Then this Montgomery guy is."

"What if he's not either?"

"Why would a man confess to a—" Bogart stopped and looked a bit embarrassed. "Okay, since that's exactly what happened in your case, I can see your point. But still."

"Can it at least be considered by the . . . team?" asked Decker.

Bogart mulled this for a few moments. "My plan was to let the team examine a number of possible cases and then vote on which ones to undertake. I have that flexibility."

"And can we lobby on behalf of certain cases?" asked Jamison.

"I don't see why not," said Bogart. "I like democracy as much as the next person," he added with a smile.

"I think we should take this case on," said Decker stubbornly.

"And we can lobby the others to do that, Amos," said Jamison quickly. "Like Agent Bogart said."

Decker stared down at the laptop. Both Bogart and Jamison watched him.

They knew that Decker was stubborn and inflexible when he had made up his mind. They also knew he couldn't help it. It was just who he was.

Bogart said, "Since you arrived early, I've changed the meeting time to two this afternoon instead of tomorrow." He looked over Decker's rumpled clothes and unkempt hair. "We'll give you time to clean up and then we'll pick you up about a quarter till and drive you over. It's not that far."

Decker looked down at his wrinkled clothes. He was about to say something, but then he nodded dumbly and stared back down at his laptop.

Bogart rose, but Jamison remained seated. When he looked at her inquiringly she said, "I'll meet you back here."

He glanced at Decker and nodded curtly. "Amos, it's good to have you on board."

Decker continued to stare at his laptop.

Bogart turned and left.

Jamison glanced at Decker. "Lots of changes," she said. "In a short period of time."

He shrugged.

"What is really fascinating you about the Mars case?" she asked. "Because you played football against him?"

"I don't like people just showing up out of the blue and confessing to a crime."

"Like what happened in your family's case?"

Decker closed the laptop and leaned back in his chair. "Tell me about the other 'team' members."

"I've only met one of them. Lisa Davenport. She's a clinical psychologist from Chicago. She's in her late thirties and very nice. Very professional."

"How is all this going to work?" asked Decker.

"Like Bogart said, we vote on the cases to take."

"But someone has to put the cases we're going to vote on together. So there's a preselection by someone."

"Well, that's true." She pointed to his binder. "In there. Fascinating stuff. But you can add this Mars case. Bogart said so."

"He didn't actually say that. He said the case was out of his jurisdiction. He said we could lobby the others to take it. But if I get voted out, we don't take it." He looked at her. "Do I have your vote?"

"Of course you do, Amos."

He looked away. "I appreciate that."

Jamison looked surprised. Decker didn't usually acknowledge things like that.

"Do you want to get cleaned up?" She added diplomatically, "I know it was a long drive. And you apparently drove straight through."

"I did. And, yeah, I should clean up some. But I don't have many clothes."

"We can go shopping if you want, before the meeting."

"Maybe after."

"Anytime, Amos. I'm ready to help."

"You don't have to be this nice to me."

Jamison knew that, unlike other people, Decker was being quite literal.

"I figure we both had big changes in our lives, and we need to stick together. There might be a case down the road I want to take. And then I'd need your support, right?"

Decker looked at her thoughtfully and nodded. "You're more complicated than you make yourself out to be."

"One can only hope," she said, smiling weakly.

6

How do I get twenty years of my life back? You wanna tell me that? How!"

Melvin Mars sat across from his attorney in the visitors' room at the prison.

Mary Oliver was in her midthirties, with auburn hair cut short and square glasses over her sparkling green eyes. Her angular, pretty face was sprinkled with freckles.

"You don't, Melvin," she said. "Nothing can do that. But they haven't confirmed Montgomery's story yet, so let's not get ahead of ourselves."

"I don't know this dude. I never met this dude. I never knew he even existed until they came and told me. So they can't say I paid him to kill my parents. And if they can't show that, I'm out of here, right?"

Oliver rustled some papers in front of her. "Look, it's not that simple. We have to let the process work, okay?"

Mars rose and smacked the wall behind him, drawing a stare from the burly guard stationed in the center of the room. He was far enough away that he could not hear their privileged conversation—at least spoken at normal levels—but close enough to step in if need be.

"Process? I let the process work before, and you see what it got me? They took my damn life, Mary."

"It's natural to feel betrayed and taken advantage of, Melvin. Everything you're feeling, it's natural."

Mars looked like he wanted to slug something, anything, as hard as he could. But then he saw the guard's hand move to the head of his baton. He also saw the guard's mouth twitch in anticipation of kicking some prisoner ass.

Just give me a reason, asshole, please.

Mars calmed and sat down. "So how much longer does this process have to work?" he said in a normal voice.

"There isn't a set timetable for this because of its unusual nature," explained Oliver, looking relieved that he was being more reasonable. "But I will keep on top of it every second, Melvin. I promise. I will push them. And if I even see them starting to drag their feet, I will call them on it. I swear. I'll file motions."

He nodded. "I know you will."

She said, "This must be so hard for you. When I first heard of it, I was flummoxed. I still don't know the connection between your parents and this Charles Montgomery."

"Well, if there is a connection, they didn't tell me.

Maybe it was a stranger thing. He breaks into the house and kills them."

"But there was no evidence of a break-in. And nothing was stolen. That was why the police started to look at you."

"But you believe me, right?" he said quickly.

"Yes, of course I do."

Melvin stared at her. Running through his mind was the thought, *Sure you do.*

"Where we lived, nobody locked their doors. And it wasn't like my parents had much someone would want to steal. You know how we lived. My father worked in a pawnshop. My mom made money on the side sewing clothes and teaching Spanish and cleaning up other people's messes." He shook his head. "I was going to change all that when I got to the NFL. Was going to buy them a house, put money aside. They could quit their jobs. I had plans."

He slapped the palm of his hand against the table. "I had plans."

"I know you did, Melvin," she said soothingly.

"I always thought this was a big mistake somebody was going to finally figure out. That I'd be out of prison in a few months and be playing ball. Then a year went by and then another and another. And then five. And then a decade. And then . . . shit!"

He grew silent, started shaking his head from side to side, his face pointed downward. A tear smacked against the laminate. Mars swiped it away with his hand.

"If I get out of here, what then? I got no family. I got no job. I got no nothin'."

"The state of Texas can compensate you."

"How much?"

"It's capped at twenty-five thousand dollars."

Mars looked up at her, incredulous. "Twenty-five grand! For twenty years of my life?"

"I know it's grossly unfair, but that's what the current law is."

"Do you know how much I could have made in the NFL?"

"A lot more. I know."

"So I walk out of here with maybe twenty-five grand, or maybe less since that's a 'cap,' and then what?"

"We'll help you with that. We'll help find you housing. And a job."

"Doing what? Pushing brooms? Maybe I can get my father's old job in that pawnshop. That part of Texas, man, pawnshops do big business, because nobody has shit."

"Let's just take it one step at a time," Oliver said, trying to keep her voice level and calm.

"Even if they let me go, they might not pardon me. Which means I got two felony murder convictions on my record. Who's going to hire my ass? Tell me that? Tell me!"

Mars could see that she was growing more nervous by the second.

Petite white woman, big, angry black man. That's what she sees. That's all she sees. And she's on my side.

He looked away and his tone changed again. "Hell, I don't know why we're even talking about this. They're never gonna let me out of here, Mary."

"Melvin, they have to if you're innocent."

"I've been innocent for twenty damn years," he snapped. "What difference did that make?"

"I mean, if there is definitive proof of your innocence, they can't keep you in prison."

"Oh yeah? There's like a dozen dudes around the country. Their innocence was proved, like you said. Years ago. Guess what? They're all still locked up. One dude, they said his time for appeal had run out, so he's screwed even though they know he didn't do it. Another guy, he served his time for crimes he didn't even commit, and because of some bullshit legal technicalities, they say he's got to serve four more years, and then maybe they'll let him out. Another dude, he punched out a guard, so he's got more time to serve, even though he never shoulda been in prison in the first place. So don't tell me they have to do anything. They do what they want. That's just how it is."

"We will make sure that does not happen in your case." She started packing up her things. "Now I have to go. But I'll be in contact with you as soon as I know anything."

As she rose he looked up at her. "I'm not mad at you, Mary. I'm just mad at . . . everything, right now."

"I understand," she said earnestly. "Believe me, I don't think I'd be nearly as calm as you."

The next moment she was gone.

Mars sat there until the guard came over and told him to get his ass up.

The chains went back on.

Reedy showed up and cattle-prodded him in the back with his baton so hard he winced with pain.

"What'd your 'lawyer' say, Jumbo?" asked Reedy.

Mars, from long habit, said nothing.

"Oh, it's privileged, that's right. Just between you and her. You wanna do her, Jumbo? Get you some white woman ass? Jump her bones? Used to be against the law, black man doing that to a white woman. Still should be. White girl don't want no animal jumping her bones. Right?"

He jabbed Mars again in the small of the back.

Mars turned to look at him. "When I'm outta here, let's have a drink, okay? I'll look *you* up. We'll hang out. Together."

Reedy snorted and then stopped as the full import of Mars's words hit him like a semi.

There were no more baton jabs on the way back to the cell.

7

When Bogart and Jamison returned at 1:30 that afternoon, Decker had showered, shaved, and put on his
other set of clothes: jeans, a flannel shirt under a
sweater, and mud-stained boots on his feet. He had
some dress clothes that he had purchased back in
Burlington when he was pretending to be a lawyer,
but they were dirty and at the bottom of his duffel.

Bogart was in a crisp suit, starched dress shirt with
a collar tab, and paisley tie. Jamison was in slacks and
jacket and a cream-colored shirt with what looked
to be brand-new stylish strappy heels on her feet.
Compared to Decker's casual appearance, both looked
ready to attend a wedding. But this was the best he
could do, and they both seemed to appreciate that
he'd made the effort.

"Ready?" said a smiling Bogart.

Decker nodded. He was holding the binder, which
he'd read and memorized. As they walked to Bogart's
car he felt his stomach start to squirm a bit. Not from
lack of food but from nerves.

The hitch with this whole arrangement was that

Decker was not really comfortable dealing with other people. His hyperthymesia caused him to be aloof, awkward, and out of sorts in the company of others. He had no control over this. His mind had bent his personality to its will. It seemed strange to think about your brain as being separate from the rest of you, but with a mind like Decker's it just seemed like the realistic thing to do.

He had known that joining a "team" would require him to work with others, but now that the time was upon them, he was starting to question his decision to come here.

Have I just royally screwed myself?

He got into the front seat of Bogart's sedan and had to put it all the way back to accommodate his long legs. He used the full length of the seat belt to stretch across his gut. Jamison sat in the back behind Bogart, to give Decker as much room as possible.

"Can you tell me about the other team members?" asked Decker. "Alex told me a little about Davenport."

"Lisa was brought on board because of her expertise dealing with psycho- and sociopaths. She's very well known in her field and has written several books on the topic. She'll be able to analyze for us the personalities and tendencies of people at the center of our investigations. Telling us what makes them tick. We have folks in the FBI who already do that, of course. But I think it's a good idea to get fresh eyes on a case, outside the perspective of federal law enforcement."

"Sounds like a workable theory," noted Jamison.

"Then there's another FBI agent, Todd Milligan. Todd's in his midthirties. He's a good field agent who competed for a slot on this team. He's excited to get started."

"And how does he feel about working with non-FBI agents?" asked Decker.

"There are no problems there," replied Bogart. "Otherwise he would have been vetted out."

Decker caught Jamison's attention in the rearview. His expression indicated that he did not necessarily share Bogart's confidence on that point.

Twenty minutes later they pulled up in front of a brick building on the grounds of the Marine Corps Base Quantico, which also housed, among other things, the FBI Academy and lab and ViCAP.

As they climbed out of the car, Bogart buttoned his jacket and said, "ViCAP gave us space in their facility to use. We'll also be operationally supported by them."

"ViCAP—Violent Criminal Apprehension Program," said Jamison.

Bogart nodded as he held the door open for them. "Formed in 1985. They're a unit dealing with serial murders and other violent crimes usually of a sexual nature. They're part of the Critical Incident Response Group."

"Which is in turn part of the National Center for the Analysis of Violent Crime," noted Decker.

Bogart nodded again. "We have lots of organizational layers."

"Maybe too many," assessed Decker.

"Maybe," said Bogart curtly.

They walked down a well-lighted corridor.

"So how does what we're going to do differ from what ViCAP already does?" asked Jamison.

"ViCAP is really a central database that other law enforcement agencies, both state and federal, use to investigate cases in their jurisdictions. There are teams of FBI agents that also investigate cases on the ground, of course. But ours will be one of the first to utilize folks from outside the FBI to be part of such an operational team. It took some finagling and negotiation. I have to say there are some in the Bureau who are not supportive of what we're doing, and think bringing in outsiders is a mistake. I hope to prove them wrong."

Decker said, "Playing devil's advocate, what if we prove them *right*?"

Bogart shrugged. "Then our funding is cut and we go off and do something else. And my career slams right into the ceiling."

Jamison said firmly, "Then let's make sure that doesn't happen."

They passed through a security checkpoint and then Bogart used his ID badge to open a door.

"Here we are," he said gesturing them inside.

The Last Mile

Before Decker passed through the doorway he felt the butterflies in his belly that he often had before stepping onto the gridiron. It was an unwieldy combination of nerves, adrenaline, and anticipation.

He had thought those days were long since over.

Obviously not.

Here we go.

He stepped into the room.

8

Decker's gaze swept the space and took everything in like radar bouncing off hard objects.

Two people were there.

Lisa Davenport was to his right. She was in her late thirties, with light blonde hair cut short, a lean, attractive face, full lips, and sparkling blue eyes. Her body was long and athletic, the hips narrow, the shoulders symmetrically broad.

She smiled at Decker as his gaze passed over her.

Todd Milligan sat across the table from her. He was about six feet tall and a buck-eighty. Like Bogart he was very fit and looked like he could run forever without getting winded. His dark hair was cut military short, his brow naturally furrowed, his light brown eyes intense, his spine assuredly as straight as his striped tie. There was nothing inviting or welcoming about the man. He just looked permanently serious.

In front of each was a thick binder. Decker noted the myriad Post-it notes sticking out from the binder's sides. Both Davenport and Milligan had evidently come prepared.

Bogart made the introductions and they all sat.

On the wall was a large-screen TV that neatly filled the space. Bogart fired up a laptop that sat in front of him and manipulated some keys. The TV screen came to life and they all focused on it.

Bogart said, "We currently have twenty cases lined up to look at. Of those we will be able to, realistically, focus on only one at a time. I'm going for quality, not quantity. The twenty cases you've been given have been whittled down from a far larger number using various internal filters."

Milligan said in a firm, clear voice, "It seems to me that the Morillo case has a lot of potential. I have some angles for approaching it that I think are rock-solid."

"Good to hear," said Bogart. "But I wanted to go through a brief overview of each of the cases so we're all starting from the same page."

Milligan's features tightened just a bit. Decker could tell he was not pleased at what he no doubt saw as a rebuke, though Bogart was actually being perfectly reasonable.

Bogart methodically ran through each case, the highlights of which were shown on the screen.

Decker noted that each of the others followed along in their binders. He saw Milligan glance over at him in mild surprise because Decker had not even cracked open his book. Perhaps Bogart had not told them about Decker's hyperthymesia. He was following along in his mind, turning the mental page in his head in synch with what Bogart was doing on the screen.

When Bogart was done he looked around the room. "Comments?"

Milligan said, "I still believe the Morillo case is the one to go after, Ross. It offers the best chance of a successful intervention. The case against him isn't that strong and one critical piece of evidence was for all intents and purposes ignored. It seems to me that there are better suspects out there. And it would be good for your program to get off to a strong start."

Bogart looked at the others. "Views on that?"

Decker said, "I think we should pass on the Morillo case."

"Why?" Milligan asked sharply.

"Because it's extremely likely that he's guilty."

As Milligan looked at him his thick neck seemed to flare out like a cobra's. "Based on what?" he asked.

"Inconsistencies."

"Such as?"

"Morillo was a civilian contractor to the Navy. On page two of the statement he told police that he left for work at Crane Naval Base in Martin County, Indiana, at nine a.m. He said he arrived at the base at eight-fifteen a.m."

"That's because—" Milligan began triumphantly, only Decker ignored him and plowed on.

"That's because at that time Martin County and

the naval base had been switched to the central time zone from the eastern time zone, effective April 2, 2006. Thus it was nine a.m. eastern standard time when Morillo left his house but eight a.m. central standard time."

"Correct," Milligan admitted grudgingly. "So what's the inconsistency?"

"Morillo had a motive for killing the victims. But there was one witness for Morillo, Bahiti Sadat. He said that he saw Morillo on the street across from his shop at six-fifteen p.m. The murders, forensic and other evidence determined, occurred at six-nineteen. Since the murders were committed about ten miles from Sadat's shop, and Morillo was on foot at the time, it was a solid alibi for Morillo."

"But the police mostly discounted that because Sadat was Muslim," interjected Milligan. "And this was right in the middle of the wars in the Middle East, and there was a lot of prejudice. Sadat's testimony was rock-solid. It gave Morillo an alibi, but the jury wouldn't buy it." He paused, scrutinizing Decker. "I hope you don't have those sorts of prejudices?"

Decker ignored this too and continued. "Sadat said he had just finished his evening prayer. That's when he said he saw Morillo. He remembered it distinctly because he had just looked up from his prayer rug and through the window of his storefront. He made a positive ID."

"Exactly," said an increasingly impatient Milligan. "You're making my case for me."

Decker said, "The prayer Sadat said he had just finished was the *Maghrib*, the fourth prayer of the day."

"Right. Devout Muslims pray five times a day. We all know that," pointed out Milligan.

"Well, actually lots of people *don't* know that, and back then a lot more folks probably didn't," said Decker. "But the point is the *Maghrib* prayer cannot commence *before* sunset. The religion is strict on that. And on that day in Indiana sunset was at seven-twelve p.m., nearly an hour later than Sadat testified he saw Morillo pass by the shop as he looked up. Now, Sadat is only human, and if he'd been off by a few minutes I don't think anyone could blame him. But at that time of day the sun would still clearly be in the sky. No Muslim would have begun their sunset prayer when it was so clearly *not* sunset. And certainly no Muslim would have *finished* the sunset prayer nearly an hour before the sun had even gone down."

Milligan's jaw dropped slightly.

Bogart and Jamison shared a glance.

Davenport kept her gaze locked on Decker.

Decker added, "And in addition to that, according to the drawing the police made that was in the file, the front of Sadat's shop faces *west* toward the street where Morillo was allegedly walking at the time."

Jamison said, "And Muslims face *east* when praying. Toward Mecca."

Bogart added, "Sadat's back would have been to Morillo. When he looked up from his prayer rug he couldn't have seen him. I'm surprised no one thought to question that."

Decker said, "A lot of Americans don't know that much about Muslim customs, and they knew even less back then, when most couldn't tell you the difference between a Sunni and a Shia. I think you might find Morillo and Sadat know each other and that this alibi was prearranged, even though it didn't work. It might determine conclusively that Morillo was guilty. But since he's in prison where he belongs, you might not want to waste your time."

Milligan sat back looking extremely miffed.

Decker glanced at Bogart. "Can we talk about the Melvin Mars case now?"

"Wait a minute," barked Milligan. "I was told you just got here today. Were you sent the briefing book earlier?"

Bogart answered. "No, he got it this morning. I delivered the binder myself."

Milligan turned back to Decker. "And from all these cases you dug up detailed stuff like that on the Morillo case in, what, a few hours?"

"I didn't have to dig anything up. I read the statements and reports. It was all right there."

"And knowing the specific Muslim prayers?" said Milligan.

Decker shrugged. "I read a lot."

"And the sunset timing?" persisted Milligan.

"I'm from that part of the country. I knew that off the top of my head."

Milligan said, "From a specific day in 2006?"

"Yes," said Decker imperturbably.

Milligan said accusingly, "Did you know beforehand that I was interested in the Morillo case?"

"Until I walked in this room, I didn't even know *you* existed," replied Decker matter-of-factly. He looked at Bogart again. "Can we discuss the Mars case now? Because I don't really think any of the others in the binder are nearly as compelling. And since Sadat was lying and Morillo killed those people and we're not here to free the guilty, I think we need to move on."

Davenport had to cover her mouth to hide her smile even as Milligan stared venomously at Decker.

Before Bogart could speak, Davenport said, "I vote that we take up the Mars case."

Decker eyed her curiously. "But I haven't described it yet."

"After what you just did, Mr. Decker, I'll take it on faith." She looked at Bogart. "Ross, can we go ahead and vote?"

Bogart glanced at Jamison and Decker and then said, "Okay. All in favor of taking on the Melvin Mars case raise your hand."

The Last Mile

Four hands went up. Milligan was the lone dis-
senter.

Decker leaned forward. "Good. Now, can we get
down to it?"

9

Two hours later the meeting ended and plans were made to reconvene the next day. As they left the building, Davenport caught up to Decker and Jamison. Bogart had stayed behind for a few minutes to talk to Milligan.

"Do you two have time for a drink?" asked Davenport, her gaze swiveling between the pair. "There's a place about a five-minute drive from the base."

Jamison looked uncertain. "We drove over with Agent Bogart."

"He can meet us there. I can text him. I just wanted to talk about the case some more before tomorrow. Then he or I can drive you back. I have a car."

Jamison looked at Decker. "You okay with that?" Decker said, "Does the bar serve food? I didn't have any lunch."

"Absolutely," Davenport said, running her gaze over Decker's large physique.

"Let's go, then," he said.

★

It was called, aptly, The Dive. A hangout for soldiers and cops and rednecks and the occasional suit.

Decker's party took a table in the back, farthest away from the bar, which was already loud and crowded on New Year's Day. A digital jukebox blasted away.

Davenport snagged a seat right next to Decker, while Jamison sat across from them. They had a fourth chair for Bogart, whom Davenport had texted. He said he would meet them there in about twenty minutes.

They ordered beers and some snacks. Decker got a mound of chili, chips, and cheese for himself. Davenport had some flatbread and Jamison French onion soup.

Davenport said, "I thought the first meeting went well, although Milligan seemed a bit brusque."

"Territorial," noted Jamison. "I'm not sure he's into us outsiders being involved in FBI investigations."

"Well, he's going to have to get used to it," replied Davenport. She took a sip of beer and studied Decker, who had already dug into his chip mound.

"That was quite impressive what you did back there, Amos. Do you mind if I call you Amos?"

Decker swallowed some of his food. Without looking at her he said, "I didn't want to waste time on a case of no interest. And you can call me Amos."

"But you are interested in the Melvin Mars case, clearly."

"Yes."

"When you were talking about the case you said you played football against him in college. Is that what piqued your interest? Or was it the fact that his case parallels what happened to you in Burlington? You didn't mention that in the meeting."

Decker slowly lifted his gaze from his food to look at Davenport, as Jamison stared suspiciously at her.

"I didn't mention it because it had no real relevance to whether we should take the case or not," he replied.

"Come on, Amos," said Davenport. "A mind like yours. Hyperthymesia coupled with synesthesia due to a traumatic brain injury suffered on the football field? You're way too smart not to see that connection."

"Bogart told you that?" he said.

She nodded. "I got here a week ago. Gave me time to get acclimated and have some nice discussions with Ross. He had just come off the case with you, and he was generous with details, seeing as how I was joining the team and all."

"I'm still not sure he should have told you about it," said Jamison defensively.

Davenport held up her hands in mock surrender. "Please don't get the wrong idea. Ross didn't tell me everything. But enough so that I know there are parallels between the murders of Amos's family and

Melvin Mars's parents. I think it could be a fascinating case study."

"But he told you about my condition?" said Decker.

"Well, yes. I'm a clinical psychologist by profession, Amos, with a subspecialty in the arena of cognitive anomalies. And I actually know some of the people at the Cognitive Research Institute outside of Chicago, though this was well after you went through there."

Decker wiped his mouth with a napkin. "But the goal would be to determine guilt or innocence in the Mars case. Nothing more. Nothing to do with my *cognitive anomalies.* Because I have no interest in being a 'case study.'"

Davenport fingered her beer. "If that's what you want. Frankly, I think it would be wasting an opportunity. But if I've put my foot in my mouth, I'm sorry. The last thing I wanted to do was offend you in any way. It was not my intent."

Decker shrugged but said nothing.

A moment later Bogart walked in and joined them. He sat down and a waitress came and took his order.

After she left Bogart said, "I want to apologize for the meeting today. Milligan was out of line and I told him so. We're not in this to fight with each other. We're a team. And those who want to remain on the team will have to start acting like it."

"He had a case and he argued for it," said Decker. "I took no offense."

"Well, he could have made his argument more professionally. The insinuation that you were somehow looking to purposefully torpedo his case was ridiculous."

Bogart's glass of wine arrived and he took a sip. "Lisa may have told you that I briefed her on some of what happened in Burlington."

"She did," said Jamison. "And she knows about Amos's condition," she added, a bit crossly.

If Bogart noticed her resentment, he chose to ignore it.

"And I was telling Amos that I've had dealings with the folks at the Cognitive Institute," commented Davenport.

"But Ms. Davenport has assured me that my *anomalies* will have nothing to do with investigating the Melvin Mars case," added Decker.

Davenport raised her beer. "Touché. And please, call me Lisa."

Bogart said, "Mars is still in prison in Texas. It seems the first thing to do would be to go there. The place where his parents were killed is hundreds of miles west of the prison."

"And then we have Charles Montgomery in Alabama," said Decker.

"Exactly."

Davenport said, "Can we learn anything about this guy before we go to see him? Is there any possible connection between Mars and this Montgomery person?"

"Well, that's what the police are no doubt trying to determine," said Bogart. "And let me tell all of you right off the bat, this will be very delicate. The state of Texas will not look kindly on federal intervention at this moment. Frankly, they may well question why we're even involved. And I can't promise that if push-back comes we can stick it out." He looked at Decker. "The cases in the binder were all preapproved for our involvement, Amos. The Mars case obviously is not."

"But we can still look into it," said Decker.

"Yes. But I've found that as a general rule Texans do not like people from Washington, D.C., messing in their affairs."

"Can you access all the records on the case?" said Jamison. "We should really go through all of that first. All we have is what Amos found online."

"I can definitely make calls and see what I can do," replied Bogart.

"Then we need to get in to see Mars," added Davenport. "Meeting with him I can give you a better insight as to his psychological makeup."

"Agreed," said Bogart. He glanced at Decker. "That was a good job back there on the Morillo case, Amos. You picked up on stuff again that everyone else missed."

Decker had been staring off and not really following the conversation. He came out of his musings and said, "We need to find out if Charles Montgomery has any family."

"What? Why?" asked Davenport.

Decker didn't answer her. He just stared off again, thinking.

After they finished at the bar, Jamison and Decker were dropped off at his place, where Jamison had left her car.

"So, that went reasonably well," she said. "Although Milligan is a bit of a jerk." She glanced at him. "What did you think?"

"I get where he's coming from."

"And Davenport?"

"I'm sure she's competent."

"But?"

"But she has her own agenda."

"Meaning you."

"Maybe."

She looked him over. "There's a men's shop about a mile from here. It's open until ten. I checked."

Decker shot her a glance. "Do I really look *that* bad?"

"Clothes make the man."

"I'm pretty sure whoever said that did not have me in mind."

"Shopping always makes me think better," she said hopefully.

"And how exactly do I pay for new clothes?"

She held up a credit card. "Bogart gave me this. For essentials. Which I confirmed includes clothes for you," she added quickly. "And you'll have your salary."

Decker looked over at her. "Salary?"

"I don't know about you, but I can't do this for free. Didn't you discuss money with Bogart?"

Decker let out a sigh.

"I'll take that as a no. But I can tell you that it's a lot more than either of us were making back in Burlington."

"Really?" said Decker.

"Really. And if this thing works out we'll have to get our own housing. Can't stay on the base permanently. And you'll need a car to replace the rental."

"I hadn't given any of that much thought."

"Trust me, I could tell."

Three hours later they walked out of the men's clothing store with numerous outfits for Decker. Nothing had to be altered. They had mainly just bought the biggest sizes the store had—pants, shirts, shoes, socks, underwear, and a couple of jackets that were large enough to use as sails if need be.

Jamison had helped coordinate the colors and accessories and commented on all the pieces that Decker tried on. As he stood in front of the tri-mirror he had said, "I look like a whale in a two-piece suit."

"It's nothing you can't work on. There's a gym a

two-minute walk from where you're staying. And a track right next to it."

When he came out of the dressing room in his old duds she held up a stack of workout clothes she had gathered for him, along with size fourteen tennis shoes. "Does quadruple-X work for you?" she asked.

"If they stretch enough, yeah."

She drove Decker back to his place and helped him carry in the packages.

"I appreciate the help," he said.

"I appreciate your giving me the opportunity."

"What, to be my personal shopper?"

"No, to have this shot with the FBI. Bogart never would've extended the invitation just to me. He let me tag along so you'd come too."

"Give yourself some credit."

"Oh, I plan to work my ass off proving myself. But you got me in the door."

"You really think this will work out?"

"Who knows? That's part of the excitement."

"I'm not sure I need any more excitement in my life."

"Then I think you came to the wrong place."

10

Six a.m.

Decker blinked awake and sat up in his bed. He looked around, for a few moments unsure of where he was.

Virginia.

Quantico.

The FBI gig.

Right. He got up and padded to the bathroom.

After that he walked into the kitchen and looked out the window. It was still well dark.

He slid out the coffeepot with the intent to make and drink a pot while he went over case notes. Then he looked down at his massive gut and the slight wheezing apparently caused by merely getting out of bed and taking a leak, and sighed.

"Shit," he muttered.

He went back into his bedroom and pulled out the exercise clothes Jamison had bought for him. He put them on—thankful they had some give—and then bent down and tugged on his tennis shoes, which were each about the size of a newborn.

He walked outside and down the steps of the apartment complex where he was staying. He looked left and saw the gym that Jamison was referring to. The lights were on and he could hear sounds coming from within.

Of course. Type A's are already at it. And this place is full of Type A's.

He trudged slowly to the building and went in. He'd remembered to bring his ID. The young attendant at the front desk gave him a towel and a locker key. He returned the latter but kept the towel.

"You look like you could squat an Abrams," said the young man, eyeing Decker's enormous girth.

"I do, every time I stand," replied Decker with another sigh tacked on as he took in the large exercise area where amazingly fit people of both genders were grinding it out with enviable ease.

Decker found one corner, put down his towel, looked in the mirror once, and decided not to do so again. He did a little cardiovascular warm-up before stretching and found himself winded. He pushed on and performed his stretching. His years of doing this as a football player had made him more supple than he looked. But he was still pretty stiff right now. Places in his spine he hadn't felt in a long time started talking to him. But he was beginning to warm up.

A young woman walked by. She had an FBI ID badge clipped to her Lycra shorts. She was pretty and supremely fit, and looked like fat would not dare attach itself to her body. When she saw Decker bend down and touch his toes and then lay his palms flat to the floor she said, "Impressive."

"Well, then I'd suggest you look away. Because it's all downhill from here."

She laughed and moved on.

After limbering up, Decker hit the weights, did what he could until his muscles screamed at him, and then grabbed a medicine ball and did some core. He was really starting to sweat and it actually felt good.

"Okay, I am totally impressed beyond belief."

He turned to see Jamison standing there in her workout gear.

"You coming or going?" he asked.

"Going. I got here right when it opened. I was in another part of the gym. I was leaving when I saw you." She smacked him on the arm. "Way to go, Decker."

He put the medicine ball back and shrugged. "Little by little, right?"

"You want to walk back with me? My place is just a little bit down from where you are."

"I thought I'd walk around the track and cool down."

"Sounds good. I'll see you at the office. And Amos, have you checked out your pantry and fridge yet?"

"I noticed there was stuff in there."

She looked a bit sheepish. "I did your grocery shopping before you got here. Don't kill me, but it's mostly healthy stuff. That's why I brought you that disgusting breakfast sandwich, sort of your last hurrah before going the healthy route."

"How healthy?" he wanted to know.

She smiled uneasily. "I'll let you have the pleasure of discovery. I'll pick you up about a quarter till."

She walked out.

A few minutes later Decker was done. He wiped his face and headed to the track, which was behind the gym and enclosed by a waist-high fence.

He walked around the track at a faster than normal pace until he felt like his knees were about to quit on him. Then he slowed. His heart was beating fast and the sweat was still coming. He felt both good and exhausted. It was cold and each of his breaths came out as tiny clouds.

Then something blew past him so fast he almost fell down. He'd never seen the person coming.

Todd Milligan turned around and jogged backward as he eyed Decker. He was wearing Under Armour and his physique was impressive. His six-pack was outlined against the compression fabric.

"Hey, Decker, you might want to pick up the pace or else you'll get run over."

He turned and sprinted away. The guy was fast and athletic.

And a prick.

A minute later Decker heard someone else coming up behind him and wondered if it was Milligan looking to lap him. He was moving over to get out of the way when he heard the voice.

"Good morning."

Lisa Davenport jogged up to him and then stopped. She was in a warm-up suit. She put her hands on her knees and breathed in and out in several long sequences.

"Good morning," said Decker.

She started stretching out her arms and legs. "I just finished my run and saw you."

"I'm hard to miss, although Agent Milligan nearly ran into me. Go figure."

"I'm sure," she said dryly.

"I'm just making my way around the track. I did the gym first."

"Exercising gives me so much energy. I love it."

"Me too. As you can see."

She broke into a smile. "But you played college and professional football. You must have been in fantastic shape."

"I was, a long time ago."

"But also more recent than that."

"Why do you say that?"

"You were a police officer and then a detective. You must have been in decent condition then too."

Decker started walking again, and she matched his stride, or tried to.

"That seems like a long time ago, too."

"But it really wasn't. It was less than, what, twenty months ago?"

"You seem to know a lot about me."

"I'm a curious person, Amos, and you're a fascinating study."

"Why, because my brain got blown up so I can't forget anything and I see things in color folks don't normally associate with red, yellow, and blue?"

"It's my field. I can't pretend I'm not interested. You realize how rare you are?"

"I actually never thought about it."

She seemed to be about to say something but then paused. "Well, it was good seeing you. I'm going to grab a shower. See you at the office."

She turned and jogged off in the opposite direction.

Decker watched her go for a long time, and then he waddled over and sat down on a bench next to the track.

He let his heart rate go back to normal and then stood, reasonably sure that he was not about to suffer a stroke. He walked slowly back to his place, showered, and changed into some of his new clothes. He had tried them on last night, but now they felt just a tad looser.

Must be my imagination.

He checked the fridge: soy milk, fresh-squeezed OJ, yogurt, apples, and a carton of organically grown eggs. The bread was nine-grain wheat. The chicken was extra lean. The ground meat was turkey. The "butter" was made with canola oil. There were also drawers of fresh vegetables. He looked in the pantry. Healthy cereal, low-sodium peanut butter, honey, low-sodium soups, organic pasta, something called orzo, bottles of vitamins, flaxseed oil, power bars, bananas, an energy drink that you mixed with water, and two dozen sport drinks in various flavors. There wasn't a bag of chips, block of chocolate, or tub of ice cream in sight.

He filled a bowl with cereal that looked like twigs a squirrel had pooped out and then poured soy milk over it and cut up a banana as his topper.

Jamison had had mercy on him, because there *was* coffee. But the cream was fat-free and the sugar was the brown unprocessed stuff Decker had seen but not used. Jamison had apparently confiscated the processed sugar he had used the day before.

He made his coffee and carried his cup and bowl over to the table in the little dining area, sat down, and ate his breakfast.

Well, that was filling, he thought as he rinsed the cup, bowl, and spoon.

He checked his watch. The team was scheduled to meet in about a half hour. He had a bit of time to kill before Jamison came for him. He sat down in a chair and looked out the window onto a street that was bustling with activity.

Quantico had lots of people coming and going at

all hours. And now Decker was a little cog in this huge ecosystem. And did he want to be? Really?

He closed his eyes, and though he didn't want it to, his infallible memory whirred back to the deaths of his family in their house. To the months of agony he suffered afterward and to the eventual tracking down and punishment of their killers. And then to the realization that even with that conclusion, he had never felt even a bit of closure.

When he opened his eyes they were moist and he felt himself trembling.

Time did not heal wounds for him. Not for someone who could never forget. Their murders were as fresh now as when they occurred. Not just the visuals, but also the emotional hatchet attached to the mental images. They would be until the day he died.

He glanced out the window in time to see Jamison's tiny car pull up out front. He wiped his eyes, rose, and slapped himself a couple of times in the face.

He could either live in the past or he could venture out and see if he was capable of having a future.

And some days the decision would be easier than others.

He headed to the door.

11

The rap on the door startled Mars. Then the door slot opened at the bottom.

"Get your ass over here," said the voice.

Mars obediently rose from his bunk, turned his back to the door, placed his hands behind his back, and slid down on his haunches until his hands were level with the slot. Handcuffs were attached to his wrists. Then he rose and stepped away from the door as it opened.

It was Big Dick. He'd been here as long as Mars had. And the years had just made him meaner.

Big Dick was so wide his bulk filled nearly the entire opening of the cell door. A scowl and a smile fought for supremacy on his features.

"What's going on?" Mars asked.

"Shut up! I tell you to talk, boy?"

Two other guards emerged from behind Big Dick and shackled Mars's feet. He was hustled down the corridor, his chains clanking like Marley's ghost.

He passed walls of cells with faces looking out the square chicken-wired windows. Then he felt on his face the rush of Big Dick's foul breath, smokes mixed with whiskey.

"You a lucky man," said Big Dick, his thick neck flexing rhapsodically with each syllable. "You off death row for now. You heading to gen pop. Folks'll be glad to see your chocolate ass, Jumbo."

Mars did not consider himself a lucky man. Going back to general population meant only one thing.

He was heading to an unofficial execution.

His own.

If you wanted to survive in prison, there were strategies and tactics.

If you wanted to kill someone, there were also strategies and tactics. His leaving his cell and the security of death row was the strategy.

The tactics of his planned murder were about to be revealed.

He was led into another building. When the second door slammed shut with the shriek of automatic hydraulic rams doing their job, he was brought to a halt by the meaty hand of Big Dick on his shoulder.

"*Last* stop, Jumbo."

His handcuffs were removed but not the leg shackles. Then the guards turned and left him.

Mars looked around.

Death row was housed in Building 12, but he was now in the prison's open area with all the other inmates. The place was filled with convicts, some in

pants, some shirtless, some in shorts cut from their
prison pants. Though it was technically winter, it was
stifling hot in here. Overhead fans spun away but
barely moved the thickened, humid, malodorous air
that hung over them all like a marine layer of toxic
gas.

A group of prisoners sat at tables bolted to the
floor. Some stood conversing. Still others were doing
push-ups, or else pull-ups on bars built into the walls.
The stench of sweat, cigarette smoke, and the fuzzy
must of prison-alchemy drugs hit him like a wave.
Guards hovered, their batons smacking lightly against
callused palms. Their eyes spun around the space,
looking for signs of trouble. But they kept coming
back to Mars.

He was obviously the special guest today.

The show was about to start. Everyone had good
seats. The only thing missing was the popcorn.

The prisoners had also turned to look at Mars.
Those doing push-ups and pull-ups stopped. They
wiped off their hands and moved back against the
wall.

And waited. Their expressions were clear.

Thank God it's not me.

The news had spread fast. Mars might be getting
out after nearly being put to death.

Getting out.

Uh-uh. Wasn't to be. At least not standing up.

Mars rubbed his wrists where the shackles had cut

into him. The pain was actually welcome right now. If you could feel pain you were alive. That status could change, surely. But right now he was breathing.

He looked up one story to the catwalk that ran around the perimeter of the open area. Big Dick was up there staring down at him. The smile on his face was something to behold. Next to him was the runty Reedy looking just as gleeful—the royals above, the gladiators below.

Mars looked back at the group of prisoners watching him. Two in particular seemed to be paying him a good deal of attention. They were both white, bigger than he was, prison-barbell-muscled, tatted, bearded, crazy-eyed, with rotted teeth, strung out on the shit they smuggled in or made right here.

Tweedle-Dee and Tweedle-Dum.

Mars didn't know them or what crimes they'd committed to be sent here. But he could easily see that they were exactly where they belonged. They weren't humans. They were animals in a cage. But they weren't in a cage right now. They were right out in the open.

With me, thought Mars. *And my legs are chained.*

He stretched out his neck and felt a gratifying pop as a kink was relieved.

Next he eyed the field in front of him like he had as a running back earning his future between the tackles in the old Southwest Conference, smashing into men bigger than he was and yet almost always somehow winning the battle. He'd always divided the field into grids, planes of existence through which he had to navigate. He was blessed to have vision that saw everything all at once. That attribute was perhaps the rarest gift in sports. And he still had it even all these years later.

His breathing slowed, his nerves calmed, his muscles relaxed. He felt good, actually.

Twenty years of my life. Twenty damn years.

The anger in him was suddenly immense. The frustration just as potent.

Somebody had to pay. And somebody was about to.

Jumbo was about to come down for an extremely hard landing.

He shuffled forward with what seemed to be the intention of joining a couple of inmates.

Mars knew the lay of the land, and the pair did what he expected them to do. They turned and walked off. Nobody mixed with the leper. The infection might rub off on you.

He looked back up at the catwalk. At Big Dick and Reedy.

He knew what they expected to see on his features: fear.

But instead, he smiled.

And on their faces he saw what *he* wanted to see: surprise.

He turned back to face Dee and Dum, who had separated from the pack and were now circling him, wild dogs on the prowl. There were lots of wild dogs in Texas and they always hunted in packs. They went after wounded animals, running them out of air and then ganging up on them for the kill.

Well, Mars was not wounded and he had plenty of air.

He wondered what their reward would be. Drugs, smokes, maybe a local skirt snuck in for an hour?

Well, he would make them earn it.

Dee and Dum were both in their thirties, years younger than he was. They were tough, scarred, hardened.

To a degree.

It was always about degrees.

He was about to find out where this pair stood on the prison hardiness spectrum.

Mars shuffled toward Dee while keeping Dum in his periphery. Dee was the linebacker looking to take him head-on because he was big and strong and that was his job. Yet he looked a little surprised that Mars was coming right for him. Then his expression told Mars that he thought this a positive. That Mars was actually making his job easier.

Maybe instead of Dee, he was actually Dum.

Now the other dude was the safety, the fail-safe. If Dee went down, Dum was the one set to take Mars out of this world.

From the corner of his eye Mars watched Dum. The dude was jacking himself up, getting ready. Part of him wanted his mate to fail, just so he could have his shot, build his cred inside here to unassailable proportions.

He could hear it now. *I took out Melvin Mars. Dude was a murderer. NFL lock. Biggest, meanest cocksucker you ever saw. And I wiped the floor with his ass.*

He'd be telling that story in here for the next forty years. Well, except for one thing. It was never going to happen like that. And Mars didn't think Dee and Dum had forty seconds, much less forty years, left to live.

Get ready, fresh meat, 'cause here comes Jumbo.

"What's up, brotha?" said Mars to Dee.

"I ain't your brotha," snarled Dee.

"Know that, man, just makin' conversation. Ain't no big deal, right?"

Words did not come out of Dee's mouth. Instead a shiv was revealed in his hand as he came at Mars with a burst of speed. The strike would be to his belly and up to his chest cavity. That was quick and clean and the bleed-out would be fast and fatal. And immensely painful.

The prisoners and guards had backed away, to give Dee room to work.

And Mars to fall.

Well, they actually had it backward.

Mars had already lowered his shoulder, squatted down, tensed his enormous thighs, and, despite the shackles, sprang forward like a launched cannonball.

As his hand clamped around Dee's wrist, holding the shiv right where it was, his right delt slammed into Dee's throat, pushing his chin up at an angle that would cause nothing but a bolt of pain right before blackness.

There came an audible crack as the spine was pushed past all point of return. And it was over, just like that.

Bleeding from the mouth, an unconscious Dee crumbled where he stood, the shiv dropping from his hand.

Linebacker down.

Mars pointed to the blade as it hit the floor. "Hey, man got a blade," he said to the closest guard. "Y'all be careful now. Somebody might get hurt."

He saw in his periphery what he expected to see.

Dum was hesitating now after the quick slaughter of his larger twin, but then how could he not follow through with all the dudes and especially Big Dick watching?

Man had to go. No choice. Else he'd get a shiv in his gut later. Just how it was.

America didn't have prisons. It had chaos pens where men were transported back seventeen centuries. Where the strong survived until it met something even stronger, and where the weak died every time.

Dum screamed and ran at Mars at the top of his speed.

It was almost too easy, really. Dum was all muscled

up and yet slow as gravy. Big in the arms, light in the quads. And the man was about to pay a steep penalty for that imbalance.

Mars again bent low, pivoted, blocked Dum's arm where his shiv was held, got his shoulder under Dum's belly, and exploded upward. It was the same move that had launched three-hundred-pound defensive linemen off their feet.

The two-hundred-and-fifty-pound Dum went airborne, soaring over Mars. The crowd parted and Dum landed hard on the concrete and slid across its smooth surface headfirst into a cinderblock wall with shattering velocity.

There was a crunch of bone as his spine compressed and he lost about an inch of height. He didn't move again. He'd just been in a car accident without benefit of a vehicle. Blood seeped from his mouth. His shiv had fallen from his hand and clattered to the floor.

Dee and Dum out for the count.

Blood from their wounds pooled on the filthy floor. Their last lines in the sand.

Adios to the Texas correctional system.

Actually, Mars didn't know if they were dead. And he really didn't care. Quads for life might be better justice.

He looked up at Big Dick and called out, "That man got him a shiv too, sir. Lotta that goin' round. Best tell the warden."

That's when the guards pounced, beating Mars with their batons until he went down.

Smiling all the way.

12

Who the hell are you?"

Melvin Mars had just awoken and was looking up from his hospital bed.

Amos Decker stared down at him. "You may be the luckiest guy in the world, Mr. Mars."

"You trying to be funny?"

Mars tried to sit up, but his wrist was handcuffed to the bed railing and it was a struggle because every part of him was hurting. His face looked like a balloon from all the swelling.

Decker dipped his big hand under Mars's waist and hoisted him to a sitting position against the pillow. He pulled up a chair and sat down.

Mars studied him. "Do I know you?"

"Not unless you remember a linebacker at Ohio State that you humiliated about twenty-two years ago."

Mars squinted and looked Decker up and down. "I humiliated a lot of people on the field. You pretty big for a backer. You put on some weight?"

"About a hundred pounds. You, on the other hand, look exactly the same."

"Who are you?"

"I'm with the FBI."

"You an agent?"

"No, I just work with them."

"Didn't know that was a thing."

"It's not really."

"Why are you here?" asked Mars.

"Because of your case. The recent development."

"Why is the FBI interested?"

"They are because I am," said Decker.

"Which gets back to my first damn question. Who *are* you?"

Decker held up his ID badge. "Amos Decker."

"Why did you say I was lucky? 'Cause I don't feel lucky."

"Three reasons: Because someone came forward and confessed to the murders you were convicted of, you might be released. And despite the beating you took, you have no broken bones and no permanent injuries. The docs said your concussion was relatively mild, which means your head is very hard."

"And the third reason?"

"Two of the guards ratted out their colleague about the ambush back at the prison. So you will not be held legally accountable for what happened."

"What *did* happen?"

"One man dead, another man paralyzed."

"And the colleague, Big Dick?"

"Is right now being processed and jailed by Texas authorities."

Mars smiled and then laughed out loud, his split lip starting to bleed. "Damn, man. Big Dick on the other side of the bars? It's a miracle."

"Forget about Big Dick. You need to focus on you."

Mars settled his gaze on Decker. "Did we really play college ball against each other?"

"You remember when your Longhorns beat my Buckeyes by five touchdowns? In Columbus?"

Mars smiled again. "Man, were you the one asked me how I did what I did?"

Decker nodded. "That was after your third touchdown."

Mars shook his head. "What can I say? Worked my ass off, but a lot of it was God-given."

"God wasn't as generous with me."

Mars looked around. "Where am I?"

"After we heard what happened, we had you transferred to a hospital near your old home."

"When did you get here?"

"We landed about six hours ago."

"You keep saying 'we.'"

"I came with a team."

"A team of FBI agents is interested in my case? Why? Just 'cause some dude confessed? Is it that unique?"

"Unique enough. But it also had some parallels to another case."

"What case was that?"

Decker said, "One to do with my family. You don't have to know the details, only that the similarities are striking."

"So that's why you're here?"

Decker studied him. He was good at sizing people up, but Mars was proving a tough one to crack.

"Tell me about your parents."

"Where's the rest of your team?"

"You don't believe what I'm telling you?"

"I don't believe nobody 'bout nothing."

"Believe him, Melvin," said a voice.

Mars looked toward the doorway where his attorney, Mary Oliver, stood. She walked over to the bed and took his free hand as he sat up more.

"Thank God you're all right," she said, her eyes moist with tears.

"I'm good, Mary. You know this dude?" Mars asked, indicating Decker.

"I just finished speaking with Special Agent Bogart," she said. "Mr. Decker is the real deal, Melvin."

Decker added, "We're here to try to figure out the truth."

Mars sat back against the pillow. "The truth? After all this time? I wish you luck."

"Luck may set you free," noted Decker.

"Do I have to go back to that prison?" asked Mars.

Decker shook his head. "After what happened, we're moving you to another place."

"Where?"

"Federal custody."

"What does that mean?"

"That means we're accepting responsibility for you. You'll have two Feds standing guard over you while you rehab here. After that, you're in our custody until the outcome of your case is determined."

"And the state of Texas is okay with that?"

"The state of Texas has its own problems," said Oliver. "Namely, you can sue them for what happened to you."

"Are you serious?"

"A conspiracy headed up by one of their guards nearly resulted in your murder. And then they almost beat you to death. So you have a plausible civil claim against them. And a criminal one against the guard and anyone else from the prison involved."

Decker said, "I wish you luck with that. But that's not why I'm here." He looked at Mars. "I'm here about the murders of your parents."

Mars swiveled his head to stare at Decker. "What do you want to know?"

"Everything."

"You got paper and pen, 'cause it's a lot of stuff."

"I have a good memory," said Decker. "I don't forget much."

The door to the room opened and Jamison came

in. She had apparently heard what Decker had said. She held up a recorder.

She said, "But my memory's not as good, so I always use this."

"Alex Jamison, Melvin Mars," said Decker. "She's also part of the team."

They shook hands.

Jamison said, "My colleague really wanted to take on this case, Mr. Mars. It's the only reason we're here."

"Yeah, that's what he told me," said Mars, staring dead at Decker.

"Tell me about the night your parents were killed," said Decker as Jamison turned on her recorder.

"If you're up to it," said Oliver quickly, placing a protective hand on Mars's shoulder. "You took a real beating."

Mars said, "I'm good. You want me to start at the beginning?"

"Yes."

And Mars did. He talked for well over an hour. Decker frequently interrupted to ask a question or to clarify a point. When Mars was done, Decker said nothing for a few moments.

"You were visiting a friend that night?"

"Yeah, like I said. Ellen Tanner."

"Where and when did you meet Ellen Tanner?" asked Decker.

Mars frowned. "What does that have to do with anything?"

"Right now, everything has to do with everything else," said Decker matter-of-factly.

Mars drew a long breath, licked his swollen lips, and said, "I met Ellen at a university alumni event the team attended. This was like a few weeks before. She was a big football fan. Good-looking woman. Fun. Smart. We hit it off. We saw each other a lot, actually. And we made plans to see each other that night."

"And you drove there?"

"Yes."

"And what did you do while you were there?"

"We had a couple of beers. She had some pot but I said no. That could blow my chance to play in the NFL."

"Did you two sleep together?"

"She testified that we did."

"What do you remember?" asked Jamison.

"We had sex, so what?"

"And then you left?"

"Yeah. I had a practice session with my trainer the next morning and wanted to get home and hit the sack. Then my car conked out. So I pulled into the motel and spent the night there."

Decker said, "The thing is, the timeline provided by Tanner and the motel clerk does not coincide with your story."

Mars rubbed his eyes. "I know. I heard them testify. All I can tell you is what I know. And I know when I left Ellen's place. And I know when I checked into the motel."

Decker sat back. "Your credit card was used at a time that backs up the motel clerk's account, not yours."

"You don't think I know that?" barked Mars.

"I'm just trying to make sense of what on the surface does not make sense. And the last thing we need is for you to lie to us."

Mars suddenly jerked against the handcuff trapping him to the bed, but it did not give. Jamison and Oliver had jumped back, but Decker hadn't moved a muscle.

Mars sat back against the pillow, breathing hard. "I'm not lying."

"Okay," replied Decker calmly.

"And maybe you're not here to help me. Maybe you're here to make sure I stay in prison the rest of my life. Or get the needle. You might be working with the state of Texas for all I know."

"Why would he be doing that?" asked Jamison.

"How the hell am I supposed to know that?" snapped Mars. "Maybe they brought you in when this Montgomery dude said he killed my parents. Maybe your job is to mess all this up so I don't get outta prison."

Everyone was silent for a few moments until Decker said, "But can you explain the time discrepancies?"

"If I could I would have twenty damn years ago, so, no, I can't."

"Okay," said Decker. "So you have no explanation? Nothing else for us to look at on that point?"

Mars shot him an angry glance. "Look, if you don't believe me, then just leave. 'Cause I got no time for bullshit if you don't want to get me outta prison."

Decker rose. "Maybe you misunderstood me, Mr. Mars. I didn't say I believed you were innocent or that I wanted to get you out of prison. I told you I wanted to find the truth. If it turns out that truth means you are guilty, then they can inject you and you can die, because you'll have deserved it. But in the meantime, we will continue to investigate this case and let it take us where it does. Is that clear enough for you?"

Jamison and Oliver exchanged a nervous glance.

Mars and Decker stared at each other. The former seemed to be trying to figure out the latter. And the latter seemed to have already turned his mind to other matters.

"I think we understand each other, yeah," said Mars.

But Decker was already walking toward the door.

After he left Mars turned to Jamison.

"Damn, is the dude always like that?"

"Pretty much," replied Jamison.

13

Decker walked down the hall, gathering momentum like a wave about to crash onto the beach as he went. He heard Jamison scurrying behind him. Up ahead, standing in the hallway, were Bogart and Davenport.

Milligan was at rented office space about twenty minutes south setting up shop. They were all staying at a local motel, which represented the best lodgings in the area.

Jamison caught up to him. She said, clearly irritated, "I wish you'd stop doing that."

Decker looked down at her. "Doing what?"

"Just walking out of a room like that."

"I was finished. So I left." He paused. "And you bought me quinoa? Seriously? Is that even a food?"

She smirked. "You're getting so skinny I'm having trouble seeing you sideways."

"Yeah, like a Mack truck coming right at you."

They reached the pair and Bogart said, "What's your take so far?"

Decker shrugged. "Early to say. There're problems

with his statement. We need to see if there are alternative explanations."

"Well, after two decades the trail is definitely cold." Davenport said, "I'm going to be speaking with him later. Then I can report on his psychological status."

Bogart focused on Decker and Jamison and said, "Not holding you to anything, but do you think he's lying?"

Jamison looked troubled by the question. "We only just met him. But if you want an answer, then, no, I don't think he's lying."

"Any particular reason?"

"He told Decker if he didn't believe him to pack up and leave. Not what you'd expect from a guy who could still be executed. A guilty guy would grasp at anything."

Bogart looked at Decker. "Anything to add?"

"No."

He turned and walked off down the hall.

Jamison let out a long breath.

Bogart looked amused.

Davenport looked curious. "Where is he going?"

"To dig. He's going to dig," answered Bogart. "And if we're going to keep up, we'll need to hustle."

They had been settled around the rented office space and staring at paper and laptop screens for some time now.

It was just the men. Jamison and Davenport had stayed behind at the hospital to further interview Mars.

Decker was wearing some of his new clothes. For the last week back at Quantico he had gotten up early and gone to the gym and then the track. He had even jogged a bit and ventured onto the elliptical. And he had eaten only the food Jamison had bought for him. Small meals, she had suggested. Four or five per day.

He was so overweight that even that little stretch of exercise and better eating had resulted in his dropping twenty pounds, mostly liquid.

He was on the third belt notch, after starting on the first. His pants were very loose on him.

And he was still morbidly obese.

Milligan eyed him and said grudgingly, "You're looking better, Decker."

"Yeah, but don't run into me on the track. I don't want to hurt you because I'm still a blob."

The comment drew a rare smile from the FBI agent. "Hey, you're making an effort. Good for you."

"Okay, let's talk about preliminary investigative possibilities," said Bogart.

Milligan said, "Ellen Tanner is no longer in the area. No record of where she went, nobody who knew her. We checked at UT. She didn't go there. And with twenty years gone by it's going to be pretty much impossible to track her down. She might have married and changed her name."

"And the motel clerk, what was his name again?" asked Bogart.

"Willis Simone. And we did track him down. He died of a heart attack in 2001 in Florida."

"Any connection you can see between Tanner and Simone?" asked Bogart.

Milligan said, "None. They didn't move in the same circles. They were far apart in age. No lines of connection that I can see."

Decker said, "Let's assume they were paid off to lie, is there any way to track those payments?"

Milligan looked at him funny. "Twenty years later? Probably the banks they used aren't even around anymore. Industry has consolidated. Plus, why would they lie? And who would pay them off?"

"For the moment I'm assuming that Mars is telling the truth. If so, we have to account for the discrepancy in the timelines offered up by Mars on one side and then Tanner and Simone on the other."

Milligan shook his head. "I think it far more likely that Mars is lying. Otherwise, you're looking at a big conspiracy against a college football player, and I just don't see the motive."

Bogart cut in. "But we're here and we will explore the angles. *All* the angles."

Milligan looked down at his notes, obviously unhappy with this. "I talked with the police department. Most of the officers from that time have retired, but there was one guy I spoke with who was around back then."

"What did he say?" asked Bogart.

"That they'd never had a murder here before. Burglary, missing person, drunks getting in fights, kids stealing cars for joyriding, and even someone taking a cow as a prank, but this crime blew the town away."

"But they latched onto Melvin Mars pretty fast."

Milligan glanced at Decker. "Well, the evidence was *overwhelming.*"

"What do we know so far about the parents? Where was Lucinda from?" Decker asked.

Milligan rustled through some pages. "I couldn't find out. Like her husband, there's not a lot on her."

"Where did she learn to sew? The police report said that was partly how she earned money. And Mars confirmed that today."

Milligan had a hard time keeping a straight face. "To sew? I really couldn't tell you."

"And she also taught Spanish," said Decker.

Bogart said, "There are a lot of Spanish-speaking people in Texas."

"But we don't know if she was from Texas," pointed out Decker. "Now, if she were Hispanic, I could understand the language thing. But she was black."

"Well, last time I checked black people *can* learn to speak Spanish, Decker," said Milligan. "And sew."

Decker didn't ignore this one. "Right now we're speculating. So to compensate for that we have to deal in probabilities. Lucinda certainly could have learned to sew and speak Spanish. I would just like to know where and how."

"Okay, if you really think it's important," said Milligan. "Feel free to check it out for yourself."

"I plan to," said Decker. "She also worked at a janitorial service?"

"Yes. They cleaned places around town."

"Busy woman. Any other family?"

"Not that I could find. Same for her husband."

"Doesn't that strike you as odd?" asked Decker. "One of them not having any family around, okay, but both?"

Milligan shook his head. "It was a long time ago. Maybe they moved around. Not everybody comes from huge families. People get lost in the shuffle. It seemed the only remarkable thing about either of them was their son. There were lots of stories about him, even before the murders. Guy was a helluva athlete. What a waste."

Bogart said, "Keep digging on the Marses."

Milligan nodded, but didn't look terribly enthusiastic.

"They were shotgunned and then burned," said Decker. "Why both?"

Milligan said, "If you think it was done to obscure identification, it wasn't. They were positively identified by their dental records."

"Then why?" persisted Decker.

"Symbolic?" suggested Bogart. "If Mars did do it he might have wanted to obliterate them from his life. Burning might accomplish that, in his eyes at least."

"But then we have Charles Montgomery saying he did it," pointed out Decker. "I need to talk to him."

"That is being arranged," said Bogart.

"The Marses' house isn't far from here," noted Decker.

"That's right. It's abandoned. I guess no one wanted to live in it after what happened."

"And the motel where Mars said he stayed?" asked Decker.

Milligan said, "Knocked down. It's now a shopping mall."

"And Ellen Tanner's place?"

"Still there, but she's long since gone. So I'm not sure what you'll find there."

"Well, that's why people look," replied Decker. "Let's go."

After he left the room Milligan put an arm on Bogart's sleeve.

"Sir, maybe the Morillo case wasn't the best one, but we have a binder full of others a lot more promising than this one."

Bogart said, "Actually, we're just getting started here."

Milligan removed his hand and said, "You're putting a lot of faith in this guy."

"Yes, I am. Because he's *earned* that faith."

Bogart walked out to follow Decker.

Milligan reluctantly did the same.

14

The house looked lost among a wasteland of over-grown bushes and fat-canopied trees. One might need a machete to hack through the tangles.

Decker just used his hands and his bulk to navigate it. Bogart and Milligan were right behind him.

They reached the fallen-in front porch and stared up at the façade. They could still see the char marks on the outside of one of the upper-story windows, which was boarded up with plywood.

"Where the bodies were found," noted Decker, and Bogart nodded in agreement.

"We'll need to step carefully," said Milligan. "I don't know how structurally sound this place is."

Decker gingerly stepped up onto the front porch, avoiding the obvious areas of weakness. He reached the front door and pushed against it. The door didn't budge.

Decker put his big shoulder to it and finally the wood cracked and the door swung inward. There was no electricity on, of course, which was why the men had brought powerful flashlights.

They moved inside to find the interior remarkably free of debris, although the smell of mold and rot was everywhere.

Bogart put a hand over his nose. "Damn, I'm not sure we should be breathing this."

Decker looked up. "The roof and windows held. That's why it's not more trashed inside."

He swung his light around the room, taking in the space bit by bit as he moved forward.

The house was small and it didn't take them long to finish with the ground floor and the attached garage. There was no basement level; that left the upstairs.

As soon as Decker hit the first step his brain popped with the color blue. It was so sudden that he misjudged the riser and stumbled a bit. Milligan caught him by the arm.

"You okay?"

Decker nodded, though he wasn't feeling okay.

He had only experienced blue like that when he had seen his family's bodies in his old house. And every time he had visited it since.

Electric blue: It seemed to overwhelm every sense that he had. It was unnerving, uncomfortable.

And I just need to get over it.

He blinked rapidly, only to find the blue reemerge each time his eyes opened.

Synesthesia is not all it's cracked up to be.

He picked his way carefully up the rickety stairs and hit the landing.

There were only two bedrooms up here—Mars's and his parents'. They had shared a bathroom.

Decker stepped into the first bedroom. He assumed it was Mars's. The bed was still there, and so were crumbling posters of R&B singers Luther Vandross and Keith Sweat. On another wall was the confirmation that this was not the parents' room—tattered posters of supermodels Naomi Campbell and Claudia Schiffer.

"Red-blooded American male," commented Milligan. "Jeez, it's like we opened a time capsule or something."

"Where was the shotgun rack?" asked Decker.

Milligan pointed to the far wall. "Over there. Single rack with a small drawer underneath to hold the ammo boxes."

They next went into the parents' bedroom.

Decker stood against one wall and thought back to the diagrams in the old police reports. Bodies were right under the front window, side by side. Roy was closest to the window, Lucinda on the side nearest the bed. The glass had blackened and shattered from the heat. The plywood had been nailed to the exterior of the house, closing this gap.

Unlike their son's room, this space had been emptied.

"What happened to the furniture?" asked Decker.

"I imagine it was all taken as evidence," said Bogart. "And the firefighters might have had to carry some of the combustibles out while they were dealing with the blaze."

Decker nodded. "Maybe we can find out for sure. And those square marks on the wall. Pictures hung there. I wonder what happened to them?"

Milligan said, "I can make some calls."

Decker opened the closet door and shone his light around the interior. He was about to close the door when he stopped and leaned farther into the closet.

"Check this out."

Bogart and Milligan joined him and stared at where Decker was pointing his light.

"'AC + RB'?" said Bogart, reading off the faded letters someone had written on the side wall of the closet. "What does that mean?"

Decker took a picture of the writing with his phone. "I don't know. They could have been there before the Marses even bought the place."

"Maybe."

"Or maybe the Marses wrote them. Which means it could be important." Decker gazed around. "Who made the 911 call about the fire?"

Milligan said, "I don't think they ever determined that."

"People really didn't use cell phones back then. And I doubt reception was great back then in this area. So it probably wasn't a car driving past."

"Well, it could have been. And then the people went to their house and called."

Bogart said, "But if they'd done that they'd know where the call came from. They could trace it."

Milligan was already nodding. "That's true. I'll have to check."

They went back downstairs.

Here Decker saw what he had seen before. A faded picture of a young Melvin Mars in his high school football uniform. It was hanging on the wall. On a small shelf were more old photos of Mars at various ages.

"Surprised they're still here," said Bogart.

"Like you said, no one wants to come into a house where people were killed. And not too many people live out this way. And strangers passing by wouldn't even be able to see the house from the road, particularly now with everything overgrown."

Decker looked around some more.

"But it's interesting what we're *not* seeing."

"What's that?" asked Milligan.

"Pictures of Roy and Lucinda Mars." He turned to Milligan. "It's like they never even existed."

15

Decker looked at his watch.

They had driven to the house where Ellen Tanner had hooked up with Melvin Mars that night. It was small, old, and set off by itself. There wasn't another home within twenty miles of it. And back then it was probably even more isolated.

"Why's a young woman living all the way out here by herself?" Decker had asked.

Neither Bogart nor Milligan had an answer.

Then they had driven back to the site of the old motel, which was now a strip mall. They had next driven to the Marses' home. All three locations were off the same main road, a fairly straight shot.

Decker said, "It's one hour in between Ellen Tanner's old house and the motel. And about forty minutes from the motel to the Marses' house."

Milligan, at the wheel of the car, nodded. "He left Tanner's at ten p.m. He said he reached the motel about an hour later, or eleven o'clock, which works. But the motel clerk testified that he checked Mars in at one-fifteen a.m. So he could have driven another

111

forty minutes to his house, killed his parents, and driven back to the motel and made it easily by one or a bit after. That's what the prosecution successfully argued."

"Not easily," countered Decker. "He had to get to the house, shotgun his parents, get the gas, and set them on fire. That would take some time."

"But it *could* be done, there's no denying that."

"And the police report said a car matching Mars's was seen leaving the vicinity of their house about the time the coroner thinks the murders occurred," added Bogart.

"That's right," said Milligan. "And the witness was a long-haul trucker who was based here and knew the Marses."

Bogart nodded. "And he died five years ago, so we can't talk to him."

Decker said, "But we have Charles Montgomery. We can talk to him."

"I got an email back from the folks in Alabama. It's all set. We can speak to him the day after tomorrow."

Decker's phone buzzed. It was Jamison.

She said, "We've talked to Mars. Davenport is writing up her report now."

"What does she think?"

"I'm not sure. She plays things close to the vest."

"What do *you* think?"

"He seems very sincere, Amos. But he could also be very manipulative. I just don't know which one yet."

"Did he tell you anything new?"

"Not really. He reiterated his innocence. We went over his actions on the night his parents were killed. He can't explain the timing. He said he went to sleep at the motel and woke up when the police knocked on his door."

"Well, he's had two decades to perfect that story. But one thing does bother me."

"What?"

"If he planned this all out, why can't he come up with a plausible explanation for the time gap? He had to know it was going to be a problem."

Bogart, who had been listening in, said, "Criminals usually slip up. And they usually slip up on the timeline, Amos. They can't be in two places at the same time. You know that as well as anyone."

"They *do* slip up, but not by that much," countered Decker. "Fifteen minutes, maybe half an hour can be fudged, but not hours. It was a huge hole. If he was meticulous in other respects, why not with that critical piece? I'm just saying it's something to keep in mind."

Jamison asked, "When will you be back?"

"In about an hour."

He clicked off and stared out at the highway as the vastness of Texas stretched ahead of them. All the way to the horizon the topography looked exactly the same. He closed his eyes and let his mind whir back to something that was gnawing at him.

Bogart glanced over and saw this, something he had seen often back in Burlington.

"What?" he asked.

Decker kept his eyes closed but said, "Shotgun then fire."

"Come again?"

"They were killed with the shotgun and then set on fire."

"That's what the police report said, yes. Why?"

In his mind Decker brought up the photos of the charred bodies. The good thing about hyperthymesia was that he saw things exactly as they were; no detail was missing. Nothing inserted, nothing taken away. Clear as a mirror.

"Pugilistic."

"What?"

"The bodies were in the pugilistic pose."

Milligan glanced at him. "Right. Fire makes muscles, tendons, ligaments stiffen and contract, whether the victim was dead or alive before the fire was started. Fists clench, arms bend, you look like a fighter in the ring in a defensive stance."

"Hence the name," said Decker, whose eyes were still closed. "The shotgun blast killed them, clearly."

Milligan shrugged. "Shotgun blasts to the head from a close distance are always fatal. Nature of the beast."

Decker opened his eyes. "So why burn the bodies?

If they were already dead? And I don't believe it was symbolic."

Bogart said, "The police reports raised that question but never answered it. If it was done to make identifying the bodies more difficult, it didn't work. They were identified by their dental records.

And even if that hadn't worked, you can still get DNA off a burned body."

"But maybe the killer didn't know that."

"You mean maybe *Melvin Mars* didn't know that?" said Milligan.

Decker ignored this. "They were positively identified as Roy and Lucinda Mars?"

"Yes. There was no question about it. The bodies were badly burned, and despite the shotgun wounds to the head, enough of their teeth were left intact to ID them through their dental records. They were the missing couple."

"Still doesn't answer my question. Why burn the bodies after they were dead?"

They drove for a few more miles in silence.

Finally Bogart said, "Maybe the killer panicked. They do. He tried to get rid of the evidence, thinking that maybe the fire would cremate the bodies."

"All it did was create a lot of smoke that someone noticed and called the fire department. If he had just left the bodies, they might not have been discovered for a long time."

Milligan interjected, "Well, if their son didn't kill

them he would have found the bodies when he got home that morning. Or more likely the house would have been burned down."

"There was no reliable time-of-death calculation?"

"With burned bodies outdoors you can have an entomologist look for insect evidence, flies laying eggs, that sort of thing. Even indoors you have that occur. But that sort of evidence wasn't available. Flies naturally won't lay eggs on a burning body. The most precise analysis for TOD on severely charred victims is an examination of the bones. Chemical and microscopic analysis. But then you're talking microradiography and electron microscopy."

Decker nodded. "But I doubt in a rural Texas county twenty years ago they were able to do any of that."

"I doubt they have the equipment to do it *today*," pointed out Bogart. "So the TOD was determined largely by the call to the fire department at ten minutes past midnight. The firemen showed up eleven minutes later. Five minutes after that they discovered the bodies."

"So twenty-six past twelve?"

"Correct."

"Let's say the bodies were set on fire around midnight."

Milligan said, "Mars would have had time to do it then. Straight from Tanner's place to the house. Do the deed, get back in his car and head out to the motel."

Bogart said, "Now, we can assume if the bodies had been burning for long that the house would have been more damaged by the spreading flames. He kills them, sets the fire, and is gone by midnight or shortly thereafter. That way the fire has only been burning for maybe less than a half hour or a bit more when the fire department shows up."

Decker shook his head. "But it's forty minutes to the motel from here. The motel clerk said he checked in at one-fifteen. That leaves a gap of about thirty-five minutes."

Bogart said, "Maybe he drove around. Maybe he sat out in the parking lot trying to calm down. I mean, he would've just killed his parents, Amos."

"He had the forty-minute drive over to do that. He waits in the parking lot he's screwing up his supposed rock-solid alibi, which was really no alibi based on the timing that Tanner and the motel clerk testified to. It doesn't make any sense."

"But it's the best scenario we have."

"But it's got a big problem."

"How do you mean?" asked Milligan.

"Over twenty years ago a credit card would probably have been manually run through the system, especially at a motel in rural Texas. There would be no electronic time stamp. So it was the motel clerk's word against Melvin's."

Milligan shook his head. "No, I checked that. The motel owner called the card in at sixteen minutes past one, to verify the account. That came out at trial."

"Still doesn't prove anything."

"I don't see why not," said an exasperated Milligan. "And don't forget, his mother's blood was found in his car. How is that possible unless he killed them?"

"I need to talk to Mars again."

"What about?" asked Bogart.

"Among other things, credit versus cash."

16

What the hell does that have to do with anything?"

Mars stared from his hospital bed at Decker, who impassively stared back. Bogart was next to Decker and looking bewildered. Milligan had elected to wait in the car and make some phone calls.

Decker cleared his throat and said, "I told you before that nothing is too important to overlook. The room rate was twenty-five bucks. Why not just pay that in cash? Why pull a credit card?"

"Where's my lawyer?" Mars demanded. "Where's Mary?"

"I suppose she left," replied Decker. "We can call her and wait until she gets here, but it would be faster if you just answered the questions." He paused momentarily. "So why the credit card?"

"It was over twenty years ago. I don't remember."

"Just take a minute, think back and try. That's all I'm asking."

At first Mars looked put out, but the genuine look of curiosity on Decker's face made him lean back against his pillow and do just that.

After about a minute he said, "Okay, my first inclination would have been to pay cash. I didn't like using the card. Only I didn't have enough cash. In fact, I don't think I had any."

"You went on a date with a woman with no cash? Did you go out to eat, take in a movie, order takeout? Did you spend it that way?"

"We didn't go out. We stayed at her place. She made some food. We had some beer."

"And no drugs. You said she had some pot?"

"Well, Ellen smoked a joint, but not me."

"Did you ever ask why she lived in the middle of nowhere?"

"No, I just assumed she had a good reason. It was probably cheap."

"Was she in college? Did she have a job?"

"I think she had something to do with PR. I think she mentioned that at some of the alumni events. She seemed the type. Really pretty, very outgoing."

"So you discovered you had no cash when you went to pay the motel guy?"

"I think so, yeah."

"Did you remember having any cash on you before you went to Ellen Tanner's?"

"Well, since I didn't have any cash after I left her place and I hadn't spent any while I was there, I guess the answer to that would be no."

"No, that really *doesn't* answer my question. Did

you look in your wallet before you went to Tanner's? And if you did, did you have cash in your wallet?"

Mars looked at Bogart. "Do you have any idea what he's getting at?"

When Bogart said nothing, Mars glanced back at Decker. "I don't remember, okay? I just don't."

"Where did you get the credit card?"

"It wasn't from any alumni booster or anything. It was all on the up-and-up."

"I don't care about that. I just want to know where you got it."

"My parents got it for me. I'd graduated from college. Made the dean's list the last two semesters. It was a reward. It had a low limit on it, but it was cool to have. Never had a credit card before." He added dryly, "Haven't had one since."

"And you used that to pay the motel room bill?"

"Yeah. Lucky too, since I had no cash."

"Did he run the card with a manual machine?"

"Yeah. One you use your hand to push back and forth."

"The motel clerk testified he phoned in the charge to confirm it was okay. Did you see him do that?"

"Yeah, I wasn't surprised. I was a young black dude showing up at night. Probably thought I'd stolen the card. Guess he wasn't no college football fan."

"So he made the call while you were standing there?"

"Yeah."

"What did he say on the phone?"

"I don't remember, okay? Whatever you say when you're trying to make sure a charge is okay, I guess. I really wasn't paying attention."

Decker nodded slowly. "And he said that occurred at around one-fifteen in the morning."

"Well, that's bullshit, because it was around eleven. It's only an hour from where Ellen lived to the motel. I know that for a fact. Been that way many times."

"And that would be the logical way for you to go home?"

"Dude, it's the *only* way."

"And then your car died?"

"Right as I was passing the motel. Lucky for me."

"Maybe not so lucky. Did you decide then to stay the night there?"

"No, my first thought was to see if I could get the car started. I couldn't. Sat in the parking lot for like five minutes trying to get it going, but it was dead. Then I went into the motel office. Dude came out from a little room in back. Told him I had car trouble. That I wanted to call a tow service."

"What did he say to that?" Decker asked quickly.

"He told me the only one around was like two hours away. And they were closed."

"And you accepted that?" asked Decker.

"Well, yeah, I'd never broken down before. My dad was good with cars. Fixed anything wrong with 'em, so I never had to think about going to a repair place.

So while I knew the area okay, I didn't know where the closest tow place was. You said you'd been to my house?"

"Yes."

"Well, this is middle-of-nowhere Texas. Back then that motel was the only one for I don't know how many miles."

"So when you knew you couldn't get a tow you decided to check into the motel?"

"Yeah. Then I planned to call the tow place in the morning. Or maybe my dad. Only then the police came, and that's when I found out what had happened."

"And they knew where you were because of the activity on your credit card?"

"Guess so," said Mars.

Bogart interjected, "Why didn't you phone your parents that night? They could have come and gotten you."

Decker looked at him approvingly and then turned back to Mars.

Mars said, "I didn't have a phone. I could've used the motel phone, I guess, but it was late and I didn't want to wake them up."

"But if they woke up next morning and found you weren't there wouldn't they be worried?" asked Bogart.

"Look, I was a grown man. I stayed out all night before. When I left I told them I might be late, or I might go straight to my practice session if I stayed over at Ellen's. I had my stuff in the car. So they wouldn't necessarily be expecting me home."

"So why *didn't* you stay at Ellen's?" asked Decker.

Mars looked down at his manacled hand. "Look, we had sex. She was really hot. Last woman I've slept with for twenty years. But—"

"But what?" asked Bogart.

"I was gonna be rich after the draft. And she . . . I think she wanted to be part of that."

"What, marriage? How long had you been seeing her?"

"See, that's the thing. Not that long. Like a few weeks. I wasn't thinking of marriage. Hell, I didn't even know where I'd be living. Depended on what team was going to draft me."

"So did you two argue?"

"I wouldn't say argue. We discussed stuff."

"And what was the result of that 'discussion'?" asked Decker.

"She politely asked me to get the hell out of her house, and so I did."

Decker took a long breath. "When I first asked you about that, you said you left to get home and hit the sack because you had your workout session with your trainer the next morning."

"Again, what the hell does that matter about any-thing!" Mars barked. "Now this dude in Alabama said he killed my parents. Why don't you go question his ass and leave me the hell alone?"

"We are going to question him," said Bogart. "But we have questions for you too."

Mars pointed his finger at Decker. "This dude thinks I'm lying. He thinks I'm good for it. Got a beef against me 'cause I ran over his ass up in Columbus. Buckeye gets gored by the Longhorn. He sure as hell can't be objective. Like the dude who prosecuted me. Did you know he was a Tennessee man? President of the boosters club and everything. Now that's bullshit, ain't it?"

Decker said, "This might come as a surprise to you, but most people's lives do not revolve around football. I haven't watched a Buckeyes game since I graduated. I couldn't care less if you played for the Longhorns or ran over my ass twenty-some years ago. I just care about what happened to your parents."

"Well, good for you. I've told you all I know about it. If that's not enough then that's too bad."

Mars rolled over in the bed and stared at the wall.

Bogart glanced at Decker, whose gaze was still on Mars.

"Your mother's blood was found in your car. Do you have an explanation other than it came from you?"

"No."

"Could she have been in the car before? Maybe cut herself or had a nosebleed?"

"No. None of that happened. She never used my car."

Decker said, "Did you get along with your parents?"

"Why?" said Mars over his shoulder.

"Well, the motive the prosecution painted during your trial was that—"

"I know what that man said," interrupted Mars. He rolled back over. His features were calmer, or perhaps just resigned. "My parents never made any demands on me when they knew I was going pro. I was going to take care of them. Buy them a house, a new car, set them up. I had it all planned out."

Decker cocked his head. "You're a good planner, right?"

"What's wrong with that?"

"Nothing. But the prosecution brought in witnesses who said otherwise about your parents. That they wanted more money than you were willing to give them."

Mars said slowly, "Not both of them."

Bogart said sharply, "So *one* of them did say things like that? The testimony was correct? Because you just told us they had made no demands on you. So were you lying to us?"

Mars licked his lips nervously. "My father. He kinda changed the last few months. He was moody and would get mad at Mom and me for the least little thing. I thought he was getting off in the head or something. But I guess it was the money thing. He figured out how much I'd probably be getting with my first contract. This was before the rookie rule. I'd done my homework, and if I went in the top three I was looking at a seven-million-dollar signing bonus. This was over twenty years ago. You know what that works out to be today?"

"Over ten million five hundred thousand," said Decker.

Mars looked at him funny. "That's right. How'd you know?"

"Lucky guess. And that was just the bonus?"

"Right. You got more over the course of the contract, but the signing bonus was the thing. And I was looking at maybe a seven-year deal that I could opt out of in three years. If I made All-Pro and led the league in rushing, I could write my own ticket. I mean, my next contract would make my rookie deal look cheap."

"But you never got that chance," said Decker.

"Does it look like I did?" he snapped.

"So what did your father say to you about it?"

"He wanted to be taken care of. I told him I would."

"But?" said Decker.

"But . . . but he said he wanted something in writing. To make it, you know, legally binding."

Bogart looked at Decker. "This wasn't part of the trial transcript."

Decker kept his gaze on Mars. "No, it wasn't. And why was that, Melvin?"

Mars sat up. "That was one of the reasons why I didn't testify at trial. My lawyer was afraid if I got asked about it I would have to reveal it."

"Reveal what?"

"That I signed a one-page contract saying that thirty percent of my rookie contract would go to my parents."

"And what happened to this contract?" asked Bogart.

"I guess it don't matter now." He let out a long breath. "I got rid of it."

"How, in a fire maybe?" Bogart said sharply.

"Hey, I know this doesn't look too good for me."

"*That* is an understatement," retorted Bogart.

17

Without taking his eyes off Mars, Decker said, "Agent Bogart, can you give us a minute, please?"

Bogart looked like he was going to say no, but Decker added, "Just two old footballers going to have a little one-on-one. That's all."

Bogart slowly rose. "I'll be out in the hall."

When the door had closed behind him, Decker drew his chair a little closer to the bed. He put his large hands on top of the bed's side rail.

Mars said, "Okay, I see how this is playing out. You're here just to trick me and make sure I go back to prison. Well, I ain't talking to you anymore without my lawyer being here."

"I already told you, Melvin, I'm here to find the truth. If you didn't kill your parents I will do everything in my power to prove that and get you out of prison with a full pardon."

"I *didn't* kill my parents. But I've been sitting in a prison cell for two decades getting ready for the needle, and then having to wait some more and then get ready for it again. You know what that's like?"

"Not even close," said Decker.

Mars looked surprised by this comment. He glanced toward the door. "Why'd you ask your partner to leave?"

"I thought you might be more comfortable just talking to me and not the FBI."

"But you're with the FBI."

"Until about two weeks ago I was living in a dump in the middle of Ohio with about sixty bucks in my pocket and not much of a future beyond shit PI cases." He paused. "If you still want your lawyer, I'll leave right now." He stood.

"Hold on. You . . . you told me my case was similar to something to do with your family?"

"Certain parallels, yes."

"What happened to your family?"

Decker sat back down. "Somebody murdered them. My wife, daughter, and brother-in-law. I found the bodies when I came home from work one night."

All the hostility in Mars's features disappeared. "Damn, man, I'm sorry."

"About sixteen months went by with no arrests. Then this guy walks into the police station and confesses."

"Shit, did he do it?"

Decker gazed at him. "It was a little more complicated than that."

"Okay," replied Mars, looking uncertain.

"But we got the people responsible. And they were held accountable."

"They in prison?"

"No, they're in graves."

Mars's eyes widened at this.

Decker said, "But that's history and it's over. Let's talk about the present. *Your* present."

Mars shrugged. "What you want me to say, Decker? I was a black man accused of killing his parents and one of them was white. Now, this is the South. This is Texas. Everybody loved me when I was a football star. But when I was charged I had no friends left. I was just a black dude fighting for my life. Hell, Texas executes more people than anybody else, and a whole lot of them are black."

"The contract with your parents?"

"I knew I was innocent, but I listened to my lawyer. I can carry a football and score touchdowns, man. But I didn't know anything about laws and courts back then."

"So your lawyer knew about the contract?"

"Yeah, I told him. But he said we didn't have to tell the prosecution nothing. It was their job to find out about it."

"I guess technically that's true."

"But morally, I know, it sucks. I wanted to get on the stand and tell my story. I wanted folks to hear it from my point of view. But he convinced me not to. So I didn't. Then we lost and I was screwed anyway."

"What'd you do with the contract?"

"I flushed it down the toilet. But let me tell you, I had no problem with giving my parents that money. I was going to make a lot more. I was working on endorsement deals that would've paid me more than my football money."

"And then it all went away."

Mars shook his head wearily. "Faster than I could run the forty."

"Tell me about your parents."

"What do you want to know?"

"I want to know about their pasts. Where they came from? Were they born in Texas? Did they come from someplace else?"

Mars looked perplexed by this. "I'm not sure what I can tell you. They didn't talk about any of that with me."

"How about relatives? That you visited or visited you?"

"That never happened."

"No relatives?"

"No. We never went anywhere. And nobody came to see us."

"That's pretty unusual."

"I guess, looking back on it. But it was just the way it was. And my parents, I guess you'd call it, doted on me. So that was cool. I liked that."

"Tell me about your father."

"Big man. Where I got my size and height. Strong

as an ox. My mom was tall for a woman, about five-nine or so. And man she could run, let me tell you. We'd go out on runs together when I was a kid. She could sprint and she had endurance. Ran me into the ground until I got to high school."

"So you got your speed from her?"

"Guess so."

"Maybe she was an athlete when she was younger. Maybe your dad too."

"I don't know, they never said."

"There were no photos of them at your house. Were there ever any?"

Mars leaned back against his pillow. "They didn't much like getting their picture taken. I remember there was one of them on a shelf in the living room that was taken when I was in high school. That was about it."

Decker scrutinized him.

Mars said, "Hey, I know it sounds kinda crazy now, but back then it was just the way it was, okay? I didn't think nothing of it."

"I've seen an old, grainy picture of your parents. But tell me what your mother looked like to you."

Mars's face spread into a smile. "She was so beautiful. Everybody said so. She could've been a model or something. My dad said he married way over his pay grade."

Decker held up his phone. "I took a picture of this in your parents' closet. Any idea what it means?"

Mars read the screen. "AC and RB? I have no idea what that means. That was in their closet?"

"Yeah."

"I don't know. I never looked in their closet."

"Okay. Your dad worked in a pawnshop and your mom taught Spanish and did some sewing?"

"Yeah."

"Who'd she sew for?"

"Some local company needed some piecework done. Didn't pay much, but she could work at home."

"And the Spanish? Did she go to a school to teach?"

"No, she didn't teach kids. She taught adults. White dudes mostly. You had a lot of folks coming over the border to work and such. People who hired 'em had to learn the language so they could tell 'em what to do. So my mom taught 'em."

"And where did she learn Spanish? Was it her native language?"

"No. I mean, I don't think so. She wasn't Hispanic, if that's what you mean. She was black. A lot darker than me. I'm pretty sure she was an American."

"Based on what?"

"She spoke like one. And she didn't have any foreign accent."

"Did you learn Spanish from her?"

"Bits and pieces, but we mostly spoke English. My dad was a stickler on that. We weren't Spanish. We were Americans, he would say. He didn't like it when she spoke Spanish at home."

"And she worked another job?"

"Yeah. The sewing and the Spanish lessons didn't pay much. She worked for a company that cleaned places around the area. And she'd press clothes. The woman could iron like a pro, I'll tell you that. Hell, she'd iron my jeans I wore to school."

"Did you ever ask them about their pasts?"

"I remember once wanting to know about my grandparents. It was grandparents' day at school when I was in the third grade. Just about everybody else had grandparents who came in. I asked Dad about it. He said they were dead. And then he didn't say anything more."

"Did he say how they died?"

Mars slapped the bed rail with his free hand. "Shit, what does that matter? You think my dad killed his parents? And you think I killed mine?"

"No, I don't think you killed your parents. I don't know if your father killed his. He might have."

Mars had been about to say something else but then stopped. He looked right at Decker. "What the hell is that supposed to mean?"

"You know nothing about your parents, Melvin. You know nothing about any of your relatives. There was one picture of your parents in their house. They never told you anything about themselves. Why do you think that is?"

"You mean you think they were hiding something?" Mars said slowly.

"At least it's worth exploring. Because if they *were* hiding something it might give someone *else* a really good reason to kill them."

18

Okay, what else have we found out about Roy and Lucinda Mars?" asked Bogart. The entire team was assembled around a conference table in the rental space.

Milligan glanced at Decker and said, "Okay, I have to admit, it's a little funny There's just really nothing on them that we can find. There were Social Security numbers issued to them, but when I dug into them nothing else came up."

"Nothing?" said Bogart. "You think they stole the numbers?"

"It's possible. And they did have driver's licenses on file twenty years ago, but I couldn't find anything else about them."

"Roy Mars had a job," said Jamison. "And so did Lucinda. They had to have FICA taken out of their paychecks and they had to file tax returns and such."

"Not that we could find," said Milligan. "The pawnshop where he worked is long since gone, but they could have paid him in cash or barter. And maybe the same for his wife. And lots of people don't file tax returns because they don't make enough money and don't owe anything."

"But you still have to file," pointed out Jamison. "It's a federal crime not to."

"And lots of people ignore that," countered Milligan. "And apparently the Marses were those kind of people, because the IRS has no record of them. And Texas doesn't have a personal income tax."

"How about the house?" asked Bogart. "Was there a mortgage on it?"

"Again, not that I could find," said Milligan. "But in the real estate records Roy and Lucinda Mars were listed as the owners."

"Okay," said Bogart. "That doesn't leave much to go on."

Milligan glanced at Decker. "I made some inquiries. The cops can't tell me who made the 911 call about the fire. If they ever knew, those records are long gone. I also asked about the interior of the house. The missing pictures on the wall and all. Apparently they didn't take crime scene photos of any of that. Just the bodies."

"Well, that was careless," opined Bogart.

"Do you think he's innocent?" asked Milligan.

"Leaning that way," said Decker.

"Why?" asked Bogart.

"The blood in the car. I gave Mars two plausible and exculpatory explanations of why her blood would be in his car. Neither could be disproved by the cops. Nosebleed or cut. He rejected both. Said she'd never been in his car. A guilty man would have jumped at either scenario. But not Melvin."

The others glanced at each other, the stark plausibility of what Decker had just said sinking in.

"So that was a test for Mars?" asked Davenport.

"And he passed it," said Decker. "At least in my mind."

He held up a sheaf of papers that had been stapled together. "This is the rest of the autopsy report on the Marses. It just came in from the coroner's office. They'd misplaced it."

"How'd you find out about that?" asked Bogart.

"The front of the report listed thirty-six pages as the length. There were only thirty-four pages attached. I made a call."

Jamison said, "And is there anything significant on the new pages?"

"One thing. Lucinda Mars had Stage Four glioblastoma."

They all stared at him, stunned.

"Brain cancer?" said Davenport.

"*Terminal* brain cancer, according to the report."

"Melvin never mentioned that," said Jamison.

"Maybe he didn't know," replied Decker.

Milligan said, "But how does that bear on the case?"

"I don't know if it does or not," said Decker. "She was dying, but then someone killed her." He glanced at Davenport. "Let's set that aside for a minute and focus on the son. What's your conclusion about his psychological makeup?"

Davenport pulled out some written notes.

"He's well above average in intelligence, with a combination of book and street smarts. He graduated from college early after majoring in business. The man is no dummy. He has an interesting combination of keeping things close to the vest but then appearing to open up, as in making very forceful claims of innocence and of being wrongfully persecuted."

"Not unusual for a man who's spent two decades in prison," noted Bogart. "He's learned how to play the system."

"Maybe," said Davenport. "And I have seen that, of course, but there seems to be something different about Mars. I just can't quite put my finger on it. He desperately wants to know more about this Charles Montgomery. He wants to know the details that Montgomery allegedly knows that would tie him to the murders. And he is wary that the authorities will try to connect him to Montgomery in some sort of murder-for-hire scenario. He's convinced that even if he is innocent he won't get out of prison. In fact, he's borderline paranoid on that."

"Well, considering how he was almost killed in prison, I don't think I would call his paranoia unjustified," said Decker, drawing a sharp glance from Davenport.

"If Mars had hired him to murder his parents

twenty years ago why would Montgomery come forward now?" asked Jamison. "Right before Mars was to be executed?"

"The timing is a little . . ." began Davenport.

"Convenient," Decker finished for her.

Bogart said, "So you think this was all planned out? By Montgomery?"

Decker shook his head. "He's on death row in an Alabama prison. How would he have even known Mars was going to be executed?"

The others just looked at him blankly.

Decker said, "So we need to hear that right from Montgomery himself."

"You think he'll tell you the truth?" asked Davenport, as she watched Decker closely. "The last words of a doomed man?"

"Not even close," replied Decker.

Holman Correctional Facility had been opened in 1969 and was filled to the brim with far more inmates than it was designed to hold. Located in southern Alabama where summer temperatures could soar to over a hundred degrees, the facility had no air-conditioning, and relied on industrial fans to move hot air around. Nicknamed "Slaughter Pen of the South" because of its reputation for violence inside the walls, and "the Pit" because of its geographical location at the bottom of Alabama, Holman housed Alabama's death row.

Decker and the rest of the team had made the trip on a commercial jet. They all wore FBI windbreakers, creds clipped to their jackets. Bogart's briefcase smacked against his thigh as they walked toward the prison's front entrance.

They were cleared through prison security after Bogart, Decker, and Milligan surrendered their weapons, and were escorted to a visitors' room by one of the prison guards.

"Tell us about Montgomery," Decker said to the guard as they walked along.

"He's a loner. No trouble. He bothers nobody and nobody bothers him. It's odd, though."

"What is?" asked Bogart.

"Well, in Alabama you get a choice on how you're executed. And Montgomery is the only one I've ever known to choose the electric chair over lethal injection. Why would you want to fry versus go to sleep?"

Bogart and Decker looked at each other. They continued on and were soon seated in a room opposite a heavily shackled Charles Montgomery while two burly guards hovered in the background.

Montgomery was white, a little over six feet, and had just turned seventy-two. His shaved head had a noticeable indentation on the top left side. His eyes were brown, his teeth even but stained with nicotine, and his once hard body had softened some. His forearms were muscled and heavily tatted and his ears were pierced for earrings, but no such hardware was allowed in here.

He raised his eyes to theirs and, starting with Bogart, went from left to right and then back right to left. Then his gaze dropped to his manacled hands.

Bogart said, "Mr. Montgomery, I'm Special Agent Bogart with the FBI. These are my colleagues. We're here to talk to you about your recent confession regarding the murders of Roy and Lucinda Mars in Texas."

Montgomery still did not look up.

Bogart glanced at Decker before continuing.

"Mr. Montgomery, we would like to hear from you the details of the night you allegedly murdered the Marses."

Montgomery said curtly, "Nothing *alleged* about it. And I already told 'em."

The tone was not hostile, simply matter-of-fact.

"I appreciate that, but we need to hear it from you, too."

"Why's that?" asked Montgomery, still looking down.

Decker had been running his gaze over the man, taking in small details of his appearance and demeanor.

"Was it a beating in here?" he asked. "Or was it Vietnam?"

Now Montgomery looked up. In that emotionless gaze it was readily apparent that the condemned man was one very dangerous person.

"What?" he asked quietly.

In response Decker touched the left top of his head. "Your skull's been partially cut away leaving that indentation. Was it a beating? Some kind of combat injury? You served in Vietnam."

"Mortar round exploded twenty feet from me. My buddy died. I got a hole in the head."

"Your file says you were in the Army," noted Bogart.

"Eighteenth Infantry, First Battalion, out of Fort Riley," Montgomery recited automatically.

"When did you come back stateside after the war?"

"Nineteen sixty-seven, mustered out a month later."

"Didn't want to be career military?" asked Decker.

Montgomery gave him a surly glance. "Yeah, it was so much fun and all."

Bogart pulled out a file from his briefcase. "So you were in Texas then when the Marses were murdered?"

"Had to be, since I killed 'em."

"Run us through that. How did it happen?"

Montgomery glanced over at him, impatience on his features. "It's all in your file. So why do I have to do that?"

"We're just trying to confirm everything. And we would like to hear it from you. That's why we came here."

"And if I don't want to say?"

"We can't force you," said Decker. "But we were wondering why you came forward in the first place."

"You know my sentence?"

"Yes."

"So what does it matter? Get it off my chest. Maybe help with the Big Man in the hereafter."

"I can understand that. But to get Mr. Mars off, your story needs to be confirmed. The FBI can do that faster than the state folks can. So if we both want the same thing, why not cooperate?"

"You look way too fat to be with the FBI."

"They made an exception for me."

"Why's that?"

"Because I like to get to the truth. Can you help me do that?"

Montgomery gave a long, resigned sigh. "What the hell does it matter? Okay." He rubbed his face with his chained hands and settled back in his seat.

"You heard of PTSD?" he asked Decker.

Decker nodded. "Yes."

"Well, they never tested me for it, but I got it. And all that crap that was burning over there? Munitions, chemical weapons. Agent Orange shit they dropped on our fuckin' heads? And who the hell knew what the Vietcong were chucking at us. Breathing all that in, day after day. It messed me up. Surprised it didn't give me cancer. Then that mortar round blew up next to me." He pointed to his head, his shackles clanging as he did so. "And they had to cut out a part of my skull. Hell, maybe part of my brain, VA never said. And then the headaches started."

"You got the Purple Heart," said Bogart.

"Big shit. That's *all* I got."

Decker interjected, "So the headaches started?"

"Yeah. And the VA didn't want to hear nothing about it. I got no treatment. But I tried to get on with my life. I got married, tried to keep a job, but it was no good. The pain never stopped. And when the docs wouldn't write no more prescriptions I took matters into my own hands."

"To get drugs, you mean?" asked Davenport. "For the pain?"

"Yeah. It was just little stuff at first. To get money to get the drugs. Then I started taking the drugs from people I knew had 'em. Cut out the middleman and go right to the source." He smiled darkly. "The Army taught me to be efficient."

Davenport said, "The drugs you were probably taking are heavily addictive. So you got hooked and couldn't stop?"

"Yeah. I was a total druggie. Do anything to get more."

"And then what?" asked Decker.

"Then things just snowballed. It was like I was a different person. Things I never woulda done before, I'd do. Hurt people, steal shit. I didn't care. I got busted a few times on petty crap but never did no real jail time. But my first marriage unraveled and I lost my job, my house, everything. Then I just started drifting across the country, trying to get the headaches to stop."

"And how did that get you to the Marses?"

Montgomery looked down again, his thumbs pressing together, his brow furrowed.

"See, I didn't know that was their name, not at first."

"Okay, but walk us through that night," said Decker.

"I come into town the night before, just passing through. Didn't know nobody and nobody knew me. It was a one-traffic-light shithole."

"You said the night before. Did you stay anywhere?" asked Bogart.

Montgomery looked at him crossly. "And pay with what? I had nothing in my pocket. Not even no change. I was hungry but I couldn't buy no food either. Much less a place to stay. I slept in my car."

"Keep going," said Decker.

"I drove past this pawnshop the next day. It was in the little downtown area. At first I didn't think anything of it, but then I got an idea. I went inside, thinking maybe I might pawn something. I had my medals, and an old service pistol. If I pawned those I could get something to eat. And I was riding on close to vapors. So I could maybe fill up my tank and head on to the next shithole. Anyways, there was a dude in there. Tall, white guy."

"That was Roy Mars," said Jamison. "He worked there."

Montgomery nodded. "But I didn't know that was his name back then. I pulled out my stuff and showed him. But he told me they weren't interested in crap like that. Lotta former soldiers in Texas, he said, and then he pointed to a case full of guns and old medals dudes had pawned and never come back for."

Bogart and Decker exchanged a glance.

Montgomery continued. "Anyway, that pissed me off. I asked the guy if he was a vet and he said that was none of my business and if I was looking for a hand-out I'd come to the wrong place because they were barely making a living as it was. Then the door opened and another customer came in. I walked over to the corner and watched. When the man opened the cash register I saw all the money in there. That's when I knew the dude had lied to me. He had money. He wasn't barely getting by. That pissed me off even more."

"What did you do then?" asked Bogart.

"Went back to my car and waited. Army teaches patience. I was hunting this dude and didn't care how long it took. He closed the shop up at nine, got in his car and drove off. I followed him. He got to his place, which was in the middle of nowhere. No other homes around. That was fine with me. He went inside. I parked my car and got out."

"What kind of car were you driving?" asked Decker.

Montgomery didn't hesitate. "Rusted-out piece of shit '77 V-eight Pontiac Grand Prix, dark blue, big as a house. You could land a chopper on the sucker's hood."

"Surprised you remember that in such detail."

"I lived in that car for about a year."

"Did you own it?" asked Decker.

Montgomery lifted his gaze to him. "I stole it from somewhere and got plates off a ride in an impoundment lot in Tennessee. Don't remember where."

"So you were waiting outside the house?" prompted Decker.

"Right. I pulled surveillance on the place. Again, what the Army taught me. I was able to see in a couple of windows without being seen. It was just the two of them. Him and, I supposed, his wife. I remember she was black, which surprised me him being white."

"Okay," said Decker. "What then?"

"I waited until maybe eleven-thirty or a little later."

"You're sure about that?" asked Decker.

Montgomery flashed him a surprised look. "Yeah, why?"

"Just trying to confirm. Keep going."

"So's I got in through the back door. It wasn't locked. I had my gun out."

"What kind of gun?" asked Bogart.

"My service piece, one I tried to pawn."

Decker nodded. "And then what?"

"They weren't downstairs. I had seen the lights go out and then the lights go on upstairs. Figured they were going to bed. I snuck up the stairs, but I got messed up on the room they were in. I went into one bedroom but it was empty. Girlie posters on the wall, athletic gear everywhere, so I was guessing it was their kid's room. I was worried maybe their kid was sleeping in the bed, but it was empty."

"And that's when you saw it?" asked Decker, which drew a sharp glance from Jamison and Davenport.

Montgomery licked his lips and nodded. "Yeah. The shotgun was in a rack on the wall. I thought if I was going to do this, I couldn't use my service piece. They might be able to trace it to me, you know, through ballistics."

"Not if they didn't have your gun," pointed out Bogart.

"Yeah, but they might arrest me and then they'd *have* my gun," countered Montgomery.

"Keep going," said Decker.

"I took the shotgun, found the ammo for it in a little drawer attached to the rack, and loaded it. Then I went into their bedroom. They were in bed asleep, but I got 'em up. They were scared shitless. Dude remembered me. I told him I wanted the money from the till back at the pawnshop. If he did that I'd let 'em live. He said that was impossible because the owner took it every night and put it in the bank's night deposit slot. That really ticked me off. See, I thought he *was* the owner, but he was just some little prick clerk. But he had talked big like he owned the damn place. I don't like people lying to me. Don't sit well. Bet the sonofabitch never wore the uniform. And he's looking down on me? Telling me he's not giving *me* a *handout*?" Montgomery shook his head with finality. "Who the hell does he think he is? No way I'm letting that pass. So I blew him away. His wife was screaming. I couldn't let her live, right? So I shot her too."

Montgomery stopped abruptly and looked around at Jamison and Davenport.

"What's wrong?" asked Decker.

"I felt bad about popping the woman, but there was nothing else I could do." He shrugged. "I've killed people. On the battlefield and off. But I never killed no woman before. It was his fault, not hers."

"And then what did you do?" asked Decker, hiding his disgust at the man's apportioning of blame for Lucinda Mars's murder onto her husband.

Milligan was busy writing all this down in his tablet, but he too looked upset at what he was hearing.

"I panicked. I mean, you get the adrenaline rush when you're doing it. But when it's done it's like you're coming off a crack high. You crash. My first thought was just to run for it. But then I looked down at the bodies and thought of something else.

When I had been scoping out the place I peeked in the garage. Saw the gas can. I ran down and got it and poured the gas over them and then set them on fire."

"But why?" asked Bogart.

"I thought . . ." He faltered. "I thought maybe if they and the house burned down they might just think it was a fire that killed 'em. And not that nobody had shot 'em."

"What'd you do with the shotgun?" asked Decker.

"Put it back on the rack."

"Then you left?"

"Yeah. I jumped in my car and hightailed it out of there."

"Did you see another vehicle while you were driving away?" asked Decker.

Montgomery shook his head. "I was so screwed up in the head right then I coulda passed a convoy of Army tanks and never even noticed it."

"Were you wearing gloves?" asked Decker.

"Gloves?"

"When you picked up the shotgun?"

"Oh yeah, I had on gloves. Didn't want to leave no prints behind. I was in the Army, they were on file." He paused and looked at Decker. "And that's . . . it."

"Not quite. How'd you find out about Melvin Mars?"

"Oh, that," said Montgomery offhandedly. "This was just within the last year. I was here in prison.

Dude told me about Mars. He said he heard it from a guy over in Texas."

"Dude have a name?" asked Bogart.

"Donny Crockett," said Montgomery promptly.

"And where is he now?"

"In a coffin. He was on death row too. They executed him four months ago."

Bogart and Decker looked at each other while Davenport kept her gaze squarely on Montgomery.

She said, "Why would he mention Melvin Mars to you?"

"Didn't you know?" said Montgomery with a brief grin. "I played some ball at Ole Miss. I was a fullback. That meant I slammed my body against other bodies all game long so the tailback could look good. Now, I never played against Mars, because I was a lot older, but I heard of him later on. Didn't connect it to what I done in Texas. But then when my buddy told me the details, I had my wife Google it for me. When I saw the pictures of the parents I knew they were the ones I'd killed."

"And you decided to come forward why?" asked Decker. "Because God might go easier on you?"

Montgomery shrugged. "Look, I'm going to die anyway. Screwed up my whole life. This dude Mars lost out on a lot because of me. Guess I'm just trying to make amends. Do one good thing before I kick off." He stopped and gave Decker a searching look.

"They are going to let him go, right? He didn't kill his parents. I did."

"We'll see," said Decker. "It's the reason we're here."

"I told the local cops stuff that I knew about the house and all. Details they didn't let out to the public. It was me. What else can I say?"

"I think you've said a lot," answered Decker.

Bogart said, "And you never met Melvin Mars?"

Montgomery shook his head. "No sir, I never met the man. If he had been home that night I would've killed him too."

They all fell silent for a few moments. Decker was studying Montgomery closely while Bogart looked down at some notes. Jamison and Davenport were watching Decker.

Decker finally said, "So you eventually remarried?"

Montgomery nodded. "A couple years later. I was already in my fifties, but Regina was twenty years younger. So we had a kid. I tried to settle down and get cleaned up, but it was no good." He motioned to his head again. "Pains came back. Had 'em all the time at that point. I just went nuts. Did shit. Regina took our son and ran for it. I started robbing banks and selling drugs, murdered a couple dudes I was doing business with. Then I killed a state trooper. That's why I'm here."

"Where does your current wife live?" asked Decker.

Montgomery's eyebrows flicked up at this. "Why?"

"We'll need to talk to her."

"Why?" he asked again.

"She's part of this chain. We have to look at every link."

Montgomery considered this for a long moment. "She lives about twenty miles from here. Prison has the address. Moved there when I got transferred here."

"And you've been married how long?"

"About eighteen years. Though I've been in prison the last nine. Like I said, she left me when I went out of control. Hell, Tommy was just a little boy then. But when I got the death sentence she came to the prison to see me. We never officially got divorced. I guess she felt sorry for me."

"How many kids do you have?" asked Decker.

"Just Tommy. He lives with his mom but he never comes here. Don't blame him. Wasn't there for him, so why should he be there for me? He's a really good football player from what she tells me."

"Does she visit you often?" asked Davenport.

Montgomery leveled his gaze on her. "Every week, like clockwork."

"That's nice," said Davenport, drawing a wary look from Montgomery.

"Anyone else ever visit you?" asked Decker.

"I don't have anybody else."

"No lawyers or anything?"

"They tried. And failed. And left."

Decker said, "When is your execution date?"

"Three weeks from yesterday."

Davenport asked, "Why did you choose the electric chair over lethal injection?"

Everyone looked at her.

Montgomery grinned. "Figure where I'm going I better get used to being hot. And why not go out with a bang?"

"What are your wife's plans after you're gone?" Decker asked.

"Start over somewhere else."

"Right," said Decker. "We'll tell her you said hello when we see her."

"I'm doing the right thing, right?" said Montgomery nervously.

"That's not for me to answer," replied Decker. "One more thing. Did you steal any money or property from the Marses?"

Montgomery stared up at him, a wary expression on his features. "No, did the cops say I did?"

"Did you commit any other crimes while you were in town?" asked Decker.

"No. I told you. I killed them and tore outta there."

"So you didn't stay around and do a day's worth of labor or anything?"

Montgomery looked at him like Decker had lost his mind.

"After murdering two people?"

"So, no?"

"Hell no."

"And how far did you drive after you left town?"

"I don't know."

"You remember a city?"

Montgomery thought for a moment. "Maybe Abilene. Yeah, that's right. I jumped on Interstate 20 and just headed east. Ran smack into Abilene."

"That was about, what, a hundred and eighty miles? Maybe a three-hour drive?"

"About that, I guess, yeah."

"Okay, thanks."

As they started to leave Montgomery called after them. "Can you tell Mr. Mars that I'm sorry?"

Decker looked back at him. "I don't really think that's a good idea."

19

They drove directly to Regina Montgomery's house, which, as Montgomery had said, was only about twenty minutes from the prison.

The skies were threatening rain, and, as the temperature dipped, perhaps even some snow, though it rarely fell in this part of Alabama.

Bogart drove and Decker rode next to him. Davenport was in the backseat writing up some notes on her electronic tablet. Milligan was next to her doing the same thing on his.

Jamison was to Milligan's left. She said, "That was one scary man."

"Well, at least the public won't have to worry about him anymore," said Bogart.

"Do you think his head injury made him do all those things?" asked Jamison.

"I don't know," replied Bogart. "In the eyes of the law it apparently didn't matter if it did or not."

"I guess not," she said doubtfully.

"Lisa, what was your opinion of him?" asked Bogart as he glanced at her in the car's rearview.

She looked up from her tablet. "My down and dirty is the guy is being truthful. He's obviously cagey as hell, but he also seems genuinely remorseful. And if he is suffering from PTSD and that head wound affected critical areas of his brain, what he later did could make sense."

She saw Decker staring out of the side window, obviously not paying attention to what she was saying.

"What did you think, Amos?" she said.

When he said nothing she reached forward and touched his shoulder. He jerked and glanced back at her.

"I'm sorry," she said. "I was asking what you thought of Montgomery?"

"I think it's more important what we think of Regina Montgomery," he said.

"And why is that?" she asked, looking confused. "I remember you saying we needed to find out if Montgomery had family."

"And I hope we're just about to get some answers."

Regina Montgomery lived in one of a line of old duplexes that looked about a few rusted nails and a few more termite bites from falling down. They parked out front. There was an old cream-colored Buick with a tattered faux leather top sitting out in a front yard that held not a single blade of grass. The entire area looked blighted. In the distance they could hear a freight train's whistle.

A light rain started to fall as they walked up to the

front door. It had a pyramid-shaped glass with a crack in it at about eye level.

Bogart knocked on the door.

Davenport said, "The place next door looks abandoned."

"Half the places here look abandoned," noted Bogart.

They heard approaching footsteps and the door was opened.

Regina Montgomery was of medium height, thin, and her hair was more white than brown. She was dressed in faded jeans, flats, and a sweater with some smears of dirt near the waist.

They identified themselves and were invited in.

The front room was small, with a few pieces of cheap and battered furniture. She led them into the kitchen, moved some boxes and stacks of paper off chairs, and motioned for them to sit down around the small table in the middle of the space. There were only four chairs, so Milligan and Davenport stood.

Regina looked nervously at each of them before settling her gaze on Bogart, who had produced his FBI shield at the front door.

"What do you want with me?" she asked bluntly.

"Just to ask some questions. We've spoken with your husband."

"Just so you know, while it's true we never got divorced, we haven't lived together for a long time. He's been in prison for years."

"But legally he's still your husband?"

"Yes."

"When did you learn about his maybe having murdered Roy and Lucinda Mars?"

She leaned back in the chair and assumed a focused expression. "When I went to the prison to visit Chuck."

"Do you remember the date?"

"No, not exactly. I go every week, though. Lemme think." She picked up a pack of cigarettes off the table, lit one, blew smoke out her nostrils, and was silent for a few moments, then said, "Maybe a couple months or so. Maybe. I'm not really sure."

"Were you surprised?" asked Bogart.

"What, that he'd killed people? Hell no. I knew he could be violent. He'd murdered other people. It's why they're going to execute him. He killed an Alabama state trooper. That's gonna get you the damn death penalty every time."

"He said he had you look up the Marses' case online to make sure he was right?" prompted Bogart.

"Yeah, I went over to the library. I don't have a computer. I printed out their pictures and some other information and brought it to him at the prison. He recognized them right off."

"Did you suggest that he tell the authorities?"

She shook her head. "That was Chuck's idea. But I thought it was the right thing to do. One way he could, you know, make up for what he'd done a little."

Decker looked around the space, his mind taking snapshots of everything he was seeing. "After your husband is executed what are your plans?"

She snorted. "Ain't got none. I live here and can barely make the rent. I work at the grocery store and then have a second job at the McDonald's down the road."

"Your son lives with you?" asked Decker.

She nodded. "Tommy. He's a good boy. He'll do all right."

"His father said he was a good ballplayer."

She nodded. "Yeah, he is."

"He doesn't visit his dad?"

She looked at him crossly. "No. Why should he?"

"It was good of you to stick by your husband through all this," noted Jamison.

"We had some good times together. A *few* good times. And he *is* Tommy's dad. And I blame the damn government. Chuck fights for his country, gets a chunk of his head torn out, and what'd they do for him? Nothing. Now that's a damn crime, if you ask me."

"I think you'd find a lot of people to agree with you on that," observed Davenport.

"Anything else you can tell us?" asked Bogart.

"I don't know nothing else." She looked at her watch. "And I got to get to work. My shift starts in about twenty minutes."

She walked them to the door and shut it firmly behind them.

Bogart looked at Decker. "Okay, what now?"

"Now we go see the Howling Cougars."

The rain had started to fall more steadily as they approached the high school that Decker had located on his phone.

"What are we doing here?" asked Bogart.

"You mentioned the Howling Cougars?" said Davenport.

Decker nodded. "The pictures at Regina Montgomery's. Her son was in his Howling Cougars football jersey."

"Okay, so you want to talk to him, but he's never visited his father," pointed out Jamison.

"I don't want to ask him about his father."

Bogart parked in the visitors' parking lot and they went into the office. A few minutes later they were headed to the gym with the assistant principal.

"Tommy has finished his classes for the day," said the man as they walked down the corridor. "But the team is doing some work in the gym."

"But isn't football season over?" asked Bogart.

The man smiled. "This is Alabama. Football season is never really over. And we won the conference championship this season. The boys want to repeat next year. Just getting in some extra work."

He left them in the gym after speaking to the

coach, who brought Tommy Montgomery over a minute later.

He was a good–looking kid, taller than his father, with broad shoulders and thick arms and thicker legs.

He looked at them all with unfriendly eyes. "Coach said you're here about my old man."

"That's right," said Bogart.

"I got nothing to say about him, 'cause I don't know him. He was never around. I'll be glad when they do him. Then he's outta my life for good."

Decker looked over at the other players, who were going through some formation reps.

"What position do you play?" asked Decker.

Tommy looked up at him. "Why? You know anything about football?"

"A little. You're undersized for the O or D line. Linebacker too. But you've got length in your arms and legs. And your calves are rocks, your thighs are ripped, and your fingers are callused. You touch the ball a lot and you run farther than the line of scrimmage. You're either a safety or a tailback or a receiver."

Tommy appraised him in a different light. "You *did* play ball. I'm a tailback."

Jamison said proudly, "Decker here played at Ohio State. And then with the Cleveland Browns."

Tommy's jaw dropped. "Damn, really?"

Decker said, "What's your best running play?"

"We call it the firecracker. Fake the A-gap blast to the fullback, pitch to me on the left edge. I cut back to the B-gap and then make a stutter to clear the line and let the tight end do a cutback scrape on the backer, then I hit the corner and I'm gone. Always good for at least ten yards until the safety makes the tackle. We run it on third and long because the box ain't stacked and the secondary's playing cover-two soft thinking we're gonna pass."

"I didn't understand a single word of that," said a bemused Davenport.

"If it makes you feel any better, neither did I," commented Bogart.

Decker glanced over at the other players running a formation. "So you obviously run the tight end on that side if his job is to scrape the backer."

"Yep," said Tommy. "Extra blocker."

"Right, but he's not being properly utilized." He looked back at Tommy. "Okay, tell your coach to scratch the stutter. The blast would've frozen the interior lineman anyway, so don't waste the time. And you want to hit the B-gap at speed. You let the left tackle crash down to seal the edge, the *guard* comes around to do the scrape on the backer, that allows the tight end to release, and you follow his butt down the field. *He* engages the safety with his left shoulder if the guy comes up and tries to make a play, and forces him to the outside while you push off hard to the inside. If the corner's in soft cover two he probably will have already committed to the outside edge because of the pitch, and you'll have a receiver on him blocking, so you don't have to worry much about him. If you've got decent wheels, you're home free down the seam for a lot more than ten yards. Maybe end zone if you're fast enough to beat the angle the other safety takes."

Tommy broke into a broad grin. "Damn, man, thanks."

"You're welcome. You got any scholarship offers?"

"I've been starting since my freshman year. I'll be a senior next year and I've already got three offers, two from D-ones and one from a D-two."

"That's great. Good for you. Look, we talked to your mom. About her future. After your dad . . ." Decker let his voice trail off and he stared expectantly at Tommy.

"Yeah."

"And then you'll be off in a year. I hope she'll be able to make ends meet."

"Oh, she'll be okay. With the money and all."

Bogart started to say something, but Decker said, "Right, the money. She started to tell us about that, but then she had to go to work."

"Yeah, it's a lot. Enough for her to be okay."

"That's what she said. Do you know from where?"

"Insurance. My scumball father had a life insurance policy. Go figure."

"And it pays off even if he's to be executed?" asked Bogart.

"Yeah. I mean, that's what Mom said."

"So a lot of money," said Decker. "Do you know how much?"

"Not exactly, no. But she said she'd be moving away from here after I graduate and then settle down wherever I go to college. She's going to buy a place and not have to work." He paused. "I mean, she's always been there for me, you know. Most guys probably don't want their moms around when they're at college, but . . . it's been rough, you know and she's . . . you know what I mean?" he finished looking a little embarrassed.

"I know exactly what you mean," said Decker. "Good luck with your ballplaying." He tapped his temple. "And never lead with your head. It's not worth it."

They left Tommy there and walked back out to the car.

"How did you know, Decker?" said Davenport.

"Know what?"

"That Regina Montgomery was coming into money?"

"I didn't know until he told me. But I suspected it."

"But why did you suspect it?" asked Bogart.

"Because dead people have absolutely no use for cash."

20

Charles Montgomery was in court today in Alabama and gave an allocution to the judge that he killed your parents."

Decker tapped his hand on the arm of his chair as he sat looking at Melvin Mars, who was finishing a full week of rehab at a facility attached to the hospital.

Mars looked pretty much normal. The swelling was gone, along with the soreness. The docs had given him a clean bill of health. He was to be released the following day.

Mars put down the weights he had been lifting and toweled off his face.

"So what does that mean exactly?"

"It's a formal statement under oath that what he said is true. It included specific details about the murders of your parents."

"And the court accepted it?"

Decker nodded.

He had come here today by himself. He wanted some time alone with Mars.

"So what now?"

Decker said, "That statement has been forwarded to the court here in Texas that has jurisdiction over your case. The court will review it and then make a determination."

"What about the people who actually prosecuted me?"

"They've retired. But the state lawyers are in the loop and they are also considering everything. If they come down on the side of believing Montgomery and throw their support to you, then I don't think the court has any choice but to set you free. Pretty much immediately."

Mars wrapped the towel around his neck, his muscles straining against the tight T-shirt, and sat down opposite Decker.

"How long you reckon all that will take?"

"I can't imagine that long."

"What was he like?" Mars asked quietly.

"Who, Montgomery?"

Mars nodded, his gaze on the floor.

"Probably like a lot of guys you've known in prison."

"So just a screwed-up asshole looking to hurt people?"

"He was a Vietnam vet. Said stuff over there gave him headaches. Couldn't take the pain. Turned to crime to pay for the drugs because the VA wouldn't help him."

"But why'd he kill my parents?"

"You really want to hear this? It can't change anything."

Mars glanced up at him. "Tell me."

"Wrong place, wrong time. Montgomery tried to pawn stuff at your dad's shop. He said your dad wasn't buying, maybe dissed him. He got pissed, followed him home, wanted money, but your dad told him he was only the clerk there, that the owner put the money in the bank every night. So . . . he did what he did, using your shotgun he found in your room. And that gas can in the garage."

Mars studied the floor. "And you believe him?"

"He had details only the person there would've known."

Mars looked up again. "But do you believe he did it?"

Decker said nothing.

"So you don't believe him, then?"

"Doesn't matter what I believe. It matters what the truth is."

"And that doesn't come close to answering my question," Mars said irritably. "Why do you have to make everything so damn hard, Decker?"

"My job is to find the truth, Melvin. I told you that the first time I met you. Right now, I don't believe anybody."

"Including me?"

"With you, I'm getting there. Faster than I normally do." He added, "It's probably because you're so lovable."

Mars laughed. "Didn't think you had a sense of humor."

"I don't. You must be rubbing off on me."

"So where do I go while all this stuff is being decided?"

"A safe house maintained by the FBI. It's in Austin."

"Haven't been back to Austin since I played at UT."

"I figured." Decker paused. "Got a question for you."

"Okay, shoot."

"I read your mother's full autopsy report."

Mars stiffened as he looked warily at Decker. "And what? Did you see something off?"

"I saw that the coroner concluded that your mother had terminal brain cancer."

Mars nearly toppled off the stool. He managed to keep his balance by slamming a hand down on the floor and righting himself.

"I can tell from your reaction that you didn't know."

"That's bullshit," exclaimed Mars.

"Not according to the report. There were pictures of the tumor. I won't show them to you because the shotgun blast had done a lot of damage. Stage Four, pretty much always fatal. It's what Ted Kennedy died of."

Mars was staring at the floor, his eyes wide in disbelief. "She never said anything to me. Nothing."

"Did she show any signs of being sick?"

Mars pressed the towel against his face and began to sob into it.

Decker, unprepared for this, sat back and simply waited.

When the sobs finally subsided, Mars rubbed his face dry and slowly sat up, his chest still heaving.

"She'd lost weight. Didn't have much of an appetite. And she had headaches. Migraines, she said."

"Did she ever go to a hospital? Receive any treatment?"

"I can't believe this. She had brain cancer and they didn't tell me? She was dying and they didn't think to mention it to their only child?"

"I know this is a shock, Melvin. But if she'd started treatment you would have known, right?"

"I don't know. I was gone a lot. But she didn't lose her hair or nothing like that. I would've noticed that."

"Was she still working at the end?"

Mars looked up. "No. Dad said he wanted her to take a break. I just thought it was because of the money I'd be getting. I never . . ." His voice trailed away.

"Would they have gone to a doctor in town?"

"I guess. They had their dentist. And Mom used a chiropractor sometimes. All the work she did made her stiff."

"Do you know the name of the doctor?"

"No." He paused. "I guess back then it was all about me, Decker. I really didn't have that much to do with my parents. I was so busy with football. But . . . but I still loved them. I was going to take care of them. But . . . shit."

He looked down, his features full of a guilty misery.

"You were dealing with a lot for a young guy, Melvin. I wouldn't beat yourself up too badly."

"This brain cancer. Do you think it has anything to do with their deaths?"

"I don't see how. But what I don't see right now could fill a library."

Mars sat up and wiped his face again. "What do I do if they let me loose, Decker?" he said in a hollow tone. He looked across at Decker like a little boy lost in a world he didn't even know existed.

Decker appeared uncomfortable at this query and said nothing.

Mars looked down and continued, "I was nearly twenty-two when I left the world. I'm almost forty-two now. I was a kid then, now I'm a man. But back then I still had plans. Lots of 'em. Now, I don't have a . . . damn clue what I'm supposed to do."

He glanced up at Decker, saw the blank face staring back at him, and looked away. "Forget it. I'll figure it out. Always do."

"Let's take it one step at a time, Melvin."

"Yeah, right," said Mars absently.

173

Decker leaned forward. It was time to discuss what he had come here to talk about.

"What if you didn't do it and Charles Montgomery *also* didn't do it?"

Mars sat up looking bewildered. "What?"

"What's the third option, Melvin? That's what I want to know."

"Third option?"

"Your parents' past is too fuzzy. Nobody looked at that back then because they had you dead to rights for the murders. But there are too many holes. There might be something in one of those holes that would explain why they were killed."

"Like what?"

"I don't know."

"But why don't you believe Montgomery? He knew stuff from my house."

"He could have been told all that by whoever really did it."

"But why would he do that? Confess to a crime he didn't commit?"

"Because he's already a dead man. What's two more murders? They can't execute him a second time. And what if someone asked him to do it in return for setting up his wife and kid for life?"

Mars slumped back in his chair. "Set them up for life? That's big money. My parents . . . why would anyone with big money care about them? Or care about getting me outta prison after all this time?"

"I don't have answers for that. I just have the questions."

Mars rubbed his face with a sweaty hand. "You're throwing me for a loop with all this shit, man. First you tell me my mom had cancer and now this," he added angrily.

"I figured you might want to know the truth. The *real* truth. If I spent twenty years of my life in prison for something I didn't do, I'd want to know exactly who put me there. And why."

Mars stared at him for a few seconds and then started to nod. "Yeah, me too. So how can I help?"

"By remembering anything you can about your parents. Something they said that seemed odd. Letters, phone calls they might have gotten that seemed off somehow. Visitors. Anything that might tell us where they really came from."

"I'll have to give that some thought."

"Well, I'm not going anywhere. And neither are you."

21

Milligan put down his cup of coffee and stared across the table at Decker.

The team was having dinner at an Applebee's in Austin, where they had moved Mars after his release from the rehab facility. The rain was pouring down outside and they had spent a long day going over the details of everything they could find about Charles Montgomery.

Milligan said, "There *is* a life insurance policy that *does* pay off when Montgomery dies."

"But it's only for thirty thousand dollars," said Jamison, who was sitting next to Decker.

"But it's big money to her, I bet," replied Milligan.

"Not enough to buy a house and not have to work," pointed out Davenport.

"So maybe Tommy Montgomery was exaggerating," countered Milligan.

"I don't think so."

Milligan said, "Why don't you just tell us why you really think Montgomery is lying? Come on, Decker, we're a team, right? We need to share information."

Decker put down his fork and wiped his mouth using his napkin.

"It's a question of cash flow."

"Excuse me?" said Milligan in an aggressive tone. "With the wife?"

"No, the husband." Decker had selected a salad, though he really wanted the ribs. When he'd made noises about ordering the rack of ribs Jamison had given him a look that had made him feel guilty enough to go with the leafy vegetables. He had dropped fifteen more pounds and his knees didn't ache all the time anymore. But in an act of defiance, he *had* ordered an Amstel Light.

He finished off his beer and looked over at the man with the expression of someone having to do something he really didn't want to be bothered doing.

"Montgomery told us he had no money when he got to town. That's why he went to the pawnshop. He rode into town on an empty gas tank and an empty stomach. He told us after he killed the Marses he tore out of town. He didn't steal anything from them, or anyone else. He didn't work a job before he left. He said he drove all the way to Abilene, which is about a three-hour trip, without stopping."

"Okay, so?"

"He was driving a '77 Impala with a V-eight. I looked it up. Brand-new that car got about eighteen miles to the gallon highway. After nearly twenty years I doubt it would get much more than twelve at best.

He'd need about fifteen gallons at minimum to make the trip. And back then gas was a little over a buck a gallon. So if he came into town on an empty tank and wallet and left with an empty tank and wallet, how'd he get all the way to Abilene without running out of gas? And on top of that he had to drive all the way out to the Marses' house to kill them. That's nearly two gallons right there. So tell me, how is that all possible?"

Davenport and Jamison exchanged a quick glance.

Bogart cleared his throat and said, "It's not. Which means he was either lying or mistaken."

Decker said, "I don't buy it that he was mistaken. He was too specific on the details. It was just a small point that was overlooked when the cover story was put together."

"Whoa," said Milligan. "Where do you get a *cover* story?"

"Someone had to put it together."

"That is a huge and, in my mind, unjustified leap of logic."

"Well, I guess that's just the difference between my mind and yours."

Milligan screwed up his face at this comment and picked up his coffee. "And remember Lucinda's blood in Melvin's car? She never used that car," he said. "So how'd the blood get there? Montgomery sure as hell couldn't have put it there."

Bogart's phone rang. He answered the call, listened for a few moments, and then clicked off.

He looked around the table. "The Texas court has just decided to give Mars a full pardon. He's being released from prison."

"That's great news," said Jamison.

"If he's innocent," said Milligan sullenly. "Not so great if he's not."

"I wonder if he wants to go to Alabama," said Bogart.

"Alabama?" asked Davenport. "Why?"

"Family members of the victims are entitled to witness the execution. And although technically Montgomery wasn't convicted of the murders, he did confess to them, and it's not like Mars will get a second chance to see him put to death."

"Well, let's go ask him," said Decker.

Mars was sitting in a room in a rental house guarded by three FBI agents out of Austin. His lawyer, Mary Oliver, had obviously just arrived, because she was hugging Mars as Decker, Bogart, and the rest of the team showed up.

"I knew it might be coming," said Mars. "But it's still hard to believe."

Oliver said, "There will be a formal court proceeding where your record will be expunged, and I've already filed for compensation from the state. I don't think you'll have any problem getting the max pay-out."

After they all had finished congratulating him, Bogart told him about Montgomery's execution coming up. "I've made calls. They'll let you attend if you want to."

Mars looked over at Decker. "What do you think? Should I go?"

Decker thought about this for a few moments. "If you think it might give you some closure, yes."

"But you don't think he really did it."

"And I could be wrong." Decker paused. "Besides, there's another reason for us to go to Alabama."

"What's that?"

"*Mrs.* Montgomery."

The court proceeding was held the next day. Mars, dressed in a cheap suit, stood next to Mary Oliver as the judge apologized for what had happened and formally cleared him of all charges.

"I can only hope, Mr. Mars, that the rest of your life will be full of nothing but positive events," said the judge. He smacked his gavel and the proceedings were over.

There were quite a few newspeople gathered outside the courtroom, all wanting a piece of Mars and his story. But by now Bogart, Decker, and Milligan had joined the fray, and Decker used his bulk like a bowling ball to move Mars through the throngs of waving microphones to a waiting SUV.

As they sped off Decker said, "You're going to be the national news story du jour."

"I'm surprised anybody still cares about it," said Mars.

"They will, but only for *one* twenty-four-hour news cycle."

Bogart handed him something. Mars looked down at it.

"A cell phone?"

Jamison answered. "It's actually a smartphone. You can get the Internet on it. Do emails, texting, tweeting, Instagram, Snapchat, take pictures and watch TV and movies. Oh, and you can also make *calls* with it." She added with a grin, "But *sexting* will just get you in trouble. So skip that one."

Mars rubbed a finger over the phone's screen. "Guess I got a lot of catching up to do."

"Well, it's better than the alternative," noted Decker.

Since Mars was no longer a prisoner, he could travel without a guard, and without being shackled. He sat on the United Airlines flight next to Decker. Bogart was across the aisle. Jamison and Davenport were in the seats behind Bogart. Milligan had volunteered to remain in Texas to keep working on the case locally.

Mars looked out the window. "Haven't been on a

plane in a long time. They look pretty much the same."

Decker adjusted his sitting position, reclining his chair the maximum one-eighteenth of an inch allowed. "There's one difference. The seats have gotten smaller. Or maybe I've just gotten a lot bigger."

Mars continued to stare out the window. "Never thought I'd be leaving Texas."

"I'm sure you thought you'd never be doing a lot of things."

"I've never witnessed an execution."

"Just so you know, Montgomery picked the electric chair over lethal injection."

Mars glanced sharply at him. "What the hell is that about?"

"Couldn't tell you. Alabama gives you a choice and that was his."

"Will his wife be there?"

"She's entitled to be. Whether she's coming or not I don't know. I doubt she'll bring her son if she does."

"And if he didn't kill my parents?"

"He clearly murdered several others. His capital sentence was justified under the law."

Mars nodded. "How many innocent folks you figure were executed?"

"One is too many. And I'm pretty sure it's more than one."

"I came within a few minutes of being part of that group."

"Like I said when I met you, you're one lucky guy, after being one really unlucky guy."

"Yeah, well, let's hope my luck holds."

Mars looked to the front of the plane and watched as the flight attendant positioned the beverage cart as a roadblock in front of the cockpit as one of the pilots came out to use the restroom.

"When did they start doing that?" he asked.

"After 9/11," replied Decker.

"Oh, right."

Mars pulled his gaze away from the front of the plane and said to Decker, "You said we were coming here for Mrs. Montgomery too."

"That's right."

"Why?"

"She was the only one to visit her husband the last few years."

"Okay, why does that matter?" asked Mars.

"If this was all set up, you're not going to do it over the phone. It's going to be face-to-face. She was the only face. She went to the prison and told her husband what he had to do. Including all the details, so he could get his story straight. She probably did this over and over to make sure it all sunk in."

"So she had to have contact with whoever really killed my parents? She initiated this, not her husband."

"That's the way I see it, yes."

"But she's not just going to tell us who contacted her."

183

"No, I don't think she will," replied Decker.

"So what do we do, then?"

"We find out as much as we can on our own and then we confront her with it."

"And hope she rolls over?"

"Yes. You ever remember anything about the stuff I asked you about?"

Mars looked back out the window as the plane descended into Alabama. "I gave it a lot of thought. Only thing I really thought about, to tell the truth."

"And?"

Mars pointed to the back of his right ear. "My dad had a scar right here. I saw it when I was a kid and we were horsing around on the floor, just roughhousing, you know. I touched it and asked him about it. He flew into a rage. I mean, I thought he was going to beat the shit out of me. Then my mom came in the room, saw what was happening, and calmed him down. After that, he was never really the same around me. And he started wearing his hair a lot longer."

"To cover the scar?"

"That's right. At least I think so."

"Did you ever ask your mother about it?"

"No. I was too scared. I'd never seen my dad like that. I mean, he was scary."

Decker stared at the seat back in front of him. "Did it look like a wound? Like from a gun or knife?"

"Not a gun. It was more like a long cut."

"So a knife?"

"Yeah, that's what I think. Look, I know it's not much."

"Well, it's more than we had, Melvin. We just have to figure out what it means."

22

Thursday at 5:30 p.m.

Charles Montgomery had a half hour left to live.

He had eaten his last meal from a vending machine.

A barbecue sandwich and a can of Coke.

His stomach would not have to digest the meal.

Bogart, Decker, and Mars were sitting in the front row of one of the viewing rooms. Jamison had elected not to come. Davenport was immediately behind Decker in the second row. There were three other people in the room. Two were journalists and one was with the Alabama State Bar. None of the families of the victims had come except for Mars.

The journalists had recognized Mars and had tried to interview him, but Bogart had flashed his badge and quickly put a stop to that.

The curtains were pulled so that the death chamber was not currently visible. In an adjacent room the family of the condemned was allowed to sit. The curtains were also closed there, so they didn't know if Regina Montgomery was here or not.

Mars was looking nervous and there were beads of sweat on his face although the room was cool.

Decker noted this and put a large hand on the other man's shoulder. "You gonna hold it together? Or you want to get out of here?"

Mars bent over and took several deep breaths. "I was just thinking how close I came to this."

Decker removed his hand. "But it's not you, Melvin. It's the other guy. But we can leave if you want."

Mars straightened. "No, I'm good."

"You sure?"

"Yeah."

Bogart leaned over and said, "They're coming."

A dozen correctional officers surrounded Montgomery as he left the holding cell where he had been brought the previous Tuesday. They were led to the death chamber by a pastor holding a Bible and saying a prayer. A hymn was being played over the sound system.

The gurney had been removed from the chamber and the electric chair had been brought out of storage. Nicknamed "Yellow Mama," because its color came from the yellow paint used on highway lines, it had been built by a British inmate in the 1920s. It was massive and sturdy-looking.

His head bowed, the pastor peeled away and went to the viewing area where Decker and the others were. He took his seat at the end of the row and began reading his Bible.

The correctional officers escorted Montgomery into the chamber. Then the curtains were opened so that Montgomery could see into the visitor rooms.

Decker and the others now saw that Regina Montgomery was indeed in attendance. Her son was not with her.

Montgomery's gaze lingered on his wife for a few moments but no words were said or even mouthed between them. Finally, Regina looked away.

The warden read the death warrant out loud and Montgomery was asked if he wanted to say any last words.

He looked at his wife again. He started to say something, then shook his head and looked away from her. Then his gaze found and settled on Melvin Mars. The two men stared at each other for a long, torturous moment.

Montgomery again looked away without saying anything. His expression wasn't one of remorse; to Decker it looked more like one of disgust.

The warden went into another adjacent room where there was a man on the phone. This was to make sure that there was no last-minute reprieve of the death sentence from the governor.

There wasn't, and the warden gave the appropriate signal.

Ten of the officers left the room, passing by the warden as he returned to the death chamber. The two remaining officers readied Montgomery by taking off his handcuffs and leg chains, placing him in the chair, and strapping down his arms, legs, and head to the wood of Yellow Mama.

The metal helmet connected to the electrodes was placed on his head and then a hood was placed over that. There were also electrodes attached to his arms and legs. The power supply to the chair was plugged in.

The warden went into the generator room, where he engaged the equipment by pulling on several levers.

Mars gripped the armrest of his chair and his breaths grew ragged.

Decker put an arm around Mars's shoulders. "Almost over," he murmured. He glanced over at Regina Montgomery. She was looking down at the floor.

Decker looked back at Montgomery. He couldn't see the man's face because of the hood, but his entire body was tensed against the yellow wood. He looked like a figure carved in stone on its throne.

One of the officers picked up a sign that read *Ready* and held it against the glass window leading into the generator room.

The two officers left the chamber and they all heard the door slam.

One of the officers gave the requisite signal by knocking twice on the door. The warden immediately sent the first of two power surges to the chair, eight amps and 1,850 volts, that lasted thirty-four seconds each.

Decker watched as Montgomery slammed back against the chair as the current hit him like a tank round. He lashed against the restraints. An electrode tore away from his leg as he thrashed. Smoke started to rise off his head. The smell of charred flesh permeated the viewing room.

There was a scream and they looked over in time to see Regina Montgomery faint and topple out of her chair to the floor. Footsteps were heard as prison personnel rushed to aid her.

The second surge of current hit Montgomery and he started to shake uncontrollably. They heard him scream, gasp, scream again, and then he fell forward, kept in the chair solely by the restraints.

The smell of burned flesh became even stronger; it seemed to be driven right into their pores.

As they watched, a small flickering flame rose from the cloth hood before dying out, along with the occupant of the chair.

"Oh my God," hissed Davenport. She jumped up and rushed from the room. They could hear her being sick outside in the hall.

Next came the sound of the generator providing the electricity powering down and growing silent.

The curtains were drawn and the image of the dead man, smoke still rising off him, was gone. They heard more rushing feet and then the sounds of a fire extinguisher being deployed.

It was over.

23

That was the longest few minutes of my life," said Davenport, who still looked gray and nauseous.

They were sitting around a table in the lobby of the hotel where they were staying near the prison.

Decker shot her a glance. "Imagine how it was for Montgomery."

She looked at him and turned a bit pink in the face. "I know. I didn't mean it that way. It was just . . . horrible."

Although Jamison hadn't attended, she seemed as distraught and subdued as the others. "Did they confirm he was actually dead?"

Bogart nodded wearily. "By law they have to. The doctor came in and did his tests. Montgomery was pronounced dead at five minutes past the hour. Regina Montgomery was revived and checked out by a doctor at the prison. Then a state trooper drove her home."

Decker turned to Mars, who hadn't said a word since they had left the prison. He looked like he had no idea where he was.

"You okay?" Decker asked.

Mars shook his head. "Dude was on fire," he said dully.

"That's why they don't use the chair anymore," said Decker. "Too many things can go wrong. I think the state of Alabama should stop giving the condemned a choice."

Davenport said fiercely, "Or better yet, just abolish capital punishment." She looked at Mars. "They came close to executing you, an innocent man. That's reason enough just to do away with it. There are no second chances."

Mars nodded curtly and looked away.

Bogart said, "Well, that's way above my pay grade and not an argument we're going to settle tonight. I think we all need to get some sleep and then regroup tomorrow." He looked at Decker. "What else did you want to do while we're here?"

"Talk to Regina Montgomery again. We need to find out where the money came from."

"She's not going to willingly tell us anything," pointed out Jamison. "She almost kicked us out last time."

"But she might slip up, or by not telling us something she might just answer our questions."

Bogart rose. "Well, again, nothing else is going to happen tonight. So let's just call it an early evening. I don't think I'm good for anything else. Witnessing an execution leaves you utterly drained, at least it does me."

Bogart headed off and a still shaky Davenport followed.

As Jamison was about to leave, Decker snagged her by the arm.

"Hold up, Alex."

"What is it?"

Decker looked first at her and then at Mars. "You two up to going somewhere? Right now? Because I don't think that we should wait."

They knocked for a long time, and only when it was clear that they weren't going to leave did Regina Montgomery answer the door. She stood there defiantly in the doorway still dressed in the clothes she had worn to the execution.

"What do you want?" she snapped.

Decker said, "We just had some questions for you."

"My husband was executed tonight. Can't you leave me in peace!" she added shrilly.

"I can understand how you feel, Mrs. Montgomery, but I wouldn't be here unless I thought it really important. Can we come in? It won't take more than a few minutes."

She looked at Jamison, and then her gaze fell on Mars and her face twisted in disgust.

"What, you mean him too?"

"Him especially," said Decker. "He's—"

"I know who the hell he is! I just . . . I mean I don't have . . ."

Decker said, "It'll only be a few minutes. And since this pertains to Mr. Mars, he needs to be included. Please, Mrs. Montgomery."

Jamison stepped forward and took the woman by the hand. "Let's just go in and sit. Have you had anything to eat? Maybe a cup of tea to help settle your nerves? I can only imagine what you've had to deal with today. I'm so sorry."

"I . . . that would be . . . I can't eat anything, but some hot tea. Yes."

"Just show me where and I'll fix it right up."

Jamison smoothly steered Montgomery inside while Decker and Mars followed. When Jamison turned around, Decker shot her an appreciative look.

After Regina Montgomery showed Jamison where things were in the kitchen, she and Mars settled around a coffee table in the small, cluttered living room. Back in the kitchen Jamison put a kettle on the cooktop to heat up the water. Then she found a cup and a box of tea bags. While the water was heating she rejoined them.

When she sat down across from Montgomery, Jamison's gaze flitted over Montgomery and held briefly on her wrist. She looked surprised.

Montgomery was staring at Decker. "Well?" she said crossly.

"Is your son here?" asked Decker.

"No," she said sharply. "He's staying at a friend's. I

thought it best. No reason for him to have to deal with . . . this."

"That was a good idea."

She glanced at Mars sitting next to Decker and her mouth curved into a frown.

Mars stared right back at her. He seemed about to say something when Decker spoke.

"Tommy told us about the insurance money."

She was startled by this. "What? When did you— how did you know where he was?"

"Howling Cougars," said Decker, pointing to the photo on the table across from them.

"Well, so what? Chuck had life insurance. I'm the beneficiary. Nothing wrong with that."

"For thirty thousand dollars?"

She jerked again. "Who told you that?" she demanded.

"We're the FBI, Mrs. Montgomery, we can find out things."

The teakettle whistle blew. Jamison rose and went into the kitchen to prepare the tea. She poured it into a cup and then, looking around for some crackers, pulled aside a curtain covering a small niche in the kitchen. What she saw inside made her start. She snagged a box of crackers and some peanut butter off a shelf, and walked back over to the sink.

"Hey, Decker?" she called out. "Can you give me a hand? I know Mrs. Montgomery doesn't need us to be here any longer than necessary."

A bit put out by her request, Decker rose and went into the kitchen. While Jamison was spreading peanut butter over the crackers she jerked her head toward the open curtain. "Check that out," she said quietly.

Decker turned, saw what was there, and glanced quickly at Jamison, who hiked her eyebrows. "And there's something else I saw," she said.

A minute later they came back into the room, Jamison with the tea and Decker with the plate of peanut butter crackers. They placed them in front of Montgomery, who was staring stonily at Mars.

"Thank you," she said. She took a sip of the tea and nibbled at a cracker, her gaze now downcast.

While Montgomery was doing that, Jamison glanced around the room and her gaze fixed on a coat tree by the front door. This time she didn't look surprised.

Montgomery put her teacup down. "Why do you care about the insurance money?"

Decker said, "Tommy also said that you were planning to move from here to wherever he ended up going to college. That you were going to buy a place and not have to work."

Montgomery didn't say anything for a long moment. Then she waved her hand dismissively. "He's just a kid. He doesn't know what he's saying. I *am* planning to move to where he goes to college. But I'll have to work. And I sure as hell won't be buying a house. Thirty thousand dollars isn't enough for me to stay home and twiddle my thumbs."

"So you will have to work?"

"Didn't you hear me? Yes, I'll have to work. Do I look rich to you? I've been working my ass off all my life. Work till I drop, unless Tommy makes it to the NFL, and then he can take care of me."

Mars said, "I wouldn't bank on that. It's like a one-in-a-million chance."

She eyed him. "You played football, so I heard."

"It's a rough sport. Tell Tommy to be a doctor or lawyer instead. He'll have a much healthier retirement."

"I'm sure you're mad at my husband, but he *did* come forward. Only reason you're out of jail."

"He was the reason I was *in* jail," countered Mars. "He murdered my parents. So excuse me for not feeling grateful."

She shook her head and mumbled something like, "You people."

Decker placed a restraining hand on Mars's shoulder, since it looked like the man was about to jump to his feet. "When do you get the insurance money?" he asked.

"Why do you care?"

"I told you I just had a few questions, Mrs. Montgomery. The sooner you answer them the sooner we're out of here. The reverse is also true."

She picked up her tea, took a sip, ate a cracker, and

then said, "I have to file the claim. It might take a few days, or maybe a week. It's not like they won't have proof he's dead."

"Right." Decker looked at Jamison and nodded.

Jamison pointed to Montgomery's wrist. "That's a beautiful watch. Cartier, isn't it?"

Montgomery immediately covered it with her other hand. "No, it's not."

"It says Cartier on the watch face," pointed out Jamison.

She looked down at her hand. "I got it for like ten bucks."

"Where?"

"I forgot."

"It's against the law to traffic in knockoffs," said Decker.

"So find the person who sold it to me and arrest him."

Decker rose, went into the kitchen, pulled the curtain aside, lifted up the boxes stacked there, and brought them back into the room and set them on the floor.

Montgomery jumped to her feet. "What the hell are you doing? You can't do that. Those are mine."

"Chanel. Neiman Marcus. Saks. Bergdorf Goodman. Jimmy Choo. They all make very nice stuff. And very expensive."

Jamison pointed to a bag hanging on the coat tree

by the front door. "And that's an Hermès bag. I wish I could afford one."

Montgomery turned pale. "They're all fakes. I can't afford none of that."

Decker said, "I wasn't aware that fraudsters shipped their goods in boxes with the names of the brands on the side. They usually just sell them on the street."

Montgomery said nothing to this. She took another sip of tea and ate another cracker.

"Can I look inside the boxes?" asked Decker.

"No!"

"Why not?"

"You got a search warrant?"

"Actually, I don't need one."

She looked wide-eyed at him. "Why not?"

"I used to be a police officer but I turned in my badge."

"But you're with the FBI!"

"As a civilian, not an agent. Never badged or sworn in."

Despite Montgomery's protests, Decker opened the boxes and snapped photos of the contents with his phone camera. Then he leaned down so his face was only a few inches away from Montgomery's. "We can easily trace all of these purchases. And since you already told us you haven't received the insurance money yet, that can't be the source of the funds. So why don't you tell us the truth, Mrs. Montgomery? How did you come by the money?"

"I don't know what the hell you're talking about!"

"Do you really want to play it that way?"

"Get out of my house."

Mars said, "Somebody paid you off to have your husband lie and say he killed my parents. Who was it?"

She looked at him and said fiercely, "Who the hell do you think you are, talking to me like that? You are nothing but—"

"But what?" interrupted Mars. "A colored boy who should keep his mouth shut 'round good white folks like you?"

"Get out of my house!" she screamed.

"I lost twenty years of my life!" Mars screamed right back.

Montgomery looked at Decker. "Get out of my house before I call the cops."

Decker said, "You can call the cops. And then we'll tell them what we know. And we'll find out about the money you've come by and why. And then you're going to be in a world of trouble. In fact, you're going to go to prison."

She looked stunned by this. "I ain't done nothing wrong."

"Try obstruction of justice. Conspiracy. Aiding and abetting a murderer."

"I did not!"

"By helping those who really did kill the Marses, you did. And the cumulative penalties for all those crimes means you won't have to worry about following your son to college. Your housing will be provided by the government." He paused momentarily. "For the rest of your life."

Regina Montgomery looked like she might faint again. She took several deep breaths and said, "Get outta my house."

Decker said, "Have it your way. We'll be back tomorrow. With the police." He pulled out his phone. "Say cheese." He took a photo of the Cartier watch.

"Get out!" she screamed. She started to throw the cup of tea at Decker, but Jamison caught her by the arm and the cup fell out of her hand and hit the floor, shattering. As they walked out, Decker took a photo of the Hermès bag.

Outside Jamison looked at Decker.

"She's guilty as hell."

"Yes, she is. By the way, that was really good work in there, Alex," said Decker.

She smiled. "I have my moments, especially when it has to do with high fashion."

Mars added, "You were right, Decker, somebody *did* pay her off."

"Now we just have to find out who."

24

Decker was dreaming in color. It was a combination of rooms, numbers, and days of the week, all outlined in different brilliant hues. This was a relatively new phenomenon for him. But as one of the doctors at the Cognitive Institute had told him, the brain was ever-evolving and Decker would find new experiences awaiting him from time to time.

But the noise kept interrupting. He had nearly gotten clear of the room and was moving on to something new, dark, and mysterious and a puzzle to figure out. But the noise came again, tickling around his ears, like a gnat buzzing him. It was disrupting all that he was trying to do.

Finally, like a swimmer clearing the depths and reaching the surface, Decker retreated from the colors and began breathing air again. He opened his eyes and saw another color.

A bright white light was emanating from his phone, which rested on the nightstand. And the phone was buzzing.

He heaved up, snagged the phone, saw that it was

three in the morning and also that the call was from Bogart.

"Hello?"

"Decker, can you meet me in the lobby in about ten minutes?"

"What's up?"

"It's Regina Montgomery."

"What about her?"

"She's dead."

Decker was in the lobby in five minutes and watched as first Davenport and then Jamison came down. A moment later Bogart strode into the lobby.

"I've got the car outside."

"Where's Melvin?" asked Decker.

"I thought it best not to involve him in this."

"You said she's dead. How?" asked Decker.

"Let's get in the car."

"What about her son, Tommy? Is he okay?"

"Yes. He wasn't home. He was staying with friends. And his football coach has taken him in for now."

He led them outside and they all climbed into the SUV. Bogart drove, with Decker next to him. The women were in the backseat.

As soon as they pulled out of the hotel and onto the road Decker said, "How did she die?"

"They're not sure."

"How can they not be sure?"

"Because the entire duplex blew up. They're still searching the rubble."

"Oh my God," said Davenport.

"But they found Regina?" said Decker.

"Yes. It was a positive ID. I mean, she was somewhat disfigured, from what they said, but it's not like the Marses' bodies. They made a positive ID on the spot."

"Okay, an explosion. Gas?"

"The property used a buried propane tank, so, yes, it could be that."

"Or it could be something else?"

Bogart shot him a glance. "How so?"

Decker glanced back at Jamison and then turned to look at Bogart. "We visited Regina earlier tonight."

"What?" exclaimed Bogart. "You and who else?"

"Jamison, Melvin, and me. It was my idea."

"Why?"

"I had a theory."

"And you didn't want to inform me?"

"You said you'd had enough for the day, and I didn't want to wait."

Bogart looked both angry and disappointed.

Jamison quickly said, "We were going to report everything we found out to you in the morning, Agent Bogart."

"Well, thanks for that," he said sarcastically.

"But," said Decker, "we found out a lot."

"Tell me."

Decker recounted everything that had happened at Regina Montgomery's house.

Bogart took it all in and said, "Decker, if you had told me this last night I would have put security around her house. In fact, I would have brought her in for questioning on the spot and she'd be alive today to tell us the truth."

Decker sat back and gazed out the side window. "Yeah, I can see that now."

"Just because your brain works better than all of ours doesn't mean you're infallible."

Decker sighed. "Okay, I'm sorry. I screwed up."

"You did more than that. Your actions may well have led to Regina Montgomery being murdered."

Decker said nothing.

Bogart added, "When I put this team together I thought it obvious that I envisioned us acting *as* a team. I don't need you going maverick on me, Decker. I'm ultimately accountable for all of it. Including what happened to Montgomery."

"I . . . I don't know what to say," said Decker uncomfortably.

Bogart gazed sternly at him. "We'll leave it for later. But this is not over. Understood?"

Decker nodded while Jamison and Davenport looked on anxiously.

Bogart said stiffly, "Now tell me what you think happened."

Decker composed himself and said, "Someone was

either watching us last night or Regina called someone right after we left and told them what happened.
And that person came and killed her. So you're right,
our going there was the catalyst for her murder." He
paused. "But I think she was a dead woman regardless."

Bogart steered the vehicle onto a highway entrance
ramp and punched the gas. "How so?" he asked.

"She was a loose end. They had to let her live
long enough so that her husband was executed and
couldn't recant his confession. They had already given
her some of the promised payout, which is how she
bought all that stuff. But why let her live after her
husband is dead? She probably knew too much. I
doubt she knows exactly who is behind this, but she's
made contact with someone. And if she told us about
that we could conceivably follow it back to the
source. So, no more Regina."

Bogart nodded. "That makes sense."

"But now that they've eliminated her, we've lost
that chance," said Decker. He slammed the palm of his
hand against the dash, making all of them jump. "I
shouldn't have left her like that. I should have known
what would happen." He looked at Bogart. "I blew it."

"Well, actually, you were the only one who suspected her in the first place," the FBI agent replied.
"But let's get out to her place and see what we can
find."

Decker nodded absently but his expression was not hopeful.

I'm an idiot. The woman is dead because I'm an idiot.

What the initial explosion had not destroyed, the resulting fire had pretty much taken care of. It was fortunate that no one had been living in the other part of the duplex. There was substantial damage to a number of other nearby units, but luckily there were no fatalities other than Regina Montgomery.

Decker surveyed the area. The fire was out. Montgomery's home had been catastrophically damaged. It was truly a miracle that there was anything left of her to identify. Apparently the blast had blown her clear of the house before the fire consumed the duplex. The firemen had reported to the police that they had found her body in the front yard.

Bogart had parked the SUV well back of the area and they had walked the rest of the way. A light, misty rain had begun to fall, which, added to the smoke from the still smoldering fire, made it seem like they were taking a stroll through fog.

They gathered at the rear of an ambulance and one of the local police lifted the sheet off the corpse in back.

It clearly was Regina Montgomery. Her face was burned but otherwise intact. It might have been the concussive force of the blast that had killed her. One of her legs was missing, as well as the lower part of her right arm.

"She still has her Cartier watch on," observed Jamison.

Decker's gaze ran over the body, and then he looked over at the ruins of the duplex. Up and down the short street, folks were standing outside of their homes, wondering what the hell was going on. Some were dressed in tattered robes, others simply in their underwear.

Since the duplexes here each had their own propane tank, the authorities had seen no need to evacuate the area, as they probably would have had it been a natural gas explosion running off a main pipe.

Bogart took a few minutes to explain to the local police their theory on what might have happened.

One of them said, "Well, we'll get the arson boys in here. They'll be able to tell if someone deliberately started this thing. Always leaves signs behind."

He left to report in, leaving the four of them there to look dismally around.

"Even if they can trace the point of origin of the blast, it might not provide any clues to who did it," said Davenport.

Bogart and Jamison nodded at this obvious point; however, Decker was staring over at where the duplex had once stood, his attention evidently elsewhere.

"What is it?" asked Bogart when he noticed the distracted Decker.

"There's only one road in or out of here. There is absolutely no cover for anyone to do a stakeout. It's far enough off the main road so that whoever came and did this would have to risk leaving their car back there and make their way on foot. Otherwise, someone would have heard something. Or seen something." He turned and looked at Bogart. "Did anyone see or hear anything?"

"I can sure find out."

Bogart fast-walked over to a group of police officers who were huddled together near the destroyed duplex watching the firefighters pour more water on the remaining embers. He spoke with them for a few minutes and then came back over to Decker.

"They went house by house soon after they got here and took statements from everyone. No one saw or heard anything until the explosion occurred."

Decker looked up and down the row of duplexes and the folks standing in front of each. "The duplex attached to Montgomery's was vacant?"

Bogart nodded.

Decker looked up and down the duplex row again. "Any others vacant?"

"I don't know."

"Well, there're people standing in front of all these places except for that one."

He indicated the fourth duplex down on the left. The lights were out and, as Decker had said, no one was standing outside it.

"There's no car there, but that doesn't mean anything. Not everyone who lives here has a car," noted Bogart. "And the place might be vacant."

Decker's mind revolved back to both times they had been to visit Regina Montgomery. He had seen nothing when he had been here with Bogart. But last night he had seen a light on in that house and a car had been parked out front.

He told Bogart this and said, "The vehicle was a four-door tan Toyota Avalon. The license plates were not visible from where I was standing. But you can see ruts in the front of the house caused by the car's wheels. They're fresh."

Bogart said, "Okay, that puts things in a different light. There might be someone there."

"Let's go see for ourselves," said Decker. "And it would make sense to get some backup."

He pulled his gun while Bogart motioned to one of the officers, who hurried over. After some whispered instructions the officer and his colleagues pulled their weapons and headed over to the darkened house. When they got there, they surrounded it. With Decker and Bogart behind the three officers in front, the lead cop pounded on the door, identified himself, and asked to be let in. No response came.

He called out one more time and then kicked the door in. The flimsy wood gave in on the first try. At the same instant the rear door was broken down and the two sets of cops flooded the small space.

A minute later the all-clear was given.

Decker and the others were allowed into the duplex.

There wasn't much to see. It was empty. Not a stick of furniture or anything else.

"Doesn't look like anyone was ever here," said Davenport.

"But someone was," said Decker.

25

Mars kept shaking his head in disbelief.

"Somebody just killed her? Blew up her house?"

Decker nodded.

They were sitting in the lobby of the hotel with Jamison and Davenport.

"But you said her son is okay?" said Mars.

"He's fine, other than losing both his parents on pretty much the same day."

"And you really think someone murdered her?"

"If not, it's the biggest coincidence I've ever seen. And I don't even believe in little coincidences."

"Do you know who might have done it?"

"Whoever was paying her off, with Cartier watches and expensive clothes, and promises of a better life with her son."

"So you think Tommy might be in danger?" asked Jamison.

"Bogart has state troopers looking after him," replied Decker. "I doubt his mother told him any-thing, but whoever killed her can't be certain of that.

It was clear when we spoke to Tommy that he just thought it was insurance money."

Mars glanced at him. "What do we do now?"

At that moment Bogart walked into the room looking agitated and upset.

Jamison said, "What is it? Not another murder?"

Bogart shook his head and dropped into an unoccupied chair next to Davenport. "No, it's not that," he said, not meeting any of their gazes. "It's actually more complicated."

Decker eyed him closely. "You want to tell us?"

Bogart lifted his gaze to Decker's. "I just got a call from D.C. We have been officially pulled from this case."

"What?" exclaimed Jamison and Davenport simultaneously.

"Let me rephrase that. HQ does not see this as a case. Not an open one. Mr. Mars has been cleared. The real killer has confessed and paid the ultimate price. That's it. They want us back home."

"But what about Regina Montgomery's death?" said Decker, still watching Bogart.

"Irrelevant, at least to them. An accident, nothing more. And certainly not the jurisdiction of the FBI."

Mars looked around at each of them before his gaze settled on Bogart. "So what exactly does that mean, Agent Bogart?"

"That exactly means that we pack up and leave and head back to Quantico. I'm sorry for the way this has turned out. It's not how I intended it to happen. I'll let Milligan know. He can leave directly from Texas."

"Well, he'll be ecstatic about that," said Decker dryly.

Bogart rose and held his hand out to Mars, who rose and shook it.

"I'm sorry to be leaving in this way, Mr. Mars. It's not how I would have done it, if it were my choice. But I wish you the very best of luck."

"Okay," said a bewildered Mars. "Sure, thanks."

Decker said, "Have a good trip, Agent Bogart."

Bogart didn't look that surprised. "So you're not coming?"

"I don't leave a case until it's finished. So I'm staying here to see it through."

"Decker, please listen to reason, you can't do that," said Bogart.

"I can do that. And I will do that."

"But you work for—"

"I resign," interrupted Decker.

Bogart took a deep breath.

"Have you really thought this through?"

"I did, though it didn't take long."

Bogart looked at the two women. "And what about you?" he asked.

Jamison said firmly, "I'm staying with Decker."

Bogart's gaze drifted to Davenport. "And you?"

Davenport didn't look nearly as certain, but after

giving Decker a sideways glance she said, without looking at Bogart, "I'm staying too."

Bogart nodded slowly. "Seems like my team and project are out of business."

"We're sorry, Agent Bogart," said Jamison.

Bogart actually smiled. "You may be. But he's not," he added, looking at Decker.

"It's nothing personal," said Decker. "But Charles Montgomery did not kill Roy and Lucinda Mars. I'm going to find out who did."

"I wish you luck. And I wish I could stay and help you do it. But unlike you, I don't have that option."

He turned and left.

Mars quickly looked at Decker. "Hey, man, you don't have to do this. I don't want y'all to lose your job over me."

"Right now my job is to find out what happened to your parents, Melvin," said Decker. "Whether it's under the auspices of the FBI or not doesn't matter a damn to me."

"But the dude is your friend."

"And Agent Bogart is still my friend. And he'll be perfectly fine. He's obeying orders."

"But they might not let you back in working with him after this is over."

Decker glanced at Jamison before turning to Mars. "That's our problem, Melvin, not yours."

Davenport said, "What do we do now?"

Decker answered, "Since we're no longer with the FBI, the police don't have to cooperate with us."

"That will make it a lot harder," pointed out Davenport.

"Which is why we won't tell the police that that's the case," continued Decker.

"Lie to the police?" exclaimed Davenport. "Look, I know I agreed to stay, but I'm not getting in trouble over this."

"We aren't going to lie. We aren't going to say anything about it. We're just going to continue on with the investigation as if nothing happened. If the police think we're still working with the FBI, that's their mistake."

"But Decker," said Davenport. "Surely Bogart is going to inform them that the FBI is leaving the field."

Decker cast a glance in the direction of Bogart, who was waiting at the elevator bank and casting furtive looks in their direction.

"No, I don't think he will."

Jamison said, "Okay, to take up Lisa's point, now what do we do?"

Decker turned his attention to her. "Catch a killer."

"But how?"

"We have clues, we just need to run them down."

"What clues?" said Davenport.

"A blown-up house. A four-door tan Toyota Avalon. And whatever the neighbors can tell us about the person or persons in that duplex. And we trace back the money that went to Regina."

Mars said, "You really think that'll provide answers?"

Decker stood. "What's the key to winning on the football field?"

"Preparation," said Mars automatically.

"That's right. Well, in the investigation field preparation means looking at all the little details in the hopes that they deliver up the big answers. And in my experience, when you look for criminals, you have to dig deep in the shit. Because that's where they live. Let's go."

He strode out of the room.

Mars looked at Jamison. "Damn, he really *is* always like that."

26

Heavy rains over the last several hours had turned the site of the duplex explosion into a quagmire.

Wearing slickers and boots, Decker, Jamison, and Davenport walked the site looking for clues and talking to the local cops. Because he was not with the FBI or the local police, Mars could only watch from the rental in which they had driven over.

"We couldn't find any evidence of an accelerant or a timer or bomb materials, Agent Decker," said the cop who had been leading them around the site.

Decker did not correct the man about his "agent" status. And his FBI creds were prominently clipped to the outside of his slicker for all to see, the same for Jamison and Davenport.

Decker surveyed the debris field. "Do you think you still might turn something up?"

"Usually by this time we would have. We're not inexperienced with explosions down here. People like to blow shit up, so we know what to look for. And we know the explosion patterns we typically see if a man-made device was used. Right now all things point to it being an accident. The duplex was really old and in bad shape. And I have to imagine the pipes and valves coming from the underground propane tank weren't in pristine condition. We've had these things blow before. It just happens."

Decker nodded. "I get that. Only I'd feel a lot better if the timing were different."

The cop nodded in understanding. "Meaning her husband just being executed?"

"Right."

"You don't think she committed suicide, do you?"

"By blowing herself up?" said Decker skeptically.

"No, but she could have tried putting her head in the oven or something like that and then it just blew. You said she was a smoker. She could have struck a match for some reason."

"That's one theory, but I don't think it's the right one."

Decker left the officer and joined Davenport and Jamison.

"What now?" asked a soaked and visibly irritated Davenport.

"Well, since they're not finding what caused the explosion, now we talk to the neighbors."

"Can we at least wait until it stops raining?" asked Davenport.

"*You* can," said Decker.

He turned and headed to the nearest house.

Jamison glanced at Davenport. "You coming?"

Davenport stared after Decker, annoyance flitting across her features. "Actually, I think I'll wait with Melvin. It might be more *productive.*"

She stalked off toward the car while Jamison hurried after Decker.

Folks in six of the duplexes had not noticed the Toyota Avalon. The seventh door was opened by a tiny, bent, white-haired woman, who looked to be close to a hundred. She wore a fuzzy white bathrobe, used a walker, and had to tilt her head back to take in the full scope of the huge Decker. Her glasses were Coke-bottle thick, and Decker was not holding out much hope that she would be able to tell them anything.

She invited them in, looking excited, because, as she said, "a G-man" was here to talk to her.

"And G-lady," she said, nodding and smiling at Jamison as they settled into chairs around a small, battered coffee table. "I guess even the FBI has learned that the women can get things done better than the men."

"Guess so," said Jamison with an impish look at Decker.

"My name is Patricia Bray, but you can call me Patti. All my family and friends do—well, they did when they were alive. I'm really the only one left now. The last of nine siblings."

"I'm sorry to hear that, Patti," said Jamison.

A fat tabby jumped up into Bray's lap and the old woman stroked it. "But I'm not alone. This here is Teddy. He's sixteen, and it's anyone's guess who'll out-live the other."

Decker said, "You heard what happened to your neighbor?"

Bray nodded, her lips curling into a frown. "I knew Regina. What a life that woman had. But I heard Tommy is okay, thank the Lord. He's a nice young man. He's helped me around the house lots of times. I watched him grow up. They moved here when that husband of hers was transferred to the prison down the road."

"We know."

"They just electrocuted him," added Bray. "And now this." She started. "My goodness, that means Tommy's an orphan. Who's going to look after him? He's still in high school."

"They're working on that right now," said Decker. "He's staying with his football coach for the time being."

"Oh, that's very nice. He's a good football player. Regina would go on and on about him. Very proud momma."

"So you two spoke a lot?" asked Decker.

"Oh yes. I used to bake and I'd bring things around. Now I'm too old for that, so Regina would do shop-ping for me, help around the house some. She'd send

Tommy over to do things too. Nicest woman in the world."

Decker glanced a bit guiltily at Jamison. "I didn't know that about her."

"Oh yes. She's had a hard life, like I said. But lately she seemed happier. I mean, it might have been because she could see the light at the end of the tunnel. What with her husband and all. And then she had Tommy in her life. I think that's what she was clinging to. Seeing him get into a good college. Being there for him."

"Did she tell you about her plans for the future?" asked Jamison.

"Oh, sure. She was going to be moving from here, which made me sad in one respect. But she has her life to lead and I don't have all that much life left. She was going to follow Tommy to college. I mean, she wasn't going to attend college, but live nearby. Look after him, you know. He was all she had."

"Did she say how she was going to manage that financially?" asked Decker.

"She said there was some insurance money. So I guess that husband of hers was good for something."

"Did you see anything last night that looked suspicious?" asked Decker.

"Suspicious? I thought it was a gas explosion."

"The police are still investigating. At this stage they have to explore every possibility."

"Oh, sure, I see. Well, I went to bed early. Something didn't agree with me that I ate apparently. Next thing I know I hear what I thought was a bomb going off. I pulled on my robe and got to the front door and . . ." Her voice trailed off and the hand she was stroking Teddy with began to shake.

Jamison swiftly put her hand on top of Bray's. "It's okay. You don't have go into that. We know what happened."

Decker said, "So you saw nothing out of the ordinary?"

"No, not that I can recall." She suddenly looked around. "Where are my manners? Would you all like something to drink? Coffee? It's raw outside."

"No thanks," said Decker. "We're good." He paused, formulating his next question. "Okay, now—"

Jamison said, "Would you like me to make *you* some coffee? Like you said, it's raw out."

While Decker looked perturbed at the interruption Bray smiled warmly at her. "Why, honey, that would be so nice. I just put a fresh pot on when y'all knocked."

"Do you take anything in it?"

"Yes, black coffee." Bray tittered and Jamison chuckled, while Decker sat there looking impatient.

Jamison fetched the coffee and delivered it to the old woman, who took a sip and placed the cup next to her on a side table. She refocused on Decker. "Now, what were you about to ask, young man?"

"Did you ever see a Toyota Avalon parked in front of the duplex two doors down from you?"

"Avalon?"

"Yes."

"You mean the tan four-door?"

Decker sat up a bit straighter. "Yes."

"Didn't know it was an Avalon. It was here yesterday."

"What time was that?"

Bray took off her glasses and rubbed a smudge off the lens using her sleeve. "Oh, I'd say about six o'clock. Must of been because the evening news was just coming on. I know folks don't watch the news on TV anymore. They use those computers and such and even their phones! But I loved watching Walter Cronkite, and though there's nobody on TV like Uncle Walt anymore, I still watch. So, about six o'clock I went to put Teddy out to let him run around. That's when I saw it. Parked right in front."

"I don't suppose you got a license plate?" asked Decker, eyeing the woman's thick glasses as she settled them back on her face.

"There was an 'A' and an 'R' and the number 4. Oh, and it was a Georgia plate."

Decker looked surprised. "A Georgia plate, you're sure?"

"Hell yes. I played that car game enough times with my kids. You know, count the state plates? This was back when people drove long distances with beds in the back of the car for the kids to sleep in and seat belts were only used to hold the groceries in place.

225

I've seen enough Georgia plates. Had the Georgia peach right in the middle. No other plate has a peach, does it?"

"No, they don't," said Decker with a quick glance at Jamison. "Did you see who was driving it?"

"See, the thing is that duplex is usually empty. I mean, the person who owns it rents it out, but the only people who live here are ones who can't afford a nicer place. Like me. All I got is Social Security. I noticed the car because it was nice, relatively new. The rule around here is most folks don't have cars. They catch the bus on the main road or ride bikes to work. Now, Regina had a car, but it was about twenty-five years old and on its last legs. You said it was an *Avalon* parked out front?" Decker nodded. "Well, it looked pretty new."

"And the person driving it?" prompted Decker again.

"Oh, right. Well, I saw him too."

"So it *was* a man?"

She looked up at him. "Well, didn't I just say it was?"

Jamison, trying hard not to smile, said, "Can you tell us what he looked like?"

"He was big. But not so big as you," she added, looking Decker up and down. "But close, height-wise leastways."

"Age?" asked Decker.

"Not as young as you, not as old as me. Maybe

seventy. He was bald, or nearly so. Fringe of white hair. No beard or nothing on his face. A hard face."

"Fat, thin?"

"Neither. He looked fit enough, sturdy. No big gut or nothing." She slapped her knee with the palm of her hand. "You see an old person in this country who's not fat, what's the first thing you think? Huh? That they got cancer, that's what. Am I right? Portion control. Always worked for me. In my day dinner plates were what people now call *dessert* plates. And they wonder why they're obese. Well, don't get me going on *that*." She again looked at Decker, who though he'd lost over thirty pounds was still considerably overweight. "Oh, excuse me, son. I didn't mean nothing by that. I'm sure you're very nice, but you might want to cut back on the carbs."

Decker ignored this and said, "You said he had a hard face. How close were you when you saw him? You said it was around six in the evening, so it must have been fairly dark by then."

In answer she pointed to her glasses. "These give me twenty-twenty, so the doctor tells me, if you're thinking that I'm blind as a bat and can't see in the day much less at night. And I never had me no cataracts. And he was standing on the front porch and the outside light was on, so I got a good look at him. Oh, and he walked with a little limp." She thought for a moment. "Seems his right leg was bad."

"Did you ever see anyone visit him?"

She shook her head. "To tell the truth, I thought he might just be squatting there for a spell. That's happened before here. People see places like this and just drop anchor and move in. No damn respect for property rights."

Jamison said anxiously, "Patti, did he see you watching him? Because that could be a real concern."

In response, Bray pulled from her robe pocket a sleek, compact nine-millimeter Beretta pistol.

"I might look frail and blind, honey, but fact is I can hit anything within ten feet with this baby. Good stopping power. Drops you on the spot, specially if you shoot 'em in the nuts."

"I bet," said Decker.

27

We'll get a BOLO out on the Avalon and this guy," said the Alabama police officer guarding the crime scene, after Decker had informed him of their conversation with Bray. "It's a little sketchy, but it's worth a shot. It's not like we have a whole lot else to go on."

Decker wasn't holding out much hope that the guy was even still in the state of Alabama. Even if he had been around when Regina Montgomery's duplex had blown up, he had a big head start.

He rejoined Davenport, Mars, and Jamison in the SUV that Bogart had rented previously. "There's no more we can do here," he said. "Let's head back to the hotel."

On the drive there Mars said, "Tell me about her son, Tommy?"

"He goes to the local high school. He'll be a senior next year. He's already got some college offers. He's a running back, like you were."

"And what happens to him when all this is said and done?"

Decker said, "If he has relatives somewhere, he'll

probably go and live with them. Or maybe his football coach will let him stay with him until he graduates."

Mars nodded and looked out the window where the rain was still beating down and showing no signs of letting up. And the weather was turning chilly.

"Why?" asked Decker, watching Mars curiously.

"No reason. Just . . . just wanted to know. Tough for a kid, losing your parents."

"Tough for an adult too," replied Decker.

At the hotel they found that Bogart had paid for their rooms for a few more days. And that the rental vehicle was good for the same amount of time.

"I hope that doesn't come back to bite him in the ass," said Davenport. "He's taking a big risk by doing that, especially after he was ordered off the case."

"We were *all* ordered off the case," said Jamison.

"It's a shame that the team didn't last," said Davenport. "It could have been really fulfilling."

"If you go now you can probably still be on the team," said Decker. "Assuming they're going to reconstitute it."

She stared at him. "Do you want me to leave?"

"I want whoever is going to stay to be one hundred percent committed to solving this case."

"I take it you're referring to me not wanting to investigate in the pouring rain?" said Davenport sharply.

"I'm referring to exactly what I just said," replied Decker in an even tone.

Davenport looked ready to fire a response back, but then her expression changed. "You're right. I'm sorry." She looked nervously down at her hands. "I just can't get that execution out of my head. It changed . . . a lot for me. Made me unsure if I really wanted to do this."

Jamison put a hand on her shoulder. "I can understand that, Lisa. I chickened out and didn't even go."

Davenport gave a hollow laugh. "I wish I had been as smart as you and done the same." She looked over at Decker. "I guess you think I'm kind of a wimp."

Decker shook his head. "I know a lot of so-called tough guys who would never have gone to see it in the first place."

"But I lost my nerve."

"I wouldn't beat yourself up over it. We need your talents to solve this thing."

Davenport glanced at Jamison, who gave her a supportive smile and then looked back at Decker. "I appreciate that. And I will give you everything I have. So what's our next step?"

"We need to get some traction on at least one lead. Either here or in Texas. The fact that Regina was killed shows that we're on the right track. She was paid off to have her husband lie and say he killed Melvin's parents. That tells us that twenty years later there are people out there connected in some way to the original crime. Including, perhaps, the real killer."

Mars stirred. "But I can't wrap my head around why someone would go to all this trouble to save me all these years later."

"That might speak to the motivation," said Decker.

Davenport nodded in agreement. "That's actually an important point." She looked at Mars. "You might have an ally out there that you don't know about."

"But how is that possible?" Mars asked. "And why now?"

Decker said, "We have to figure out the timing."

It was past dinnertime and they were all hungry. They had a quick meal at a restaurant a block over from the hotel. Back at the hotel they said their good nights after Decker admonished each of them to think about the case and come ready the next morning with ideas to pursue.

Decker took the elevator to his room, washed up, and was just about to undress and climb into bed when someone knocked on his door.

He rose and said, "Yeah?"

"Do you have a few minutes, Amos? I'd like to talk."

It was Davenport.

He debated silently for a few moments.

Obviously sensing his hesitation, she said, "It really won't take long."

He opened the door. She stood there with a bottle of beer in each hand.

He eyed them and then looked down at her. "I'm on a diet."

"Which is why I got light beer. Only ninety calories. After today you probably need the carbs."

They sat and sipped their beers.

"Well?" asked Decker.

"We got off to a bad start."

He shrugged. "It's good."

"I think being open and honest is the best policy."

"Okay."

"So here's my open and honest statement. I made my decision to join the team only *after* Bogart told me about you."

Decker took another drink of his beer, sat back in his chair, and listened to the rain falling outside. "And why was Bogart telling you about me a deciding factor?"

"Don't get me wrong, I sincerely was interested in the offer from Ross. It sounded fascinating and I had pretty much done everything I could in my field. And I like to seize opportunities. I'm a classic Type A overachiever. Only child, two academic, doting parents. Excelled at every level. I was also a distance runner in college at Stanford before I went on to Columbia."

"Impressive. But it didn't answer my question."

"I wasn't meaning to brag about myself. The fact was, it was *you* that led me to join the team when Ross called."

"You mentioned something like that when we first met."

"I know I did."

"And the parallels in my case and Melvin's. You thought it might make a fascinating case study."

"Exactly."

"And I told you it would have nothing to do with my *cognitive anomalies.* That the focus would be on Melvin's guilt or innocence."

Davenport sipped her beer. "And I told you that would be a wasted opportunity."

"I know, but how exactly?"

"I wanted to see if you would allow me to include you in a professional study. The fact that you have turned your unique mental abilities to fighting crime only heightened the uniqueness. I thought it would make a wonderfully compelling paper or even a book. It might even be a bestseller," she added enticingly.

Decker finished his beer. "I have no interest in that whatsoever."

She looked at him resignedly. "Which I knew would be the case about five minutes after I met you."

"So where does that leave you?"

"I already told you that I'm here until the end. I'll give you my all to solve this case."

"Why?"

She started to say something but then hesitated, tearing off a bit of the bottle's label. "I could give you a standard professional answer that would be mostly gobbledygook. Or I could go with the truth."

"I'll take the latter."

She sat forward and stared directly at him for the first time. "It was the execution. The way that man died. Maybe he deserved it. I'm not going to get into a debate on the pros and cons of capital punishment. But Melvin Mars *is* innocent and was very nearly executed. How many other innocent men have been put to death?"

"As I said before, one is too many," replied Decker. "So why did you show up here tonight?"

"Like I said, we got off on the wrong foot. Don't get me wrong, it was all my fault. I just wanted to square things before we moved forward to tackle this case to the end."

"Okay, consider us square."

She smiled weakly. "Just like that?"

"Just like that. But tomorrow is a new day."

Davenport nodded as she got his meaning. "I guess we all have to prove ourselves. Every day."

"That's the way I've always seen it." He held up his bottle. "Thanks for the *light* beer."

She rose. "Thanks for listening." She turned to leave but then looked back at him. "Ross told me about your family. I'm so very sorry, Amos. So very sorry."

He stared back at her but said nothing.

"How hard is it not to ever forget?" she said, her expression matching the sad tone of her words.

"Harder than you might think."

She left.

Decker put the bottle down and went over to the window where outside the rain was now bucketing down.

He let the frames of his perfect memory whir back to their encounter with Regina Montgomery.

Cartier watch.

Three boxes from Neiman Marcus.

Two boxes from Chanel.

Two from Saks.

One from Bergdorf Goodman.

One from Jimmy Choo.

Then there was the Hermès purse.

He pulled out his computer, went online to each of those retailers, found the items he had seen, and priced them out.

He totaled them in his head.

Fifty-four thousand dollars and change.

The Hermès bag had cost over nineteen thousand alone. The watch was another fourteen thousand. The Jimmy Choos another grand.

Decker shook his head.

To carry stuff, tell time, and encase your feet, *only* thirty-four thousand bucks.

But that told him that whoever was behind this had deep pockets. Regina Montgomery had evidently expected a lot more money to be coming through.

The big payoff for a life of misery with Charles Montgomery.

Only she never really got to enjoy it, did she? Once Charles was dead, Regina was expendable. It was cruel. It was heartless.

Decker would have expected nothing less from people who had let an innocent man rot in prison for twenty years.

He got undressed and climbed into bed.

They had worked this case for a while now and he was desperately fearful that the minimal progress they had made would be all there ever was.

28

The gym was small, with only one treadmill, a rack of dusty dumbbells, an ancient stationary bike, and a solitary medicine ball.

Decker walked on the treadmill, slightly increasing the pace every few minutes. As he walked he watched the TV bolted to the wall.

The news was on, and the top story was the execution of Charles Montgomery, followed by the death of his wife when her home had exploded.

"What are the odds?" asked one of the newscasters. "Both dying on the same day like that."

They didn't die on the same day, Decker thought. Regina had actually died *after* midnight, meaning she had perished on the following day.

But still, he couldn't dispute the man's overarching point. What were the odds?

Well, Decker knew they were actually really good if someone had murdered Regina as soon as her husband was safely dead.

The door to the gym opened and in walked Melvin

Mars dressed in workout clothes. He nodded at Decker and started doing some stretching.

Then he began his workout, and Decker forgot all about what he was doing and simply watched. He couldn't believe the intensity, even the insanity of the routine. Once, he nearly fell off the treadmill because he was so enthralled by what the nearly forty-two-year-old Mars was capable of doing.

Finally, Decker just turned off the treadmill and watched.

When Mars was finally done, he picked up a fresh towel off a table and wiped down.

"How often do you do that?" asked Decker.

"Every day. For the last twenty years."

"Impressive. I felt like I was having a heart attack just watching you."

Mars shrugged. "Kept me going. Kept me sane. You know?"

Decker nodded. "I can understand that."

Mars sat on a stool and looked up at Decker, his expression wary. "What do you think is going on, really?"

"Someone hated you. And then someone felt sorry for you."

Mars looked surprised. "What?"

"They framed you, put you in prison, and nearly let you be executed. Then they paid off the Montgomerys and a false confession got you out of prison."

"You think it's the same folks?"

"It's been twenty years, but it's certainly possible."

"Why the change of heart? They kill my parents, see me go to prison, and then get me out? Doesn't make a lick of sense."

"I agree. They pinned the crime on you because you were the most likely suspect."

"So why kill my parents?"

"Because of something they knew, saw, heard, did."

"They were just ordinary folks in a little town in West Texas, Decker."

"They were that when you knew them. But they might have had a whole other life before you came along, Melvin. And maybe they came to West Texas to get away from it."

Mars nodded. "I guess that makes more sense than anything else. You think they were involved in something bad?"

"The probabilities lie there. People involved in something *good* do not often get murdered."

"It's hard to see my parents in that light."

"The scar on your father's face?"

"Yeah, I know. Been thinking about that. He got so mad. Never seen my old man like that before."

"Maybe he was like that a lot when he was younger."

"You think somebody cut him? Bad dudes that later found 'em and killed 'em?"

"Not necessarily."

"What, then?"

"It could have come from a bad plastic surgery."

Mars nearly fell off his stool. "Whoa, what?"

"If your dad was on the run from people, he might very well have wanted to change his appearance. Plastic surgery is a way to do that. But he might have not had the money or maybe the opportunity to go to a legitimate surgeon. So he opts for someone in the back-alley trade. Hence the scar."

"But what about my mom? She didn't have any scars."

"He might have met her after he was on the run. She might not have been involved in the bad world he was in."

"Yeah, okay. I can't see my mom being a criminal. She was really a sweet lady. Never raised her voice to me. Always calm."

"The question is, how do we trace them?"

Mars rubbed some more sweat off his face. "Do we have to?"

Decker looked at him with a puzzled expression. "Have to what?"

"Push this any further. I mean, my parents are dead. I'm outta prison."

"So you don't want to find out the truth?"

"I don't want to find out if . . ."

"If your dad was actually a bad guy?"

"Would you want to find that out about your old man?" said Mars defensively.

"They put you away for twenty years, Melvin. They killed your parents. You don't want them to be held accountable for that? You don't want to see your parents' killers brought to justice?"

"I know, I know," said Mars miserably. "Look, I don't want nobody getting away with any of that. It's just that—"

"What?" said Decker sternly. "That you have something else going on in your life that takes priority over *this*?"

"Why do you care so much?" barked Mars. "It's not your damn family."

"But it *was* my damn family," rejoined Decker. "Somebody killed them. I could have walked away from it and gone on with my life. But I can tell you this, Melvin. You can try to walk away, but the life you'll have if you do? It's not worth living."

Decker grabbed his towel, stepped off the treadmill, and started to leave the gym. He stopped at the door and turned back to Mars.

"For what it's worth, you should have won the Heisman that year. The guy who got it lasted only a few years in the pros and never really did much. You would've been Offensive Rookie of the Year too. Hands down. Just because you never got the chance doesn't mean you weren't a superstar. Because you were."

He closed the door behind him.

Mars remained sitting on the stool staring at the floor.

29

Decker said into his phone, "Agent Bogart?"

"Decker. How's it going down there? I assume you're still in Alabama."

"Yes. It's going, slowly. We might have got a lead on the guy who killed Regina Montgomery. He might have been seen. The cops down here are following up."

"I'm glad for you."

"I appreciate you paying for some more nights at the hotel. And the rental car too."

"You're welcome. It was not my intent to leave you high and dry."

"Are you back at Quantico?"

"Yes."

"What do they have you doing?"

"Right now, not much."

"Why is that?"

"I can't really get into that."

"Does it have to do with most of your team opting to continue the investigation?"

"Would it matter to you if it did?"

"I don't want this to hurt your career."

"I think that ship has sailed."

"I'm sorry to hear that."

"Way it goes sometimes. Maybe my big idea to have this team of folks from different walks of life was stupid anyway."

"I don't think it was stupid," said Decker bluntly.

"Face it, Decker, you don't need anyone working with you. You can figure pretty much anything out by yourself."

"I needed help in Burlington. To find my family's killers."

"You would have gotten there without us."

"Maybe. Maybe not. Is everything else going okay?"

"What, you mean my marriage? I got served with divorce papers this morning, as a matter of fact. Funny, after all this, I thought we might make it work."

"So it was a surprise?"

"Yes, it was a surprise. And my soon-to-be ex apparently has a new boyfriend who's a struggling artist, so she's coming after me for substantial alimony."

"You need a good lawyer."

"I *have* a good lawyer. Problem is, so does she. Look, what can I do for you? I know you better than to think you called to chitchat."

"I know this might sound crazy, but can you run something down for me?"

He heard Bogart sigh, but he also heard the clicking of a pen. "Like what?"

"Like whether Roy and Lucinda Mars were in the Witness Protection Program?"

"What?" Bogart exclaimed.

"They have no past that anyone can find. I think they might have been relocated."

"But why Witness Protection?"

"It would be a great motive for someone other than their son to kill them."

"And Charles Montgomery?"

"His wife was bribed to make him confess. The stuff I saw in her little duplex totaled over fifty grand. A down payment only. But they killed her so they wouldn't have to pay anything else. And also we were putting pressure on her. She might've cracked and let something slip. She had to die."

Bogart was silent for a few moments. "You know that the U.S. Marshals have never lost a protectee before."

"And maybe they didn't want anyone to know they'd lost the Marses."

"That's a big accusation."

"And it's a pretty big case, so that's symmetry for you."

"And if they were in Witness Protection, why didn't the U.S. Marshals come forward during Mars's trial?"

"Well, if no one knew they were in Witness

Protection no one would know to ask them. And I doubt they would volunteer anything if they didn't have to."

"But they would know about the trial. They would know that an innocent man might have gone to prison."

"The evidence was pretty substantial against Melvin. They might have believed that he actually killed them, and thus it had nothing to do with why they were put into the program in the first place."

"Okay, let's say I look into that for you. And I'm not saying I can. That would be potentially opening a big can of worms with the Marshals."

"I understand."

"But if I did, and they were killed by someone from their past, how do you explain Montgomery being paid off to lie and spring Mars from prison?"

"I can't explain it. Not yet, anyway."

"Did Mars suggest this?"

"No. It was my idea. He knows nothing about his parents' past."

"You can't know that for sure. His parents might have told him."

"They might have," conceded Decker. "But if they were in the program it might give us a handle on who killed them."

"It might indeed," said Bogart. "I'll let you know one way or the other."

"Agent Bogart, I am sorry for what happened. It wasn't my intent."

He heard the other man sigh. "I know. For you it's all about the case."

"Actually, it's all about finding the truth."

"Well, good luck with that."

Bogart clicked off and Decker set down his phone.

The Witness Protection angle had occurred to him several days ago actually, but after thinking about it in the shower after his workout he had decided to ask Bogart to make an official inquiry with the U.S. Marshals.

If Roy and Lucinda Mars had been in Witness Protection it would explain a lot of things: their lack of personal history, their showing up in a small town in West Texas, the scar on Roy Mars's face, ultimately their murders.

But what it couldn't explain away was what had so recently happened. Namely, someone paying off the Montgomerys to get Melvin Mars out of prison.

Who would do that? The same people who had killed his parents and framed him, sending him to prison and nearly to his execution over the course of the last twenty years?

No, it could not be them.

So who?

Unless he answered that question, Decker feared he would never bring this case to a satisfactory end.

He went downstairs to the hotel lobby to find Jamison waiting for him.

"Have you eaten?" she asked.

He shook his head. They went into the restaurant off the lobby.

When Decker started to order the All-American Breakfast, complete with fried eggs, pancakes, sausage and bacon, grits, and fried toast, he got a piercing gaze from Jamison.

Instead, he ordered orange juice, plain toast, and an egg white omelet.

As they ate he told her about his idea.

"Witness Protection?" she said. "That's interesting. I guess it could explain some things."

"But not the main thing. Why Melvin is free."

"No, I guess not that."

He didn't mention his meeting with Mars in the hotel gym, and the man's sudden reluctance to see the case through. It didn't matter to Decker what Mars thought. If he wanted to quit the case that was fine. Decker would continue on alone if need be.

He did tell Jamison about his talk with Davenport.

"Well, at least she brought light beer," said Jamison. "So, a book deal, huh? I wondered about that."

Decker looked at her, slightly surprised. "Why?"

She looked uncomfortable.

"Why?" he asked again.

"Because back in Burlington I sort of had the same

thought when we were investigating the murder of your family."

"That what, you'd write a book about it?"

"About it. About you. You are fascinating, Amos, you can't deny that."

"If I am fascinating, it's only because of a traumatic brain injury suffered on the football field. It's not like anyone should be encouraged to duplicate what happened to me."

"But your mind, your memory capability?"

He put down his fork. "So, do you *still* want to write a book on me?"

She looked at him, annoyance followed by guilt flitting across her features.

"Not anymore, no."

"Good, because if you did it would have to be done without any help from me, Jamison."

"I get that. I mean, I know that about you now." She looked around the room. "So what do we do? Stay in Alabama and see what the police come up with?"

Decker shook his head. "The events in Alabama are just part of the effects. Charles Montgomery being executed. Regina Montgomery being killed. The cause of it all is back in Texas. That's where we need to go."

"But didn't this really start before Texas? I mean, if the Marses were in Witness Protection?"

"Absolutely, Jamison. But to get to there we have

to go through Texas first. Because, for Melvin, that's where all this started."

The next moment Decker froze.

"What is it, Amos?"

Decker mumbled, "Heisman?"

"Heisman. What, the trophy?"

Decker rose. "No, all the hoopla associated with it."

"How is that connected?" she said.

"I think it might be the catalyst for all the rest."

30

I don't know," said Mars.

Decker, Davenport, and Jamison faced him across the width of a table in Mars's hotel room. Like Decker, he had showered after his workout and changed into fresh clothes.

"You have to know *something*," said Decker doggedly. "You were a Heisman Trophy finalist. You went to New York for the awards ceremony. Did they go with you?"

"No," said Mars immediately. "I asked but they both said no. Dad had to work, and Mom didn't like to travel without him."

"Your father couldn't get time off from his pawnshop job to go see whether his son won the *Heisman*?" Davenport said skeptically.

Mars looked at her. "I know it sounds weird now. But it didn't back then. I was going to the ceremony. Sure, I wanted them to come, but man, it was just cameras and microphones in my face all the time. I wouldn't have had much time to spend with them anyway."

Decker sat back. "Did anyone try to interview them about you in the lead-up? I know that it's typical to do stories about the backgrounds and families of the finalists."

Mars nodded. "Yeah, I mean we got requests. They came through UT. ESPN and some others wanted to do a story on my parents. The newspaper in Austin, even the *New York Times* came calling."

"And?" asked Decker.

"My parents turned all that down. They didn't want to talk to nobody."

"Didn't you find that strange?"

"Well, looking back, yeah. But you got to understand, man, everything was going a million miles an hour for me right then. I barely had time to breathe. It was like every week somebody was honoring me with something. Hell, even my old elementary school had a Melvin Mars Day that I went to speak at. So I didn't have a lot of time to dwell on my parents. I knew they were proud of me. That was all cool."

Jamison said, "I'm sure they were, but their reluctance to be in the public eye may mean something." She glanced at Decker. He nodded.

She said in a low voice, "Decker thinks your parents might have been in Witness Protection."

Mars's eyes widened and he gaped at Decker.

Davenport said, "That would make sense, actually. And explain a lot." She looked at Decker. "Can we verify it?"

"Working on it," said Decker as he continued to study Mars.

Mars said, "Why would my parents be in Witness Protection? Isn't that for, like, criminals who ratted people out?"

"Not always, no. Innocent people have gone into Witness Protection because they helped bring down bad elements and because of that their lives were in jeopardy."

Mars mulled over this. "I guess that might make sense. But they never said anything to me about it."

"I would imagine not," said Davenport. "Telling you might lead to bad things. You might slip up and mention something. I'm sure the protocols for the U.S. Marshals are to have as few people as possible know."

Mars nodded but still looked stunned by this possibility.

Decker stirred. "Did your parents go to the elementary school event?"

Mars composed himself and said, "Yeah. It was the only thing I remember them going to, actually. It was just a little ceremony in the auditorium. I spoke to the kids and teachers. Then some little kids brought up this plaque and presented it to me. I got my pictures taken with the principal and some of the teachers I had when I was there."

"And your parents?"

"Well, they were in the audience."

"They didn't come up onstage?"

"No way. They would never have done that. They hated stuff like that. Wanted to keep in the background."

"And did you leave together?"

Mars knitted his brows, obviously thinking back. "Yeah, we did, actually." He flinched a bit and then eyed Decker. "When we were coming out of the school there was a local TV film crew there. We didn't know they would be there. Sort of a surprise. But they talked to me. I did a little interview right there. Talked about my time at the school, the award I'd been given. All feel-good stuff."

"And your parents?"

"They were behind me."

"And in the camera's eye."

"Well, yeah, I guess. The dude was doing sweeps of the crowd."

"And did you mention your parents?"

"Yeah. I turned and pointed them out—" Mars stopped.

"And did the footage play on TV?"

Mars dumbly nodded. Then he said, "And ESPN picked it up and played parts of it over the next couple days. I remember seeing it."

Decker sat back. "So that's what started all this."

"What do you mean?"

"Your parents being on national television."

"But you said my father probably had plastic surgery done. To change his face."

"Maybe he did but it didn't change it enough."

Davenport said, "Decker, are you saying someone saw the Marses on TV and then came to Texas and killed them?"

"It's one theory, yes."

"And the people who did it were the reason the Marses were put in Witness Protection in the first place?" asked Jamison.

Decker nodded.

Mars said, "But you're talking a long time ago."

"Some people never stop looking," said Decker. "I speak from experience. So the passage of time means nothing."

Jamison shot him a quick glance but said nothing.

"So can we find out for sure if my parents were, you know, in Witness Protection?"

"I have Agent Bogart running that down for us."

"Bogart?" exclaimed Davenport.

"But it may take time," added Decker.

"Then what do we do in the meantime?" asked Jamison.

"Like I told you before, we head back to Texas."

"What about the guy who might have killed Regina Montgomery?" asked Davenport.

"I think he might already be in Texas."

"Why?" asked Davenport.

"Because there's a big piece of this that makes no sense to me."

"Such as?" asked Jamison.

"Such as a man who kills. And saves someone at the same time."

31

Decker and Mars didn't have the money for airfare, though Jamison and Davenport did. They were willing to put the men's airline tickets on their credit cards, but both refused the offer. Mars said he did not feel right about accepting anything from anyone.

"We'll drive back to Texas in the rental the FBI is paying for," said Decker. "You two fly and we'll meet you at the same motel."

"Are you sure?" asked Davenport. "We can drive back with you."

"Melvin and I can talk. And you two do not want to spend all that time in a car with us. When you land, you can get rooms there. Bogart emailed me and told me he had authorized government vouchers for five more days each for all of us. I'll forward you the info and you can use them. When you get back, check in with the local police to see if anything has happened since we've been gone."

"Happened?" said Jamison. "Like what?"

"Anything inexplicable."

"And you don't like inexplicable, that I know."

"No, I don't. I hate it, in fact."

The women made their flight arrangements while Decker gassed up the car and packed his few belongings. Mars had done the same. The state of Texas had given him some money after he left prison, to purchase some clothes, shoes, and other essentials, along with a duffel bag to carry it in.

Decker had spoken with Mary Oliver before they'd left to return to Texas. She was busy preparing the paperwork to get Mars his official compensation from the state. She had also hinted to Decker that she had another strategy in mind and would fill him in later.

"What strategy?" he'd asked.

"To get Melvin what he really deserves after two decades in prison. Because twenty-five grand just doesn't cut it."

"How long will it take to drive?" asked Mars as he and Decker set off in the rental.

"Seventeen hours or more. It's over a thousand miles."

"We driving straight through?" asked Mars.

"I don't know. We'll switch off. See how it goes."

"Decker, I ain't driven a car for twenty-some years. I don't even have a license."

Decker looked askance at him. "What, you worried about getting pulled over?"

"Well, yeah. They'll probably throw my ass back in prison."

"I wouldn't worry too much about that. If it comes to it, I'll say I forced you to drive at gunpoint because I'm a prick."

"Still a long drive, even for two."

"I like to drive. It helps me think."

"Well, if we're going to switch off I should sleep while you drive. Then vice versa."

"Before you do, let's talk."

"Still thinking about what I said in the gym?"

"Of course I am."

"You got to see it from my perspective. It's been my ass sitting in prison all this time. Sure I want to know the truth. But I've also got to figure out what I'm going to do with the rest of my life. And I'm scared shitless something is gonna mess this up and I'll be going back to jail."

Decker fingered the steering wheel and gazed out the windshield. They had reached Interstate 20 heading due west and he pressed his foot down on the gas. He set the cruise control and settled back in his seat.

"You can do both."

"Can I?"

"When my family was murdered I spent every waking hour of my life trying to find out who killed them. Even when I slept I wasn't away from it. I was obsessed."

"And do you think that was good for you?"

"No, it wasn't. I lost everything because of it. My job, my house, pretty much everything. But it didn't matter to me."

"Why not?"

"Because I'd already lost the only things that really meant something to me."

Mars sighed and gazed out his window. "What were their names?"

"My wife was Cassandra. But I called her Cassie. My daughter was Molly. My brother-in-law's name was Johnny."

"And you found 'em dead?"

"Yes."

"That must've been the worst thing could happen to you."

"I saw them in blue."

Mars shot him a glance. "Huh? Come again?"

"I have synesthesia."

"Synes-what?"

"Synesthesia. It's when your sensory pathways are commingled. I see certain numbers in color, for instance. And I saw my family's murder in blue. I see death in blue. I also have hyperthymesia."

"What's that?"

"A perfect memory."

"Damn, that's lucky. Were you born with it?"

"No. I never had it until I played in the NFL."

Mars looked at him skeptically. "*You* made it to the NFL? I thought you topped out at college ball."

"I made it onto the roster of the Cleveland Browns and lasted one regular-season play."

"One play? What the hell happened?"

"Guy laid me out on the kickoff. I died twice on the field. When I came out of the coma my brain had been changed. I was a different person."

When Mars said nothing in response, Decker looked over at him to find the man gaping at him.

"That's how you got that, that hyper thing, a perfect memory?"

Decker nodded.

"Come on, you're bullshitting me," Mars blurted out.

Decker shook his head. "Bullshitting is no longer really in my wheelhouse, because along with a perfect memory my personality also changed. You see, the brain controls that too. Or certain areas of the brain do."

"But what happened to you must be rare."

"Extraordinarily rare."

"But doing what you do, an investigator and all, it must come in handy to be able to remember everything."

"It does. But the rest of the time, not so much."

They drove in silence for a few minutes.

"Why'd you tell me that?" asked Mars. "I mean, you strike me as being pretty private. And it's not like we're good buddies or anything. We barely know each other."

"I wanted you to know that there is no right or wrong answer for what you're faced with. I know what I want to do. I want to find out what happened to your parents, and who set you up. But that's me. You have a different set of circumstances, like you said. Other priorities. But I also want you to know that I'm really good at what I do. I'm not good at anything else, but I am good at this. So if you'll work with me on this case, there's a really good chance that we'll get to the bottom of it eventually."

Mars appraised him. "You know, I do remember you now. From the game, I mean. You had perfect technique, did everything on the field right. Covered me coming out of the backfield just like the coaches drew it up."

"But you can't teach speed, or nimbleness, or the ability to change direction on the fly, or field vision. And you had all of that."

"It wasn't a fair fight," said Mars matter-of-factly. "But I also had the added motivation that this was my only way out. That's the way it is for lots of guys like me. You had other options."

"Good thing, because I was not going to be in the NFL for long, hit or no hit."

"I *do* want to find out what happened to them. And I know you can help me get there."

"So that means you're in?"

"Yeah, I guess so."

"One more thing, Melvin."

"What's that?"

"Sometimes the truth hurts more than not knowing."

Mars scowled and said, "Thanks for waiting to tell me that until *after* I agreed to keep going."

Mars put his seat back, closed his eyes, and went to sleep.

32

They were back in Texas.

But they still had over five hundred miles and another eight hours-plus to go.

Everything in Texas *was* big.

It was dinnertime and they were both starving. And they had to use the restroom.

Decker pulled off the highway and into the parking lot of a huge facility that had a bar-and-grill component as well as a grocery store and a gift shop. The parking lot was pretty full, mostly with oversized pick-up trucks sporting gun racks in the back and semis pulling double trailers.

They could hear the music blaring twenty feet from the door to the place.

They went inside, hit the bathroom, and then made their way to an open table near the back and away from the bar and live music. They ordered drinks and their food.

Mars looked around at the men and women, many wearing cowboy hats and boots, line dancing. Off to the right was a pool hall. To the left was a video game arcade.

When the live band took a break they could hear the smack of pool balls and the trash talk of the men playing. Decker noted a group of young men with pool cues in one hand and beers in the other watching them. When he looked away he saw Mars take a sip of his beer and smile.

"What?" asked Decker.

"Haven't had a beer in twenty years, man."

"Right."

Decker took a drink of his water.

Mars eyed him in amusement. "How's the diet coming?"

"It's coming."

"Trying to get back in football shape?"

"No, trying to live to celebrate another birthday."

Mars's smile faded. "Yeah, me too." He looked at his watch. "The girls will be back by now."

"They actually landed six hours ago. I tracked their flight on my phone."

"You can do that?" said Mars. "On a phone?"

"You have a lot of catching up to do."

"Yeah. So what do you think they can do?"

"Find out what's been going on. The local police still think we're FBI. So we can coordinate with them."

"What do *you* want to do?"

"I want to take you back to your old house, let you look around. It might jog something."

"And if I don't want to go there?"

"Then you don't go. I'm not going to force you."

"What else?"

"Bogart is running down the Witness Protection angle. We're still going to try to trace the funds Regina used to buy all that stuff."

"Okay."

"You remember anything else about your parents?"

"Been thinking about it, but nothing's come yet."

"So maybe a trip back to the old homestead is in order."

"Maybe."

"It was an elaborate setup, you know. They paid off the girl and the motel clerk."

"Come again?"

"Ellen Tanner. She was part of it. It was her idea to meet that night at her place, right?"

"Well, yeah."

"And she kept you a certain amount of time. Then had the argument and then you left. And she lied about the time. And she checked your wallet when you weren't looking and cleaned out any cash you might have had, so you'd have to use your credit card."

"Why would she do all that?"

"Same reason Regina did. She was paid to do it."

"And the motel clerk?"

"He was waiting for you."

"How did he even know my car would break down right in front of his place?"

"A car that worked perfectly the next morning when the police showed up?"

"So you're saying they messed with my car?"

"Maybe while you were at Tanner's."

"But wait a minute, I heard the clerk call in the credit card info."

"Yeah, at about eleven or so when you actually got there. Only he wasn't talking to the credit card company. He might have been talking to a dial tone for all I know. Doesn't matter. He probably wrote down the credit card info and then made another call later, at about one-fifteen, to the credit card company so that the official record reflected that as your check-in time. The manual machine he ran it through doesn't have a time stamp of course. He just wrote in the date, not the hour or minute. But he had to call the card company, so they have a time record of the call. And voilà, your alibi goes out the window."

Mars put down his beer. "Sonofabitch!"

"Yeah, I was thinking that too. Sonofabitch."

"That's a lot of work. A lot of planning."

"And that means there had to be a really good reason."

Decker bit into some of his salad with no dressing.

"How is it?" asked Mars, eyeing the lettuce, cucumbers, and carrot strips.

"Actually, I'd rather be eating a turd."

David Baldacci

Mars snorted and waited for him to finish the bite.

Decker said, "They framed you in an elaborate conspiracy, and then they got you out of prison. Why?"

"If it's the same people."

"I'm pretty sure it is."

"Then like you said, why?"

"That's the million-dollar question, Melvin. Why?"

They finished eating, paid the bill, and left. On their way to the car Decker said, "Shit."

Mars shot him a glance. "What is it?"

Before Decker could answer, the same men who had been watching them inside appeared from in between two parked cars. They quickly surrounded the pair. It was five versus two, and the other men were in their twenties, tall, muscular, and tough-looking.

Decker eyed the guy who seemed to be in the lead. "Can I help you?"

The biggest of them pointed at Mars. "You that dude got off death row, ain't you? Saw you on the TV."

Mars didn't answer him.

"Hey, I'm talking to you, boy," said the man.

Decker did not really want to deal with these punks, but he also didn't want Mars to get really ticked and kill the guy. So he said, "Why don't you go back to playing pool, okay?"

The man ignored him and kept staring at Mars.

"You killed your parents and you're outta prison? Tell me how that makes sense, asshole."

Decker could see the expression on Mars's face and didn't like what he was seeing.

The lead guy continued. "They said you played football? Shit, I bet my little brother could run right over your ass, boy."

Decker said to the man, "Just move on. Now!"

The man looked at him. "Who the hell are you telling me what to do?"

Decker held out his FBI cred. "This is who I am." He opened his coat to show he had a gun. "And this gives me the right to tell you to back the hell off."

The man looked at the FBI ID and then at the gun and his look became even more disgusted. "Hey, boy, is he your *babysitter*, or what?"

Decker saw Mars tense and he put a hand on his shoulder, though his gaze remained on the man. "Move on."

The man looked back at his buddies. "You think that pussy is wetting his pants yet?" They all laughed.

"I said move on."

Decker looked at Mars. "Just head to the car, I'll deal with these guys."

Mars looked at Decker as though he had lost his mind.

"Just go, Melvin!"

Mars reluctantly turned to walk off.

The man stepped forward and slapped the back of

Mars's head. Mars slowly turned back around as Decker looked at the man and said, "Do you have a death wish?"

The man said, "I think *he's* got the death wish, man. Or he'll wish he was dead once we're done with him."

Decker took a deep breath and glanced at Mars, who looked like a massive bull straining against the gate.

Decker swore again and turned to the man. "What's your name?"

The man gave Decker a patronizing look. "Why? You gonna write me up?"

"No, I just like to know who I'm dealing with."

"My name's Kyle, asshole. And by the way, we don't give a shit if you're a Fed. That don't mean nothing down here." He opened his jacket to show a gun. "And just so you know, we all got guns too."

"Okay, Kyle, you want to fight this guy, let's set some ground rules."

Kyle snorted. "Ground rules, what the—"

"Shut the fuck up!" roared Decker, who had just reached his limit with these guys.

Kyle froze.

Decker drew a calming breath and tried to pretend he was alone rather than in front of all of these people. He drew his weapon. "Rule number one, anybody pulls a gun, I will shoot you right in the nuts. Rule number two, you have to orally agree to what

I'm about to recite." He took out his phone and activated the video recorder function. Holding it up to capture his image, he said, "Regardless of the outcome of the fight, none of you will attempt to press charges against Mr. Mars for any reason, ever. If one or more of you dies, none of your survivors may make any legal claim, civil or criminal, against Mr. Mars."

"Are you shitting me?" said Kyle.

"You can't have a problem with any of that."

"Why not?"

"Like you said, because he's a pussy." Decker pointed his phone at Kyle. "You have to say, 'I agree.'"

The four other men looked at Kyle. He snapped, "I agree."

The other men looked at each other and one by one they too said the same thing, but not with the same level of enthusiasm.

"Good," said Decker. He eyed Kyle. "Now, give me a phone number of your next of kin."

Kyle said warily, "What, why?"

Decker looked at Mars and then back at Kyle. "Because he's gonna kill you, dumbass."

Decker stepped back and nodded at Mars, who stepped right up to Kyle and said, "Throw the first punch."

"Why?" barked Kyle.

"'Cause I don't want nobody saying I started this."

Kyle turned to look at his buddies, quietly mouthing instructions. Then without warning he whirled around and landed a haymaker right on Mars's chin. Or he would have, if Mars hadn't easily blocked the blow with his arm.

Kyle screamed and fell back a step. "You broke my damn ar—"

He didn't finish the sentence, because Mars slammed his fist into Kyle's face with such force that the man was lifted off his feet and landed unconscious on the pavement.

Kyle's buddies had all jumped back and now looked down at him. Blood was coming out of his mouth, his nose was broken, and three of his teeth lay on the asphalt next to him.

"Next," said Decker, looking expectantly at the other men.

The other guys hauled Kyle up and ran for it.

Decker holstered his gun and walked over to Mars. "Let's go," he said quietly. They strode to their car, climbed in, and drove off. Mars rubbed his knuckles and looked out the window. Decker eyed him and said, "Didn't make up for it, did it?" Mars shook his head. "Never does."

33

Mars just stood there for a few moments staring up at it.

The day was dry, the sky clear, and the heat building, though it was January.

He glanced over at Decker. Next to him stood Jamison and Davenport.

Decker said, "You good?"

Mars nodded slightly, his gaze fixed tightly on his old home. They were a foot from the front porch.

"You said you been in it?" said Mars.

Decker nodded.

"What's in there?"

"Not much. But that's not the important thing. The important thing is you being here and something occurring to you."

They had arrived back in town and immediately met with Jamison and Davenport at the motel they had checked them all into. The women had spoken with the local police to find that not a lot of progress had been made. Indeed, now that Mars had been pardoned, it seemed the Texas authorities considered the case closed.

"We did meet with Mary Oliver," Jamison had told Mars. "Melvin, she's filed a request with the state for compensation for you."

"How long will that take?" Mars asked. "I don't have any money or any job."

"She wasn't sure but she did say she filed for an expedited review. She seemed optimistic that you'd receive the maximum allowance."

"Yeah, twenty-five grand," he'd muttered before heading out to the car to come here.

Now Decker led the way into the house, the old door's hinges, broken from when Decker had forced it, giving a torturous shriek. Mars winced slightly as he followed Decker in. The women brought up the rear.

They stood in the front room for a few minutes. Jamison and Davenport looked around, while Decker kept his gaze on Mars.

The man looked frozen, as though he had just been teleported back to the 1990s.

"Take your time," advised Decker.

Mars went over to the photos on the shelf. He picked up the one of him in his football uniform and stared down at it.

"Walk down memory lane," said Decker.

"But it's like this isn't even me," replied Mars. He

looked at the other photos one by one. "None of these. It's like they're all someone else."

Davenport said, "That's because your life changed so dramatically, Melvin. Your past has become so detached it's nearly unrecognizable."

"So no pictures of your parents?" noted Decker. "Other than the one you mentioned that was taken when you were in high school?"

"Yeah, like I said, they didn't care for that. That was the only one of them when I was living here."

"Who took the photo of your parents?"

"I did."

"Who took all these pictures of you? Your dad or your mom?"

"My mom."

"Okay."

"Why?"

"Just wondering."

They covered the ground floor, Mars stopping and staring at various spots.

Decker said, "You had the shotgun for hunting. Did your parents have other weapons?"

Mars nodded dumbly. "My dad had two pistols. A nine-mil and a forty-five. Pretty pieces. He kept them locked up. But at night he would take one out and carry it up to bed with him."

"What happened to them?" asked Jamison.

"I don't know."

Davenport glanced at Decker. "Except for the

shotgun there was nothing in any of the police reports about finding weapons here."

"And Charles Montgomery didn't mention taking anything from here," added Jamison.

Decker nodded. "And if your dad had been surprised by an intruder in bed he would have had a gun to defend himself."

"What does that tell us?" asked Davenport, looking suddenly intrigued.

"That they forgot that part of the story," said Decker. "Melvin, did you tell anyone about the pistols?"

"No, nobody asked me."

"And you didn't testify at trial," added Decker. "So what happened to the guns?"

Davenport looked around. "Well, somebody could have come along and taken them later."

Decker shook his head. "The police would have searched this place from top to bottom long before any souvenir hunter could have taken anything. And if they had found two pistols it would have been listed in the inventory. They weren't, so that means the pistols were not found here." He looked at Mars. "You said he kept them locked up. Where?"

"Portable gun case he kept in the hall closet."

"How big?"

"About two feet square."

"Show me."

They trooped to the closet and Mars pointed to the

spot, a shelf above the clothes rack. Decker already knew there was no gun case there, because he had looked in the closet during his first visit here.

Decker said, "Your parents were killed by the shotgun you had and which was found here, and then their bodies were burned. No reason to inquire about handguns. And the police didn't." He shot Mars a glance. "Who would have known about the gun case?"

Mars shrugged. "I knew. My mom knew. We never had visitors here. So maybe nobody else knew."

"Well, someone must have, because they're gone." Decker added, "Why did he have two pistols?"

"Everybody in Texas has guns."

"Shotguns, rifles, yeah, but why two handguns?"

"We lived in the boonies. For protection, I guess."

"Did you see them any other time except when he took one up to bed with him?"

"One night my dad was cleaning them."

"That the only time you saw him cleaning them?" asked Decker.

Mars nodded.

"When was that?"

"Why does that matter?" snapped Mars, but then he calmed. "I'm not sure. Sometime around—"

"Around the time you went to the elementary school? Maybe a few days after?"

Mars looked at him in surprise. "Yeah, how'd you figure that?"

Jamison answered. "Because your dad might have

assumed someone saw him on the telecast and recognized him."

Davenport added, "So your father was getting ready in case someone from his past came calling."

Decker concluded, "And they apparently did."

Jamison gave Decker a curious look. "Okay, I get them taking out their revenge or whatever on the parents, but why frame Melvin for it?"

"Maybe payback by association," said Decker. "They wanted to take out the whole family."

"But why not just kill me too?" asked Mars. "Why set up this elaborate frame?"

"I wish I could answer that, but I can't," said Decker. "But for some reason they wanted you to pay the penalty for their crime."

Davenport cleared her throat and the others turned to her. She glanced nervously at Mars. "I'm not saying this is the case, Melvin."

"What?" he said abruptly. "What's not the case?"

"Whoever killed your parents may have mimicked whatever wrong, or *perceived* wrong," she added quickly, "that may have been committed against them."

"Wait a damn minute, are you saying my parents committed crimes against someone else? Killed somebody and they did what they did to get even?"

"It's a possibility only," said Davenport delicately. "And probably not a plausible one."

"I can't believe my parents were criminals!"

"As I said before, lots of people get put into Witness Protection who are not criminals," said Decker. "And your parents may well be in that category."

"Yeah, well, when will we find out for sure?"

"I hope soon. You want to go upstairs now?"

"No." But Mars nonetheless headed for the stairs.

34

I can't believe this stuff is still here."

They were in Mars's bedroom. He eyed the posters hanging on the wall.

"And my bed too." He put a hand on the head-board. "It's like it's twenty years ago," he said absently.

"Only it's not, Melvin," said Decker. "It's today."

Decker had placed his broad back against one wall to steady himself. The color blue had hit him as soon as his foot touched the first riser coming up, just like when he was here with Bogart.

Jamison had observed this, but not known the cause. Davenport had glanced curiously at Decker too, and given him a supportive smile.

Now that they were in the bedroom, Decker was able to come to terms with the color, at least enough to function again.

"Anything strike you?" he asked.

Mars walked around the small footprint of the room. "What happened to all my other things?"

"Did you come back here after your parents were murdered?"

"No. They wouldn't let me. It was a crime scene. I stayed with some friends. And then they arrested me. This is the first time I've been back since they died."

Davenport walked over to him. "It may help to sit on the bed, close your eyes, and just let your mind wander back to the last time you were in this house, or in this room. Then you may remember something that will help us."

"You really think that'll work?"

"Or I can hypnotize you."

Mars scoffed. "You can't hypnotize me."

"Really?" she said, smiling. "Would you like to bet?"

His skeptical look faded. "How would you do it?"

"Sit on the bed."

He looked at Decker and then Jamison, as though wondering when they were going to put a stop to this nonsense. Neither said anything.

Mars looked back at Davenport.

"Sit on the bed," she said. "This won't hurt. I promise."

He sat. She stood in front of him and took a pen out of her pocket. She held it up in front of him at an angle that made him lift his gaze a bit.

"Can you keep your eyes on this pen?"

"This is silly."

Decker said, "Melvin, just do it, okay? It's worth a shot."

Mars sighed and focused on the pen. "Okay, now what?"

"Just follow the pen."

Davenport started to move the pen slowly up and down and then from side to side. She spoke in a low, conversational voice the entire time.

Mars did as she asked and his gaze went wherever the pen did. The movements were slow, rhythmic, and her voice began to modulate, matching the movements of the pen.

Then Mars shook his head. "This is stupid."

Davenport kept the pen raised and said, "I know many athletes get into a zone before they play a game. Did you?"

"Well, yeah."

"Pretend you're getting ready to play a football game. Get your head right. Relax. But focus." She glanced sideways at Decker. "You're about to play Ohio State and run over Decker again." She then pointed to the pen. "This is the zone, Melvin. You can get there. The big game. For all the marbles. Just concentrate. This pen is the goal line. Go get it."

Mars settled back and stared at the pen, his gaze still slightly elevated due to the angle at which Davenport was holding it.

In a whisper to Decker she said, "Give him some football direction, low even tones."

Decker looked wildly uncertain about this.

Davenport said in a soothing voice, "You can do it,

Amos. Just like when you were talking to Tommy Montgomery."

Decker nodded and began speaking in a halting low voice as he gave Mars the scenario on the field: The ball was snapped. Mars took the handoff. The A-gap was clogged, the B-gap a possibility. Mars had to read the linebacker's eyes, strong safety coming up on the left, right guard just had to maintain his block for another second, a glimpse of daylight.

Davenport motioned for Decker to stop talking.

As Decker had been speaking, Davenport had slowed the movements of the pen and Mars had matched this with his gaze. Finally, she held the pen steady in the air and Mars stared at it, his eyes glassy and fixed, his features relaxed.

"Melvin, can you hear me?" she asked.

"Yes," he answered, his voice unlike his usual one.

Davenport slowly lowered the pen, but Mars's gaze remained fixed on the same spot.

She said, "You're in college at the University of Texas. Do you remember that?"

He nodded.

"You're home now with your parents, though. Okay?"

"Yes."

"This is after ESPN showed your parents on TV. They found out, right?"

"Yes."

"How?"

"Somebody at the pawnshop told my dad. He was pissed."

"They're acting strange now, aren't they?"

"Yes."

"Can you tell us how?"

"Nervous. And angry. My dad was really upset."

"Because it showed him on TV?"

"Yes."

"Did he say why that had upset him?"

"No."

"What about your mother? Did she talk about it?"

"She said to just leave Dad alone and he'd be okay. She . . . she didn't want to talk about it."

"Did you see your father doing anything unusual during that time?"

"He worked late a lot. And he didn't eat. And he drank a lot."

"Did he and your mother argue?"

"I could hear them yelling, but I couldn't really hear what they said."

"Could you hear anything?"

Mars's brow furrowed. "Some Spanish word. Funny one. My mom said it."

"What was it?"

The brow furrowed more deeply. "*Ch-chocha.*"

"*Chocha*, you're sure?"

Mars nodded. "*Chocha*. I looked it up. It actually has a couple of meanings in Spanish. It could refer to a prostitute, or"—here he squirmed a bit—"or the private parts of the female anatomy. I didn't know what they were talking about. It made no sense."

"Can you remember anything else about that time?"

Mars was silent for a few moments and Davenport waited patiently.

"I came home one night and he was sitting in his chair. Mom wasn't there."

"Okay, go on."

"I asked him how he was doing. And he looked at me in a way . . ."

"Yes."

Tears had appeared in Mars's eyes. "In a way that scared me. Like . . . like he hated me."

"Okay. Did you talk to him?"

Mars shook his head. "I was scared. I was going to go up to my room, but then he said something."

"What did he say?"

"He said . . . he said he was sorry."

Davenport glanced at Decker and Jamison. By her expression, she had evidently not been expecting this answer. But Decker didn't look surprised.

She turned back to Mars. "Did he say what he was sorry about?"

Mars shook his head. "Then he just got up and walked out."

"Do you have any idea what he was referring to?"

Mars shook his head again. "I asked my mother about it the next day."

"And what did she say?"

"She just started to cry, and then she ran out of the room."

"Did you tell the police about this?"

"No. I didn't think to. I mean, I didn't know what was wrong. I never thought that was connected to whoever killed them."

Davenport looked at Decker. "Anything else?" she whispered.

Decker stepped forward but kept out of Mars's line of sight. In Davenport's ear he said something. She started, looked at him strangely, and then turned to Mars.

"Melvin, did your father . . . did your father ever tell you that he loved you?"

Jamison shot Decker a surprised look.

Mars kept staring straight ahead. "No. He never did."

"Okay. When I count to three you're going to wake up. You're not going to remember anything that we discussed. Okay?"

Mars nodded.

She counted to three and his eyes slowly refocused. He looked up at them.

"I told you that you couldn't hypnotize me," he said.

"*Chocha,*" said Decker.

Mars shot him a glance. "What?"

"You *were* hypnotized. Do you remember your

mom saying the word *chocha* while she and your dad were arguing?"

Mars looked surprised and then slowly nodded. "Yeah, now that you mention it, I do. Do you think that's important?"

"It could be."

Decker looked over at a corner of the room. "Those scratches on the floor? What was there?"

"A bookshelf."

"What sort of books were on it?"

"Different kinds. From when I was little to when I got older. I didn't read as much as a teenager." He suddenly smiled.

"What?" said Decker quickly.

"It's nothing."

"Tell me."

"It's just that my dad would read a book to me when I was little. It was funny, you know, this big, tough guy reading a book to a little boy."

"What sort of books?" asked Decker.

"It was just the *one* book." Mars smiled again. "He would even act it out, you know, all goofy like. Never did that any other time."

"What book was it?" asked Decker in a very serious tone.

Mars laughed. "*The Three Little Pigs*. He told me he was the Big Bad Wolf, gonna eat those little pigs up. Sometimes he got into it so much it kinda scared me."

Decker stared at him for a long moment while Jamison and Davenport glanced at him.

"Decker, what is it?" asked Jamison.

Mars added, "It was just a picture book, Decker. A fairy tale."

"Yeah," said Decker, evidently lost in thought.

His phone buzzed. He looked down at the screen. "It's Bogart." He answered, listened, and asked a couple of questions. "Thanks, Agent Bogart, I really appreciate this." He clicked off and looked at the others.

"Well?" said Jamison. "Don't keep us in suspense."

"Bogart got an answer from the U.S. Marshals."

"So my parents *were* in Witness Protection," said Mars numbly.

"No," said Decker. "They weren't."

35

The two women stared back at him. One grown, one still a child and who would forever remain so, while the other would not grow a minute older.

Because both were now dead.

Decker sat in a chair in his motel room and stared down at the photo of his wife and daughter.

He took out the picture whenever he was feeling sad or hopeless and simply needed to see their faces. He would never have to worry about forgetting them. About their memories fading into the dim recesses of his mind.

His mind had no dim recesses.

It was like Times Square all the time.

He was feeling claustrophobic, as though a compression of his entire being was taking place and he had no power to stop it.

The news that neither Roy nor Lucinda Mars had ever been in Witness Protection had been a staggering blow. He had been so certain that he was right about that. Yet Bogart had checked and then double-checked. And the U.S. Marshals would have had no reason or basis to lie. If they had lost a protectee they would have documented it seven ways from Sunday.

He had leads, he had developments, but that was all. Yet none of these things appeared likely to give him what he so desperately wanted.

The truth.

At times it seemed the most elusive thing in all of creation.

He had notched another belt hole as his appetite seemed to weaken along with the prospects of solving the case. Given a choice, he would gladly have packed the pounds back on to find out who had killed the Marses.

Even if they hadn't been in the U.S. Marshals' care, they could still be running from a dark past. In all likelihood they were. He just had to find out what that past was. And to do that he needed information.

That was the first part.

The second part was figuring out who had paid off the Montgomerys and why.

He rose and went to the window. The rain had started again, pushing the heat away. The day was overcast, chilly and miserable. Matching his feelings perfectly. It wasn't supposed to rain much in this part of Texas, but the current weather was certainly bucking that trend.

Because of his perfect memory it seemed that some people regarded him as a machine. And while his social skills were not close to what they had once been, and in some ways he did appear to be unfeeling, even robotic, Decker did still *feel* things. He grew sad and depressed. And there was nothing his perfect memory could do about that. If anything, it made it worse.

He was surprised by the knock on the door.

"Yeah?"

"It's me."

He slipped the photo into his pocket and opened the door to see Mars standing there.

"Got a minute?"

"Yeah."

Mars came in and they sat a foot apart from each other. Before Decker could ask him what he wanted, Mars took out something and handed it across.

Decker looked down at the photo.

The man was very tall. His hair was brown with a bit of white and curled around his head. The face was rugged but good-looking. The nose had been broken and not reset very well. The eyes were flat, appeared lifeless. The mouth was small and drawn as a slash across the lower part of the face.

The woman could not have created a greater contrast. She was tall and lean and her luxuriant hair cascaded down around her broad shoulders. Her skin was dark brown and flawless. The face held no imperfections that Decker could see. The eyes danced with life. The mouth swept up into a beaming smile that was infectious. Indeed, Decker felt his own mouth tug upward as he looked at her image.

He glanced up at Mars. "Your parents, obviously. This was the picture you mentioned before, the one you had taken?"

Mars nodded.

"Where'd you get it?"

"Always had it. Took it to prison with me."

"You could have shown it to me before."

Mars wiped at his eyes. "Yeah, I could've."

"So why now?"

"Because I wanted you to see them as real people, not just little puzzle pieces, Decker. And I wanted you to see my mom's smile. And my dad's eyes. I just wanted you to know that . . . that they existed."

Decker looked back down at the photo, his features a bit strained by the other man's frank admission.

And maybe my frank omission.

"I can understand that, Melvin. When was it taken?"

"When I graduated from high school. They were real proud. I'd already committed to UT. I was going away. My mom cried a lot."

"And your dad?"

Mars hesitated. "Not so much."

"Sometimes it's that way with fathers."

"Yeah."

"Your mom was beautiful. Truly stunning."

"Yeah, she was."

A long moment passed as the two men stared at each other.

"Got something else on your mind?" Decker asked.

"It's like I don't exist, Decker."

"Why do you say that?"

Mars glanced at him. "I don't know anything about the two people in the photo. Where they came from. Who they really were. Why they were killed. Nothing. And since I came from them, meaning nothing, what can that make me?" He put up his hands. "Nothing."

A minute of silence passed as the rain started to pick up outside. The drumming of the drops seemed to march in parallel with the heartbeats of each of the men.

Decker took out the picture of his wife and daughter and handed it across to Mars. Mars looked at it.

"Your family?"

Decker nodded.

"Your little girl is super cute."

"*Was* super cute."

Mars looked uncomfortable. "I know you must miss them."

Decker leaned forward. "The point, Melvin, is that I knew *everything* about them. Everything. There was no mystery at all."

"Okay," said Mars slowly, evidently unsure of where this was going.

"And they're gone. And I'm ... nothing too. Same as you."

Mars looked like he wanted to hit something. "So is that it? There's nothing else? Then what the hell are we doing this for?"

"We're doing it because there *can* be something else. It's up to us."

"But you just said—"

"I said I am nothing. Today. Tomorrow I may be something. That's the only guarantee any of us have. It's a big, free country. There are opportunities for all to do something."

"It's different for me."

"Why?"

"Damn, why do you think? I'm black. You're white. Biggest difference there is."

"You think?"

"And you don't? You got a bigger one?"

"I was thinking more along the lines of Longhorns and Buckeyes. Race doesn't matter there, just winning."

Mars gave him a smirk. "Nice one. But it don't change reality. I'm a black ex-con, pardon or not. Remember them assholes from the truck diner?"

"Forget them. They're a shrinking segment of society. But finding out who really did this can change things, Melvin."

Mars shook his head, but Decker continued. "Half the people still think you killed your parents."

"I don't give a shit what they think."

"Hear me out."

Mars was about to say something else, but he stopped and nodded curtly.

Decker continued, "There are few things more powerful than the truth. Once you get truth on your side, good things tend to happen, black, white, or anything in between."

"But you thought they were in this Witness Protection thing. They weren't. So we're right back where we started."

"In a game when the play broke down and the first hole was plugged, what did you do, fall on the turf and give up?"

"Hell, what do you think?"

"So what *did* you do?"

"I found me another hole to run through."

"Well, that's what we're going to do, Melvin. We're going to find another hole to run through."

"How?"

"Did your dad keep a safe at the house?"

"A safe? No."

"Would he have used one at work? That only he would have access to?"

"They had a safe there, but my dad told me the owner was a real prick. Hovered over him all day, afraid he was stealing. Even after working there for years. So there's no way that my dad would have been the only one to have access to that safe."

"Then that really leaves only one alternative."

36

Decker and Mars faced the stone building as fresh storm clouds built overhead. Darkness had arrived early thanks to this new weather system.

"Texas First National Bank?" said Decker. "You're sure this is it?"

"I had an account here when I was in high school, and later in college. My parents brought me here. It's where they kept their money, what little they had."

"They might have had more than you think."

"If they'd had money why didn't they spend some of it?"

"I wasn't necessarily talking about cash," replied Decker as he began to mount the broad steps leading to the bank's front doors.

Inside, he made his request to a teller and they were quickly shuttled off to the assistant branch manager.

The man was short, in his early forties, bespectacled, with a paunch that protruded from between the flaps of his suit jacket. As he put out his hand he glanced at Mars and his jaw dropped.

"Melvin Mars?"

Mars nodded. "Do we know each other?"

"I'm Jerry Bivens. We went to high school together."

Mars eyed him more closely.

Bivens said apologetically, "I didn't play football. Not really built for it."

Mars shook the man's hand and forced a smile at Decker's slight elbow nudge. "Yeah, Jerry, I remember you. How you doing?"

"All right. Married, four kids. Working my way up the corporate ladder. In five or six years I'll probably be the branch manager."

"Good for you, man."

The two men stared awkwardly at each other.

"I heard you, um, got out of prison," said Bivens nervously.

"Yeah, another dude confessed."

"What an injustice," said Bivens. He looked over Mars's impressive physique. "You look like you could still suit up."

"Yeah, if only," said Mars.

Decker cleared his throat and Bivens focused on him. Decker flashed his FBI credentials, which did not include a badge, but nevertheless seemed to impress Bivens, who immediately stood straighter and buttoned his jacket.

"Yes, Agent, um, Decker, what can I do for you?"

"We need some information."

Bivens glanced around to find both tellers and three customers in line staring at them.

"You want to step into my office?" said Bivens hastily.

Bivens's "office" was a cubicle partially enclosed by glass. He indicated chairs for them to use and then seated himself behind his desk.

"What sort of information?" he asked.

"I understand that Roy and Lucinda Mars had an account here."

Bivens said nothing but clasped his hands together and placed them on his desktop.

"Is that a yes?" asked Decker.

"I'd have to look that up."

Decker glanced at the computer sitting on the desk. "Okay."

"I meant, I would with the proper authorization. We respect a customer's privacy."

"I appreciate that, but the Marses are both dead."

Bivens changed color, glanced quickly at Mars, and then lifted his hands off the desk and placed them on the arms of his chair. "Well, yes, of course I know that. But then their legal representative—"

"They don't have one," interjected Decker.

"Or their next of kin."

Decker tapped Mars on the shoulder. "Sitting right here."

Bivens again stared at Mars. "Right."

Mars said, "You have my permission to look it up and tell him, Jerry."

Bivens began tapping keys on his computer. He

read through a couple screens. "They had an account, but it was closed twenty-some years ago."

"Can you give us the exact date?" asked Decker.

Bivens told him.

Mars said, "That was two days before they died."

Decker nodded. "Can you tell us how much was in the account before it was closed?"

Bivens tapped some more keys and pulled up the transaction history. "About fifty-five hundred dollars."

Decker and Mars both looked disappointed.

Bivens said, "I'm sorry if you were looking for any funds, Melvin." He paused. "I know you were in prison a long time."

Decker said, "No other accounts?"

Bivens glanced at the screen. "No, just the checking account."

Mars looked crushed, but Decker appeared to just be getting started. "How about a safe deposit box?" he said.

Mars jerked and glanced at him.

Bivens hit some more keys. "Right, they had a box. How did you know?"

Decker said, "Just a lucky guess on my part. What can you tell us about it?"

"Well, it was closed out at the same time as the account. We have all records on computer now. Your father closed it and signed all the necessary documents."

"And there's no way to tell what was in the box?"

Bivens shook his head. "No inventories are kept of safe deposit boxes unless a client specifically requests that it be done. Otherwise it's strictly private."

"But he closed it and took everything?" said Decker.

"Yes."

"How large was the box?"

Bivens hit some more keys. "Our largest. A double. It could hold a lot."

"Is there anyone here who worked at the bank back then that we could talk to?" asked Decker.

"Oh, no. I've been here the longest. Fourteen years. The branch manager was transferred in from El Paso three years ago. The others have all been here less than five years." Bivens glanced over Decker's shoulder and then said to him, "Is there anything else I can do for you?"

Decker looked behind him to see two people lined up waiting to talk to Bivens.

"No, but we appreciate your help."

They walked outside, smack into the dreary weather.

Mars barked, "I can't believe this shit. My mom was dying from cancer and no one told me. And now I find out my dad kept a safe deposit box loaded with who knows what. It's like I'm living somebody's else's life."

"And he closed it two days before he died," noted Decker.

The Last Mile

"You think my dad knew something was coming?"

"Of course he did. And the question is, what did he do with the items from the box?"

37

They met up with Jamison and Davenport in a private area adjacent to the motel lobby later that day. Decker filled them in on the meeting with Jerry Bivens at the bank.

Jamison said, "So even if the Marses weren't in Witness Protection, it seems like they had some secrets."

Davenport added, "The history that no one can uncover, not even the FBI." She glanced at Mars. "Roy and Lucinda Mars are probably not even their real names."

Decker said, "AC and RB. We found those initials written on the wall of their closet. Those might be their real initials."

"Shit," said Mars, shaking his head and looking away from them. He seemed like a man stumbling through a dream he'd had no hand in creating.

Decker said, "So they weren't in Witness Protection, but they may have been on the run from someone."

"Or some group," amended Jamison. "Like the mob."

"The mob!" barked Mars. "Okay, just stop right there. My parents were not in the damn mob, okay?"

Decker said sharply, "The fact is, Melvin, right now none of us knows what they were involved in, including you. But whatever it was, it was bad enough that they created new identities and moved to a little town in Texas to escape it."

"And the safe deposit box contents might have something incriminating to whoever these people are," said Jamison.

"But there's no way for us to find out what was in the box," added Davenport. "I mean, it was twenty years ago. And whoever killed your parents, Melvin, may have taken it."

"Or not," said Decker.

They all turned to him.

"Care to elaborate on that point?" asked Davenport.

"The one question that can't be answered by any of this is, why would someone pay off the Montgomerys to get Melvin out of prison?" He glanced at them one by one.

"I give up," said Mars finally. "Why?"

"They might if they didn't find what was in the safe deposit box. And it's still out there somewhere. And they may think you know where it is."

"That's quite a theory," said Davenport.

"But if so, why wait all this time?" asked Jamison.

"It may be that once Melvin was scheduled to be

executed they panicked, figuring this might be their last chance to retrieve it."

Mars looked puzzled. "But Decker, no one's tried to contact me. Or kidnap me and make me tell them what I know, which is zip."

"They may plan to simply let us do what we're doing, searching for it."

"And rush in when we find it and, what, kill us all?" said Davenport skeptically.

"Perhaps," said Decker. "Or perhaps not."

"Well, I'm glad we cleared that up," said Davenport, clearly frustrated.

"Investigations are not always simple," retorted Jamison. "The case we worked in Burlington took a ninety-degree turn, but it took a ton of legwork and asking questions to get us there. And what seemed unimportant at first turned out to be critical."

"Okay, but Decker, your theory is riddled with holes," said Davenport.

"It *is* full of holes," admitted Decker, drawing a surprised look from Davenport. "That's why it's only a theory. It may well be disproved later on. But we have to run down the possibility anyway."

Mars looked at him nervously. "So you think someone may still try to come after me?"

Decker considered this. "If they're following us, which they may very well be, they would know that we're searching for answers too. If they saw us at the bank and deduced what we were doing, they also know we left the place empty-handed."

"So they might simply let us keep going until we do find something," said Mars slowly.

"Right."

"They have long memories," said Mars. "If this goes back before I was born, we're talking over forty years ago."

"Well, I have a long memory too," said Decker.

"Amen to that," replied Mars. He looked up and saw Mary Oliver walk into the lobby.

"Mary, over here," he said, rising and motioning to Oliver, who was heading toward the front desk. She was wearing a beige pantsuit and a smile.

"You look happy about something," prompted Davenport.

"The state of Texas has agreed to the maximum of twenty-five thousand dollars in compensation to you, Melvin."

"Well, it's something," said Mars.

"And I'm filing suit against them for what happened to you in prison. To the tune of fifty million dollars."

Mars stared dumbstruck at her. "Are you kidding me?" he finally said.

"Melvin, you almost died. This was a conspiracy that included guards who were representatives of the state's correctional system. And I discovered that these same guards have had other lawsuits filed against them and no disciplinary action was ever taken against them. That constitutes, at the least, willful negligence on the part of the state."

Decker said, "This was the strategy you mentioned before?"

She nodded. "Yes, it is."

Decker looked at Mars. "Well, at least monetarily fifty mil will make up for your not being able to play in the NFL."

Oliver added, "Look, I won't blow smoke up your butt. It's a long shot and there's no guarantee, but I'm going to give it my best effort."

Mars was speechless for a few moments. Then he hugged her. "Thank you, Mary. Thank you."

They sat down and the others let Mars compose himself.

No one noticed the three state troopers and plainclothes detective heading their way until they were right on top of them.

Decker spotted them and said, "Can I help you, Officers?"

They ignored him and surrounded Mars. "Mr. Mars, please stand up," said the plainclothes, after he flashed his badge and told them he was a homicide detective.

"What? Why?" said Mars.

"Please stand up," said the man more firmly.

"What is this about?" said Oliver, who did stand. "I'm his lawyer."

"And you'll get a chance to talk to your client. Just not now. Please stand, Mr. Mars. Last time I'll ask."

Mars glanced at Decker, who nodded. Mars stood and automatically put his hands behind his back. The plainclothes motioned to an officer, who came forward and handcuffed him.

The plainclothes said, "You are under arrest in connection with the murders of Roy and Lucinda Mars." Then he read Mars his Miranda rights.

"He was pardoned for that!" snapped an incredulous Oliver.

"His pardon has been revoked. That's why we're here."

"They can't do that!" said Oliver.

The plainclothes handed her a sheaf of papers. "The court order doing just that. Let's go, Mr. Mars."

As they led Mars away, Oliver called after him, "Melvin, I'll see you at the station." She then read down the first page of the document.

"What does it say?" asked Jamison as she rose.

Oliver's face paled as she finished skimming. She shot a glance at Decker.

He sighed. "I didn't believe they would do this," he said quietly.

"Do what?" snapped Jamison.

"You knew?" demanded Oliver.

"I suspected."

"Will someone please tell us what the hell is going

on?" barked Davenport, who had risen and was standing next to Jamison.

Decker said, "Our investigation has shown that it's entirely probable that the Montgomerys were paid off to lie about Charles Montgomery killing Roy and Lucinda. That confession was the only reason Melvin was released and pardoned." He looked at Oliver. "Am I right?"

She nodded but said nothing.

"Oh my God," said Jamison.

"That means—" began Davenport.

Decker interrupted, "That means that as far as the state of Texas is concerned Melvin killed his parents. Hence his pardon was revoked."

"How did they find out what we discovered?" asked Jamison.

"Texas sent its own people to Alabama to investigate Montgomery," replied Decker. "And we talked about our suspicions and findings with the Alabama authorities. They must have relayed that to the Texas folks."

"But he had nothing to do with the Montgomerys lying about this," said Jamison.

"That doesn't matter legally in Melvin's case," said Oliver. "It's as if nothing has changed now. No confession, the sentence is reinstated. The allocution Montgomery made is no good if he lied."

Jamison turned, horrified, to look at Decker. "So

our work has sent him back to prison and maybe to his death?"

Decker didn't answer. He had pulled out his phone and was heading toward the motel exit where a minute before Mars had left on his way back to prison. As he watched Mars being driven off, he punched in a number. After two rings there was an answer.

"Agent Bogart, it's Decker. I'll understand if you tell me to go to hell, but I have a big favor to ask."

38

"All rise," said the burly bailiff.

All the persons in the courtroom rose, including the only one wearing shackles.

Judge Matthews, a wizened, balding man with a lumpy Adam's apple, appeared through a doorway behind the bench, ascended the stairs, and sat down in his chair.

"Be seated," commanded the bailiff, and everyone returned to their respective chairs.

Mary Oliver sat next to the shackled Mars. Decker, dressed in the suit he had bought while shopping with Jamison, sat on the other side of him.

The state prosecutor held forth at the other counsel table. He was in his midfifties, with a patch of soft white hair that didn't come close to covering his pink scalp. His shirt collar was stiff from being overstarched, and this attribute neatly matched the man's demeanor. He had a file in front of him labeled *Mars, Melvin*. He was silently moving his lips, as though rehearsing what he was about to say.

In the second row of the courtroom sat Davenport

and Jamison. There was a goodly number of reporters present because word had gotten round that Mars had been arrested. There were also a few dozen gawking local citizens to round out the audience.

The judge eyed both counsel tables and their respective occupants, cleared his throat, and said, "The defendant filed the motion, so let's hear from him first."

Oliver rose and straightened the jacket of her two-piece suit and adjusted her shirt cuffs.

"Your Honor, the state's actions in this matter can be summed up as follows: It wrongly convicted my client, Mr. Mars, locked him up for over twenty years and very nearly executed him until it saw the error of its ways when presented with evidence of his innocence. It then granted him his liberty and with it a full pardon, and also ordered that he be paid the maximum compensation for his erroneous incarceration, not that twenty-five thousand dollars can make up for over two decades in prison." She took a breath and seemed to swell with righteous indignation. "And now, shortly after granting him his freedom, it has unilaterally revoked his pardon and his liberty, placed him under arrest, and he now sits shackled before us. All of this was accomplished without benefit of a trial, or representation by counsel, thus denying him due process. That is why I filed the habeas corpus petition, because it is clear beyond doubt that the state is illegally detaining my client. I therefore ask that he be released forthwith, and that both the terms of his pardon and compensation be fully honored and enforced by this court."

Oliver put a hand on Mars's shoulder and added, "Anything less would be a travesty of justice and establish an unsustainable and dangerous precedent should the state be allowed to unilaterally renege on its agreement with my client, since we may assume that it will try to do so with other defendants in the future."

"Understood," said Judge Matthews. He turned to the state's prosecutor. "Mr. Jenkins, counsel has made some excellent points. I don't like the idea of the state going back on its word. It would wreak havoc with the system if defense counsel could not rely on agreements provided to them by your office."

Jenkins rose, buttoned his jacket, smoothed down an errant strand of hair, glanced disapprovingly at Mars and Oliver, and then turned his attention fully to the judge.

"Your Honor," he drawled. "The action which the state took was the only one, in good conscience, that it could take. While I'm the first to admit that the situation here is a little unusual—"

"That's an understatement," interjected Judge Matthews.

"Be that as it may, there was only *one* reason that Mr. Mars was released from prison." Here he paused and held up a single finger for emphasis. "That was because another man, Charles Montgomery, now dead, executed by the state of Alabama for assorted heinous crimes, confessed to the murders for which Mr. Mars was previously convicted. After due investigation, it appeared that Mr. Montgomery did indeed have information and knowledge of the crimes which only the true perpetrator would have possessed. Now, due in large measure to the work performed by the FBI, it appears clear that Mr. Montgomery, and his wife, who, significantly enough, was likely murdered to cover up what went on, were paid a great sum of money to make that confession. Thus it is almost a certainty that Mr. Montgomery had no more to do with the murders of Roy and Lucinda Mars than you or I, Your Honor. Thus the state's position is that the original conviction of Mr. Mars was right and just, and his incarceration at this time is warranted *and* legally proper."

Jenkins glanced once more at Mars with an expression of cold contempt. "And let me add that the state of Texas will vigorously explore whether Mr. Mars was in any way connected to what amounts to a bald-faced attempt to deceive the criminal justice system of Texas, as he stood to benefit the most from this so-called confession by Mr. Montgomery."

Oliver jumped to her feet. "There is not a shred of evidence that my client was in any way involved with this, Your Honor."

Jenkins bristled. "Well, the fact that this now discredited confession came at the eleventh hour prior to the defendant's scheduled execution seems an awfully large, and well-timed, coincidence."

Oliver gave him an incredulous look and said in a tone dripping with sarcasm, "Yes, I'm sure that Mr. Mars waited until minutes before they were to put him to death before arranging from death row for this miracle confession to come along in the nick of time and save him."

"There is no need to take that unprofessional tone," snapped Jenkins.

"Regardless," said Oliver, addressing the judge, "the state had ample time to investigate the veracity of Mr. Montgomery's claims. It did so with the result that a full pardon was issued to my client. If the state is now allowed to go back on this agreement, the sanctity of the pardon will have been destroyed and no person may rely in the future on the state doing so without fear that it will once again renege."

Jenkins said, "But the state clearly has a vested interest in seeing that convicted murderers are not set loose upon the public."

Judge Matthews interjected, "Well, it appears to me that the state got itself into this mess, Mr. Jenkins. And if it can unilaterally reject its own agreements, then Ms. Oliver is right in saying that makes the entire pardoning system untenable."

Jenkins spread his hands. "All we desire, Your Honor, is the ability to more fully investigate the matter. And during that time the defendant's incarceration is duly warranted. The pros certainly outweigh the cons. If he is innocent then no harm will have been done. And if he is guilty, which we believe that he is, he will not have the opportunity to flee. He has no ties to the community, and we consider him a likely flight risk."

Oliver retorted, "He has no passport, no valid ID of any kind, and, thanks to the state of Texas, no job or money. I hardly consider him a flight risk."

"And the Mexican border is only a hop, skip, and a jump away," countered Jenkins. "And while it is porous for those seeking to enter this country, it is equally porous for those seeking to do the opposite."

Judge Matthews looked uncertain as he stared down at them. He glanced at Oliver. "Well, I can't say I totally agree with Mr. Jenkins's position, but it seems to me that there's no harm in allowing the state to retain custody of Mr. Mars while the investigation is ongoing."

At that moment Decker stood and all eyes in the courtroom turned to his towering presence. Decker felt the mingled gazes, and his gut was lurching and his nerves were fraying, because he just didn't like interacting with other people.

And he certainly didn't like having to be less than completely honest with a judge. But this was the plan he had come up with, and he had no choice but to follow it through.

"With your permission, Your Honor, may I speak?" he asked.

"And you are?" said Judge Matthews expectantly.

Decker rubbed a bead of sweat off his face. He could feel the wetness under his armpits. He suddenly felt nauseous. He briefly wondered if he might faint right here in court. In a slightly tremulous voice he said, "Amos Decker. I'm here representing the FBI."

Jenkins quickly said, "I don't see that the FBI has any standing to be involved in a case that is completely under the jurisdiction of the state of Texas."

Decker kept his gaze on the judge. "The FBI *has* become involved in this case, Your Honor. Indeed, as counsel has already pointed out, it was our efforts that led to the doubts being cast on Mr. Montgomery's confession."

"But—" began Jenkins. However, Judge Matthews held up his hand.

"That's a valid point. Let Agent Decker finish what he was saying."

For the first time in his life Decker was suddenly seeing everything in the most vivid shade of blue even though no one in the room had died. He closed his eyes.

"Agent Decker?" prompted Judge Matthews as Jenkins snorted and looked derisively at Decker.

Do it, Decker. Right now. Fill the A-gap. Make the tackle. Now.

Decker opened his eyes. In a firm, confident voice

he said, "The FBI believes that this case is far more complicated than it first appeared. We also believe that Mr. Mars is innocent."

"Based on what?" interrupted Jenkins testily.

"Based on discoveries made in our ongoing investigation. We believe that this case may involve forces that operate across state lines, bringing it solidly into the purview of the Bureau."

Judge Matthews said, "And is the court to be provided the results of your discoveries, Agent Decker?"

"My superior, Special Agent Ross Bogart, heads up a special task force, Your Honor. He has authorized me to have the court contact him directly, and he will provide full particulars."

Jamison and Davenport shared a surprised glance.

"The court, but not the prosecutors for the state of Texas?" barked Jenkins.

"Is there a valid reason why the information cannot be conveyed in open court?" asked Judge Matthews.

"Agent Bogart will explain everything, Your Honor. It is truly a sensitive matter, and we believe public disclosure at this time may have an adverse impact on our investigation and allow the guilty parties to escape arrest and prosecution for their crimes."

"Nothing you've said explains why Mr. Mars cannot remain in custody until the issue is resolved," pointed out Jenkins.

Before the judge could speak, Decker said, "I'm sorry, I would have thought that the fact that Mr. Mars was nearly beaten to death by prison guards after two prisoners, paid off by another guard, tried to kill Mr. Mars, would have made that point rather obvious. Along with the fact that Mr. Mars has filed a multi-million-dollar lawsuit against the Texas correctional system for this heinous and illegal act. I would imagine that Mr. Mars is very much persona non grata for those folks, including any friends or coconspirators of the guard in question, who remain unknown and still on duty. Thus, returning him to prison here should in no way be considered to be a safe haven for Mr. Mars. On the contrary, it would be most likely signing his death warrant."

Judge Matthews shot a glare at Jenkins. "Is this true?"

Jenkins turned a bit paler under the judge's wrathful look. "Your Honor, while that unfortunate act *did* occur, we believe that Mr. Mars is in no further danger while in the state's custody."

"To err on the side of caution," said Decker, "we should avoid *any* possibility that Mr. Jenkins is incorrect. If Mr. Mars is found to be innocent, but ends up dead in his prison cell, I fail to see how that benefits him. Perhaps the state of Texas has a different opinion?"

The judge snorted at that comment.

Jenkins simply glared at Decker, who continued. "The FBI, with the state's approval, took custody of

Mr. Mars after he was beaten, and we stand ready to do so again."

Judge Matthews refocused on Decker. "And this has been approved by the FBI?"

"Again, Agent Bogart will provide all necessary assurances and details."

The judge turned back to Jenkins. "I am hereby ordering that the defendant be released into the custody of Agent Decker and the FBI until such time as future facts dictate another course of action."

"But, Your Honor," began Jenkins in a reproachful tone.

"That's my ruling, so don't go there, Frank! I can't say I like the way y'all have handled this, so be happy I didn't order the defendant released on his own recognizance. This court is adjourned." Judge Matthews smacked his gavel, rose, and disappeared into his chambers.

Jenkins looked over at Decker as the court officers unshackled Mars. "I hope you know what the hell you're doing," he said.

So do I, thought Decker. *So do I.*

39

Mars sat in the passenger seat and rubbed his wrists where the cuffs had cut into his skin.

"Thanks," he said to Decker, who was driving.

Oliver, Davenport, and Jamison were in the backseat.

Decker had said nothing as they had left the courtroom, shoving past the journalists who were sticking mikes and notepads in their faces.

Jamison and Davenport had peppered him with questions as they walked across the parking lot to their car, but he had remained silent. Now Jamison reached over the front seat and tapped him hard on the shoulder.

"Are you going to explain what just happened or am I going to have to get physical with you?"

Decker shot her a glance in the rearview and noted her irresolute demeanor. "I asked Agent Bogart for a favor and he provided it."

"So this is all on the up-and-up?" asked Jamison, drawing a startled look from Oliver.

She said, "Decker, please don't tell me I was an

unwitting participant in perpetrating a fraud on the court?"

"There was no fraud. Melvin is in our custody. And everything I said to the judge was true."

"He thought you were an agent," pointed out Davenport.

"He said that. I never did," countered Decker.

"But you didn't correct him either," she retorted.

"That wasn't my job, but it doesn't matter either. Bogart *is* an agent and he will back me up on this." He eyed Oliver. "And you did file the lawsuit?"

"Yes."

"Then we're good."

Mars said, "Well, *I'm* not good if they come and arrest my ass again. You heard what the judge said. If future facts come out then he could let them do that. Another course of action, he called it. And that Jenkins dude was pissed. I bet he's right now working on something to get my butt back in a Texas prison."

"I'd be stunned if he wasn't," conceded Decker. "We just have to make sure that that doesn't happen."

"How?" asked Davenport.

Jamison answered. "By solving the case."

Decker's phone buzzed and he answered it, cupping the phone against his ear with his shoulder as he drove toward a sky that was growing dark and promised still more rain. The inclemency of the weather didn't faze Decker. He had other things on his mind as he listened to the other person on the call. He thanked the person and put his phone away.

"That was the Alabama police. They ran down the rental car, the beige Toyota Avalon with the Georgia plate with the partial number Patricia Bray gave us. It was leased by a man named Arthur Crandall." He looked at Mars. "Ring any bells?"

"No."

"Didn't think so, since it was a false name. The credit card he used was a forgery. The license was probably a phony too."

"Are we sure it's the same guy?" asked Jamison.

"They're trying to verify that right now."

"What the hell is going on?" wondered Mars.

"Loose ends," said Decker. "Just loose ends."

"So the guy we think killed Regina Montgomery after paying them off to have her husband confess is this Arthur Crandall?" said Mars.

"That's not his real name."

"Yeah, that I get. But by doing what he's doing he helped me get out of prison."

"And as we discussed, that could be because he thinks you have something that can hurt him or whoever he's working for."

"But that makes no sense, Decker. Even if I knew something, which I don't, why not just let them execute me and I take it to my grave?"

Davenport said, "Maybe they need to really get

whatever it is they think you have. So they spring you from prison hoping you'll go and get it."

"But then why frame me for murder in the first place?" asked Mars.

"Maybe back then they thought that was the best course," suggested Jamison. "Kill your parents, frame you, and you get sent away for life. That's really the only explanation that works."

"No it's not," disagreed Decker.

"What, then?" asked Jamison curiously.

"We're assuming that whoever framed Melvin and murdered his parents is also the one looking now for what was in the safe deposit box. The fact is, we could be dealing with two different sets of people, with dissimilar goals."

"Jesus," said Davenport. "Wasn't it complicated enough?"

"Apparently not," acknowledged Decker.

He glanced at Mars. "Who was your mother's doctor?"

"Her doctor? Why?"

"Well, someone had to diagnose her with terminal brain cancer."

"I don't remember."

"Give it some thought."

"Do you think the identity of her doctor is really important?" asked Davenport.

"Right now, in this case, there is nothing that *isn't* important."

40

Decker slept soundly until five in the morning. The rain was beating down outside and he rose and stumbled over to the window to look out. Rain, wind, the occasional flare of lightning, and the tagalong boom of thunder. The weather was as miserable as this case, he thought.

He looked down at his feet, surprised for a moment that he could see them. His belly had shrunk sufficiently for that to be the case. It had been a long time . . .

He sat on the edge of his bed and stretched out his legs. His hamstrings were tight, his lower back tighter still.

Physically, he was what he was.

But mentally?

He closed his eyes and let his perfect memory wander back to the point nearly twenty months ago when he had lost everything he had.

He knew the color would come, piggybacking on this memory like a parasite attached to a big fish.

Blue.

The color blue poured across the memory of finding his family slaughtered. It was like someone had callously thrown a bucket of paint on top of the most treasured possession he had. Or a giant pen had gone wacky and was releasing its ink everywhere.

Had being the operative word.

Molly and Cassie were gone. Nothing he could do to bring them back. He would remember them in perfect detail until he took his last breath. But that was both a blessing and a curse.

He showered, changed into clean clothes, and opened the door to his motel room, which led directly to the outside. He was on the first floor, which had a covered porch running the length of the building. They were all on the first floor, with him at one end, Mars and Jamison in the middle, and Davenport at the far end.

The rain continued to bucket down as Decker leaned against a support post and gazed out into the darkness.

Decker didn't like deceit. He didn't like lies. He didn't like bad acts with no consequences. People did wrong, that was a given. And that was their choice. And they needed to suffer the repercussions of those bad choices.

He checked his watch. It was a little after six. The sun was still making its way from the other side of the world. And even when it did rise it would be hidden behind the thick curtain of storm clouds. There was a coffee shop attached to the motel. He could reach it under cover of the roof overhang.

It took him two minutes. Three people were already there having breakfast. A tired-looking waitress was pouring out coffee. She swept her arm around the small dining room when she saw Decker come in.

He apparently had his pick of unoccupied tables. He chose one as far away from the other people as possible. He sat, picked up a menu, and ran his gaze down it. Heart attack city, all of it. Cholesterol mania with every bite.

When she came around he ordered coffee, a glass of orange juice, and toast.

"Do you have egg whites?" he asked.

When she stared back at him blankly he said, "Maybe a fruit cup?"

She eyed his ample form and a sympathetic smile appeared on her face. "Sure, hon, coming up. All healthy stuff, I'll see to it."

She walked off.

A minute later she brought the coffee. He took a sip. Nice and hot, and it warmed his bones as the rain lashed the windows outside.

He settled back in his chair, half closed his eyes, and focused.

Point One: Roy and Lucinda Mars had a secret life dating from before their son was born. They had changed their names and moved here to get away from whatever that life had been. The scar on Roy Mars's face might be from plastic surgery.

Point Two: They were seen on a national sports program some time before they were killed.

Point Three: Roy Mars had emptied a safe deposit box right before his death. The contents of that box and its current whereabouts were unknown.

Point Four: Lucinda Mars had terminal cancer.

Point Five: They were murdered and their son framed for the crimes.

Point Six: Mars had been scheduled to be executed but was saved by the confession of Charles Montgomery.

Point Seven: Mars was released from prison.

Point Eight: Charles Montgomery was executed.

Point Nine: Charles Montgomery had almost certainly lied.

Point Ten: Regina Montgomery had received the monetary fruits of her husband's confession.

Point Eleven: Regina Montgomery had been murdered, possibly by the man in the Toyota Avalon.

Point Twelve: Someone wanted what was in that safe deposit box.

Point Thirteen: And that someone might be different from whoever had framed Mars.

Now the questions poured forth, principally among them: Who had paid off Montgomery? If Avalon man, why? To set Mars free so he could be followed and they could use him to locate the safe deposit box contents? If so, it was a very clumsy way of doing it. How could they know that Mars even knew about the contents, much less its whereabouts, now? And why now, twenty years later? Why not back then? For that matter, why not torture the Marses before you killed them and make them tell you where the contents were?

Maybe they were tortured. But took the secret to their graves.

Decker could think of no plausible theory that would reconcile all of those questions.

And this was clearly frustrating the hell out of him.

His memory was perfect, but that did not mean that the answers were always there. If someone told him a lie, he would remember it clearly, not knowing that it was false until he could compare it with other facts that would, hopefully, demonstrate the inconsistency of the statement.

But it wasn't inconsistency that was his chief enemy here. It was simply not knowing enough.

"You look like your brain is gonna catch fire."

He looked up to see Mars standing there.

Decker motioned for him to sit. Mars did.

"Did you give the things I asked about some thought?" Decker asked.

Mars nodded. "Thought about 'em all night. And I got nothing to give you, Decker. I feel . . . I feel like an idiot. I didn't even know my own parents. My whole life was wrapped around playing football." He clearly wanted to say something else, but apparently couldn't find the words with which to do so. He ended up by just shaking his head.

"Don't give up on yourself," advised Decker. "Something still might occur to you." He glanced at the waitress, who was heading their way with his food.

"You want some coffee or food?" she asked Mars.

"Just coffee."

The waitress put the toast and a bowl of fruit down in front of Decker. "There you go, hon. Bet you'll be wearing skinny jeans in no time."

Mars gave Decker a curious look but made no comment. He ordered his coffee.

After the waitress walked off, Decker took a forkful of the fruit and a bite of the toast.

"So did *you* think of anything?" Mars asked him.

"I thought of lots of things. Mostly questions to which I have no answers."

"You know, I did remember one thing."

"What's that?" asked Decker quickly.

The waitress appeared again to deposit Mars's coffee. She left and he said, "The only medical practice in town back then was over on Scotch Boulevard. If my mom talked to a doctor, it would have been there. That's where they went to the dentist too."

Decker nodded. "Good. We'll check that out today."

"But I still don't see how that's going to help us."

"Investigations are not exact sciences. You plug along until something starts to make sense."

"I talked to Mary. She's still pissed about what happened. This is making her even more determined to sue the crap out of Texas."

"She's a good friend to you."

"I thought I was done for when my last lawyer resigned. Then Mary came along and took up the case. We had lots of long talks. She wasn't just my lawyer. She was, like you said, a friend. And we didn't just talk about legal stuff. I learned about her family and she asked questions about mine, though it wasn't like I could tell her much. But she was still interested. Was willing to listen for as long as I wanted her to. She knew how I felt about my mom and dad. She knew I could never have killed them."

"I'm sure, Melvin."

Mars glanced around. "You know, I thought Jamison would be here with you."

"Why?"

"Her room is next to mine. I knocked on the door when I was heading over here to see if she wanted something to eat. Nobody answered."

"Did you hear her inside?"

"No, nothing. Why?"

"Where else would she be at this time of the morning?" Decker put some dollar bills down on the table and rose.

Mars did too.

"Do you think something's wrong?" he asked.

"That's what we're going to find out."

They hustled outside and down to Jamison's room. Decker knocked loudly on the door.

"Alex? Alex, are you in there?"

When Decker reached down and pulled his gun, Mars took a step back. "You want me to knock the door in?" he asked Decker.

"What are you two doing?"

They turned to see Jamison walking toward them.

"Where the hell were you?" asked a relieved Decker as he put his gun away.

"They didn't have any shampoo in the room. So I went to get some at the front desk, and that took forever because I couldn't find anybody. And then I went into the little gift shop for a bottle of water. Is everything okay?"

"It is now," said Mars. "We were just worried."

"Well, I appreciate the—"

She stopped when a woman ran up to them. She was in her sixties, dressed as a maid, and clearly out of breath. "I think there's something wrong," she said.

"What do you mean?" asked Decker.

"Please hurry." She turned and jogged back the way she had come.

They raced after her. They turned a corner and reached the other end of that wing of the U-shaped motel. The woman pointed to a door that was half open.

331

"That's Davenport's room," said Jamison.

Decker pulled his gun once more, approached the door, and slowly pushed it open.

He peered inside to find the room in a shambles.

They quickly searched it.

Davenport was gone.

And not voluntarily.

41

Bogart and Milligan are on their way down," said Decker.

He was sitting in his room with Mars and Jamison after just getting off the phone. The police had come and done an investigation in connection with Davenport's disappearance, but they had left with virtually no helpful findings. It was clear that she'd put up a fight. No one had heard anything, because that wing of the motel had been largely unoccupied at the time.

"FBI reengaging on this?" asked Jamison dully as she rubbed wearily at her eyes.

"It appears that they are taking her abduction as a personal attack on the Bureau, even if she wasn't technically working for them at the time."

Decker studied Jamison. She was pale and clearly shaken.

"Alex, do you have a gun?"

She gave him a sharp glance. "A gun? No. Why?"

"I'm going to get you one and then show you how to use it."

"Do you really think that's necessary?"

"Given this latest development, do you think it's unnecessary?"

Jamison looked away, her hands nervously clasped in front of her.

Mars said, "I don't get this. Why take Davenport? Why not me? I'm the guy they want. Davenport could know nothing about what was in that safe deposit box."

"They can't know that for sure, Melvin," pointed out Decker. "And let's face it, Davenport is an easier target than you. And the room was still wrecked, so Davenport put up a fight. Could you imagine if it had been you instead? You might have killed them."

Mars slowly nodded. "I guess you're right."

Decker suddenly looked pensive. "Actually, I might not be." He rose.

"Where are you going?" asked Jamison.

"To look at Davenport's room."

"The locals have already gone over it."

"And now it's our turn."

Decker entered the motel room and walked over to one wall, put his back against it, and surveyed the room in elongated sweeps, his head running side to side like a lighthouse beam. Jamison stood next to him. Mars hovered near the doorway, looking nervous and uncertain.

"See anything?" he asked anxiously.

"Davenport weighed about one-ten?" Decker said.

Jamison looked surprised by the question but said, "About that, I guess. She was about my height. And very lean."

"She's a runner," said Decker thoughtfully. "So she would be lean."

His gaze ran over the overturned table, upended chair, smashed lamp, the drywall by the bed, and finally the unmade bed.

Jamison said, "She was asleep when it happened. The intruder woke her."

Mars said, "Well, she might have gotten up and gone for a run and not made her bed before she was kidnapped."

"You're both wrong," said Decker.

"How can we *both* be wrong?" said Jamison.

Decker pointed to the floor of the open closet. "Her running shoes are there. And so are her workout clothes. It's bucketing outside and has been all night. The shoes and clothes aren't even damp or mud-splattered. She wouldn't have run in this weather anyway. There aren't any paths and the road outside gets busy with traffic. Not very safe."

"Okay, so she was attacked while she was sleeping," said Jamison. "Meaning I was right."

Decker pointed to the door and then the window. "No forced entry on either. The cops confirmed that. A key was needed to get in. The motel office has been checked. These are old-fashioned locks with real keys. There are no duplicates."

Jamison was not giving up easily. "Well, maybe they got one from the cleaning staff. They must have masters."

Decker moved forward near the bed and said, "Look at the table that was knocked over."

They stood next to him and looked down at it.

Mars said, "It was the one next to the bed. It had a lamp on it. The lamp got knocked over and smashed when the table went down. So what?"

"Look at the table leg."

They did so.

Decker said, "There's a piece of the lamp embedded in it."

Jamison examined the leg and nodded in understanding even as Mars still looked confused. Jamison said, "If the table was knocked over in a struggle the lamp would have flown off and landed well past the table. There is no way the lamp would have hit the table so hard a piece would embed itself in the wood."

"Exactly," said Decker. He pointed to the drywall. "And look there."

They stared at where he was pointing.

Mars said, "There's nothing to see."

Jamison shook her head. "No, Amos is right. There are no marks on the drywall. Yet the table is set next to the bed. If there was a struggle the table would almost certainly have been knocked back against the wall and a mark would have been left." She looked at Decker. "This was all staged. The table was turned upside down and the lamp smashed over it. Someone knocked on her door and she answered it. She was taken and the room later wrecked to make it look like a fight had happened."

"That's how I see it," agreed Decker.

"But why would they do that?" asked Mars.

"Because they didn't want us to know that Davenport *knew* the person who took her," replied Decker.

Jamison snapped her fingers and said, "At that hour she wouldn't have let anyone in her room she didn't know. That's why there was no forced entry."

"Right," said Decker, his gaze still swiveling around the room.

Mars said admiringly, "Damn, you figure all that out 'cause you got a perfect memory?"

"No, I figured all that out because I was a cop for twenty years and know what to look for."

Mars looked at Jamison. "And you're good at this too."

She smiled. "Amos has rubbed off on me."

"No," said Decker. "You see things, Alex. Sometimes you see more than me."

"But Decker, Davenport didn't know anybody in this town," noted Jamison.

"Well, obviously she did. And it was someone she trusted."

Mars said, "So it comes back to why take her?"

Jamison leaned back against the wall and said, "Do

you think they'll try to find out what we've learned by . . ."

Decker stared at her. "Beating her? Torturing her?"

Jamison paled but nodded.

"I think it far more likely that they'll use her as a bargaining chip," observed Decker.

Mars looked puzzled. "Bargaining chip? For what?"

"For you."

42

I should never have left."

Bogart stared across the table at Decker.

The men were sitting inside an office of a small building the FBI had turned into a makeshift command center.

Bogart and Milligan had flown in with a half dozen other agents. They were in the other part of the building working away on trying to locate Lisa Davenport.

"You had no choice," said Decker.

"Everybody has a choice," retorted Bogart, who was looking distraught. His tie was unknotted, his shirt wrinkled, and his hair mussed.

"*Realistic* choice, then," countered Decker. "And even if you had been here, the same thing probably would have happened."

"We can't find anyone here that she would have known well enough to let into her room at that hour. Any ideas on that?"

"It's possible that she knew someone that we didn't know she knew."

"If they are using her as leverage we can expect a communication."

Decker nodded. "The problem will be the exchange. That's always the problem with scenarios like this."

Bogart said, "You don't think we'll get her back alive?"

"She saw who took her. She *knew* the person."

Bogart sighed and slumped back in his chair. "And she can't be allowed to tell us who that is."

"The odds are certainly against it."

"Who do you think is behind this?"

"There's more than one."

"Meaning what exactly?"

"Motivations and actions tell us a lot. We have irreconcilable motivations and actions. That means there's more than one player out there."

"Something changed," said Bogart. "Mars was in prison for twenty years and nothing happened."

"What changed was he was going to be executed. He had never gotten that close to the death chamber before. That was the catalyst for them to act."

"To pay off Montgomery?"

"Yes."

"So which 'faction' did that?"

"I don't know. It could be one or the other at this point."

"They want what they think he knows. The stuff in the safe deposit box that his father took."

"That's the golden ring. His father took it and put it somewhere. They may think the son knows."

Bogart said, "What are the irreconcilable motives and actions?"

"The party that wants the information could have let Melvin be executed. The information hadn't surfaced for twenty years. They could assume it was lost. By getting Melvin out of jail they gave him an opportunity to go get it, assuming he knows where it is. Then they hope to be there when he does and grab it?" Decker shook his head. "That's a huge risk. So huge that they wouldn't have done it. They would have let sleeping dogs lie."

"But then who got Mars out of prison?"

"The other party."

"But why?"

"That's the irreconcilable issue, Ross. And I haven't gotten it figured out yet."

Bogart rubbed a hand through his hair. "We *will* figure it out, Amos. We have to. Failure is not an option."

Decker looked him over. "I appreciate you covering for me with the court."

"The court called. I told them what they needed to hear."

"Are things square back in D.C.?"

"I'm back on the case, so I guess that means the higher-ups saw the error of their ways."

"And the divorce?"

"Not much of a silver lining there. But I'm getting to the point where I don't care. I've got my work. That's enough."

"You sure about that?"

"No, but it's my story and I'm sticking to it." He looked over some files on his desk. "We don't have very many leads."

"No, we don't. I'm getting Jamison a gun and showing her how to use it."

Bogart looked at him in surprise. "You think they might try another kidnapping?"

"No, but I've been wrong before."

"Join the club."

Decker rose.

"Where are you going?"

"To get Jamison her weapon, and then I'm going to the doctor's."

"Are you sick?"

"No. Keep an eye on Melvin."

He walked out, leaving Bogart to stare after him.

Decker selected a compact nine-millimeter for Jamison. Texas had a concealed handgun permit requirement, but when Jamison showed the store owner her FBI credentials and Bogart emailed him an official letter from the Bureau detailing her membership in an FBI task force along with the authority to carry such a weapon, the owner skipped those steps and handed the gun over.

When Jamison used her personal card to pay for it the man said, "Damn federal government so hard up for cash you got to buy your own guns now?"

"No, just the bullets," shot back Jamison.

The shop had a gun range in the back. Decker showed her how to properly load, handle, and aim the weapon. Then he had her fire about a hundred rounds until he was satisfied.

She holstered the weapon and they left together.

"It feels funny carrying a gun," she said.

"It's better than *not* carrying a gun when you need it."

They got back into their rental and drove off.

"Where to?"

"The doctor's."

"Is this about the Marses?"

"Yes."

"Decker, we should be back there helping the others to find Davenport."

"What we can do is solve this thing. That might be the best way to find out who took her and where she is."

They pulled into the parking lot of a small brick office building. The office directory inside the lobby showed that all of the tenants were medical practices. It took nearly an hour and many exploratory questions until they arrived at the right one.

The nurse, in her late sixties, and nearly as wide as

she was tall, nodded. "Yes, the Marses were patients here."

Decker said, "Can you tell us about them?"

"It was twenty years ago."

"Anything?" said Decker.

The woman sat down behind her metal desk. "Well, they sort of stood out because they were the first mixed-race couple I'd ever seen. First one in town in all probability. Back then lot of folks didn't care for that, I can tell you."

"Did a doctor from this practice deliver Melvin Mars?"

"Yes. Doc Turner. He's been dead, oh, about seven years now."

"Was he delivered at the local hospital?" asked Jamison.

"That's right. I actually assisted. We're a small town. Doc Turner was a general practitioner, but here you do what needs doing. There aren't enough people living here to justify a practice devoted only to ob-gyn." She looked wistful. "I remember that Lucinda Mars was probably the most beautiful woman I'd ever seen. Her face was flawless. Her body, well, let me tell you, I wish I'd had one like hers. Her legs were longer than my whole body."

"Did they start coming here when she got pregnant?" asked Decker.

"Oh, she was about five months along when they moved to town. I remember because I'd just come here about a year before and she was asking me where I shopped and what kind of jobs were available."

Decker glanced at Jamison and then back at the nurse. "So she was already pregnant when they came here?"

"She was already showing. She didn't gain much weight. Me, I put on forty with the first, thirty with the second, another thirty with the third, and it's been with me ever since. She delivered Melvin and within a week she looked like she'd never been pregnant. Some people are just lucky that way. And Melvin, let me tell you, that boy was big. Nearly ten pounds. You could tell he was going to be a big man. His daddy was really big. About your height and about two-fifty, and none of it was fat. Wouldn't want to get that man on the wrong side of you."

"Did he have a temper?" asked Jamison.

The woman pursed her lips. "He just never looked, well, happy. I mean, he had this gorgeous wife. And his son grew up to be the best damn football player this town and maybe Texas has ever seen. Now, I know what happened later, but he just always had a scowl on his face."

"Did you think there were problems in the marriage?" asked Jamison.

"Honey, every marriage has problems, and some are better at hiding it than others. But I'd have to say that I have *never* seen a man who loved his wife more than Roy did Lucinda. He was so gentle with her.

When she was pregnant he wouldn't let her lift a finger. I'd see them from time to time around town. And he would open the car door for her. Hold her hand while they were walking. The only time he looked happy, in fact, was when he was looking at her." She sighed. "If my hubby looked at me like that just once in my life, I'd keel over from a stroke at the shock."

"When was her brain cancer diagnosed?" Decker asked.

The nurse sat up in her chair. "Excuse me?"

"Her brain cancer. When was it diagnosed?"

"She didn't have brain cancer."

"Her autopsy showed a malignant glioblastoma. Stage Four. Inoperable. She maybe had a few months left to live before she was killed."

The woman stared at Decker like he was speaking another language. "Well, it wasn't diagnosed here, I can tell you that," she finally said. "Glioblastoma. Are you sure?"

"It's what the coroner found. I assume he wouldn't be mistaken about something like that."

"No, I guess not," she said absently. "I never would have thought. She looked so healthy. And the papers never said she had cancer."

"Probably because the police knew that the cancer certainly didn't end up causing her death. So they had no reason to divulge that personal medical information. And I don't think a murder-suicide pact was ever contemplated. You can't set yourself on fire after you've killed yourself."

They left her sitting in her chair still pondering this news. They were walking down the hall when Decker saw the sign stenciled on one of the doors along the hallway. He veered toward it, forcing Jamison to do a quick about-face and follow him.

He opened the door and walked up to the reception desk. Jamison came to stand next to him.

Decker held up his FBI card and said, "We need to talk to someone about a patient of the practice twenty years ago."

The woman stared openmouthed at Decker and picked up the phone. "Just give me a sec."

A minute later a man in his early thirties appeared dressed in a white coat. He had a stainless steel dental tool clutched in one of his gloved hands.

"I'm just finishing up with a patient. You can wait in my office."

The receptionist led them down the hall and showed them into an office. They sat facing the desk.

Jamison shivered.

Decker looked at her. "Problem?"

"I hate the dentist. I had more cavities than teeth growing up."

"Relax, we're here for information, not fillings."

"Yeah? I bet he'll take one look at my teeth and start singing, 'Drill, baby, drill.'"

A couple of minutes later the dentist walked in. He

had taken off his white coat and his hands were no longer gloved. He had on a white dress shirt and a striped tie. Jamison shifted uneasily in her chair as he passed by her and sat down.

"I'm Lewis Fisher. What can I do for the FBI?"

Decker explained the background of why they were here. He added, "I assume from your age that you were not the dentist to the Marses."

"No. I was still a kid. This was my grandfather's practice back then. I took it over when he retired."

"Would you still have the records of the Marses here?"

"No. Not after twenty years. And of course, because of the fact that they're dead. I heard Melvin was released from prison," he added.

"He was. Did you know him?"

"No, but we went to the same high school, at different times, of course. Everybody knew who Melvin was. I was stunned when he was arrested for the murders."

"And his parents' identities were established through their dental records here?"

"I guess that's right, yes. I remember there wasn't enough left of their . . . Well, you know."

"Right. Is your grandfather still alive?"

"He is. And he still lives in the area."

"Any chance we can talk to him?"

"You can try."

Decker cocked his head. "Meaning?"

"Meaning he has dementia and resides at an assisted living center."

"Does he have lucid moments?"

"Occasionally. He used to have more. But I'm afraid he's slipping away at an alarming rate. It's very sad when your own grandfather can't recognize you."

"I'm sure it is," said Jamison sympathetically.

Decker said, "Can we give it a shot?"

"With what goal in mind?" asked Fisher.

"Information," said Decker. "You never know where a new piece might help the investigation."

"And what exactly are you investigating?"

"That's not something we can comment on publicly," said Decker, his tone becoming very official.

"Oh, right, of course." Fisher quickly wrote the address down on a slip of paper and slid it across. "I'll call and tell them you're going to come by."

Decker looked at the name. "Lewis Fisher Sr."

"I'm Lewis Fisher the third. My father is the junior."

Decker and Jamison rose. He said, "Thanks, I appreciate it."

Fisher turned to Jamison, who quickly closed her mouth so her teeth weren't visible.

"You should smile more often," said Fisher. "You have very nice teeth."

Outside the office Jamison said, "Let's hope Fisher Sr. can give us a lead. We could sure use one."

"It's why we do the drill, Alex."

"Please don't use that word so close to a dentist's office."

43

Lewis Fisher Sr. had obviously done well for himself, because the facility he was in was an upscale private one. The building was designed to look like an antebellum plantation, with tall, broad columns and a huge porch that was filled with rocking chairs and residents doing the rocking. The interior was decorated with bright wallpaper, wooden chair railing, six-inch crown molding, and thick plush carpets. There was even a game room with a pool table and an old-fashioned soda fountain.

The bulletin board in the lobby was filled with activity sheets. Senior citizens were walking or rolling to their next appointments. The place was full of energy and enthusiasm as Decker and Jamison strolled down the wide corridor accompanied by one of the staff. She was dressed in crisp blue scrubs. Her name tag read *Deb.* She waved and greeted residents as they walked along.

"Nice place," said Jamison. "Everyone seems really happy."

"A lot better than anything the state offers," said

Deb. "But you have to pay for it, and it's not cheap. This is definitely for the upper echelon. We get folks from like a two-hundred-mile area because the facility is so unique and this part of Texas is big and isolated." She sighed. "I could never afford to come here when I get to be their age."

They reached a set of double doors with a sign reading *Memory Unit* overhead. Deb had to use her key card to access the doors.

"Is that so no one in the unit can wander away?" noted Jamison.

"Exactly," she said as they passed through the opening. "We don't want anyone getting lost."

She led them down the hall and then turned toward a door about halfway down. She knocked.

"Dr. Fisher, you have visitors."

They heard a grunt from inside.

Deb turned to them. "He has good and bad days. I'm not sure which one this will be. He gets very frustrated, like many of our memory unit patients." She eyed the FBI credential that rode on Decker's hip. "Is Dr. Fisher in some sort of trouble?"

"He's in no trouble at all," said Decker.

"Well, that's a relief. You know, when he first came here his memory was razor sharp. Probably better than yours."

"I seriously doubt that," said Decker as he pushed open the door and went inside.

A startled Deb looked at Jamison, who gazed at her

awkwardly. "It's a long story," she said. "We'll let you know when we're done. Thanks." She joined Decker inside the room and closed the door.

Fisher was sitting up in the chair next to his bed. He had on a hospital gown and his feet were resting in white slippers. He looked to be in his late eighties, bent and frail. When he looked up at them, Decker could see a lot of the grandson in the man.

"Dr. Fisher?" he said.

"Who the hell are you?" Fisher barked.

"This might be one of the bad days," whispered Jamison.

Decker grew closer. "I'm a friend of your grandson. So is she."

Fisher turned his gaze to Jamison. "She's not my grandson."

"No, she's a *friend* of your grandson's."

Fisher looked down at his lap.

Jamison knelt next to him. "This is a very nice room."

Fisher looked up at her. "Do I know you?"

"I'm Alex and this is Amos."

"Amos and Andy. Like the show?" said Fisher.

"No, *Alex* and Amos. He's Amos. I'm Alex."

He glanced at Decker. "You're very large."

"Yes, I am." He pulled up another chair and sat down. "Your grandson told us you were a dentist for a long time. You had a lot of patients."

Fisher looked puzzled. "Dentist? My grandson, my grandson . . ."

"Lewis," said Jamison helpfully.

"My name is Lewis," he barked. Then he added in a quieter, desperate tone, "Isn't it?"

"Yes, and he was named after you."

Fisher rapped his head with his knuckles. "This just all . . ."

"I know," said Jamison soothingly. "I'm sure it's frustrating."

Decker said, "You were a dentist, Dr. Fisher. You had lots of patients. Do you remember the Mars family? Roy and Lucinda? And Melvin?"

"Mars? Like the planet? Are you talking about the planet Mars? It's . . . it's the red planet." He smiled and looked pleased.

"No, not the planet. A family named Mars. They were killed. And the records in your office were used to confirm their identity."

"Killed? The planet was killed? Are you . . . crazy?"

Jamison put a hand on Decker's arm. "Let me try."

She turned to Fisher and said very quietly, "They were patients of yours a long time ago. Twenty years. They were killed. Their bodies were burned, so they had to use their dental records to identify them. Records from your office."

She looked at Fisher hopefully, but all she got back was a blank stare.

A minute went by and no one broke the silence.

Decker was about to say something when Jamison held up a hand.

"Dr. Fisher, I have a tooth problem. Do you remember me? I'm Lucinda Mars. This is my husband, Roy Mars. He has a tooth problem too. Can you help us? We're your patients. You have our records."

They waited a long moment. At first it didn't seem Fisher would answer her.

Fisher said, "Maxillary second premolar."

"What was that, Dr. Fisher?" said Jamison.

"Maxillary second premolar," he repeated, shaking his head.

Jamison said, "What about it?"

"Not right."

"What wasn't right?"

"The second premolar. Just not right."

Jamison knelt down next to him. "Whose? Roy's or Lucinda's?"

"Just not right. Should've said. Not right." He looked up at Decker. "Who the hell are you?"

"A very grateful man." Decker rose and said to Jamison, "Can you stay here and see if you can get anything more out of him? I'll come back and get you."

"Where are you going?"

"To find a maxillary second premolar."

44

A premolar?" said Bogart. "Seriously?"

He and Decker were standing in the musty warehouse where old police records were kept.

"That's what he said. The maxillary second premolar. Something was not right with it."

They stared at the shelves full of haphazardly stacked boxes.

Bogart said, "The sergeant I talked to said the records were a little—"

"Unorganized?" finished Decker. "I'd say he was seeing the glass half full." He took off his coat and rolled up his sleeves. "Well, let's get to it."

The files were indeed in a shambles. The years were sometimes mixed up and the boxes themselves were not well inventoried. On more than one occasion the filing papers inside were just blank.

Six hours went past without any success.

Decker's phone rang. It was Jamison and she was not happy.

"I took a cab back to the motel. When you said stay

here and see if I could get something more out of him, I didn't think you meant *forever*."

"I'm sorry, Alex, I got distracted."

"Gee, what a shock!"

"Did he say anything else that might be helpful?"

"Only that something wasn't right. He just kept repeating that."

"No clue on whether we're talking about Roy or Lucinda?"

"No. Then he just fell asleep. I've been calling you for the last three hours, by the way."

"I took my coat off. I heard this call because I had picked up my coat when you phoned."

"Where are you?"

He told her. "But we're not having much success."

"Until now," called out Bogart. He had lifted a box off the shelf and opened it.

"I gotta go," said Decker, and he clicked off.

They pulled all the items out of the box and laid them on a table. Decker found it first. He pulled up the X-ray sheets for the two Marses that were labeled with their respective names.

"I Googled 'premolar' before I got here," Decker said. He pulled out his phone and brought up an image of a mouth full of teeth. "These are second premolars." He pointed at spots on the X-rays. "They help with mastication or chewing. The one on the right is the four and the left is the thirteen, in dentist numbering vernacular."

"All fascinating," said Bogart sarcastically. "But what was *wrong,* according to Fisher? The dental records for the Marses from Fisher's office matched the dental records taken from the bodies at the crime scene."

"Alex couldn't find out. The guy has dementia. But he just blurted out 'maxillary second premolar'—" He stopped, pulled out his phone, and punched in a number.

"Alex, did Fisher mention any numbers?"

"Numbers?"

"Yeah."

"No."

"Okay," said Decker, obviously disappointed.

"But it was weird, he held up four fingers a couple of times."

"Four, you're sure?"

"Yes. And he kept looking at them like they meant something."

"Thanks."

"De —"

Decker clicked off and turned to Bogart.

"Okay, it was the right premolar."

They studied the X-rays.

"I don't see anything on Lucinda's X-ray," said Bogart. "But Roy's number four has a filling."

Decker looked at it. "You're right."

"So was Fisher saying that Roy Mars *didn't* have a filling in number four? That's why something was wrong? But if so, why wouldn't he have pointed that out back then?"

Decker picked up his phone again, called Fisher's office, and a minute later was talking to the dentist.

"Your grandfather was very helpful," he said. "But I have a question for you."

"Okay, shoot," said Fisher.

"Tell me the procedure for when the police want to get copies of your records."

"They send in a court order and we answer it."

"How so? Do you personally pull the records?"

"Not always. But if not me then someone on my staff does."

"Who checks for accuracy?"

"Well, all of our files are carefully organized, cross-checked, and labeled seven ways from Sunday. We also have electronic copies of everything. Nature of a medical practice these days. No room for error."

"But twenty years ago?"

"Well, it was different. My grandfather still kept excellent records. But they were stored manually and labeled with the patient's information. Name, address, Social Security number, and individual patient file number."

"Do you have anyone on your staff who worked with your grandfather twenty years ago?"

"Yes, Melissa Dowd."

"Can I speak to her?"

"Where is all this going?"

"Please, time is of the essence."

"Hold on while I get her."

A minute later a woman answered the phone. "This is Melissa."

"Melissa, Amos Decker with the FBI. I was wondering about your filing system twenty years ago."

"Yes, Dr. Fisher told me. Well, lots of practices had transitioned to some sort of computer system by then, but Fisher Sr. was old school, so our operation was still manual. We used a typewriter. Labels were made up for all patient files. It was all very organized. We never made any mistakes with recordkeeping."

"Do you remember getting the court order to turn over the Marses' records?"

"I didn't personally pull those files, but I do remember the request. We'd never had such a request before, for a murder anyway."

"Did someone have to authenticate the records during the trial?"

"Yes. I was the one who did that, because I was the one who really maintained the records."

"So Dr. Fisher wasn't involved in that?"

"No, he was very busy and couldn't take time off to come to the trial. It was the only time I was called on to do that. It was kind of exciting."

"Did Dr. Fisher ever mention to you that there might be something wrong with the records?"

"No, not that I recall. *Was* there something wrong?" she asked anxiously.

Decker ignored this question and said, "Do you remember who cleaned your office building back then?"

"Cleaned our office building?"

"Yes."

"Um, well, it's the same firm that does it now. Quality Commercial Cleaners. They do all the offices here."

"And so they had keys to your office?"

"Well, yes, that's normal practice, but we've never had any problems."

"Thanks."

Decker clicked off and looked at Bogart.

The FBI agent was studying him. "Is this going where I think it's going?"

"I don't think Roy Mars died in the bedroom that night. I think a nurse or technician pulled those records and sent them to the police and then Dowd authenticated them at trial. But she would just be looking at the names and other file criteria in order to do that. Maybe sometime later, maybe a lot later, Fisher Sr. looked at the records and saw a filling in the number four premolar where he hadn't put one."

"Well, we can't assume it wasn't the other way around. It might be he was referring to Lucinda's records. She didn't have a filling, but maybe Fisher had put one in there."

"Agreed. And why he didn't come forward then I don't know. Maybe he was starting to feel the effects of the dementia by then." He sighed and added, "Well, this opens up a lot of questions."

Bogart nodded. "Well, the big one for me is, if it wasn't Roy's or Lucinda's body, whose was it?"

45

How are you going to break this news to Melvin?" asked Bogart. They were driving back to the motel from the warehouse.

"It's not a fact, it's a theory. I have no proof."

"But it's a pretty good theory based on some facts," replied Bogart.

"If we assume it was Roy Mars that faked his death, that would explain the shotgun to the face. And the bodies being burned. Dental records would be the first way to ID the bodies. The teeth were relatively intact."

"But he would have had to get into the dentist's office and swap out the records with those of the body that was discovered."

"Lucinda worked for a cleaning company in the area. I'm betting it was Quality Commercial Cleaners. That would have given her and Roy access to the dentist's office after hours."

"Wait a minute, do you think the other body was Lucinda's?"

"I don't know. Maybe not. If Roy is alive and he

killed the two people that were found, I have a hard time believing he would have shotgunned his wife in the face and then set her on fire."

"And set up his son for the crime? Because that's a big part of this too."

"And maybe the most inexplicable."

"But I keep coming back to the two people. It's a small town. How could two people just disappear and no one know?"

Decker said, "They could have been drifters, not from here. But—" He stopped and closed his eyes. The frames in his head whirred back and forth as he searched for the precise statements he'd been given by the police and Melissa Dowd.

There were two of them.

Burglary, missing person, drunks getting in fights, was the first.

We'd never had such a request before, for a murder anyway, was the second.

He took out his phone and punched in a number. A minute later he had Melissa Dowd on the line again. She sounded a little put out at being called away from her work again, but Decker brushed right past the annoyed tone in her voice. He had put the phone on speaker so that Bogart could hear.

Decker said, "When we last spoke you said that you'd never had a court order for dental records for a murder investigation before."

"That's right."

"But the way you said it implied that you *had* received other court orders."

"Well, just the one time. It was right before the one for the Marses' murder, actually, now that I think about it. Sort of odd."

"Was it for a missing person?"

"That's right, how did you know that?"

"Educated guess. Can you tell us about it?"

"Well, it was one of our patients, and the police thought they had found his body in the woods, but it had been disfigured by some wild animals. They had learned that we were the man's dentist and thus asked for the records. But it wasn't a match. It wasn't him."

"And this was before the Marses' murder, you're sure?"

"Yes. Just shortly before."

"Do you remember the man's name?"

"I do, as a matter of fact. His name was Dan Reardon. To my knowledge they never found him."

"Do you have any records for him?"

"No. They would have been disposed of by now."

"Can you describe him. Race, height, weight, anything?"

"Well, he was a big man. Tall, about six-four or so. Over two hundred pounds. Dan was in his fifties back then. Strongly built."

"White, black?"

"White."

"Did he have any family?"

"No. His wife had died. And they had no children. He lived on the outskirts of town and kept to himself."

"What did he do for a living?"

"Not much. Odd jobs here and there. Always in hock for something. He'd get some money and then it would be gone. We often had to write off his charges because he just didn't have the money."

"Well, thanks, Melissa, this really helped a lot."

Decker clicked off and looked at Bogart. "Always in hock. Get some money and then it would be gone. What are the odds he visited the pawnshop where Roy worked? And then Roy found out they had the same dentist?"

"Clearly, the physical descriptions tallied, which would have been the reason Roy would have picked him. And with the bodies being burned and the faces obliterated you would just have to be close enough to sell the deception."

"So Roy kidnapped Dan to later substitute his body in the house. Then he killed Dan and either killed another woman or his wife and set the bodies on fire."

"And set up his son for the murder. He must have paid off the motel clerk and Ellen Tanner to lie about the time."

"And messed with the car so it would break down right in front of the motel. Melvin told us his dad was good at working on cars."

"But why, Decker? Why go to all that trouble to implicate your own son and send him to prison?"

"I don't know," admitted Decker.

"Could he have hated Melvin for some reason?"

"Hating your son is one thing. Doing all of this to put him in prison is something else altogether."

"Unless Roy Mars is some sort of psychopath."

"He lived here for twenty years without harming anyone," pointed out Decker. "This was an elaborate scheme and it had to have sufficient motivation."

"Which brings me back to my earlier question: How are you going to tell Melvin?"

Decker looked out the car window, where yet another storm was descending upon them. "Not a clue," he replied.

46

When they got back to the motel, Mary Oliver was in the small lobby with Jamison. Both women rose when they walked in.

"Any word on Davenport?" asked Oliver breathlessly.

Bogart shook his head. "We're doing everything we can, but so far, nothing. The locals are reporting in to me every hour. There have been no sightings."

Oliver glanced down, obviously distraught.

"Are you okay?" asked Bogart.

She balled her hands into fists. "God, this is just so frustrating. First, this man Montgomery comes forward and that gets Melvin out of prison."

"Well, you helped too," said Jamison. "You kept him alive to get to that point."

Surprisingly, Oliver shook her head in disagreement. "I wish I could claim credit for all that, but I can't. I came on relatively recently. I filed a petition to stop the execution, but the court declined to act on it. Melvin's other lawyers had washed their hands of him. I think they thought he was guilty. I read about the case and contacted Melvin. I just had a feeling, you know, that something wasn't right. And then Montgomery coming forward seemed to be a miracle. And now it turns out all of that may have been a lie."

"But you don't believe that Melvin is guilty, do you?" asked Jamison.

"No. There's something else going on here. Something far deeper. But now Davenport has been kidnapped and we may never see her again."

"Well, we do have some news," said Bogart.

He told them about the discoveries with the X-rays and the possible switching of the dental records. When he was done both women stared at him, stunned.

"I . . . I can't believe this," stammered Oliver. "Why would Roy Mars have done all that?"

"A good question," said Decker. "And one we don't have an answer for."

Oliver said, "Would it be okay if I worked with all of you on this? I know that you're the professionals, but I don't think anyone wants to get to the bottom of this more than Melvin and I do. And I'm a criminal defense lawyer, so I do know my way around investigations."

Bogart glanced at Decker and Jamison before saying, "Another pair of eyes never hurts."

"Where's Melvin?" asked Decker.

"In his room," said Oliver. "I've just come from there. Are . . . are you going to . . . ?"

"I'm going to try," said Decker, and he set off.

A minute later he knocked on the door.

"Who is it?" Mars called out.

"Decker."

Decker heard footsteps coming toward the door and it opened. He said, "You up for a walk?"

Mars gazed at him suspiciously. "Why?"

"Got something I want to talk to you about."

"Is it bad?"

"It might be. In fact, it probably will be, to you."

"Is it about Davenport?"

"No. It's a little more personal. And I just want you to hear me out, okay? And then you can, well, say what you want to."

"Shit, Decker, you definitely got my attention."

"Let's go, we might be able to beat the rain. And you might need some air."

They started walking on the shoulder along the road. Decker had his hands shoved deeply in his coat pockets.

Mars shot him anxious glances. "Come on, man, don't go quiet on me now. My belly's on fire."

Decker took a long breath and plunged into what they had discovered. To his credit, Mars said nothing until he was finished. In fact, he didn't say anything until Decker prompted, "Well?"

"What do you want me to say?"

"I don't know. Something."

Mars stopped walking and so did Decker. The two men stared pointedly at each other.

Mars said, "It's pretty clear I knew nothing, really, about my parents. So what you just told me, I guess, hell, it could be true."

"Can you think of any reason why your father would want to frame you for murder?"

"Not off the top of my damn head, no," barked Mars. "How would you answer if someone asked you that question about your old man?"

"I'd be pissed, like you are now."

"Well, there you go."

Mars started trudging along again and Decker matched his stride.

A truck zipped past them, and then another car. They moved farther off the road and were soon walking along the edge of a drainage ditch.

His gaze on the ground, Mars said, "If it wasn't my dad's body, do you think it was my mother's?"

"I have no facts to support it, but, other things being equal, I *do* think it was your mother. One missing person in a small town was enough. Two would have been a red flag to the police, when it was followed by two burned-up bodies."

"So my father just killed her? And then burned her up? How could he do that? I mean, I know he loved her. If I know nothing else about the guy I know that!"

"There might be an explanation."

"Like what?" snapped Mars.

"Like she was dying anyway. And it would not be a painless death. It might be months of agony. Maybe they thought this way was better, I don't know."

"Okay, but my mom never would've been part of framing me for a murder."

"Maybe she didn't know about that."

Mars considered this and then said in an exasperated tone, "Shit, I don't know. I'm not smart enough to figure this out."

"Maybe I'm not either."

"Hell, if you don't, who will?"

"So the murders and the burning were done to allow your father to get away. Your mother's death is explained by her cancer. She wasn't going to go with him, so that was the only way."

"To get away from his past, you mean?"

Decker nodded. "That also might be why he told you he was sorry that night."

"What?"

"When you were hypnotized by Davenport, you told us you came home one night and your dad was there. He was looking sort of scary but he told you he was sorry. That was it, no explanation. Then he left the room."

"Damn. I forgot about that."

372

"And it must be something really bad because he had to take such extraordinary steps. He killed this Dan Reardon, Melvin, and used his body as part of the deception. You need to come to grips with that."

"That my old man was a cold-blooded killer? Yeah, let me just come to grips with that. Probably only take a few seconds," he added sarcastically.

"Well, he might have been one in the past, but it looked like he reformed until something happened to throw everything out of whack. I think the sequence of events went something like this: Your mother was diagnosed with cancer. It wasn't here because the doctor's office knew nothing about it. So they went somewhere else to get that diagnosis. I don't know where."

"Okay," said Mars. "Then what?"

"They probably *were* going to tell you the bad news and deal with it like every other family does in such a situation. But then the ESPN piece aired, someone recognized your dad and/or your mother, and everything changed."

"Do you think they threatened them?"

"Maybe, or maybe they didn't wait for the threat to come. They just acted. They switched the dental records. Your father snatched Reardon. You said Ellen Tanner was a recent acquaintance. Your dad could have arranged all that. Same with the motel guy. They're paid off to lie. Then Tanner disappeared and the motel guy retired to Florida. He probably used the money in his bank account to pay them."

"So you're telling me they lied and sent me to prison for, what, less than three grand each?"

"I've run into people who'd slit your throat for a cup of coffee," Decker replied bluntly.

"Damn."

"And you said your dad was good with cars."

"Yeah, he could fix anything."

"So he could easily have sabotaged your car so it would stall by the motel. He probably drugged your mother and Reardon, shot them, and then burned the bodies. And then he left. He also probably planted the blood in your car." Decker paused. "He might have driven over to the motel to do it, and at the same time he reversed whatever he'd done to disable your car so it would start when the police showed up there. And that would explain the person who saw a car in the vicinity of your house that night. Only it was your dad's car, not yours."

"Our cars *did* look alike. But what if I'd called my house that night from the motel and told him to come get me?"

"I don't think he would have picked up the phone, Melvin. And that would leave you stuck at the motel."

"So he did all that knowing that I'd be arrested for the crime? But why?"

"The folks coming after him would suspect a deception because they so conveniently died with no faces left and the bodies burned. But they would probably never think that Roy would frame his own son for the murder. That throws the suspicion off effectively and makes the deaths seem legit. That gives Roy breathing room. He gets away with whatever was in that safe deposit box."

"And twenty years later everything starts exploding. Montgomery being paid off? Me out of prison? Davenport being kidnapped? Why?"

"They want what's in the box, Melvin. They see you as the last chance to get it."

"You still think they'll contact you about Davenport?"

"I hope they do. It might be the only chance we have to get her back alive."

47

Decker sat in his motel room staring at his laptop.

He had typed one word in and was checking the search results. Most people faced with pages of information tended to skim. Decker did not skim. He read it all thoroughly. And down near the bottom of the third page he found something of interest.

This took him to another search, and he read down these pages.

This, in turn, had led him to something of greater interest.

Then he sat back and drank from the glass of water next to his elbow as he listened to the rain beating down outside. He had heard that Texas had been in a prolonged drought. Well, they might just be coming out of it. He had never seen this much rain before, even in Ohio, where the weather could go through long stretches of inclemency.

He put the glass of water down, lining up the water ring precisely, though his thoughts were not nearly as aligned.

Chocha did mean "prostitute" in Spanish. And

Decker had learned that the "female anatomy" that Mars had refused to say out loud under hypnosis was "vagina." But *chocha* also meant something else in another regional dialect of Spanish. In a country other than Spain or Mexico. And that something else might be both informative and problematic.

And Decker didn't know how to deal with the problematic part, at least right now.

Lucinda had said the word, not Mars's father.

Yes, problematic.

A couple minutes later he was knocking on Mars's door after speaking to the FBI agent standing guard there.

"I can tell from the look on your face you got more questions," said Mars wearily when he opened it.

"I do."

"You never get tired?"

"I get tired all the time. I'm fat and in crappy shape."

"You're not as fat as you were, Decker. You want to start working out with me?"

"I'd be dead in five minutes."

"I'll start off slow."

"Maybe. Let me ask you something."

Mars sighed and motioned him in. They sat in chairs next to the bed.

Decker said, "Did your mother have any family heirlooms?"

Mars laughed out loud. "Heirlooms? Shit, Decker. What, you think she had a pot of gold or something? You think we'd have been living like we were if she'd had damn *heirlooms*?"

Decker was unperturbed. "Maybe not gold. But how about silver?"

Mars looked like he was going to laugh again, but then he abruptly stopped. "Damn."

"What?"

"She had a silver teapot."

"Where did she say it came from?"

"Like her great-grandmother or something."

"What happened to it?"

"I don't know. She kept it in the bedroom in her closet."

"Did she polish it?"

"Yeah, sometimes."

"How did she polish it?"

"What do you mean?"

"With a cloth?"

"Yeah." He paused and concentrated, evidently thinking back. "But she would finish off the polishing with her—"

"With her fingers?" Decker interjected.

"How'd you know that?"

"You finish off polishing fine silver with your fingers. At least well-trained servants do. Or used to do."

"Servant?"

"House cleaner, expert seamstress, silver polisher,

professional clothes presser? Those are all skills of someone working as a servant in a very wealthy household. And that may be where the silver teapot came from."

"Where would my mom have been a servant in a wealthy household? I mean, you're talking like *British royalty* stuff."

"Actually, you'd be surprised. And maybe it was also the place where she learned Spanish."

"You think rich folks would've just given her a silver teapot?"

"No. I think she probably stole it."

Mars rose and looked down at Decker. "My mother was no thief."

"I'm not saying she was."

"Then what the hell are you saying?"

"She might have been a *slave* in that household."

"A slave. Are you serious? Where?"

"Did your mother use foul language?"

"Never. She was very proper in that way."

"But she used the word *chocha*? Which could translate to 'whore' or 'vagina'? That doesn't seem very proper."

Mars sat back down, looking confused. "Yeah, but she was upset. I told you that."

"But it doesn't fit the context of the argument she was having with your father. Where would a whore come in? Was she accusing your father of using a hooker or of being some kind of pussy?"

"No, my old man would never have cheated on her. And I don't think anyone would call my father a pussy. And it wasn't like she was angry at him. She was more scared than angry, really."

"Which reinforces my point that the word doesn't make sense. *If* you were using the typical Spanish translation," he added.

"Is there an atypical one?" asked Mars warily.

"Spanish is obviously spoken in many countries. And other countries and other regions of other countries sometimes have very different translations for the same word."

"And did you find one for *chocha*?"

"I did."

"What country?"

"Colombia. More specifically the Cali region. That location is the basis for the theory I've come up with."

"Wait, you're saying my mom was from Colombia?"

"I'm not saying she was from there for certain, but at some point in her life I think she ended up there. Maybe against her will. Which is where the slave thing comes in."

"Who the hell in Colombia was in the slave trade?"

"The drug cartels in Cali. I did some research. Back when the cocaine trafficking was centered in Colombia, drug czars would threaten the families of people and use that as leverage to keep them in harness. Or they would kidnap people, especially women, and use them as servants in their households. They took people from other countries, including the United States. I think your mom might have been one, but I think she escaped. And she took that silver teapot with her as partial repayment for what they did to her. It really was a shot in the dark on my part, and I could have been wrong. But I thought she might have taken something with her, just to get back at whoever was holding her."

"And you're sure it was Colombia? But how can you be?"

"Because of the translation. Apparently it's particular only to the Cali area."

"But you haven't told me what the translation was."

"*Chocha* in the Valluno dialect means 'possum.'"

Mars stared blankly at him. "And why would a possum make any more sense than the other translations?"

Decker drew a long breath and then just said it.

"Principally, Melvin, because possums can play *dead*. Which seems to be exactly what your father did."

48

So you think a cartel is behind all this?" asked Bogart.

Decker sat across from him, Milligan, and Jamison in Bogart's room at the motel. Decker had filled the others in on his deductions and his conversation with Mars.

"I don't know for sure, but one certainly could be. If Lucinda escaped and also stole from them, they could have come after her. She might have married Roy then and they fled to Texas together."

Milligan shook his head. "So twenty years later they get seen on ESPN and the cartel comes after them again? According to you she was a house servant. Why would they care? And back then the cartel wars were going hot and heavy. Drug bosses were getting killed left and right or else put in prison. And now forty years after the fact they're still coming after the Marses?"

"Unless she had something else on them," said Jamison. "Something really damaging or valuable that would still be important all these years later, and the leaders today want it back. That could be what was in the safe deposit box."

"Still a stretch," said Milligan.

"It *is* a stretch," conceded Decker. "But it can't be discounted. Not yet. We have to follow it up."

"How?" asked Milligan. "You're talking forty years ago, Decker. The people involved are either dead or geriatric. And, since we're talking cartels, most likely dead. There are all new players now. And Colombia has really cracked down on drug trafficking in the last two decades. Most of the business has moved to other places, like Mexico."

"All true," said Decker. "But one way to follow it up is to find Roy Mars."

Bogart said, "We have people looking for him, but it's a long shot. He hasn't been seen in a long time."

"You're wrong there," said Decker. "He was seen very recently."

"What are you talking about?" asked Milligan. "Where?"

"In Alabama."

"No one saw him in Alabama," countered Milligan.

"Patricia Bray did. She saw the guy in the Avalon."

"Wait a minute," interjected Bogart. "Are you saying that the man who blew up Regina Montgomery was Roy Mars?"

"Of course it was. Right age. Right physical description."

Jamison said, "Have you told Melvin that you suspect that was his dad?"

"No."

"Are you going to?"

"I don't know," said Decker. "What do you think?"

Jamison looked at the others and said, "I think he has more than enough on his plate right now. Until we know for sure, I say we tell him nothing."

"Agreed," said Bogart, and Milligan nodded.

"But, Decker, why would Roy Mars have killed Regina?" asked Jamison.

"She screwed up. She spent the money he paid her. We went back there a second time. That told Mars something was up. He was staying nearby for this very reason. To see how interested we were in her. Charles Montgomery was dead. The kid would have been told nothing. Regina was the loose end. Maybe Roy intended on killing her regardless. He had no trouble dispatching Reardon and burning up his body. The guy is a killer."

Milligan said, "Do you think he might have worked for the cartel? Maybe as an enforcer for them? He could have met Lucinda that way."

"It's possible, although the cartels didn't cast a wide net back then and kept their muscle pretty much homegrown, so bringing in a white guy from America was probably not in their protocols. But he could have been in South America and met Lucinda there. Maybe he helped her escape from the cartel."

"But this is all still speculation," countered Bogart. "We have no proof that any of this is true."

Jamison said, "So Roy Mars paid off Montgomery to lie to get Melvin out of prison. But if Roy committed the murders for which Melvin was convicted, he framed Melvin. Why would he work so hard to get him out of prison now?"

Bogart said, "I was wondering the very same thing. That seems very inconsistent."

Decker turned and gazed off.

"Decker?" said Jamison. "Can you explain that?"

He glanced back at her. "Maybe it all comes down to a promise made."

"A promise made? To whom?" said Jamison.

"To Lucinda Mars."

Bogart shook his head. "You've totally lost me."

Decker turned to Jamison. "You remember that I asked Melvin when he was hypnotized if his father had ever told him that he loved him?"

"Yes. I was pretty shocked that you asked that."

"I did it because I wanted to know the lay of the land."

"The lay of the land?" said Milligan, looking supremely confused. "Come on, Decker, it's like you're speaking in tongues."

"I don't think Roy loved Melvin, but Lucinda did. I think Lucinda knew what Roy was going to do. Kill her to spare her from suffering with the brain cancer. They probably planned that part out together.

Remember, this was twenty years ago and they were in a small town, with little money, and I doubt her end would have been painless. So they made that compact. Roy would kill Reardon, Lucinda switched the dental records to cover that end. Roy cleaned out the safe deposit box. He had an argument with Lucinda in which she used the word *chocha*. That told me she had spent time in Cali and learned her Spanish there. It also told me that she was aware that Roy was going to pretend to be dead—a possum, in other words."

"But if she was part of the plan, why the argument?" asked Bogart.

"Buyer's remorse. She loved her son. She was sick, dying. Even if she knew what the plan was that doesn't mean she had to love it. She obviously didn't."

"How much could she love Melvin if she let him be framed for her murder?" asked Jamison. "He spent two decades in prison."

"Maybe his mother thought he would be safer in prison."

This statement came from Milligan. The others looked at him.

He said, "Look at it this way, if they were afraid the cartel had found them through the ESPN piece— maybe they'd actually received a warning or threat— then they knew if they didn't disappear their death warrant was signed. But how could Melvin disappear with them? The guy was a college superstar, everyone knew him. He was going to be drafted, play in the NFL. They could sneak off and fade away, but not him. Yet they couldn't leave him behind because the cartel would come and either kill him or torture him for information about his parents and then kill him."

Bogart said, "But the cartel could have reached him in prison."

Milligan replied, "Yeah, but not as easily as him being on the street. It was probably the lesser of two evils. But they also might have thought the cartel would believe that in prison Melvin was no threat to them. And if they believed he had killed his parents then they might have assumed that Roy and Lucinda had told him nothing about the cartel and their secrets," he added.

Decker appraised the man. "Agent Milligan, nice reasoning."

Milligan grinned. "Thanks. And Decker, you can call me Todd. We are on the same team."

Jamison said, "Well, I'm not buying it."

They all looked at her.

She continued, "To protect your son you frame him for murder? And he gets the death penalty? Yeah, a real softer option."

Milligan said, "I'm not saying it's the right answer, Jamison. I'm just saying it's possible."

Bogart said, "Okay, for argument's sake, let's suppose it's true. Then why did Roy come back and do what he did to get Melvin out?"

"Melvin was going to be executed," said Decker immediately. "And I'm thinking that Roy made a promise to his wife that if that ever came to be he would step in and save Melvin. And he did."

Jamison said, "That's what you were referring to when you said a promise had been made?"

Decker nodded.

"All these years later?" asked Bogart. "He might have died, and then Melvin would have been up shit creek."

"But he *didn't* die. And he *did* fulfill the promise."

"In a way he must have loved his wife very much," said Jamison.

"I believe that he did," said Decker. "I can only imagine what it took to pull the trigger on that shotgun and end her life. Even if he knew he was sparing her six months of agony."

"Could you really do that to someone you loved?" asked Milligan skeptically.

"I think you could *only* do that to someone you really loved," said Decker. "It would be the hardest thing you ever had to do, but you would do it because of that love. And I think a part of Roy Mars died that night. The only positive thing in his life was gone."

"And Melvin?" asked Jamison.

"Father did not love his son. He was sorry for what he was about to do. Remember he told Melvin he was sorry that night? It was for the mother's sake, not the son's. But there's something off there, only I can't figure out what. So now the question becomes, where is Roy Mars?"

"Wait a minute," said Jamison. "Maybe the cartel isn't even involved in this. Like Todd said, after forty years they could all be dead. Roy paid off Montgomery, got Melvin off, and then killed Regina. He could be the only one out there."

Decker shook his head. "Then who kidnapped Davenport?"

"Roy?" offered Jamison.

"Why?"

She started to say something but then stopped. "I don't know why."

"There is someone else out there. But Melvin getting out of prison triggered their interest."

"Do you think they believe that Roy Mars is actually alive?" asked Milligan.

"Maybe, and/or that Melvin getting out of prison has once more piqued their interest about whatever was in that safe deposit box. They may hope he can lead them to it, like I suggested before."

"So if the cartel took Davenport?" said Jamison slowly.

Milligan and Bogart exchanged glances.

Bogart said, "I won't try to sugarcoat this. The odds of us getting her back safely don't look very good."

"So how do we find Roy Mars?" asked Milligan, breaking an awkward silence.

Decker said, "Well, I'm convinced he's close by. So

one way or another we might just run into each other."

"You're joking of course," said Milligan.

Decker didn't answer.

49

Decker was walking in a gray drizzle along the same route that he and Mars had earlier taken. His thoughts had turned to another facet of the case. One way to find Roy Mars was to figure out his connection to Charles Montgomery. If Mars had paid off Regina, then he had to have some connection to the Montgomerys. He hadn't picked them out of the blue. There had to be a reason. And that answer might lie in the man's past.

Charles Montgomery had not told them all of the crimes of which he'd been accused. This was understandable since the list was lengthy. But Decker had done some digging.

Montgomery had come back stateside and left the Army in March 1967. In January 1968 he had been arrested in Tuscaloosa, Alabama, for driving while intoxicated and for possession of marijuana. Bail had been posted and he'd skipped town. A month later he'd been stopped in Cain, Mississippi, for illegal possession of a stolen gun and drunk and disorderly. Again he'd posted bail, and again he'd skipped town.

The crimes had not been serious enough to warrant much of a follow-up, and he apparently had never returned to either state until shooting the Alabama state trooper. And back then there was no central database for cops across state lines. But the crimes were relatively minor and the police no doubt had more pressing matters to claim their time than chasing a petty criminal.

In his mind Decker listed the offenses in chronological order:

DUI and pot possession in Alabama.

A stolen gun and drunk and disorderly in Mississippi.

Bail posted each time.

And he'd skipped town each time.

There was no reason to think it important, but as the drizzle hit him, Decker couldn't think it *unimportant*, he just didn't know why.

He went back to his room and sat in his chair and stared out the window at the gathering gloom. It was barely five in the evening and it looked and felt like midnight. His energy just seemed sapped. If this weather kept up they might all well drown without even stepping into the water.

But Decker's desire to find the truth trumped the weather. His brain hit the reset button and the key question popped up again.

Why did Roy Mars pick Charles Montgomery?

Montgomery's explanation of seeing Melvin's name

and putting two and two together obviously had been a lie. The process had actually worked in the reverse. Montgomery hadn't found Mars. Roy Mars had selected Charles Montgomery.

The only possible reason was that the two men had known each other before. And perhaps Montgomery owed Mars for some reason. And that reason, coupled with the inducement of the money to be left to Regina Montgomery and their son, was enough for the condemned Montgomery to lie about killing Roy and Lucinda Mars.

But how and where had they previously met?

Both men were about the same age. Roy Mars was not the man's real name, so he could have been in the military with Montgomery over in 'Nam. They had no fingerprints from Mars to search for in the military database.

Yet had they been in the military together? Maybe Mars had saved Montgomery's life over there? That seemed plausible.

But if not in Vietnam, where?

Had Mars been a petty criminal too? If he were connected to the cartel then Montgomery might have been in South America at some point. Or in Mexico. Or in some way had been connected with the drug trade. He had told them of his pain problem and his quest to steal money and drugs in order to deal with his headaches.

Had Montgomery known Lucinda?

Was that the angle to come at this by?

Decker rubbed his eyes and then closed them.

Even for his exceptional mind this was a staggering conundrum. He could not find traction anywhere. Every time he thought he had something figured out, another question of even greater complexity took its place, like a vanquished cancer cell being replaced by an even more malignant and entrenched one.

But something in the back of Decker's brain told him that if he could find the connection between the two men, many other questions might be answered.

He opened his eyes and looked out the window. Somewhere out there Lisa Davenport was being held against her will and perhaps tortured.

Or she might already be dead.

Decker had concluded that his first assumption had been wrong. They had not taken Davenport to later exchange for Mars.

And he wasn't even convinced they had taken her for information purposes.

But if not either of those two reasons, why? What else was there?

What was a possible third reason?

He closed his eyes again. The answer simply wasn't coming.

He ate dinner in his room while the others gathered together in the small restaurant off the motel lobby. An apple and a bottle of water. Only two months before he would have laughed at such a meal. It would not even have constituted a snack. Now it filled him up. He wanted nothing else.

He notched his belt a hole tighter. At this rate he would have to cut another hole in the belt or get a new one. He was losing weight rapidly. Not in a good way. His inability to solve any significant part of this case was pretty much eating him from the inside out.

He finished the water, tossed the bottle and the apple core, undressed, and got into bed. But though his eyes closed, his mind did not turn off. If anything it hit another gear and raced even faster.

Every conceivable explanation was run through his brain and came out the other end with an imagined "rejected" stamped on it. Some conclusions seemed promising right up until the moment they ran into a fact that could not be explained away and were discarded into his mental rubbish pile.

Again and again he seemed to be close, but something always came around to screw it up. It was like having one move left on a Rubik's Cube and being unable to seal the deal. The truth was, he was no closer to working this out than he had been on the very first day.

And he had this oddly creeping feeling that he was running out of time, though he could think of no plausible reason why that would be the case.

He opened and closed his eyes, and his brain,

perhaps taking a cue that it was overworked and not anywhere near success, also shut down.

Decker slept.

And he awoke for only one reason.

A knife blade was pressed against his throat.

50

Decker didn't move.

The room was very dark, the moonlight that would normally be coming in through the window obscured by the cloud cover. He could hear the rain drumming on the roof.

But his focus was on the knife blade. It was pressed against his left jugular, a superhighway of circulation. If it was severed, he would bleed out in under a minute.

He could hear the other person's breathing, slow, measured —no panic or lack of control there. That gave him some comfort. The breath was also foul: coffee, cigarettes, and garlic. The confluence of smells swept into his nostrils, nearly making him gag.

By casting his gaze downward he could just make out the very large hand holding the knife.

The voice said, "You're fucking everything up." It was calm, low, and still managed to be intimidating.

Decker thought about this candid opening. He wondered if the follow-up would be to slash his neck open. "Not my intent," he said.

"Don't play stupid with me. I know you're a cop. I know you got brains. But you leave it be. Go home. And leave it be."

"What about Melvin?"

Decker felt the knife blade press harder against his skin. So hard in fact that it cut into him. Something slid down his neck. A drop of blood. But only a drop. The jug was still intact.

"What about him?" asked the voice.

"He's got nothing."

The knife pressed still harder and Decker could feel another little prick of the blade. And another drop slid down his neck and was absorbed into his T-shirt.

"He's got his freedom. That's enough."

"After twenty years?"

"He should be grateful."

"I'm not saying he's not," replied Decker calmly, even as he felt the blade push deeper against his skin. His jugular was exposed, right at the surface from the pressure. The guy knew exactly what he was doing, and had probably done it before. Which did not make Decker feel any better.

"I'm just saying that he's feeling vulnerable."

"Tell him not to worry. I've got his back."

"Because of his mother?"

The blade withdrew just a hair. "What the hell do you know about anything?" the man growled.

"I don't know much. In fact, there's a lot I don't

know. But I know Lucinda loved her son. And you loved *her*. And she made you promise, didn't she?"

The blade pressed more firmly against his artery. "You're making this difficult on yourself."

"I'm just trying to help Melvin."

"I told you I've got his back."

"Against the cartel?"

The man snorted.

Decker said, "So not the cartel?"

The man fell silent.

"Why did you pick Montgomery to get Melvin out of prison? What's the connection?"

"Not going there."

"You don't have Davenport, do you?" asked Decker.

The man didn't answer right away. "Who?"

"She was with us. Someone took her."

Decker felt the blade slowly move away from his neck. "When?" The voice was not intimidating now, just wary.

"A few days ago. She must have known them. They took her from her room and made it look like a fight. But it was all staged. She knew the person. And that narrows things down."

"Why would they take her?"

"I don't know. I thought for leverage against us. Maybe to ask for Melvin in exchange, but they've made no attempt to contact us."

"Maybe they want information."

"Maybe they do. And maybe they got it from her. But I think what they really wanted was Melvin."

"Why?"

"The stuff in the safe deposit box. They think he has it."

"How do you know about that?"

"I'm a detective. It's what I do."

"*Mellow* knows nothing about it."

Decker didn't understand this name, but he didn't think right now was a good time to get into it. "I know he doesn't, but they don't know that. They think he will lead them to it."

"Shit." This was said more to himself than to Decker. "I didn't think . . . after all this time."

"Right, I get that. But it did happen and it's a problem," said Decker. "You had to be aware that might happen. You sprung him and now we see the consequences. They didn't buy Montgomery's story. And they know you're alive . . . *Roy.*"

Decker steeled himself for the blade to return to his jugular, because he had finally named the man. He added, "Even though that's not your real name."

"I told you to back off."

"I know you did. I'm just telling you what I know. Lucinda's dead, you're not. You set up your own son."

"No I didn't."

"Then what happened?"

"I don't have to tell you nothing."

"No, you don't. You've got the knife. I'm just saying

that they're out there and they want Melvin, and I'm not sure you can cover his back."

"You're with the damn FBI, what can *you* do?"

"We're doing all we can. I just don't know if it's going to be enough, considering I have no idea who else is out there. Maybe you can help me there."

Decker waited for the man to say something. He knew he was still there. He could hear him. And smell him.

Outside the rain continued to pour down. Decker wondered if this would be the last time he would hear the miserable rain. He imagined himself bleeding out on this crummy bed in the middle of nowhere in Texas.

"You there?" he asked. "You got something to say?"

"If they took your friend, I'd stop worrying. It's too late for her. Just the way it is."

"Okay. I hope you're wrong, but you're probably not."

"And you need to stand down. I'll take care of this."

"Like you took care of Regina Montgomery?"

"You want me to kill you?"

"No, but I want to understand what's going on."

"Why?"

"I told you why. I want to help Melvin."

"Nobody can help him, not really. He got screwed. No fault of his, just the way it turned out."

"He had his whole life planned out."

"So did I. It happens. Life is like that. Plans go to shit."

"He went to prison because of you, Roy."

"It was better than the alternative. He's alive, isn't he?"

"For now."

"Just go back to wherever you came from and let me take care of this. Take Mellow with you. As far away as you can. I won't ask a second time. The next time I'm just going to gut you, you understand what I'm saying?"

"I understand."

"No, I don't think you do. I really don't."

Decker braced for the strike.

When the blow fell, it wasn't the knife, but something hard and heavy.

It struck the side of his head and all Decker saw after that was darkness.

51

Now it's *you* who's lucky."

Decker blinked his eyes open.

Mars was staring down at him.

"I don't feel lucky," he groaned.

"Join the club."

Decker looked around. "Where am I?"

"Hospital. You got a concussion. Side of your head looks like you got in a fight with Ray Lewis."

"That's what I feel like, actually." He tried to sit up, but Mars put out a restraining hand. "Whoa, big fellow. You ain't going anywhere."

Decker lay back. "Where are the others?"

"Bogart and Milligan are trying to figure out what happened. Jamison sat next to your bed for hours. She just left to use the bathroom. Expect her back any second. Pretty loyal to you, that lady."

Decker gazed up at him. "I guess I don't always realize those things."

Mars pulled up a chair and sat down. "I did some research on your *condition*." He tapped his head. "Up here."

"Why?"

"Because I wanted to understand you better. It's like studying film and then making a game plan."

"And what did you find out?"

"That it's complicated. You're complicated. No two cases are really alike. You could change tomorrow if your brain keeps rewiring itself. Pretty dicey."

"I guess that's why I live for today," quipped Decker.

Mars grinned. "You and me both." Then his grin faded. "Was it him?"

"Who?"

"You know who, Decker. My old man. Did he do this to you?"

The door opened and Jamison appeared there. When she saw that Decker was awake she rushed over. "Omigod, Amos. How are you feeling?"

"Alive. That's about it. But I'll be fine."

Mars said, "Decker was just about to tell us who walloped him."

Jamison gasped. "You know? You saw the person?"

"It *was* your father, Melvin. At least I'm ninety-nine percent sure it was."

"So you didn't see him?"

"I heard him. He had a knife against my jugular during our conversation. He knew about everything."

"Did he use my name?" asked Mars.

"Yes. Well, sort of."

"What exactly did he call me?"

"Mellow."

Mars looked away and rubbed his chin with his hand. "Right."

"What's the reference?"

"His joke. Since I was the exact opposite of mellow. He was the only one who ever called me that. The *only* one."

"So it *was* him," said Jamison.

"Pretty sure, yeah," said Mars.

"He was also a smoker," said Decker.

"So was my father."

"What else did he say, Amos?" asked Jamison.

Decker slowly told them, but leaving out some parts, particularly those in reference to how Roy Mars really felt about his son.

Mars said slowly, "So he's saying he did this to protect me? And he got me out probably because my mother made him promise?"

"He didn't actually say that, but when I made the statement he didn't dispute it. But one thing puzzles me. He said he hadn't set you up. When it was clear that he had."

Mars nodded. "But my mom knew what he was going to do. That he was going to frame me and then play dead. *Chocha*, like you said."

Decker and Jamison gazed nervously at him.

"She probably thought you'd be safer in prison, Melvin," suggested Jamison.

"Yeah, so safe I nearly died."

"She had terminal brain cancer, I doubt she was thinking all that clearly. And it was pretty obvious that she didn't like the plan. That was why they were arguing."

"But he still went ahead and screwed me over. And she went along with it."

A long moment of silence passed.

"We can argue forever about what was in their heads, Melvin," said Decker at last. "But it won't change things."

"Right. I know."

"But it still sucks," said Decker.

"Yeah, it does."

Jamison glanced at him and attempted to quickly change the subject. "But now you don't think it's the cartel out there behind this?"

"Roy snorted, because he thought I was going down the wrong path when I mentioned the cartel. When I reversed course on that, he clammed up."

"And Davenport?" asked Jamison in a tremulous voice.

"Unfortunately, he didn't sound so hopeful about her."

"But he said he was covering my back," said Mars.

Decker looked at him. The pleading look on the man's face was painful to see.

"He did say that, Melvin. He was going to do his best to protect you."

"Because of my mother."

"I don't think it's all that. He said you got screwed. Maybe he feels remorse."

"I don't think so," said Mars slowly. "I'm not sure the guy can feel anything."

"Whatever your father feels or doesn't feel about you, Melvin, has nothing to do with you," said Jamison firmly. "It's *his* issue, not yours."

Decker said, "The man could wield a knife. And though he's in his seventies, he's still physically formidable. I'm not easy to knock out. But he managed it."

"He always was strong as a bull," said Mars absently.

"There *is* a connection between your father and Montgomery," said Decker. "He as good as admitted that. If we can find that nexus we may be able to determine who is behind all this."

Jamison said, "Maybe we should take Roy's advice and get Melvin far away from here."

Mars said immediately, "I'm not going anywhere."

Decker added, "I agree. If I'm reading this right, it won't matter where Melvin goes. It was also clear that Roy felt that whoever he was hiding from is after what's in the safe deposit box."

"But no clue as to what that is?" asked Jamison.

"It's obviously something important."

"But if not a cartel, what?" asked Mars. "What could my old man have been involved in all those years ago?"

Decker said, "He's a dangerous man, Melvin. That may be an indicator. He kills people."

"What, like he was some sort of hired hit man?"

"I don't know for certain. I'm just saying that it wouldn't have surprised me if someone had used him as muscle."

Mars rose, went over to the window, and looked out. The man was a picture of confused despair.

In a low voice Jamison said to Decker, "This is really hard on him. I can't even imagine."

"I *can* imagine," said Decker. "But the only way to get him out of this mess is to figure it out. Otherwise he's going to be looking over his shoulder the rest of his life."

"You really think we can do that?"

"Yes. If they don't kill us first."

52

I'm having the local police post round-the-clock security at the entrance to the motel, Amos," said Bogart. "I should have done that after they took Davenport," he added apologetically. "I had someone posted outside Melvin's and Jamison's doors, but not yours. I just didn't think anyone would go after you."

He and Decker were walking together down the hall of the hospital.

"It's okay," said Decker. "I'm good to go."

"So it *was* Roy Mars?"

Decker nodded. "I think we can safely say that. Although I'd like to know his real name."

"Wouldn't we all."

They left the hospital, got in Bogart's car, and drove off.

Bogart glanced at Decker as they hit the main road.

"How are you feeling?"

"Stupid and slow. So my status hasn't changed since we got on this case."

"I mean physically."

"It hurts, but I've felt worse. A lot worse. Look, we

need to get all of the arrest records for Charles Mont-gomery."

"We have the major ones. The ones that led to his execution."

"I want the minor ones. The ones where he skipped bail. We have some of those details, but I need it all."

"You think that's important?"

"We have to trace the connection between Roy Mars and Montgomery. It wasn't random. Which means it's important. If we can find that connection we may discover who's behind this. We get that, then the whole thing starts to unravel."

"But maybe it has something to do with the mur-ders that Montgomery was convicted of."

"No, those were fairly recent. Whatever the con-nection with Roy Mars, I believe it goes back forty years or more."

"That may be true," conceded Bogart. "But that long ago, finding detailed records will be very diffi-cult."

"Montgomery got back from Vietnam in 1967. He mustered out of the Army shortly thereafter. Then he was involved in a series of petty crimes."

"But he told us he was having headaches. Messed up from the war. Maybe he was rebelling. He was young and stupid."

"Did Montgomery strike you as stupid?"

"No, but he was a lot older, more hardened, when

we met with him. A young punk back then, he was probably capable of anything."

"I think the guy we saw hadn't changed much from when he was young. He fought in Vietnam and was wounded. He was no punk. He was a soldier who'd been through hell and back. And there's something else too."

"What?" said Bogart quickly.

"I'm having trouble pulling it out."

"What, your brain going wacky on you?"

"My brain *is* wacky, all the time."

"I meant, is it starting to work like the minds of the rest of us poor shmucks?"

"It was something," said Decker, ignoring Bogart's comment. "Something I saw or heard." He touched the bruise on the side of his head. "Maybe Roy hit me harder than I thought."

"You'll think of it. In the meantime I'll dig up as much detail as I can on Charles Montgomery."

They drove on.

Later that evening, Mary Oliver met them all for dinner at a restaurant a few blocks from the motel.

Milligan looked at Decker's face and said, "Damn. I think you're lucky he didn't crack your skull."

"He probably wanted to," said Decker. "But if he wanted me dead, he could have just slit my throat."

Mars put down the knife he was holding to cut his salad.

"Sorry, Melvin," said Decker, noting this.

"Hey, it is what it is. My old man's nuts."

"No. He knows exactly what he's doing and why. He understands that him getting you out of jail caused these folks to come after you. They want what was in the safe deposit box."

"So he has those contents?" asked Oliver.

"Probably," said Decker. "I mean, not on him, but somewhere. Somewhere safe that only he knows."

Oliver said, "If we could find him, he could take us to it. Then we could go after whoever's implicated by those contents. They must have been the ones who took Lisa."

Milligan added, "Well, that's easier said than done. We went over Decker's room and didn't find one usable print or shoe mark. The guy's a pro. No one saw him come and no one saw him go. And the lock was expertly picked."

"He is a pro," said Decker. "And he knows who's after him, and he knows what they want."

"But how do we find him?" asked Oliver. "There must be some way."

"He's been watching us. He knows about us. Knows we're the FBI. He knows we're investigating all of this. I think he must be close by."

Milligan said, "If he is, we should be able to find him. We have a description. And the town's not that big."

"But he also likely knows every bit of this place,"

pointed out Jamison. "And there are probably lots of abandoned houses and farms in the area where he could be staying."

Decker looked at her oddly. "That's true."

"That he knows lots of abandoned places to stay?"

"That he might know *one* abandoned place to stay."

"You don't mean my old house?" said Mars.

"Why not?"

"It's too obvious, for one."

"So obvious no one's checked it?" said Decker.

"But you were there," pointed out Jamison. "And we later went with you and Melvin."

"But no one's watching it all the time," said Decker. "No one's watching it right now. And if he wanted to hide the contents of that box?"

Oliver said, "You think it might be somewhere there?"

"There's no guarantee, but it might be worth a look." He glanced at Mars. "Can you think of any location there that might be a good hiding place?"

Oliver pulled her phone out of her pocket and looked at the screen. "This is about Melvin's lawsuit." She typed in a response and smiled at Mars. "Things are looking up, Melvin. I've got a friend in the state government. She just let me know that the state correctional system got my motion on your punitive claim and apparently the whole department is in an uproar, running around like chickens with their heads cut off. That means they know they're vulnerable. And that also means they might come to the settlement table sooner rather than later."

"Well ain't that a miracle!" said Mars.

"I think public opinion is on your side now."

Decker said, "That is good news but let's not lose focus. Melvin, can you think of any place in the house it could be?"

Mars said, "I can't think of anything off the top of my head. The house ain't that big and I never had cause to hide anything."

"How about in the garage?"

"Well, there was a loose board in the wall next to the door leading from the kitchen. I remember I looked in there once when I was a kid and saw an old coffee can. It didn't mean anything to me. And I doubt my dad was hiding an old coffee can."

"Well, it's worth a look. Melvin and I can go check it out later tonight."

Bogart said, "Todd can go with you, just in case. I'm expecting to get in some information on Montgomery shortly. Alex, Mary, and I can go over it while you guys are checking out the house."

"Sounds like a plan," said Mars.

53

Milligan led the way through the mass of trees and bushes in the front of the property, with Decker and Mars close behind. The rain had stopped, at least for a bit, but the clouds were heavy with moisture and they all expected another dousing at any moment.

They reached the front porch and Milligan eased the door open, his hand on the butt of his gun. Decker was doing likewise.

They entered the front room and looked around. It was dark outside, but darker still in here. Milligan swept his flashlight beam around the space.

Decker led them into the kitchen with his flashlight and then to the door going into the attached single-car garage. He aimed his light around the space, while Milligan did likewise.

"It's over there," said Mars, pointing at a section of the wall near the side door leading to the outside. "You can see where the wood is uneven."

They headed to that spot following Milligan's flashlight beam.

Decker gripped the board and pulled on it. It came

away easily enough. Revealed behind it was a small compartment, really just a space between the wall studs. It was six inches deep and about eighteen inches wide. The "floor" of the compartment was a cross-beam of wood connecting the studs.

It was empty.

"It *could* have been the hiding place," pointed out Decker. "It's probably large enough for whatever was in the safe deposit box."

"But it's not here," said Milligan. "So that doesn't help us." He aimed his light around some more and then cast it on the floor. It was clean except for what looked to be fine dust and a small strip of wood. "Probably happened when you pulled the wood out," he said.

"I checked the floor *before* I pulled the wood out. That pile of dust and woodchips was already there. And if you look at the board, it has a strip of wood out of it that corresponds to the one on the floor. When I pulled on it, it came out way too easily. Place like this, abandoned for decades with rot and moisture, I'd expected the wood to be far more difficult to get out. I think it was in that state and the wood strip broke off when it was forced out."

"Which means that someone else was already here," said Milligan.

Decker nodded. "And recently. Because we searched this place before and I don't remember seeing the strip of wood. And I would have if it had been there."

Mars said excitedly, "So you think my old man did hide the stuff in there?"

"I can't say for sure either way," replied Decker. "But *someone* checked it for some reason. Maybe him. Or someone else." He looked around. "And by the way, the initials of your dad's real name are A and C."

"How the hell do you know that?"

"It's carved in the closet and also matches the ones he used when he rented the car in Alabama. Arthur Crandall?"

Milligan tensed and gripped Decker's arm. "I think someone just entered the house through the back door."

They all stood stock-still, listening.

"There," said Milligan.

"That was definitely footsteps," said Mars.

"Yes," agreed Decker. He eyed the overhead garage door. "Do we go out that way?"

Milligan said, "I bet that door hasn't been opened in twenty years. We try to it'll make a noise like a train going off the rails. Probably the same for the door over there. And we saw earlier that bushes and shit have grown up right in front of those entrances. We'd be tangled up and sitting ducks."

"But they must know we're already in the house," said Mars.

"Not necessarily. Not if they came through the back," countered Milligan. "And even if they do know we're here, they may not know we're in the garage."

417

"You don't think it's Bogart?" asked Mars.

"He would have called," said Decker. "He's not sneaking in here when he knows we're here. There might be an unpleasant result."

"Right," said Milligan.

"Then who is it?" asked Mars.

Decker and Milligan drew their guns at the same time.

"Get behind us, Melvin," said Decker.

"Hey, I can take care of myself."

"Not with people with guns, you can't," pointed out Milligan.

Decker punched in numbers on his phone. He looked at the screen. "It's not going through. No bars."

"Still the middle of nowhere out here," said Mars. "Even twenty years later."

Milligan squared his shoulders. "Okay, do we wait here and let them come through the door? Good firing line and we can probably take them out if they make a run at us."

"That sounds like a good strategy to me," said Decker. "But we need to split up. I'll take that corner, Todd, and you can take the other one. That way they'll have two fields of fire to cover. Melvin, get down on the floor over there by the workbench. It'll give you some cover."

"Look, guys, I don't want you two putting your asses on the line for me."

"We did that the second we took on this case," replied Decker. "Now just do what I say, because I hear them coming this way."

They all took up their positions. In the far corners, on either side of the overhead garage door, Decker and Milligan knelt down and assumed firing positions, their muzzles aimed at the doorway leading into the house. Mars got down on the floor on the far side of the workbench, keeping his eyes peeled on the same doorway.

"Do we wait for them to fire first?" said Milligan.

"On the off chance it's some kids exploring, I think we have to wait," said Decker. "I'd call out and identify ourselves, but I really don't think it's kids."

"Me either."

"If you fire, roll to your left. I'll fire next and roll to my right, if I can manage it."

"Roger that."

The next sound they heard was the door leading into the kitchen slamming shut. Then they heard the lock turn. Then there was the sound of something hard hitting against something else hard.

Decker and Milligan glanced at each other.

"I don't like the sound of that," hissed Milligan. "What game are they playing?"

"Hey, guys," said Mars softly. "Do you smell smoke?"

54

Decker hit the door leading to the outside and bounced off. He tried the lock. Then he stepped back and fired his gun, shearing the knob off. He tried the door again. It wouldn't budge.

"I think it's been jammed or nailed shut," he cried out.

Milligan was attempting to force the garage door up. "It's jammed too."

The smoke was pouring into the garage from the door leading into the kitchen.

Decker and Mars raced over there, coughing and gagging as they did so, Decker's light stabbing through the smoke and darkness.

Decker put his hand against the door and jerked it away with a groan. "It's red-hot. The fire must be on the other side of the door. We can't get out that way."

"Well, there's no other way to get out," yelled Milligan from across the garage.

Mars turned and took off running. He hit the door leading directly to the outside so hard that it broke off its hinges. But bushes and vines had grown up all over

420

the house, blocking the door from falling away. He pushed and kicked, but the door was inextricably tangled up in the heavy shrubs and stout vines and would not give.

"Shit!" he yelled.

Decker's lungs were heaving. He dropped low to the floor since the smoke was rising. He called out to the others to do the same. He belly-crawled over to the overhead door. Milligan was sprawled on his stomach next to it.

"Somebody's got to see the fire from the road," gasped Milligan.

"But by the time they call the fire department and they get here, we'll be asphyxiated," warned Decker.

"Get out of the way," said Mars.

They looked over in time to see him sprinting full speed toward the door. Both men slid out of the way as he catapulted past them and slammed his shoulder into the overhead garage door. It cracked, but did not give.

Mars, gasping for air after having sucked in a huge amount of smoke, dropped to the concrete and was sick to his stomach.

"Someone's trapped us in here," said Milligan. "Set the fire and jammed the doors leading out."

Decker knew that he was right about this, but how would someone know they were even coming here?

He reached under the bottom of the garage door and heaved upward. The door did not budge. This was an awkward angle for him, preventing him from using most of his strength and none of his bulk to defeat the obstacle.

He let go and thought for the first time—

We're going to die in here.

The next moment he heard it.

Gunshots, just outside. He instinctively rolled to the side, not knowing if the rounds would rip through the door.

"Who's out there?" shouted Milligan.

Something hit the door. Blow after blow rained against it. Then another gunshot. It hit the door, near where it met the wall. Decker pushed himself farther back. He readied his gun just in case.

But Milligan shot forward, gripped under the bottom of the door, and pushed upward.

The door slowly started to rise.

"Help me," he said.

Decker and Mars hurtled forward to assist him.

The door moved upward faster.

"Go, go!" said Milligan.

He pushed Mars forward.

As with the side door to the garage, thick vegetation had grown in front of the garage door. There had been no concrete driveway, only gravel, which had long since been reclaimed by the soil.

Mars kicked and thrashed and tore at vines and branches until he was clear of it. Decker was right behind him.

As Milligan stumbled out he got caught between a prickly holly tree and the side of the house. When he cried out, Decker and Mars rushed to his aid and with their combined strength soon had him free. The three men staggered away from the house and collapsed onto the ground, retching and coughing.

Mars rolled over onto his back and looked at his old home. Flames were visible at the front windows. Black smoke was pouring out of fractured glass.

Mars laid his head back against the ground and closed his eyes. But Decker was on his feet looking wildly around. He had heard a car start up but couldn't see where it was.

"There," shouted Milligan, who had his gun out and pointed to the left.

The two men reached the road in time to see the taillights of a car disappear into the darkness.

"Shit!" exclaimed Milligan. He pulled out his phone and tried to make a call, but there was still no cell reception. He shoved it back into his pocket and then raced after Decker, who was already at their car. He jumped in and put the keys in the ignition. It wouldn't start.

"What the hell?" exclaimed Decker.

The car's engine wouldn't even turn over.

Decker said, "Hit the hood release."

Milligan did so, raised the hood, and shone his light around the engine compartment. "Battery cables," he said. "They've been cut."

Decker got out of the car as Mars walked slowly over to them.

The house was fully on fire behind them, but Mars didn't look back. He leaned against the car, his arms folded over his chest, after looking at the severed battery cables.

"I wonder who the hell that was," said Milligan. "In the car."

"That," said Mars, "was my old man."

Decker shot him a glance. "How do you know that?"

Mars pointed to the cut cables. "When I was seventeen I rolled the car my dad had given me. It was a piece of crap he got for nothing and fixed up. I was being stupid and going too fast. Luckily I wasn't hurt. My father brought the car home, repaired it, and when I went out to drive it again, it wouldn't start. I looked under the hood."

"And found the cables cut," said Decker.

Mars nodded. "He said he was teaching me a lesson. If I made a mistake there were consequences. After working my butt off around the house for six months he replaced the cables."

Decker stared after the long-gone car. "He saved our lives."

"How do you figure?" said Milligan. "I was thinking he almost killed us."

"Someone almost killed us," said Decker. "But it wasn't Roy Mars."

"You sure?"

In answer Decker led them back over to the open garage door, keeping back because of the smoke and flickering flames. He pointed to the right side where the door met the wall of the house.

"You can see that something was jammed in there," he said. He picked up several pieces of flattened wood that were lying nearby. "Probably these. Roy pulled these out, although I think he might have shot one out, which accounts for the gunfire we heard by the door. That allowed us to lift the door."

"And the other gunfire?" asked Mars.

"Your dad was engaged in a gunfight with whoever did try to kill us."

Milligan looked around. "You think there might be some bodies around here?"

"I don't know."

Mars looked at him. "So my dad saved our butts?"

"Yes, he did."

"Well, I'm glad he was here today, otherwise we wouldn't be."

Mars looked off in the direction of where his dad had fled. "If he would just come and talk to me, maybe we could work together."

"He can't do that, Melvin."

"Why not?"

"Because he's murdered people. If he did come forward we'd have no other option than to arrest him."

Mars slowly nodded. "I guess so."

"Don't try to make your father out to be something he's not."

"Like what?"

"I don't think I have to say it," replied Decker. "And keep in mind that I'm here to find the truth. And while I know that you're innocent, I also know that your dad isn't. Nothing can change that. Nothing you can do can change that. It is what it is. You have a life to lead. Don't think it's going to be with your dad. Because that's not going to happen."

Decker headed toward the road, while Mars stood where he was, looking down at the dirt.

Milligan joined Decker. "I think you were a little harsh back there, Decker. Why come down on him like a ton of bricks?"

"You think it's better to give him false hope?"

"You can use some tact."

"I don't have any. And Melvin's already lost twenty years of his life. I don't want him to waste another second over a lost cause."

55

Bail.

Money put up to secure the freedom of a human from incarceration.

At least temporarily.

The practice had been around nearly as long as there were bars with people put behind them.

It was just a way to make money off another's misfortune. There were many businesses built on that concept, and they were all thriving, because misfortune was always in abundance.

Decker sat at the table in his motel room.

The fire at the Marses' old house had been put out, but the place was heavily damaged. The doors in the garage *had* been jammed shut. And the door leading from the garage into the house had been blocked off by wedging a long metal pipe between the door and the opposite wall. The police had found an accelerant in the kitchen, which meant that the fire had been set deliberately.

They had looked for the car seen racing away from the scene, but there had been no sightings. Decker was convinced that Roy Mars was in that car. He had no idea who had set the fire, or how they had escaped.

Several bullet holes had been found in the exterior walls of the house near the garage. That could have been evidence of a gun battle between Roy Mars and whoever else had been there.

More FBI agents had traveled down to Texas to help with the investigation, now that an FBI agent had nearly been killed.

What Decker was looking at now were incomplete records. In Charles Montgomery's first arrest in the 1960s, part of the bail record had long since been lost, including who had posted the bail.

But in the records of the second arrest, Decker found the name of the person posting bail.

"Nathan Ryan," he muttered.

Ryan had posted bail for Montgomery in Cain, Mississippi, on the morning of February 22, 1968. Who was Ryan, and why would he have put up a bond of five hundred dollars—significant money back then—for Montgomery?

Did they know each other? Were they friends? He obviously couldn't ask Montgomery that.

He closed his eyes and his mind cast around for a fresh angle from which to pursue the matter.

He opened his eyes and also the notebook that lay in front of him.

January 11, 1968, Tuscaloosa, Alabama. DUI and pot possession.

February 21, 1968, Cain, Mississippi. Drunk driving and illegal gun possession.

Both states in the South, and both within a short time period.

Both involved driving a car under the influence.

Was that a theme or pattern, or just the shenanigans of a young, disillusioned former soldier from Vietnam acting out his immense frustrations?

He had mustered out in March 1967. So why the approximately ten-month period where he had not been arrested for anything at all? Wasn't it more likely that he would do his petty crime spree right after he'd gotten back?

What had happened to him in the intervening ten months? And after his arrest in Mississippi it seemed that Montgomery had cleaned up his act, at least until he had started committing far more serious crimes later, culminating in his execution.

He closed his eyes again and let his mind wander.

I wonder how many police officers it took to corral Montgomery on those two occasions?

Was it one cop car, two, four, six?

Only to find the driver drunk?

Back then drunk drivers were treated far more leniently. With a wink and a nudge and a night to sleep it off, with lots of coffee thrown in. That happened even when others were hurt or killed. And Montgomery apparently had hurt no one.

Tuscaloosa and Cain.

Both in 1968.

There might be one obvious common denominator.

He opened his laptop again, went online, and did another search.

January 1968, Tuscaloosa, Alabama.

On January 10, an NAACP office had been bombed. Four people were killed. Three civil rights activists and a lawyer from New York. All black.

No one had been arrested for the crime.

And Charles Montgomery had been there, arrested for DUI and possession of marijuana, and he'd posted bail the next day.

He did another search.

February 1968, Cain, Mississippi.

There were many things that had happened there that month. But one event was predominant and carried the most headlines and, now, the most digital ink.

On February 21, fifteen members of an African-American church, including the pastor and four young girls performing in the youth choir, had perished in a bombing.

And the next morning Charles Montgomery had had bail posted for his gun possession and drunk and disorderly charges.

Decker couldn't fathom the odds of the man being in the two cities at the same time these bombings were being perpetrated. If it were merely a coincidence, it was the mother of all serendipity.

He typed the name Nathan Ryan and added "Cain, Mississippi." Then he put in the word "bombing" and hit the return key.

He read through the first few results.

When he hit the fifth result, Decker found something that made him focus totally on the screen. It was an obituary of Nathan Bedford Ryan of Cain, Mississippi, who "left this life" on March 2, 1999.

He had been involved in local politics for thirty-seven years, rising to assistant mayor. He had actually died at his desk from a heart attack. That meant he had been on the job when he had bailed out Charles Montgomery, if it was indeed the same Nathan Ryan, and Decker felt sure it was.

He looked at the bail report again. The name listed was Nathan B. Ryan.

The name on the obituary was Nathan Bedford Ryan, probably after the Confederate general, Nathan Bedford Forrest.

As Decker continued reading through the obituary he stopped on one sentence:

"The deceased had been one of the first on the scene of the church bombing that had killed fifteen people."

So that's why Decker's addition of the word "bombing" had brought this up.

Thank you, Google.

The articles he had read on the church bombing did not list any survivors. So Decker wasn't sure what, if anything, Ryan had done when he'd arrived on the scene. Perhaps he had just been able to help retrieve bodies.

There was a grainy picture of Ryan. He was obviously white. Thus Decker wondered why Ryan had been so close to a black church that he had been one of the first on the scene. He imagined that in 1968, Cain would have been heavily segregated.

So Ryan had posted bail for Montgomery.

Ryan worked in the mayor's office.

Ryan was one of the first on the scene of the bombing.

And five hundred bucks for an assistant mayor in Cain in 1968 was not small change. And thus Decker wondered if the source of the funds had actually come from someone else.

These events had happened nearly fifty years ago. If Decker traveled to these places, would anyone still be around to talk to him about it?

He rose and went in search of Bogart.

After giving the FBI agent a thumbnail sketch of what he'd found, Bogart said, "What do you propose doing?"

"I propose going to wherever we need to go to solve this," replied Decker.

56

Decker, Bogart, Jamison, and Mars took a turboprop to Dallas and then a nonstop flight to Memphis. From there they were going to drive on to Cain in Mississippi. They had left Milligan back in Texas to oversee the search for Davenport and work with the other federal agents on the attack at the Marses' old house. Oliver had some casework to finish up and was to join them later.

The drive to Cain took nearly three hours. They had to drive through Tupelo to get there.

"Birthplace of Elvis," said Jamison when they passed the sign for Tupelo.

Bogart looked out the window and said dully, "At least it's not raining."

When they reached Cain, they drove directly to a police station. Bogart had called ahead, and a middle-aged woman from administration who introduced herself as Wanda Pierce was waiting for them. Pierce was dressed in slacks and a dark green blouse and also wore a nervous expression. She led them to a small conference room with a scarred table and banged-up chairs. The walls were cinderblock painted yellow.

They all sat.

"We don't get, um, many visits from the FBI," began Pierce awkwardly.

Bogart said, "We appreciate your taking the time to meet with us."

Decker said, "Can you tell us more about Nathan Ryan?"

She nodded and opened a file she had carried in. "I've lived in Cain all my life, and know some of the Ryans. But when Agent Bogart contacted the department I looked Ryan up to get some more details. He worked in the local government here for a long time. He died at his desk from a heart attack. This was nearly twenty years ago."

"He was the assistant mayor?" said Bogart.

"That's right." She looked at Mars. "Wait a minute, aren't you—?"

"He is," said Decker impatiently. "Who was the mayor at the time?"

"I thought you were interested in the *assistant* mayor," replied Pierce.

"I was. Now I'm interested in the mayor."

"Why?"

"Because in my experience assistant mayors never do anything without their bosses telling them they can. In this case bail out a drunk named Charles Montgomery."

"Oh, well, the mayor at the time went on to become a congressman."

"His name?"

"Thurman Huey."

Bogart said immediately, "I know that name."

Pierce nodded. "Mr. Huey is the son of Travis Huey, who was a governor of the state and then went on to the United States Senate in the 1950s and had a very distinguished career."

Bogart said, "And Thurman Huey isn't just a 'congressman.' He's the chairman of the Ways and Means Committee. Arguably the most powerful committee in Congress."

"Because it controls the federal government's purse strings," added Jamison.

"Yes," said Pierce. "And it's rumored that he might be the next Speaker of the House. That would put him number two in line to the presidency," she added proudly.

"And Thurman grew up here in Cain?"

"Born and raised. The Hueys are political royalty in Mississippi. And they've taken good care of us."

Decker said, "Meaning you get your full share of pork from Washington."

"Meaning we get our *fair* share," Pierce replied stiffly.

"And how old is he now?" asked Decker.

"I believe he's in his early seventies."

"So in 1968 he would have still been in his twenties?"

"I suppose so, yes."

"And he was *already* the mayor?"

"Well, his father was a real powerhouse. When his son decided to run, I think it was a foregone conclusion that Thurman would win election. No one was going to buck the old man. His political machine was too strong. Thurman could have won election solely on the Huey name."

"About the church bombing?" began Decker, switching gears. "Agent Bogart told you we were interested in that too."

"Yes, the Second Freeman's Baptist Church," said Pierce. "But I don't understand the connection between this Charles Montgomery person having bail posted by Mr. Ryan and the bombing."

"Join the club," said Decker. "What can you tell us about the bombing?"

"I wasn't even born when it happened, but it was one of the most horrible events ever to take place here. Fifteen people, including small children, died. The girls were in the youth choir. I think of them singing their hearts out and then that bomb going off. So terrible."

"And they never caught who did it?"

"No, they never did."

"Did they ever have any suspects?" asked Bogart.

"I took a look at the files after Agent Bogart made

his inquiry. This Montgomery person was never mentioned, if that's what you want to know."

"Anyone else?"

"Well, the KKK was around back then. Threats had been made. Other places in the South had been bombed, including that church in Birmingham in 1963. It was right at the height of the civil rights movements. Lots of bad things were happening. Hell, there were so many explosions in Birmingham they started calling the place 'Bombingham.'"

"How was the bombing *here* accomplished?" asked Decker.

"Dynamite."

"And no one saw anyone place the explosives?" asked Jamison.

"Apparently not."

Decker said, "In the information your office earlier provided to Agent Bogart it was said that the church was actually under police surveillance because of threats made against the church pastor, who had marched with Martin Luther King Jr. on numerous occasions. And the pastor had also joined in a lawsuit against the city of Cain and the state of Mississippi for discriminatory acts under the Civil Rights Act."

"Yes, that's right."

Decker said, "So how could someone plant a bomb large enough to blow up a church and kill fifteen people when the police were watching the place and no one sees them?"

Pierce simply shook her head. "That's anyone's guess."

"We need more than a guess," replied Decker.

"But it was so long ago, I don't see how you can find a definitive answer now."

"Well, in the Birmingham case they finally prosecuted some of the men for the crime many years after the fact. So maybe we can do the same here. Can you tell us about Thurman's father, Travis Huey?"

"What about him?"

"His politics."

"He was a good man. Did right by the state."

"I meant what was his position on the Civil Rights Act?"

Pierce frowned. "I have no way of knowing that."

"I would assume if he was governor and then the U.S. senator from Mississippi during the 1950s and beyond that his politics leaned more toward George Wallace than Hubert Humphrey?"

"I really couldn't say. I never knew him."

"But assuredly there must have been histories written about such a prominent man."

"Look, if you're asking whether Mr. Huey was a racist, I will just say that, based on my limited knowledge, he was a man of his time. And a states' rights man."

Decker said, "Does his son share those views?"

"This is not the 1950s," replied Pierce.

"The problem is not everyone seems aware of that," said Decker.

"If you want to know about Thurman Huey's beliefs, I suggest you take it up directly with him."

"In Mr. Montgomery's arrest record, only part of which we've seen, does it note *where* he was arrested?"

Pierce looked down at the file and sifted through a few pages. "Yes, it does."

"And how close was that location to the church?"

She seemed to stiffen, as though she had finally connected the dots in her mind. "Um, well, it actually seems that it was only a few blocks away from the church."

"And is it possible that the officers who were guarding the church were also the ones pursuing and then arresting Mr. Montgomery?"

"I have no way to determine that."

"You have the arrest report and the officers' names were surely on it."

"Yes, but I don't think there's any way to determine which officers were watching the church at that time."

"But it's possible that they were one and the same?"

"Anything is possible," she replied sharply.

"And what was the explanation given at the time as to how the bomb was planted and detonated while the church was supposedly under police protection?"

"I'm not sure any explanation was ever given, because no arrests were made. It seemed that folks assumed whoever did it slipped past the officers somehow."

"And the officers' testimony regarding their whereabouts at the time?"

"There was nothing in the file about that."

"But if they *did* pursue Montgomery and arrest him, that means the church would have been left unguarded, correct?"

"Accepting your premise, which I don't necessarily, the answer is yes."

"And the time of Mr. Montgomery's arrest was nine-ten in the evening?"

"That's what the files indicate, yes."

"And the time of the bombing?"

Pierce's gaze dropped to the file. Her voice shook slightly when she said, "The best guess was about nine-fifteen."

"Interesting coincidence," said Bogart sternly.

"Well, don't look at me, as I said, I wasn't even born at the time," retorted Pierce indignantly.

"And his obituary said that Nathan Ryan was one of the first on the scene," said Decker.

"I read that too, after Agent Bogart contacted me. I wasn't aware of it before."

"But the church was in a predominantly black area. It was nighttime. Why would Ryan have been in the area at all? Did he live close by?"

Pierce shrugged. "I have no idea."

"You said you know some of the Ryans?" asked Jamison.

"Yes."

"Could you get us their contact information?" said Bogart.

Pierce looked across at Decker with unfriendly eyes. "Are you really suggesting that this Montgomery person was used as a distraction to get the police on guard to leave their posts so the bombing could take place?"

"No, I'm suggesting that the local police knew exactly what was going on and were ordered to leave their posts to arrest Montgomery so the bomb could be planted and then detonated."

She paled. "*Ordered*? By whom?"

"Well, that's for us to find out," replied Decker.

57

After several phone calls made to various Ryans in town, they arrived at a small, neat bungalow in a modest suburban neighborhood. The houses were shaded with mature trees, and the laughter of children playing filtered through the air.

Mildred Ryan was in her late eighties and wispy white hair covered her pink scalp. Time had bowed her back and shrunk her frame. She wore large black-rimmed glasses that seemed to swallow her tiny face. She sat huddled in a shawl in a comfortable chair in a bedroom of the bungalow, which was owned by her daughter.

That daughter, Julie Smithers, was eyeing Decker and his group suspiciously as they stood in the doorway of the bedroom.

"I really don't see what my mother can tell you. It was a long time ago and her memory is not that good."

Smithers was short, built like a bulldog, and her face held the same stubborn features of that canine breed.

Bogart said smoothly, "We just want to ask a few questions. If she's not up to it we'll leave and come back another time."

Ryan looked up from the Bible she was reading, her finger touching each word. "Just tell them to come on in, Jules, and ask their questions. I'm up for it," she said in a drawl that signaled her Mississippi roots.

Decker said, "Doesn't seem to be anything wrong with her hearing."

"Just don't overtire her," warned Smithers.

She left and Decker and the others moved slowly into the room.

Ryan pointed to two chairs, one of which Jamison took, and the other one Bogart offered to Decker. He sat down and slid the chair closer to Ryan. Bogart and Mars stood behind him. She looked up at all of them.

"Haven't had this many visitors in years," she said.

Bogart showed her his badge and said, "Mrs. Ryan, thank you for meeting with us."

"You're welcome. And what is this about?"

Decker said, "Your husband, Nathan?"

"He's dead. Long time ago."

"We know. But we wanted to ask some questions about him. Having to do with the church bombing back in 1968. Do you remember that?"

The shrunken woman seemed to collapse inward even more at these words. "Hell, who could forget? All those little colored children. It . . . it was such a shame." She shook her head. "It's the devil's work. I said so then and I say so now."

"We understood that your husband was one of the first on the scene of the bombing. That's what his obituary said."

She froze for a moment and then looked up at Decker. "What exactly is all this about?"

"You know that no one was ever arrested for the murders?"

"I know that."

"Well, we're here to see if we can find out who did it."

"They're all probably dead."

"Maybe, but maybe not. If they were young back then they could still be alive. Like you are," he added.

She shook her head. "I don't know anything about that."

"But you might know more than you think," said Bogart.

She looked up and suddenly registered on Mars. "When I said 'colored' just now, I didn't mean any disrespect. Just the term we used back then. Should've said African American, or black. I'm sorry, young man."

"That's okay," said Mars.

"It was just different back then," mumbled Ryan. "Just different."

"But maybe you can answer some of our questions," prompted Decker.

"I'm old. I don't remember much. It was a long time ago. I ... I just want to be left alone." Ryan looked back down at her Bible, her finger moving along the words, her mouth opening as she silently read them.

Decker glanced at Jamison, who said, "Do you read from your Bible every day, Mrs. Ryan?"

Ryan nodded. "I'm on Deuteronomy. The fifth book of the Hebrew Bible. Do you know it? I find young people don't read the Bible anymore. Rather play video games or watch filth on the TV."

"Moses's three sermons to the Israelites," replied Jamison. This drew surprised stares from all the men, and Ryan as well.

Jamison explained, "My uncle was a minister. I used to help teach Sunday school. The Israelites were on the plains of Moab. They were about to enter the Promised Land. This was after the forty years of wanderings, which was explained in the first sermon."

"I'm impressed, child," said Ryan.

"Now, if memory serves me correctly," continued Jamison, "the third sermon talks about how if Israel is unfaithful and the loss of their lands follows, it can all be made right so long as they repent. I guess that was great comfort to them."

Ryan was staring at her. "Why?" she said in a fierce whisper.

"Well, like us, the Israelites were only human. They made mistakes. God understood that. So if they fell down, they had another chance to make it right. So long as they repented, repented of their sins. Tried to do the right thing. That takes real strength. And real faith."

Jamison fell silent and closely watched Ryan.

The old woman slowly closed her Bible, set it on the table next to the bed, clasped her hands in her lap, and said, "What sorts of questions do you folks have?"

Decker gave Jamison an appreciative glance and then turned back to Ryan.

"Do you know why your husband would have been so close to the church that night that he was one of the first on the scene after the bombing? From what we found out, there were houses all around the church, where I'm sure people ran out when the bombing happened. Was he driving by for some reason? Did he tell you about it?"

Ryan cleared her throat and took a moment to drink from a glass of water that sat next to her Bible. "Nathan was a good man. I want you to understand that. He *was* a good man," she said more emphatically.

"I'm sure he was," said Decker.

"Mississippi was falling apart back then. Hell, the whole South was. From the forties to the sixties and on. Riots, lynchings, shootings, things blown or burned up. Folks murdered. Federal marshals all over the place. The National Guard. Coloreds"—she stopped and shot Mars a glance—"I mean, African Americans, demanding things from the whites. It all shook us to our souls. That Thurgood Marshall winning all those court cases. Dr. King marching around like Sherman to the sea. Many folks saw it as the apocalypse."

"Did *you* see it that way?" asked Jamison.

"I was scared," she admitted. "The world I knew was turning upside down. Now, don't get me wrong. It didn't surprise me. Hell, if I'd been them, I'd have been demanding the same damn things. But, see, I wasn't them, if you can understand that." She glanced at Mars and then looked away. "And I was raised a certain way, and taught things that, thankfully, they don't teach anymore. At least out in the open," she added, with another nervous glance in the direction of Mars.

She grew quiet and no one interrupted the silence.

She continued, "Reverend Sidney Houston was the pastor at that church. He could deliver a sermon like no one else, I can tell you that."

"How did you know that?" asked Decker. "Did you ever attend a service?"

Her eyes grew wide behind the spectacles. "Oh my goodness, no. I would've been tarred and feathered and run out of town. But you see, Reverend Houston would sometimes take the sermon outside on the front lawn of the church. And his voice carried. It was deep and powerful. And, well, some of us would get close enough to hear. The man knew his scriptures. And delivered the message forcefully. Made the

church I went to seem downright boring by compari-
son."

"Okay," prompted Decker.

Ryan started talking faster and with more assur-
ance. "He was a firebrand, that man was. He was taking
on Cain like King was doing to Selma. Like that Marshall fellow had been doing to every court in the
South. And that brought him up against some very
powerful people hereabouts."

"Do you know who they were?" asked Decker.

"Nathan worked in the mayor's office. He was
assistant mayor, in fact, at the time."

"And the mayor was Thurman Huey," began
Decker.

She waved her hand dismissively. "The only reason
Thurman Huey had that job was because of his daddy.
He was barely out of college, still more boy than man.
Nathan rightly should have been the mayor, but once
Travis Huey spoke, that was that," Ryan added, the
bitterness clear in her tone. "You know, Travis Huey
was a hero to many of us back then. We saw him as
our protector."

"And now?" asked Jamison.

Ryan pointed to her Bible. "He was a false prophet,
spewing evil and hatred. And violence," she added.

"Do you think he had anything to do with the
church bombing?" asked Decker.

"Not Travis Huey. He'd never get his hands dirty."

"And his son?"

Now Ryan seemed to shrink once more. She shook her head. "I don't know one way or another."

"What about your husband?"

She let out a long sigh. "I think . . . I think Nathan had some inkling. Some . . ." Her voice trailed off and she suddenly looked panicked, as though these long-ago memories were surrounding her and there was no escape from them.

"He had an idea that something bad was going to happen?" suggested Decker. "And that was why he was near the church that night?"

She nodded almost imperceptibly, her frail shoulders quivering.

Jamison reached out and put a comforting hand on the old woman's arm. "Mrs. Ryan, it's okay. I think that your husband was trying to do the right thing."

Ryan sniffled, reached for a tissue and blew her nose. "He was a good man. But he didn't work with such good people."

"Did you know he posted bail, for five hundred dollars, for a man named Charles Montgomery?"

She rubbed her nose with the tissue. "He told me about that. Money sure didn't come from him. We didn't have that sort of cash to throw around. Certainly not for posting bail for someone we didn't even know."

"So he was told to do it? And given the money with which to do it?"

"Yes."

"Do you know by whom?"

"He was *assistant* mayor. Doesn't take a genius to figure that one out."

"So Thurman Huey?"

"Maybe his daddy gave him the money. I don't know. Travis was a Dixiecrat," added Ryan. "And he found good company in Washington. He almost derailed Thurgood Marshall being a Supreme Court justice, did you know that?"

"No, I didn't," said Decker.

"I didn't follow things like that, but my husband did. He didn't think much of the Hueys. But he lived in Mississippi and he kept his mouth shut. He went into politics to try to do good. But it was hard to do good in Mississippi back then if it meant doing good for black folks."

"That stance probably didn't make him popular," said Bogart.

"If you wanted a career in Mississippi back then you toed the line. He had a family to support, but that doesn't mean he believed what those others did. Because he didn't."

"I'm sure," said Jamison.

"But he did things, little things to help folks. He did it under the radar, so to speak." She looked at Mars. "He helped folks like you, to the extent he could."

"Sounds like a man ahead of his time," replied Mars.

She nodded. "Old LBJ lost the South when he got the Civil Rights Act passed. Southern Democrats turned their backs on him. Travis Huey sure as hell did. He was furious, Nathan told me."

Decker said, "You said that Travis Huey wouldn't get his hands dirty by being involved in the bombing and you said you didn't know if his son would, but do you think Thurman Huey might have been involved in the bombing?"

Ryan looked over at her Bible, reached for it, and opened it to where she had been reading. For a few moments Decker thought she was not going to answer.

"I will tell you that the apple doesn't fall from the tree, certainly not with the Hueys."

Decker looked at the others. "So you do think Thurman Huey was involved?"

"I don't know, but I can tell you that Thurman had two very good friends. The Three Musketeers, folks called 'em back then. They were right famous in town."

"Why was that?" asked Bogart.

"What else? High school football."

And despite Decker's asking several other questions, those were the last words the woman spoke.

58

They all sat in the car in front of Smithers's house staring out the windows.

Bogart spoke first. "The chairman of the Ways and Means Committee and possibly the next Speaker of the House. I have to admit, I didn't see that one coming."

Jamison said, "He was one of the Musketeers. I wonder who the other two were."

Decker said, "Easy enough to find out."

"Where?" asked Jamison.

It was Mars who answered. "High school football stars? Why don't we start there?"

Decker looked at him. "We'll make a detective out of you yet, Melvin."

Cain High School was smack in the center of town. They found the school office, made their request, and were quickly shuttled off to the library. There a young woman in slacks and a sweater greeted them.

"The Three Musketeers?" she said in response to their question. "I *have* heard that. It has to do with—"

"Football," answered Mars. "Back in the sixties. Thurman Huey?"

"Right, okay. I just started here a few years ago, but I can show you where all the yearbooks are."

They were led to a shelf on which were kept all the yearbooks for the school, dating back to the 1920s. They had already determined Thurman Huey's exact age, so they knew when he probably graduated from high school. Jamison found the right volume, and they gathered around looking over her shoulder as she slowly turned the pages.

Mars saw it first, probably because it was on the pages dedicated to the football team.

"The Three Musketeers," he said.

It was a photo of three young men in football uniforms. The caption below the photo read, "Thurman Huey, Danny Eastland, and Roger McClellan, the Three Musketeers."

Mars took the book and pointed to the three figures. "See how they're lined up? Huey's the QB, and the other two are the halfbacks. They're running a version of the veer offense. Off that they can run the triple option. We used to do a variation of that at UT sometimes."

"And that formation came into being during the 1960s, when they were in high school," added Decker.

Bogart studied the pictures of the young men. "So, Danny Eastland and Roger McClellan? Doesn't ring a bell."

"Already Googling," said Jamison.

She hit the keys on her phone, waited, and then studied the results. "Let me make sure this is the same Danny Eastland." She hit a few more keys and the results came up. She read quickly.

"Damn!"

"What?" said Decker.

"Danny Eastland has done well for himself. He's the founder and CEO of a government defense contractor. It says here they used to build weaponry, but about five years ago moved more to intelligence gathering, which turned out to be a smart move. Last year it had revenues of more than five billion dollars, most of it with the DOD. It's based in Georgia, but there's an office in Jackson, Mississippi, too, among many others. This article says he has a net worth of over a billion dollars and his primary home is in Atlanta."

"How about the other Musketeer?" asked Bogart.

Jamison did a search for Roger McClellan. "Holy shit!" she said when the results came up.

The three men looked at her.

"Well?" said Bogart.

She looked up at him. "Roger McClellan is the current police chief of Cain, Mississippi."

Decker said, "Ironic, if he was part of a terrorist act against a church in the very same town."

Bogart said, "Okay, we need to start marching very lightly here. Folks here already know we're making inquiries about the Hueys. And I bet Pierce from the police station has already reported our meeting to McClellan."

"And he's probably already contacted Huey and Eastland," said Jamison.

"I'm sure he has," agreed Bogart. "So we have to be very careful. The last thing we need is to get pulled off the case because the FBI director gets a call from a pissed-off Huey."

"There's no statute of limitations on murder," Decker pointed out.

"Granted, but in D.C., Thurman Huey is an eight-hundred-pound gorilla."

"Wait a minute," said Jamison. "Do you think they're the ones who kidnapped Davenport? That would make it a very recent crime."

Bogart shook his head. "I can't believe Thurman Huey would be involved in something like that."

Decker said, "If Roy Mars has evidence that Huey was involved in the church bombing, and that evidence comes to light, Huey won't just lose his career, he could very well end up in prison for the rest of his life. Given that, I think the man might be capable of anything."

Mars said, "What sort of evidence would my dad have?"

"Whatever was in the safe deposit box," said Decker.

In a shaky voice Mars said, "You think *he* was involved in the bombings?"

"I don't know, Melvin. But somehow he ended up with something that will bury some very powerful men. No wonder he went on the run and changed his name."

Mars tried to say something but nothing came out. He finally just shook his head.

Decker returned the book to the shelf while the others headed to the door. He had a sudden thought, opened the yearbook to a certain page, scanned down it, and then ripped the page out and put it in his pocket. He did this one more time with another page. He replaced the book on the shelf and joined the others as they headed back to the car.

They all climbed in and Bogart started it up. He said, "Okay, we have a lot of work ahead of us. But as I said before, we step lightly. I don't want any specific details getting out to the locals."

"Oh crap," said Jamison, who was looking out the rear window. "I think it's too late."

They all turned.

A police cruiser was pulling up behind them.

59

Two male officers got out. They were both in their forties, a bit gray around the temples, a bit soft around the middle. They walked up, one on either side of the car.

Bogart rolled down his window. He already had his FBI ID out.

The officer leaned in. "How you folks doing?"

"Just fine, Officer," said Bogart.

The man looked at the ID. "Right. We heard y'all were in town. It's why we're here. Chief McClellan wanted to know if there was anything at all that we could do to assist you in whatever you're investigating?"

"We appreciate that very much," said Bogart. "But right now I can't think of anything."

Decker was staring out the passenger window at the officer parked there staring back at him. One of the man's hands rested on the butt of his service pistol.

Decker gave him a nod and a smile.

Neither was returned.

The officer at Bogart's window said, "Just as a

matter of professional courtesy do you think y'all could find the time to come meet with the chief? He prides himself on knowing all that goes on here, and I think you might find him an asset to help you in whatever it is that brought you to our fine town."

Though it was spoken as a request, the tone of the words suggested that a refusal would not be very welcome.

"Certainly," said Bogart.

They followed the patrol car back to a different station from the one where they had met Pierce, parked, and then the officers escorted them inside and down the hall. One of them rapped on a door that was fronted with a plaque reading *Roger G. McClellan, Chief of Police.*

"Come on in," said a firm voice.

The officer opened the door, motioned the four in, and then shut the door behind them.

The office was large, twenty by twenty, with fine paneling and shelves holding a lifetime of awards and commendations in the law enforcement field. One wall was the photo wall of fame, showcasing McClellan in the company of various dignitaries, professional athletes, and famous singers, mostly country and western. In one area of the space were leather chairs and a comfortable couch and a coffee table with an assortment of magazines on it, predominantly cop and gun publications.

The state flag of Mississippi stood in a holder behind the enormous, intricately carved desk.

There was no sign of the Stars and Stripes.

Sitting behind the desk was a tall man who, despite his advancing years, looked fit and trim. He was wearing his dress uniform, the chest festooned with medals and ribbons. His gray mustache was trimmed and his thinning hair was slicked back. His face looked like a slab of granite that had been worked over by rushing water for a couple of centuries.

He rose and put out a hand. "Chief McClellan," he said, shaking hands with each of them. "Please, take a seat." He came around the desk and directed them to places among the couch and chairs before sitting down across from them.

"Y'all want something to drink? Coffee ain't half bad, but we got some bottled water too."

They politely declined.

McClellan sat back and looked them over. "I appreciate you coming on in. Sure you can understand that when the FBI comes calling I prick up my ears."

"Absolutely. I take it you talked to Ms. Pierce?" said Bogart.

"Hell, I didn't need to rely on that. Fact is, in a small town, news travels fast. Eyes and ears everywhere." He reached over with a long arm and picked up a mug off his desk and took a sip from it.

Decker noted that the cup was imprinted with the words *Virtute et armis*.

McClellan saw him looking and said, "Official motto of the great state of Mississippi."

"'By valor and arms,'" said Decker.

"You read Latin?"

"No, I just remember seeing it somewhere."

McClellan put down the mug. "So what brings you folks here?" He gazed around until he stopped on Mars. "Now, I know you. But you're not FBI."

"No, I'm Melvin Mars."

"Damn, yes you are. Watched you play football when you were in college. Now, I'm an Ole Miss grad, played ball for 'em too. Glad I never had to tackle you. Like a Mack truck with a Ferrari engine. Helluva player, son."

"Thanks."

Decker closed his eyes while McClellan was talking, and then a light seemed to click on in his head as he made the relevant connection.

Ole Miss.

He opened his eyes.

McClellan said, "And I heard about your, um, situation. Glad you're out now. Seemed like quite an injustice."

"I saw it that way," said Mars tersely.

McClellan swiveled his attention back to Bogart. "So, anything you can tell me?"

"We're just looking into some things from the past that may have bearing on a more recent case."

McClellan nodded. "Look, I'm not going to waste

your time, Agent Bogart. I'm busy and I know you're busy. I know you've been making inquiries about the bombing of the church that took place here in 1968. As you know, no one was ever arrested. Damn frustrating. When I joined the force many moons ago I had a go at it, just like everybody on the Cain Police Force seems to do."

"And did you make any progress?"

"Not a lick, but it wasn't for lack of tryin'. It's a black mark on the town's reputation, I can tell you that. Would like nothin' better than to solve the thing, but after all this time?" He shrugged. "So, do you see any daylight?"

Bogart shrugged too. "It's early days yet."

McClellan looked at Mars again. "And since Mr. Mars is here, am I to take it that he is in some way connected?"

"That remains to be seen. We have a long way to go and other stops to make."

"Where might they be?" asked McClellan.

"Not in Mississippi. This is a multistate inquiry. I can tell you that if we require any assistance in Mississippi, you'll be the first one we call."

"Well, a man can't ask for more than that."

He rose and so did the others. They shook hands again.

McClellan lingered the longest on Mars. "Glad you got a second chance, young man. Sure you'll make the most of it. Hope the future is good to you. Better'n the past. Just keep looking forward. Not back. You'll do fine."

Mars looked at him strangely but nodded.

They walked out of the police station and back to their car.

Jamison shuddered. "Okay, he was polite enough so why do I feel like I just had a powwow with a sociopath?"

Mars said, "And he wants me to focus on the future, not the past."

"I think that particular message was meant for all of us," said Decker.

"And he also made it clear that nothing happens in this town that he doesn't know about," said Bogart.

Jamison said, "And Pierce will have told him what we were asking about. He's probably going to send over some thugs to grill poor Mrs. Ryan and she'll tell them about the Three Musketeers reference. Then he'll know he's in the crosshairs."

Bogart said, "I might need to call in some more agents. I'm feeling exposed here."

"We shouldn't have come in so hard," said Jamison. "But then again, we didn't know one of the major players was the freaking police chief."

"And maybe we turn that to our advantage," said Decker.

"How?" asked Bogart.

"Let's send in the dog to flush the birds."

The Last Mile

"How do you propose to do that?" asked Bogart.

Decker said, "I'll meet you at the hotel." He turned and walked back into the police station.

60

A few minutes later Decker sat across from McClellan in the latter's office.

The man looked him over. "Don't take this the wrong way, son, but you look a little out of shape to be in the FBI."

"You should have seen me *before* I went on the diet." Decker fell silent, studying the policeman.

"Is there something else you'd care to discuss?" asked McClellan. "I take it your friends have headed on?"

"They've got other things to check out. But I thought I'd come back and talk to you."

"Really? About what?"

"The Four Musketeers?"

"Come again?"

"The Four Musketeers?"

"You mean the Three Musketeers, don't you? Like in the story? Or am I missing something?"

"I was thinking more local. And I was counting Charles Montgomery as the fourth Musketeer."

"Who?"

"You played football with him at Ole Miss, didn't you? Because he was on the team at the same time you were."

"Couldn't tell you. Long time ago. Memories fade."

"But you don't have to worry about him. He's dead. Executed by the state of Alabama. But I'm sure you knew that."

"No, I didn't."

"I might have misspoken."

"Do tell."

"The Three Musketeers, like it said in the Cain High School yearbook. You, Danny Eastland, and Thurman Huey. You guys ran the veer, two halfbacks and one quarterback. Huey was the QB, you and Eastland were the bangers. Did it work well for you?"

"Danny was more of a scatback. I did the hard running. But we won two state championships in a row. And in Mississippi, football rests only one rung below going to church as a state pastime."

"I'm sure. So anyway, the Three Musketeers. Friends for life."

"Is this going somewhere that I can understand?"

"Try this one on. Was it your idea to have Montgomery drive by drunk so the cops on duty would have an excuse to give chase and let you boys do your little dirty deed? Or was that the QB Huey talking? Because that was Montgomery's role: the drunk driver who diverted the cops from guarding the NAACP office in Tuscaloosa and then later at the church here in Cain."

McClellan gave him a pitying look. "You're speaking gibberish, I'm afraid. Do I need to check you for being intoxicated?"

Decker sat back and assumed a deliberately thoughtful expression, though he had very little to think about, actually. He knew exactly how this was going to play out.

"Now, it might be that Roy Mars, or whatever his name was, was the *fourth* Musketeer, not Montgomery, though Chucky did provide the distraction at both bombing sites. You would have known Roy under his real name, not the fake one. His first name begins with an 'A' and his last name begins with a 'C.' That's all I know." Decker paused before delivering the hammer blow. "He didn't tell me what his real name was when he met with me a short time ago."

The only discernible reaction by the police chief to this information was a slight facial tic that Decker had not observed previously because it wasn't there.

Decker pretended to look confused. "I'm sorry, maybe you didn't know he was still alive. The stuff back in Texas? All smoke and mirrors. Cost Melvin twenty years of his life for something he didn't do."

McClellan licked his lips. "So you're saying this Roy person is alive?"

"Very much. He stuck a knife against my throat while I was sleeping. Very formidable guy. Kill you without blinking. But then you knew that he might still be alive. Or at least you had to assume that when Montgomery came forward to get Melvin out of prison. The only reason he would have done that is if Roy had come forward and bribed him. And Roy couldn't do that if Roy was dead. The Three Musketeers weren't going to pay a dime to get Melvin out of prison."

"Actually, I don't know what the hell you're talking about. I think we already established that."

"Don't worry. I'm not wearing a wire. Probably illegal if I even tried. But you want me to keep talking, right?" Decker half rose. "Or do you want me to just head on out? Your call."

McClellan spread his hands. "In my book knowing more is always better than knowing less."

"I thought you'd see it that way," said Decker, sitting back down. "So anyway, he has the goods, Chief. I know you don't want to hear that, but he does. All these years coming back to bite you in the ass. I know it can't be easy."

"The goods?"

"Hard evidence. No statute of limitations on murder. You know that."

"I do indeed, though I'm missing a few steps that you seem to have already made." He chuckled. "You're too quick for me."

"I'm not here to ask you to confess. That's not

going to happen. You'll play stupid till they lethal inject you."

McClellan took a sip from his mug. "You've lost me again, big fella. What's your name again?"

"Amos Decker. Did you know I played football for Ohio State? Melvin ran all over my ass when we played UT. Best running back I've ever seen, and I saw and played with some good ones." He leaned forward. "But the thing is, Chief, I'd take Melvin any day with his cleats in my face over his old man."

"Really? Why is that, son?"

"Because Melvin has a conscience. His old man doesn't. It was clear that he believed you boys screwed him over. And then when you found him out and came after him in Texas, that cost him everything. Roy had to shotgun his wife in the face. Only person he probably ever loved. Sent his son to prison. But that was small potatoes next to losing Lucinda. The guy's only thinking about revenge now. And when he had that knife against my throat he told me what he was going to do to all of you."

"Did he now?"

"I have hyperthymesia, do you know what that is?"

McClellan shook his head. "No idea. Sounds like that ADD thing."

"It means I have perfect recall. Can never forget anything. So for me, time doesn't heal all wounds. Because I remember them just as clearly this moment as the day they happened, regardless of the interval of time."

"Doesn't sound too good."

"It sucks, actually."

"And your point?"

"Roy Mars may have that same condition, but only with *one* memory that he holds. His wife. Time has not healed the man's wounds over her. He has to blame someone. And he blames the three of you. And that is not good for your future well-being."

McClellan edged forward. "Excuse me, son, but are you threatening me?"

"You're a police chief, but face it, this is a podunk town. Roy could take you out when you're drinking a beer at the local watering hole, or flipping burgers on your Weber, no sweat. Danny Eastland, now maybe he's a tougher nut because he's got money, but eventually he'll go down too because even a mountain of cash means nothing when you have a psychopath like Roy coming after you. And then we have Thurman Huey, the big congressman on the Hill. But even he doesn't have special protection unless he gets elected as Speaker. So bang-bang-bang. And see the biggest advantage that Roy Mars has is he doesn't care if he dies. In fact, I believe he wants to die. But not before finishing the game."

"So you think this is a game, do you?"

Decker rose. "Actually, I don't. No more than those people in the church or the NAACP office thought it was a game when you assholes blew them into the next life."

"You're making some very wild accusations. I could get you on slander."

"By the time you file the papers, you'll either be Roy's next victim and resting on a morgue slab, or else we'll have enough evidence to take it from a slander case against me to a capital murder case against *you*."

Decker headed to the door, but then turned back.

"Oh, one more thing. Roy Mars murdered Charles Montgomery's wife. You don't have to know why, just that he did. And his choice of murder weapon was an explosive device so sophisticated that the police could find no trace of it. Boom, she was gone, just like that. Sort of like the church, right? I wonder, did he make the explosive in that one too? If so, the man knows what he's doing, that's for damn sure." Decker looked around. "Maybe he's already planted one in here. Or in your car. Or at your house."

"What the hell do you want from me?" asked McClellan.

"That's the thing, Chief. I don't need anything from you. Nothing at all."

Decker opened the door and walked out.

61

So what did you think you'd accomplish?" said Bogart to Decker.

The two sat in Bogart's room at the hotel in the town square of Cain.

Decker drank down a Coke and wiped his mouth. "I told him what I told him. He's not going to stand pat. He's going to do something. Make a call. Send an email. Get in a car. Jump on a plane."

"You really think he's going to crack? He struck me as a pretty hardened guy."

"I told him somebody even tougher is after him."

"Roy Mars?"

Decker nodded. "And did you notice something about McClellan's office?"

"What in particular?" said Bogart.

"On his photo wall of fame."

"There were lots of pictures. I saw one of him and Thurman Huey, in fact."

"I wasn't talking about that. I was talking about one that wasn't there."

"I don't get that," said Bogart.

"There was a picture on the wall that's no longer there. You could see where the wall was darker."

"Why would he take a picture down?"

"Only one reason," said Decker. "We would have recognized whoever was in it."

"Who the hell could that have been?"

"I don't know."

Bogart glared at him. "Why don't I believe you?"

"And there's something else. McClellan tried to act surprised, but he knew Roy was alive. I mean he really knew. Not just speculation."

"How?"

"I don't know, but McClellan is going to make a mistake. We just need to be there when he does."

"And if, instead, he and his buddies get their acts together and stonewall us?"

"That's always a possibility."

"I wish that you had discussed your strategy with me before you went ahead and deployed it."

"I was just trying to seize the moment. What do we know so far?"

"I put tracers on his phones and his Internet connections. I have local agents watching his movements. If he does snap and goes running or emailing to one of the other Musketeers, we'll know about it. But so far, nothing."

Decker checked his watch. It was late.

"I think we need to get some sleep."

★

Melvin Mars was tossing and turning when his phone buzzed at two in the morning. He snatched it up and looked at the screen.

Out by the car in ten. We need to talk. Decker.

"Shit," muttered Mars.

He struggled into his clothes and left his room. It was a short walk to the parking lot. He found the car and looked around.

"Mellow?"

Mars froze at the name. Then he slowly turned.

His father stood ten feet away, next to another parked car.

"How did you—" began Mars.

"I got your contact info off your buddy's phone when I broke into his motel room before. He should really use a password. You just assumed the text was from Decker because I used his name."

"Dad, what the hell are you doing?"

"Not here. Let's take a ride." He pointed to the car.

Mars took a step back.

"Come on, Mellow, if I wanted to hurt you I could have done it anytime I wanted."

"Where are we going?"

"Just for a ride. Then I'll bring you back here. I promise."

"But do I get back breathing or not?"

"I promise, Mellow. I'm not going to hurt you. I figure I did a good enough job of that already."

Mars looked around and then walked toward his

father. They climbed into the car and Roy backed out, reached the main road, and accelerated.

There were no stars out, the clouds were gathering, and not another car was on the road.

Mars eyed his father. "You got a limp?"

"Yeah, getting old." He glanced at his son as he drove. "You have to hate me, Mellow. If you don't, something's wrong in your head."

"I want to try to understand why you did what you did."

"I told the fat guy some."

"Yeah, he told me some too, but not all. Probably to spare my feelings."

Roy laughed. "I don't have that problem."

"You did with Mom."

The smile vanished on Roy's face.

"You killed her, didn't you? Shot her in the face with my gun."

"The cancer was going to eat her brain. We had no money for treatments. The doctors told us . . ."

"Where did you go to get the diagnosis?"

"Mexico. Your mom and me spent time there. And they had experimental stuff, but nothing to help her. And we didn't want anyone in town to know. Just in case."

"Decker said she might've been a slave in Cali. And that she stole that silver teapot when she got away."

"The fat guy has a big brain, then. She wasn't exactly a slave, but she wasn't free either. They had plenty of money. She got fed. Had a roof over her head. But . . . she wasn't free to go. And they weren't exactly nice to her."

"So how did she get away?"

"That's how we met. I was down there working a job. The folks holding your mom knew the people I worked for. They had car problems. I went there to fix them. They lived in a damn castle, drove Rolls-Royces and Bentleys, never worked a day in their lives. But when I went there I found out about your mom. We had talks. Then we made plans. Then I got her out of there."

"Did you kill them?"

Roy looked at him. "And would it matter to you if I did?"

Mars looked out the window.

Roy said, "We took the teapot, not to sell. You know we kept it. Your mom just wanted something from them, after all they did to her."

"How could you have killed her, Dad?"

Roy noticeably winced. He pulled the car off the road, cut the lights, and put it in park.

"You think I woke up one morning and decided to shotgun her in the head? Do you!?"

"What I know is that you planned this meticulously. You killed some guy and made it look like you were dead too. And then you set me up to take the fall. Instead of playing in the NFL, I spent half my life behind bars. I was almost executed."

"I wasn't going to let them kill you, Mellow."

Mars slammed his fists so hard against the dashboard that it dented.

"My damn name is Melvin."

The only sounds for the next minute were the breathing of the two men.

"Okay, *Melvin,* everything you just said is true. I killed the dude. Your mom switched his dental records. I killed her. I set the bodies on fire. I got the chick and the motel dude to do what they did. I disabled your car. I framed you. You went to prison because of me."

"Why? Why did you do that to me?"

"It was the safest place for you. Your mom thought so too."

"Bullshit!" roared Mars.

In response, Roy pulled out his gun. But instead of pointing it at Mars, he laid it on the seat between them.

"Then pick up this gun, point it at my head, and pull the fuckin' trigger, *Mellow.* If you got the balls."

Mars looked down at the gun, disbelief on his features. Then he slowly reached down, picked it up, and pointed it at his father.

"Shit, you don't even know how to hold a pistol the right way. It's not a shotgun. Use your dominant hand to make the pull, the other to brace, even at this distance. Hell, it don't matter, you can hardly miss from where you're sitting. But my blood and brains will literally be on your hands."

Roy calmly looked away and stared out the windshield, aimlessly whistling a tune under his breath.

Mars said, "I think you want me to kill you."

"Part of me does. Just end it. I'm tired, Melvin. It's been a long time. None of it good."

"And the Three Musketeers?"

To this Roy laughed out loud. "Saw you going to talk to McClellan. How is old Roger? He likes dressing up with all those medals on his uniform. After he graduated from Ole Miss he got multiple deferments from 'Nam. Same for Thurman and Danny. Their dads saw to that. They were all way too busy back here killing coloreds to go fight the Vietcong. And the Vietcong fired back. Big, damn difference."

"Were you in Vietnam?"

"You going to shoot me or not?"

Mars slowly lowered the gun and placed it on the seat between them.

Roy gave him a disdainful look and put the weapon away in his shoulder holster.

Mars said, "You were at the house. You saved us from that fire."

Roy shrugged.

"Why?"

"Why not."

"Because you don't seem to be the sort who really minds people dying very much."

"That was *our* house. Your mother's and mine. They had no right to come there. And I told the fat guy I had your back."

"That's why you did all this, right? The ESPN thing?"

Roy shrugged. "You were so famous, Mellow. It was gonna happen one day. Your mother prayed every night that it wouldn't, but in our hearts we knew those prayers were not going to be answered one day. And then that day came."

"And did they contact you? Threaten you?"

"Let's just say that they never let the grass grow under their feet."

"But didn't you have plastic surgery? That scar?"

Roy laughed. "I didn't have two dimes to rub together. That scar was from a fight over a girl."

"What girl?"

"Your mother. You're right. I did kill the people who had her. All of them. They deserved it."

"And Mom still went with you? A killer?"

"You wouldn't ask that question if you saw what they did to her."

"I thought you said it wasn't that bad."

"I lied. It was hell. She was the family hooker and maid. They even let the guests have a go."

"Did you kill Regina Montgomery?"

"She was an idiot. All she needed to do was go off into the sunset. But before her husband was even fried she was out buying shit and screwed it all up."

"Why did you approach them in the first place?"

"Isn't it obvious? To keep you from being executed."

"You let me stay in prison for twenty years."

"But I wasn't going to let them kill you."

"Why?"

"Because I promised your mother I wouldn't."

"I just don't get you. I don't know who the hell you are."

Roy turned to him. "All you need to know is that I loved your mother more than anything. I sacrificed everything I had for her. I would have done anything for her."

"You killed her!"

Roy screamed, "Because she told me to!"

The interior of the car suddenly did not seem large enough to hold both men at the same time. Mars just stared numbly out the windshield, seemingly unable to turn his gaze toward his father.

Roy said in a strained voice, "And I did it. Because I always did anything she asked of me. Even that." He turned to Mars. "She wasn't the only one who died that night. Because I died too."

"And you put me in prison."

Roy rubbed at his face. "They would have killed you, don't believe otherwise."

"Because they think I have what was in that safe deposit box."

Roy's features hardened. "Decker again? He's one

smart prick. I should've slit his throat when I had the chance."

"*Chocha*," said Mars.

Roy looked at him. "What about it?"

"It means playing possum. Playing dead. Like you did."

"As I said, better prison than a grave. These guys were serious people. Kill you to look at you."

"Did you bomb the church? And the NAACP office? Did you?"

"You're getting way ahead of yourself."

"Simple questions. Yes or no?"

"What, you want a confession?"

"They were little kids, Dad. In a choir."

Roy looked away. "They weren't supposed to be there. Choir practice ran late, I guess."

"But you still did it."

"That part was out of my hands."

"Okay, so you're completely innocent?"

Roy laughed. "You'll never hear those words come out of my damn mouth."

"Decker told McClellan that you were coming for them. To scare them."

"Is that right? Like I could give a shit."

"Really? Aren't they the reason you had to kill Mom? I mean, if they weren't around, if you'd had the balls to finish them off way back when?"

Roy stared down at his hands. "It wasn't that simple."

"So why don't you tell me about it, Dad? You brought me out here. You obviously wanted to talk. So why don't you tell me how a guy who married a 'colored' woman that he loved more than life itself could be part of a group that blew up black kids? Why don't you tell me that?"

"Easy enough. I was a racist asshole. Just like McClellan and his buddies."

"Was?"

"Until I met your mother."

"What, then all your racist tendencies just vanished?"

"No. But I never hurt anyone like that again."

"You hurt me! I'm black. You stole my life. Your own son."

Roy turned to look at Mars. "The thing is, Mellow, you're *not* my son. Your mother was pregnant when I rescued her."

Mars sat there staring at him. "You're not my father?" he finally managed to say.

"No. I'm not."

"Then who was?" gasped Mars.

"A prick who raped your mom over and over. Until I made him stop. By slitting his throat."

62

Mars stood in the parking lot and watched the tail-lights of the car disappearing as the rain started to sprinkle. He had never felt this disconnected from every other person on earth. It was like the plague had come and he was the only one left breathing. He actually would have welcomed the absolute solitude. He didn't want to talk to anyone else ever again.

When the last wink of car lights vanished, it was as though someone had cut off his blood flow. Mars sank to the asphalt, first on his knees and then onto his belly.

He had so much rolling through his head that he couldn't process it. He couldn't even try. He felt sick. His limbs didn't seem to work.

He just lay there for a while until the rain picked up.

He finally stood, staggered to his room, and collapsed on the bed and just lay there. An hour went by, and slowly he rose and sat on the side of the bed.

His father was not his father.

The man was a killer.

He had set him up for murder. He had cost him twenty years of his life.

His entire life was bullshit.

He left his room and knocked on Decker's door. A few groans and mutterings later the door opened.

"Why are you up this early?" said Decker. Then he saw the look on Mars's face and quickly ushered him in.

Mars sat down and told Decker what had just happened.

Decker didn't say a word until he had finished.

"I'm sorry, Melvin."

"I don't want your damn sympathy. I just want to get to the bottom of this."

"Well, I'm working on it," said Decker.

Mars slowly lifted his head. "Did you know he wasn't my father?"

"Why do you ask me that?"

"Because you seem to know every damn thing, that's why. So, did you?"

Decker didn't answer.

"Decker!"

"Does it really matter?"

"Yes."

"Okay, I *suspected*."

"How?"

"Guy never said he loved you."

"How the hell did you know that?"

"You told us. When you were under hypnosis. And he framed you for murder, Melvin. Don't know many dads who would do that. What he did with Montgomery he did for your mom. And when he said he hadn't framed his son, he was being quite literal. You *weren't* his son. But none of that is your issue. It's on him."

"It doesn't feel that way."

"Maybe not now." Decker shifted in his seat and then did the same to the direction of the conversation. "Any idea where he went?"

"Really wasn't focusing on that."

"What else can you tell me?"

"I told him you had threatened McClellan and those guys with my da— I mean, with Roy going after them."

"And what did he say to that?" Decker asked.

"That he doesn't give a crap about those guys."

"And you believe him?"

"Well, since he's lied to me about pretty much everything, I really don't know."

"I don't believe him. Maybe he didn't want those guys before, but now I think he does."

"Why?" asked Mars.

"He strikes me as a guy who doesn't like to lose. The Three Musketeers need what Roy has. And they'll do anything to get it. Including killing Roy. And you. And us. That's the setup. And I don't think Roy will go quietly. Did he say anything about what he has on them?"

Mars shook his head. "But it was in the safe deposit box. I'm sure of that."

"And did he help bomb the church here?"

"He didn't say. But he did say he was a racist ass-hole like the other guys."

"Until he met your mother?"

"Shit, Decker, are you a mind reader or what?"

"Pretty simple, Melvin. A guy who's still a racist would not marry a black woman."

"Yeah, right," said Mars dully. "He said . . . he said he killed my real father. Who was a rapist."

"Yeah, you said."

"So I've got a rapist for a father and a killer for a stepfather."

"And what does that have to do with you person-ally? You didn't pick either of those scenarios to happen."

"I'm still in the middle of it."

"And we're going to get you out of it, Melvin."

Mars shook his head. "I don't think even you're *that* good. I'm screwed, man. For all I know Texas is going to find a way to put my butt back in prison. Maybe that's where I belong."

"If you really think that, go turn yourself in."

"What?"

"I don't do self-pity, Melvin. Never had time for it. And neither do you. You told me you were with me on this. I don't need you to rethink that. It's a waste of both our time."

"You don't sugarcoat anything, do you?"

"My brain's not wired that way."

"Lucky you."

"You'd be surprised at how unlucky I am sometimes."

"It was like I was living with a stranger all those years. The man I thought I knew, I didn't know at all."

"The point is, Melvin, you knew your mother. And she *did* love you. There's no fraud there. And her love made a guy like Roy do things he ordinarily wouldn't do. Like saving you from execution. So maybe he didn't love you. So he wasn't your father. I think your mom had enough love for you to make up for all of that."

Mars was silent for a few moments. "I thought you said your brain wasn't wired for stuff like that."

"I understand love and what it can do to people, Melvin, both good and bad. No matter how much my brain has changed I'll always understand that."

63

Decker sat on the edge of his bed. It was still dark outside and Mars had gone back to his room. Decker had told him to say nothing of what had happened to anyone for now.

Decker wasn't sure why he had wanted this, only that something didn't feel right.

Should they go on to Tuscaloosa? When he knew the answer to the mystery was right here?

The Three Musketeers.

McClellan, Eastland, Huey.

Decker felt like he knew the truth. He just had no way to prove it. What he needed was evidence. Apparently, Roy Mars had that in abundance. The only problem was, he had no way to get to Roy Mars. And even if he did, how would he convince him to give up what he had? Mars was a killer too. They knew he had murdered Regina Montgomery. He had practically confessed to Melvin that he was involved in the bombings. If they caught up to him he would be going to prison for the rest of his life. Maybe he would be facing the death penalty.

The man had no incentive to cooperate. Even if they could offer him a deal, there was no way it would not involve lengthy prison time. And at Roy's age, that equated to a life sentence. Not something he could see the savvy Roy readily accepting.

So the Three Musketeers suddenly became the Three Untouchables.

But Decker could not leave it at that. People had to be held accountable for what they did. He didn't care how many years had passed. People were still dead because of what they had done. And the killers had all gone on to fine careers and, in Eastland's case, great wealth.

Decker pondered some more.

Contents of a safe deposit box. There was no way Roy would carry it around with him. Too easy to lose if he got caught.

He wouldn't leave it in any place he was staying for the same reason.

On the other hand, it would have to be easily accessible.

That narrowed things down a bit, but hardly enough.

It still involved lots of possible hiding places.

It had not been in the home. Too dangerous. Lots of eyeballs all over it. And now the fire.

So where?

He flipped his frames of memory back to his lone meeting with Roy Mars. He went over every observation, every word spoken. Next, he considered what Roy had told Melvin, searching for anything helpful.

It wasn't like he thought Roy had purposefully put some sort of code or reference to the hiding place in his words. It would be subtler than that.

It might even be unintentional.

Was there something?

If there was, it was not coming to him.

And they still had heard nothing from Davenport's kidnappers. Why snatch someone for no reason?

Well, one didn't. There had to be a reason. But if not for ransom or leverage, what then?

Again, Decker couldn't think of an answer.

So back to the original question: Should they head to Tuscaloosa? They would see where the bombed NAACP office had been. They knew Montgomery had been there. Bailed out by a confederate or lackey of one of the Three Musketeers?

They couldn't show that, because the records were long since gone.

They had nothing to even take into court. They couldn't even get a search warrant. And what would they be searching for anyway?

Three guilty men were potentially going to walk.

Decker slumped back on the bed, as depressed as he'd been in a while.

His phone rang. He checked the time.

Five minutes past six.

It was Bogart. His voice was strained.

"I'm being recalled to D.C. along with my whole team."

"Why?"

"The FBI is trying to build a new headquarters. The Hoover Building is falling apart."

"And what does that have to do with you?"

"Apparently there have been inquiries from Capitol Hill about the Bureau wanting appropriations for the new facility at the same time that we are, quote, 'wasting taxpayer funds on needless investigations.' So I'm being recalled to go and testify on the Hill and this investigation is being suspended."

"Let me guess, the Ways and Means Committee?"

"Thurman Huey is apparently more subtle than that. It was one of the subcommittees, of which there are apparently an endless number. He won't appear in this at all. His hands will be clean. But I have to go."

"Understood."

"Anything I need to know before I do go?"

Decker debated whether to tell him about Mars's run-in with Roy. But what could Bogart do about that? He had to go to D.C. to save his career. Let him focus on that.

"Nothing. Good luck."

"I think you'll need more luck than me, Decker. And I'm sorry about this. Seems like I keep popping in and out of this."

"Nature of the beast."

Decker clicked off and lay back down again.

The Last Mile

The Three Musketeers' counterattack had begun.

Huey had fired his salvo.

He just wondered what McClellan and Eastland were planning.

His plan to spook them might just have backfired.

Big-time.

64

"Gone?"

Jamison stared across at Decker at their table in the motel's dining room.

Decker nodded. Mars was beside him.

"It's Huey's doing." Decker glanced at Mars. "Tell her about last night."

Mars took a few minutes to fill her in.

When he'd finished she said, "Okay, so Roy's not going to help us. The FBI's been knocked off the case. We have no proof of anything. Which means we're right now in the lion's den with no cover."

"You want to get out of town?" asked Decker.

"I don't know. What do you want to do? And don't say find the truth, because that one I get. I'm talking about what do we do today, right this very minute, in fact. And staying alive might be a good goal."

Mars said, "She's making sense."

Decker said, "If we can only find what Roy has." His face suddenly brightened. "Melvin, where is your mother buried?"

"She's not. She was cremated, her ashes were scattered."

"You know this for a fact?"

"I was there, Decker. I scattered them. This happened before I was arrested. I did the same with my da— well, with the guy I thought was my dad. But of course we know it wasn't him. It was ashes of the guy he killed."

Mars fell silent and looked down at his plate. He hadn't touched any of his food.

Decker rubbed his chin while Jamison watched him.

"Well, you guys look cheery."

They watched as Mary Oliver walked toward them pulling a rolling suitcase. She sat down in the fourth chair and wearily rubbed her face.

"Left before the crack of dawn. Three connections later, here I am . . . Obviously, haven't even checked into my room yet." She looked around. "Where's Agent Bogart?"

"He and his team have been recalled to Washington," replied Jamison.

"Not again. Are you joking?"

Jamison shook her head. "I wish I were."

"Any news on Davenport?" asked Oliver.

Decker answered. "No ransom demand, no nothing."

Oliver grabbed a piece of toast from the stack on a plate in the middle of the table and started buttering it. "Sorry, they didn't even have peanuts on any of the flights. And all the planes were like the size of my car, by the way." She bit into the toast and sighed.

Mars said nervously, "How's it going on the legal end?"

She looked at him sympathetically. "I don't think you have to worry about that, Melvin. From what I can tell the prosecutors in Texas have decided that you are a pit of vipers that they don't want to go near. At least right now. If they were going to try anything I would have had to have been notified."

He breathed a sigh of relief. "Well, that's something good at least."

Oliver studied him. "Melvin, what's wrong?"

He glanced up at her. "What do you mean?"

"I've been around you long enough to know your moods. Something's bothering you."

Jamison said, "He got a visit last night from his father."

"Only he's not my father."

Oliver choked on her toast. "What?"

Mars took a few minutes to explain.

Oliver looked stricken. "My God. I never would have thought . . . I mean." She touched Mars's hand. "That's awful."

Decker said, "And it also means Roy has no incentive to help us."

"But wait a minute. I need to get filled in. What have you discovered so far?"

Mars and Jamison looked at Decker. He cleared his throat. "We have some persons of interest. We have no proof against them."

"Who are they?"

"The police chief of this town, for starters," said Jamison. "Roger McClellan."

"The police chief! Wait a minute. What crimes exactly are we talking about?"

"Bombings in the 1960s," answered Jamison.

Oliver looked bewildered. "You have totally lost me. Bombings?"

Decker said, "We followed some leads. We learned some things. But we still need proof."

The waitress came over and asked Oliver if she wanted some coffee. She said, "Yes, and make it extra strong."

The waitress smiled and picked up the cup in front of Oliver. "Let me just swap this out, hon, it's dirty."

"Thanks."

Decker flinched like he'd been slapped. He mouthed one word: *Swap*.

Oliver turned back to Decker, who instantly refocused. "Do you think you can get the proof?"

"We have some avenues to get there. But it won't be easy."

The waitress came back and poured out fresh coffee for Oliver and everyone else. After she left Oliver said, "What can I do to help? If it's legal issues, I can definitely provide assistance."

Decker nodded. "Thanks. It may very well come to that."

Jamison added, "The key will be to find what was in Roy Mars's safe deposit box. We think that will be more than enough proof."

Oliver said, "And since he met with Melvin, we know he's nearby."

"He *was* nearby," corrected Decker. "He could be a long way away by now. Particularly if he got on a plane."

Mars looked at the others. "I'm not sure we should pursue this."

They all looked at him.

Oliver said, "Melvin, we have to."

"Why? To correct the wrongs of the past? By my count a mother has been killed and her son left as an orphan because of our investigation. The guy I thought was my father is a stone-cold killer. My mother was dying of brain cancer before he blew her head off. Decker, Milligan, and me almost died in a fire set by these assholes. And these crimes from the sixties? I'm not saying I don't want to nail the bastards responsible, but at what price? Are you going to get killed next, Mary? Or Alex? Or Decker?"

Decker said, "We all signed on for this."

"Well, I didn't. I think maybe I need to get on with whatever life I have left." Before they could say anything else, Mars rose and left.

"He's upset and frustrated," said Oliver. "I'll talk to him."

"Let him be for now," said Decker. "He's had to deal with one body blow after another. Those punches add up. I'm surprised he's still standing."

"He's tough," pointed out Oliver.

"He's going to have to be," replied Decker. "We all are."

65

Once more Decker was awoken from a dead sleep.

This time the man wore a mask. The hand over his mouth was gloved. The other held a semiautomatic pistol. The muzzle was placed against Decker's temple.

It was a hell of a way to wake up.

"You need to really listen to what I'm going to say," said the man in a low voice. "Nod if you understand."

Decker nodded.

"You have two choices. One, you abandon what you're doing and go home. Your buddy is out of prison and he'll stay out. We'll see to that. You will pursue this no further. Do you understand the first choice?"

Decker nodded.

"The second choice is that you continue investigating. The consequences of that will be that you start to lose people close to you. Jamison first, then Oliver. It won't be pretty. But it is guaranteed. There will be no second request. One step more and they die. Then you. Do you understand the repercussions of the second choice?"

Decker nodded once more.

Then something stuck him in the neck, his eyes rolled back in their sockets, and he passed out.

Sometime later his eyelids fluttered a bit and then popped open.

Decker sat up so fast he felt nauseous. He thought he was going to be sick, but he took several deep breaths and his stomach quieted down. He rubbed his neck where they had injected him. Powerful stuff. It had knocked him out in a second.

He slowly touched his toes to the floor and stood. He was shaky at first, but his balance returned and he walked into the bathroom and splashed water on his face.

He checked his watch.

Six a.m.

He had no idea how long he'd been out.

Whoever had been here was long gone, of that he was sure.

He went back to his bed and sat on the edge.

Two choices. Two very different choices.

He groaned and covered his eyes with one big hand.

He just sat there for a while and then made up his mind.

He dressed, walked to Mars's room, and rapped on the door.

"Yeah?" the voice said immediately.

Mars apparently was already up. Maybe he hadn't even gone to sleep.

"It's Decker, we need to talk."

Mars opened the door and Decker strode in. Mars closed the door and the two big men faced off in the center of the room.

"Look," began Mars. "I know what I promised you, but this was before the case took this detour to the sixties. It's not just Roy out there. He's bad enough. We got killers coming after us, Decker."

Decker said, "I know. They were just in my room."

Mars simply stared at him for a few moments. "Come again?"

Decker quickly explained the two choices.

"So you're abandoning the case?"

"I'm not, but I want the three of you to get the hell out of town. I'll contact Bogart and tell him what happened. They can arrange for protection until this is all over."

"You mean until you're dead."

"I can't tell the future, Melvin."

"Seems pretty clear to me. You pursue the case, they kill you."

"And that's my choice."

"Why are you willing to die for this? It's not even your problem."

"It *is* my problem, because I chose to make it mine."

"I don't get you, man, I really don't."

Decker sat in a chair and stared up at him. "It's all about radio timing, Melvin."

Mars slumped on the edge of the bed. "Well, that clears everything up, doesn't it?"

"I was driving from Ohio to my new job in Virginia. For some reason I turned on the radio. And right that second the story comes on."

"What story?"

"*Your* story, Melvin. A minute off here or there and I never would have heard it. And nothing that's happened since would have happened."

"So you believe in fate?"

"No, I believe in not ignoring something staring me in the face."

"They said they'd kill you."

"And that gives me hope."

"Are you losing your damn mind?"

"Why threaten me unless they're afraid?"

"*You* should be afraid."

"I *am* afraid. I was afraid every time I stepped on the football field. Or did a patrol round as a cop. Still didn't stop me from doing my job."

"So you're staying?"

"Yes, I am."

Mars sighed and looked around the small room, as though all the answers he needed would be there.

"Well, then I'm staying too."

"You're not going to do that, Melvin. You lost

twenty years of your life. I'm not going to be the reason you lose the rest."

"Well, like you said, it's a choice. They already tried to kill us once. And that pissed me off. And when I got pissed off on the field I played my best ball. I called it controlled chaos."

"You must have had it when you played us."

"I did. Second play of the game your nose tackle told me I ran like a girl."

"He always was an idiot."

"I'm staying, Decker. I walk away now and something happens to you, I've got to live with that for the rest of my life."

"So? It's not like we're lifelong friends."

"But you've risked your life for me. You discovered truths about my past that I never would have known. I can't walk away from you now."

Decker nodded slowly. "Jamison and Oliver aren't going to take this well."

"They will if you tell them that Bogart wants them to come to D.C. to work on the case from another angle while we keep looking here."

"And you think they'll buy that?"

"If you tell Bogart what happened to you tonight I think he'll be able to sell the deal. Maybe Mary goes back to Texas to work on my stuff. Perfectly natural for her to do that. And Jamison heads to D.C. We can go with her initially so she won't get suspicious."

"Sounds like a game plan. And if things get hairy, bring your controlled chaos tactic."

"In my back pocket and ready to go."

"It's the fourth quarter, Melvin."

"Where I always played my best ball."

"I think we're going to need everything you can bring to the table," replied Decker.

"And it's not like anyone would want to swap places with me. Not even you, I bet."

Decker stared at him for a long moment.

"What?" asked Mars.

"That word again. The waitress back at the restaurant used it too."

"What word?"

"Swap."

"Swap? How does that help us?"

"Believe me, it does. In fact, it pretty much changes everything."

66

What the hell are we doing here, Decker?" said Jamison.

They had flown into D.C. and were in a spare office at the FBI's Washington Field Office.

He pointed to the binders spread over the desk. "Working on another case," he replied.

"But why?"

"Because we ran into a dead end on the other one. I'm not saying we won't pick it back up, but for now, we focus on something else."

"What about Mary Oliver?"

"She's back in Texas working on Melvin's legal claims. There's more paperwork to be filed. And he needs that money. Otherwise, he has nothing."

"And Melvin? Where is he?"

"He's around, just laying low for now."

She slumped back in her chair, her arms folded over her chest, her features stubborn. "I can't believe you're just giving up."

"I'm *not* giving up." He paused, looked resigned, and said, "I got threatened, in my hotel room back in

Mississippi. Masked guy with a gun. He said if we didn't back off, they would take out everybody. You, me, Melvin, Davenport, Oliver, the Montgomery kid, everybody. Dead."

Jamison sat forward. "Holy shit. So these people have Davenport? Did you tell Bogart?"

"Yes, but his hands are tied. Huey has seen to that. He's stuck here."

"So we just do, what, nothing?"

"Nothing now. But maybe something in the future."

She looked at the briefing books in front of them. "None of these cases are as interesting as the one we were working on."

"I agree. But we have to be smart about this."

She shot him a glance. "If you're worried about me, I can take care of myself. I have a gun."

"The fact is, I'm more worried about Melvin and Mary Oliver."

"So the criminals win, that's what you're saying?"

"For now they do. But it's a long game, Jamison. And I always play for the long game."

Decker met with Bogart later that day.

Bogart said, "I'll be here preparing our senior people for Hill testimony for several weeks. I have officially been taken out of the field during that time."

"So Huey is nervous?"

"Which may not be a good thing."

"It is a good thing if they think we can prove murder charges against them."

"You were threatened in your hotel room, Decker. These people are not messing around."

"Agreed, but we still have no proof."

"You may never have any proof."

"If we can get to Roy Mars we might."

"He's probably in a country with no extradition back here."

"We still have a chance."

"You have a far better chance of dying. My advice to you is to lay low and let this whole thing cool off. I can't offer you any protection." Bogart stared keenly across at Decker. "But of course you're not going to take my advice."

"That doesn't mean it's not good advice or that I'm not grateful, because it is and I am. But, no, I can't do that. These guys are killers. They need to go down for it. Simple as that."

"And if you die in the process?"

"What law enforcement officer doesn't have to answer that question every day? And they still put on the uniform and walk out the door."

"But you're no longer a cop."

"I still feel like one."

"And Mars?"

"He's along for the ride."

"You're sure that's smart?"

"He's a big boy. There's nothing I can do to stop

him. And we might be safer together than apart. Two old helmet heads blocking for each other."

"Your original plan for us to track McClellan if he tried to contact the others won't work now that we've been pulled from the case."

"I know. We'll have to go at it from another angle."

"And you want me to keep Jamison here?"

"I'd appreciate it. She knows nothing of what I'm planning."

"While you two go off into harm's way? Sounds very 1950s. Jamison is hardly a damsel in distress."

"No, she's not."

"So?"

"So it's the way I want to play it. Jamison, despite her street creds, is not a cop."

"Neither is Mars."

"And he's tougher than you and me put together. I can't say I don't feel better having him next to me on this. And he has a bigger stake in this than anyone. And he's determined to be there at the end."

"Muscle against guns? Which do you think wins?"

"Muscle against brains? Which do you think wins?"

"So you have a plan?"

"I have a plan."

"Care to share, just in case something goes wrong?"

"I can't."

"Why the hell not?"

"Because it's not exactly legal and I don't want to get you into trouble."

"Can you at least tell me what it's based on?"

"Yes. It's based on a swap that took place."

Bogart eyed him suspiciously. "Meaning what precisely?"

"Meaning *that*, precisely."

67

The three musketeers were all accounted for.

On a private plane no less.

It was owned by Danny Eastland. Or, rather, by the company he'd built largely with government defense contracts. It used to be primarily the land of thousand-dollar wing nuts and million-dollar tires. Now it was more often software and counterintelligence platforms at a billion bucks a pop.

Eastland's plane had gotten bigger now that he dealt more with cyber than guns. The manufacturing costs were a lot lower and the ability to gouge Uncle Sam under a trillion bytes of bullshit was even higher.

The three men were in their seventies now, their trio of birthdays within two weeks of one another. They had been superstars in Cain, the three best known citizens to emerge from the small town.

Eastland, the mega-capitalist.

Huey, the über-politician.

McClellan, the perennial cop.

They were the only passengers on the G5. The two pilots up front sat behind a closed door.

McClellan poured out drinks for all and the three men faced each other across the width of a polished mahogany table at thirty-seven thousand feet.

Their visages were worn. Their bodies had started to wither. They each benefited from excellent health care, so they might have ten or even twenty more years, but maybe not all good ones. They clearly understood this.

Younger women still chased after Eastland, but only because of his wealth. His third wife had cost him enough that he was reluctant to indulge again in legal matrimony. He now focused on his business, and when he needed sex, a woman was provided, paid for, and then taken away. It worked well. He had three children by three different wives, and all of them had been a disappointment. They were largely silver-spooners, because he had made his fortune early. And he had no grandchildren since it seemed his worthless kids couldn't even manage to do that. He was wondering lately to whom he would leave his fortune.

Thurman Huey was a widower, his wife of forty-plus years having lost a long battle with breast cancer the past summer. He was currently being consoled by his four children and twelve grandchildren, and also by one eligible D.C. mover and shaker who had recently lost her husband of three decades. Yet his deceased wife could not be replaced. He felt lost without her, but he had a country's purse strings to manage. That was growing harder and harder to do as each election cycle sent more people to Congress who were ever more determined to obstruct rather than govern. He could have left the Hill years ago and earned a fortune as a lobbyist or consultant and his only real work would be to make calls, have lunches and dinners, and let the young bucks do the heavy lifting. But he hadn't. He expected to die at the job he currently held. He believed he was doing good work for the country. It was really the only thing he had left.

Roger McClellan was dressed in civilian clothes. He was the poorest of the lot, because being a cop in a small town never paid much. The woman he'd married over forty years ago was alive but had divorced him fifteen years back. "Irreconcilable differences" had been the term, nearly ubiquitous in all separations now. If his ex had listed years-long physical abuse on her divorce papers, it would have been more accurate. The same went for his kids. They were grown and scattered and had never come back, because why would they?

McClellan had had a temper from a very young age. Whenever they had lost a football game in high school or college—because the men had gone to Ole Miss and played ball there as well—his fellow Musketeers had had to hold him back from attacking members of the victorious team.

Huey sipped his drink. Eastland took a larger swallow.

McClellan downed his in one gulp and rose to pour himself another.

When he sat back down, Huey cleared his throat and said, "I truly believe we may have passed the worst of it. The FBI is officially off the case and back in D.C."

Eastland nodded, but McClellan looked at his friends like they had told him the earth was flat.

"That's bullshit, Hugh," he said. "Hugh" was a nickname that only these two men ever used.

Eastland shook his head. "I don't agree, Mac. They've gone back to D.C. with their tails tucked between their legs."

"Don't believe that for one minute. I sat in my office and listened to the fat guy—"

"Decker," interjected Huey.

"—the fat guy," continued McClellan, "go on and on about how he had us dead to rights and didn't need a damn thing to close the cell door on us. You two didn't hear that. But I sure as hell did. That man is coming for us. I've stared down many a criminal in my time. You two haven't. I've seen that look before. That man is *coming* for us."

"That was wishful thinking on his part," said Huey. "I have it on good authority that the investigation is officially over."

"Good authority!" said McClellan incredulously. "In D.C. I didn't think there was such a thing."

Eastland said, "I've had my intelligence people look

into it, without telling them anything, really, of course, and they've come to the same conclusion."

"Are these the same intelligence folks who thought I-raq had WMDs?" countered McClellan. "Because if so, I wouldn't bet the farm on your damn *intelligence*."

Huey bristled. "Mac, please don't make issues where none exist. They have no proof. They have no way to get proof."

"You're forgetting Aaron Callahan, a.k.a. Roy Mars. He has the proof. And the asshole's alive."

"We were *told* that, but we've seen no definitive evidence of it," pointed out Huey.

"Who the hell else would have gotten that colored kid out of the lockup 'cept his old man? How the hell could Callahan have married a colored? I just don't get it. He was one of us."

Eastland said, "He was *never* one of us. He was brought in, bought and paid for. He never believed in our cause. He just wanted the money."

"He thought like we did," persisted McClellan. "He thought like a white man should. That's what I meant."

"And if you hadn't gone after him when you saw that piece on ESPN we wouldn't be in this predicament," barked Eastland. "Have you never heard of the phrase 'let sleeping dogs lie'? He hadn't given up our secrets for decades, Mac. And then you poked the hornet's nest, and now look where we are."

McClellan exclaimed, "I'm not living with that

sword hanging over my head. You got tons of money and all the fancy lawyers that come with it. If he talked you could fight it all off. But not me. I spent my life protecting the public, Danny, while you got richer and Hugh got the big office in D.C. So excuse me for protecting my own ass." McClellan was so enraged that for a moment it looked like he might go over the table at Eastland.

Obviously sensing this, Huey said quickly, "Okay, let's just calm down and think this through. We can't lose our heads. Come on, Mac. We're not the enemy here."

McClellan glared at Eastland for a moment longer and then settled back in his seat.

Huey said, "Let's say he is alive, why would he come forward now? He'll go to prison too."

"Jesus, you guys," exclaimed McClellan. "You two have risen so high in the world you'd think you'd have better brains. He doesn't have to come forward. Just mail what he has to the *New York Times*. Or CNN. Or the Justice Department. You damn well know the stuff he has. He stole it from us. It was stupid of us creating all that crap, evidence of what we'd done."

"He could have done that at any time in the last forty years," pointed out Eastland patiently. "And yet he hasn't."

"And if we let sleeping dogs lie this time, like Danny suggested, then we survive this intact," added Huey.

"And things just go on like they've been going," added Eastland. "Don't rock the boat."

McClellan was shaking his head. "You boys just don't get it. You did not see the look in Decker's eyes. And I did some digging on him. He was one smart cop out in the Midwest. He was asked to work with a new task force the FBI formed. But forget that, I can read a man's eyes. Just like I used to read the QB's eyes on the field. Who had more interceptions than me in the high school conference the last three years, huh? Who? Tell me!"

"Nobody," replied Eastland wearily. "Two-way Mac, O and D."

"Exactly. And I'm telling you that this Decker dude is not going down that easily."

"Yes, you made that point quite clearly," said Huey.

Eastland said, "What exactly would you have us do, Mac? Just lay it out there."

McClellan finished his drink and took a few moments to consider his response.

"In the old days the answer would have been clear enough."

Eastland looked at Huey. Huey kept his gaze on McClellan.

"Are you suggesting that we, what, blow him up?"

Huey said, "That was fifty years ago, Mac. This is a different time. A far different place."

McClellan slammed his fist on the table. "Our way of life was threatened back then and we took action.

We didn't let no damn sleeping dogs lie. Now we're threatened again. And I say we have to take action. The world hasn't changed that much. In fact, I see the pendulum swinging back to where it should be. You can see it all over the place. People want to take their country back. Politicians are saying it. Laws are being passed. Hell, Hugh, you see that from where you sit. People don't want to take this crap anymore. And it's about damn time. Hell, for future generations of Americans if nothing else."

Huey looked out the jet's window at the white clouds down below. "What we did back then was stupid. We were young and hotheaded. It was a mistake."

"You don't believe that," said McClellan.

Huey looked at him. "Of course I believe it. I'm a lawyer. I've been a member of Congress for over three decades. I'm the chairman of arguably the most important committee on the Hill."

"Blah-blah-blah," said McClellan, waving his empty glass. "That means shit right now. Shit! So don't pull that crap on me, Mr. High and Mighty."

"I'm the CEO of a publicly traded company, Mac," said Eastland. "This isn't the 1960s anymore. Hugh's right, we're not young punks anymore with our brains in our ass."

McClellan pointed a finger at them. "It's attitudes like that that have led this country to the sinkhole it's currently in. Bad things happen when good men do nothing."

Eastland traded another glance with Huey.

Huey said, "We've always put things to a vote before, right?"

Eastland said, "Right."

Huey said, "And I vote that unless the situation on the ground changes, we pull back and take no further steps."

"I second that," said Eastland.

McClellan glared at them for a long moment before saying, "You two have turned into a couple of real pansies."

"We're being practical, Mac," said Huey. "And we've voted. Will you honor that vote?"

McClellan said, "I will. For now. But if the ground situation changes will you honor the fact that we will kill these sons of bitches?" When the two men said nothing, his voice rose. "Will you? Or you gonna take another vote and run away with your damn tails tucked?"

"If the ground situation changes we will act," said Eastland, and Huey nodded.

"We will *kill*, you mean," amended McClellan.

"If that's what it takes," said Eastland. "I'm not going to prison over this. It was too long ago, and I believe I've made up for it. We've done a lot of good in the world."

"Amen to that," said Huey. "A lifetime of service. It

517

balances things. Even the things we did," he added. "Fifty years of righteous living versus a few hot-headed acts that we regret now. I've helped many people over the years. My conscience is clear. God has forgiven me, I truly believe that."

"I feel the same," said Eastland. "I've given millions to charities. Tried to make the world a better place. I've even funded programs for black kids and Mexicans. Given them a helping hand. You know so many of their fathers are in prison. Very sad. But I've made peace with my past. I feel good about who I became as a person. Everyone makes mistakes when they're young. As we did. But we've repaid the debt, so to speak."

"Maybe you regret the past, I sure as hell don't," snapped McClellan.

"You need to stop talking like that," said Eastland warily. "The climate has changed. You can't be a police chief, even in Mississippi, and talk that way. You just can't. You can think those things if you want, but for God's sake, keep those thoughts in your head."

"Sure, the PC police crap," snarled McClellan. "Don't tell me you're turning into one of those pricks."

Eastland said, "I'm telling you that the world has changed. I have several generals I deal with who are black. My CFO is black. I even have a close friend who's black."

"And I have black committee members," added

Huey. "And representing Mississippi I sure as hell have a lot of black constituents. Not that I agree with most of what they want, which are basically government handouts. But they're there and they're not going anywhere."

"Bullshit, I bet you love 'em all right," said Mc-Clellan dismissively. "Love 'em like they were white."

"Of course we don't," said Eastland. "But we still have to deal with them. That's the point."

"We fought the good fight way back," said Huey. "And unfortunately, we lost. We have to deal with that. It doesn't change what we think, but it does have to change how we act. Otherwise I lose my seat and Danny loses his company. It's a lot harder now, Mac. You know that. We have to account for that. We really do. But I do regret the killing. There were other ways to get our points across. We didn't have to kill, not the kids anyway. I still think about that."

"If your old man could hear you talking," said McClellan disgustedly. "He'd be rolling in his grave. Now there was a man who knew his beliefs. You give an inch and they take a mile. And little coloreds grow up into big coloreds. And now it's the homos and the lesbos. And the trans-freaks. You telling me you think this looks like America? Are you?"

"If the conditions on the ground change," said Eastland, "I promise you, we'll take action. I have the resources. It will get done."

"I want to be there too," said McClellan. He

glanced at Huey. "But I doubt our fearless congress-man does. He's got too much to lose to fight the good fight anymore, right, Hugh?"

McClellan poured himself another drink as Huey and Eastland sat stonily in their seats. He held up his refilled glass. "Hell, boys, let's at least go through the motions. To the Three Fuckin' Musketeers."

The other two men reluctantly raised their glasses.

McClellan drank his down, dropped his empty glass on the carpet, and muttered, "And let's just kiss the good old US of A goodbye."

He pointed a finger at Eastland. "But when the ground conditions change, and they will, fat boy is mine. He threatened me in my own damn office. Nobody does that and gets away with it. So Decker gets done by yours truly. Understood?"

Eastland said, "Trust me, he's all yours."

68

"You sure he's not here?" asked Mars.

They were staring across at Roger McClellan's modest home, which was set by itself on a heavily treed lot off a rural gravel road about twenty minutes outside of downtown Cain, Mississippi.

"He's at a police chiefs' convention in Jackson. He won't be back until tomorrow."

"How'd you score that info?"

"I do have the resources of the FBI behind me."

"Alarm system?" asked Mars nervously.

"No. The guy's the police chief. Who's going to break into his house?"

"Well, apparently we are."

"I can do it. You can stay in the car."

"No, it'll go faster with two."

"Are you sure?"

"No, but let's do it," said Mars.

They climbed out of the car and swiftly moved across the gravel road and around to the back of the house. Decker flashed his light at the lock. "Just a single tumbler. I won't need the heavy guns. Hang on."

He inserted a pick tool into the lock, made a few manipulations, and the door swung open.

They moved inside and Decker closed the door behind them.

"What exactly are we looking for?" Mars asked.

"There was a picture missing from McClellan's office."

"Okay."

"That's what we're looking for."

"But what will that prove?"

"It'll prove that there really was a swap."

"But what does that *mean*?"

Decker looked at him strangely. "Let's just find it first and then we can talk about it later."

"But why would it be here?"

"McClellan is cagey. The guy has his plan. When he learned we were in town, I'm certain he took the picture down, because his strategy was to invite us in and have a 'chat.' After we left he wouldn't put the photo back up."

"Why? Would he think we'd break into the police station and try to steal it? That's nuts."

"No, because the son of a bitch is paranoid. He's not even going to trust his own people. And he wouldn't destroy it either. To him, that would be defeat. He's going to bring that sucker home."

They searched the lower level of the two-story house.

"Damn," said Mars as they finished going through the books on a shelf. "The dude is definitely living in the past. All these books are about the supremacy of the white race, suppression of people like me, arming whites to take back their country."

"I wasn't aware that we'd lost it," said Decker.

"Funny."

"It's actually not. A lot of these books were written in the last five years. So apparently there's still a readership for folks hankering for the 'old days.'"

Mars shook his head. "Are we ever going to get past this?"

"Couldn't tell you. I just want the photo. Let's head upstairs."

There were only three rooms on the second floor. One was a bathroom, one was a bedroom, and the last was McClellan's home office. It was about fifteen feet square. There was a computer on an old knotty pine desk. The shelves were full of books and magazines, and a black journal lay next to the computer. A globe was perched on one side of the desk. There was a landline phone next to it, and old-fashioned pens housed in a glass showcase box. An ink blotter and silver letter opener completed the items on top.

Decker studied the computer while Mars paged through the journal.

"Anything helpful?" asked Decker.

"Do you mean is there a signed confession in here? No. It's mostly just crap. Mostly depraved crap. His thoughts on what the world should look like. And guess what? Folks my color don't really have a place in it." He put the journal down and started searching the desk drawers.

Decker sat down in front of the computer and hit some keys. "It's password-protected. Understandable."

He typed in some possible passwords. None worked.

Decker sat back and thought about this for a few moments while Mars started going through the contents of the shelf.

"Go page by page, Melvin, like we did downstairs. He might have taken it out of the frame and stuck it in a magazine."

Decker kept trying passwords. "Got it," he said finally.

Mars came to look over his shoulder. "What was it?"

"The segregation king, 'George Wallace,' all caps."

"Are you kidding me?"

"Let's see what our fine police chief is into online."

Decker opened a Web browser and looked over the man's search histories.

"Well, he's into white supremacy groups, vigilant-ism, and all sites that are basically not really into diversity of any kind."

"What a shocker."

"Now let's look at emails."

Decker came away disappointed. "Okay, the guy's either really smart or just old-fashioned. No emails. I can't even find an account."

"Anything else?"

"Pretty clean hard drive. Not very much on it. He must use this principally to troll for crap from his bigoted buddies."

Decker closed out of the computer and helped Mars go through the books and magazines on the shelf. An hour later they had gone through every page and had come up with zip.

Mars said, "I hope we didn't waste a breaking and entering on nothing. Because if they catch us, I'm going back to prison. And you'll be heading there too."

"If McClellan catches us, going to prison would be a cakewalk compared to what he'd do to us."

"Right."

Decker looked around the room. "We searched everywhere."

"Well, it might not be here. He might have another hiding place he uses."

Decker said, "Maybe, but something tells me this guy likes to keep things close to home."

"We've looked at everything that could hold a picture."

Decker shot him a glance. "You know, you can't hide something three-dimensional in something flat. But the reverse is not true."

"What are you talking about?"

Decker put his hand on the globe.

"I'm not following."

"McClellan doesn't strike me as a worldly guy. Too much diversity around the globe, so why this thing sitting right on his desk within easy reach? So he can check out where the other half lives? Don't think so."

Decker bent lower and examined the globe's surface. He ran a finger along the equator, pushing and probing with his nails. Then he started at the Arctic Circle and headed south. His finger stopped at one spot near the bottom of Greenland.

"Give me that letter opener."

Mars handed it to him.

Decker carefully inserted one end into a small crevice in the globe. He very gently worked it back and forth.

"The damn thing's coming apart," exclaimed Mars.

The globe did indeed open into two metal halves, with a lip from one half inserting under the other.

And inside the space was a rolled-up photo.

Decker slid it out. "I noticed the edges didn't line up exactly. It had been opened before. We'll take a picture of it and then put it back and jigger the globe back together. I don't want him to know we've discovered it."

Mars was staring at the rolled-up photo like it was a rattler about to strike.

"Decker, do you know who's in the picture?"

"I think I know."

He slowly unrolled it and looked at the image.

"Were you right?" asked Mars.

Decker slowly turned the photo toward him. "Yes."

When Mars saw the people in the photo his knees buckled. Decker had to grab him with his free hand to keep him upright.

"Holy shit, I can't believe it," exclaimed Mars as he held on to the side of the desk.

"Pretty much sums it up," replied Decker.

"What the hell does this mean?"

"This means we finally have a chance."

69

Six people sat inside a conference room at the FBI's Washington Field Office: Decker, Mars, Bogart, Milligan, Jamison, and Oliver.

Bogart said, "As you know, we've been called off the case to work on, well, other matters. But we haven't given up on finding Lisa Davenport. We're working nonstop on that."

"Are there any leads?" asked Jamison.

Milligan spoke up. "A couple, but they ultimately led to nothing. No ransom demands. No communications of any kind. It's bizarre."

Mars looked at Oliver. "How's the court stuff coming in Texas?"

"Good and bad news," she said. "The good news is it doesn't seem like Texas is going to try to put you back in prison, as I said before."

"That's *great* news," said Jamison.

"The bad news is it looks like to compensate for that they're going to fight tooth and nail against the lawsuit I filed for damages from the attack on you at the prison."

"Not surprising," said Decker. "It's their way to try to save face."

Bogart said, "Decker has filled us in on Roy Mars meeting with Melvin, and the fact that he's not Melvin's father. And while I believe there's a connection with the 'Three Musketeers' and all this, including Davenport's disappearance, without strong evidence my hands are tied."

Decker leaned forward. "Roy more or less affirmed our theory of the case. That he was on the run after falling out with his racist buddies. But he has the evidence against them. That was in the safety deposit box. That evidence will topple some pretty powerful men for crimes they committed five decades ago."

"Did he say who these men were?" asked Oliver. "You mentioned the police chief."

"Yes, he did. Our job now is to find Roy and get that evidence."

"Decker, that's what we've been trying to do," said an exasperated Jamison.

"I know, Alex. I just feel like our chances are better now."

"Why?"

"We might have an ace in the hole."

"Can you explain that?" asked Milligan.

"Melvin and I went exploring. And we found something that might prove to be the thing that busts this whole case wide open."

"Well, don't keep us in suspense, Decker," exclaimed Jamison.

"It proves that a *swap* did indeed take place."

"A swap?" said Milligan.

"Right."

"What does that mean exactly?"

"It means in this case one person swapped for another." He pulled something from his pocket. "And here's the proof." He turned the copy of the photo around for all to see.

A chair was knocked over and feet rushed toward the door.

The locked door.

Mary Oliver turned back around to look at all of them, her face contorted into an ugly mass.

"You son of a bitch!" she screamed at Decker. Then she launched herself at him, but Bogart caught her by the arm and flung her back against the wall.

Milligan and Jamison looked bewildered.

"What is going on?" asked Milligan.

Decker looked at the picture he held. "This is a photo of Cain chief of police Roger McClellan." He paused. "And Mary Oliver."

Bogart righted the overturned chair and pointed at her. "Sit."

Oliver barked, "You can't order me around. I want out of here now. This is false imprisonment."

Jamison said, "But that's you in the picture. With McClellan!"

"So what? Is there a law against having your picture taken?" She whirled around at Bogart. "If you
don't let me out of here right now, I'm going to file
such a massive lawsuit against the Bureau that your
next posting will be at the unemployment office."

"I don't think so," said Decker. "As I explained to
Agent Bogart before, you will be arrested and charged
in the abduction of Lisa Davenport."

"Davenport? Are you nuts? You have no evidence
at all tying me to that crime."

"She would have opened her door that late at night
only to someone she knew. The crime scene was
rigged to let us think a terrific fight had ensued. It
hadn't."

"And why don't you tell me the motivation I
would have to kidnap her?"

"The *swap*. With Davenport gone you volunteered
to help us in the investigation. You played the heartfelt
comrade wonderfully, even throwing in a dash of self-
guilt. But with Davenport gone you were right in the
middle of the investigation. You fed the results of all of
our efforts to McClellan, who probably had men in
Texas. When we were planning to visit Melvin's home
you grabbed your phone. You said you were responding to a text from your friend in Texas having to do
with Melvin's lawsuit. But the thing was, I was sitting
next to you and I never heard the phone ring, buzz,
or vibrate. You just used that as an excuse to warn
your colleagues what we were going to do so they

could get there first and search the place. Later, I'm sure you texted them again and told them about the hiding place in the garage that Melvin told us about. That's why it already had been searched when we got there."

Milligan said angrily, "And then they tried to kill us!"

"You're nuts. I don't even know McClellan. That photo was from some event. Lots of photos were taken."

"Let's cut to the chase, Oliver," said Decker. "You didn't just happen to decide to take up Melvin's case. You were ordered to do so."

Mars looked at her. "All those questions about my family, my father, or at least who I thought was my father. You were pumping me for information before they were going to execute me. You were trying to see if I knew where the stuff from the safe deposit box was."

"I worked my ass off for you."

Bogart said, "After Decker showed me the photo earlier, I did some digging. Your legal work was merely perfunctory. And when Melvin was rearrested, it was Decker who saved him in court, not you. And I also checked on the 'lawsuit' you filed against the state of Texas on Melvin's behalf. Never happened."

"I guess being a disciple of a racist like McClellan, you couldn't bring yourself to actually help a black guy," noted Decker. "But all that's beside the point.

We have you for the kidnapping. That's twenty to life in a federal pen. And if Davenport's dead, you could be looking at the death penalty."

"You have no proof! And the lawsuit in Texas? It's not like I'm being paid by this guy," she added, hooking a thumb at Mars. "It was probably a filing error. I'll be sure to rectify it," she added with a smirk.

Decker looked at Bogart. "She needs more persuading."

"We got a search warrant on your phone and online accounts."

"Based on what?" screamed Oliver.

"Based on the fact that you are a close confidante of a principal player in our investigation. Coincidences that large don't exist. The judge issuing the warrant agreed with our logic."

Decker said, "And there are four lengthy emails between you and McClellan. You were keeping him posted about our investigation. That right there is obstruction. There's also a text where you use the initials LD and ask for the status of the person." Decker leaned forward. "Now, if you still don't think we have a case against you, get up and try to walk out of here."

"I want a lawyer."

"You haven't been charged yet," said Bogart. "So you're not entitled to one."

Oliver gazed around at the others before dropping into her chair and glaring at Decker. "What the hell do you want?"

"I want Lisa Davenport back safe and sound. You help us do that, and also help us nail McClellan and his buddies, then I think the DOJ will cut you a nice deal."

Oliver said nothing.

Decker leaned forward more. "Is Lisa Davenport still alive?"

Oliver said nothing.

Decker abruptly stood. "Okay, Agent Bogart, I say charge her and arrest her. We'll nail the Musketeers without her help and they all go to prison for life or get the needle, including her."

"Sounds like a plan to me," said Bogart, who nodded at Milligan.

Milligan gripped Oliver's arm. "Please stand."

When she didn't respond he jerked her to her feet. "Mary Oliver, you are under arrest for—"

"Wait, wait," she said, her breath accelerating.

They all looked at her expectantly.

"I . . . I don't know if she's still alive."

"Then I suggest you find out," said Bogart. "And then tell us where she is."

"I . . . I don't know where they took her. They wouldn't tell me."

"You don't seem to be trying," said Decker. "If you want a deal, you need to earn it. You *find* out where she is."

Bogart said, "And we'll be watching and listening to your every move. You so much as think about telling your buddies that you've been found out, I will find enough to charge you with that you won't see the light of day ever again."

Oliver's chin dropped to her chest and she started to quietly sob.

Decker said dismissively, "We've got no time for that. If they haven't killed Davenport yet, there's no telling when they might. You need to act. Now."

"But how do I find out?" wailed Oliver.

"I'll tell you exactly how," said Decker.

70

Why the hell didn't you tell me this before?" screamed McClellan into the phone.

Oliver said, "I just found out about it, Roger. I called you immediately."

"She hypnotized Mars? And he told her things?"

"Yes, that's what I just heard from Decker."

"But you mentioned the things in the safe deposit box. Did he talk about them?"

"Apparently, yes. Decker was going to meet with her to get some more information, but we'd taken Davenport by then."

"Shit. I've had her all this time and she might know? I mean really know?"

"It's certainly possible. So you need to talk to her." She paused. "Please tell me she's still . . ."

"I'll handle this," snapped McClellan, and he hung up. He hustled out of the building and jumped into his car.

It was a full hour's drive to the small farmhouse in the middle of a hundred acres that McClellan had inherited from his father. He skidded the car to a stop in front of the frame house with a falling-in porch. There was another car parked out front.

A man appeared at the door as McClellan rushed up to it. "Got your call," he said. He was short and broad-shouldered with thick hands. A pistol was shoved into his waistband.

McClellan pushed past him and into the front room. He crossed it in three strides and opened the door to the small bedroom.

On a chair sat Davenport. She was bound, gagged, and blindfolded.

McClellan pulled up another chair and sat facing her.

She had tensed when the door opened, her spine rigid against the back of the chair.

McClellan reached over and pulled the gag out. "We need to talk," he said.

Davenport licked her lips and swallowed several times. "I need some water."

McClellan grabbed a plastic bottle off a table, unscrewed the top, and held it up to her lips. She drank some, coughed, and then drank some more.

McClellan said, "You hypnotized Melvin Mars?"

She nodded slowly. "Yes."

"What did he tell you?"

"Not much."

"I need to hear it. In detail."

"I need to think. I'm just so tired."

He grabbed her by the shoulder and shook it. "Think faster."

He heard the footsteps and turned to see the other man standing there. He looked back at Davenport. Her clothes were dirty, her face the same. There was a bruise on her cheek and a cut on her forehead. She was thinner, pale, and her voice hoarse from disuse.

"Why are you doing this?" she said. "Please, I don't know anything. Just let me go."

McClellan slid out his service pistol and placed it against her temple. She stiffened when she felt the metal against her skin.

He said, "Just compose yourself and tell me what he told you. Then we'll talk about your future."

Trembling, Davenport recounted for him what Mars had said under hypnosis.

"That's it?" he said when she was finished.

"Yes," she said.

"And you're not holding anything back?" He pressed the gun muzzle harder against her temple.

"I swear to God I'm not."

McClellan removed the gun and slid it back into his holster. He looked at her closely, trying to piece together in his head what all of this meant.

He heard the other man move behind him.

"Okay, we need to take care of her," said McClellan. "And we need to do it right now."

"I think we got that covered," said the voice.

McClellan jerked around to see Agent Bogart standing there with his gun pointed at him.

The other man was being cuffed by Milligan.

Decker, Mars, and Jamison came into the room.

Bogart said to McClellan, "Stand up and put your hands on your head. You even think about going for the gun I'll drop you right here. With great pleasure."

McClellan slowly stood and put his hands on his head.

Davenport cried out, "Agent Bogart?"

Mars and Jamison hurried over and untied her, sliding off the blindfold. Her eyes were puffy and she blinked rapidly to adjust to the light. Assisted by Mars, she rose on shaky legs.

McClellan only had eyes for Decker. As Milligan came over and cuffed him, he screamed, "You fat son of a bitch. You used Oliver to trick me."

"Yes, we did," said Decker. "She'll get a better deal. And you can too. If you give up the other two Musketeers."

McClellan lunged, trying to get to Decker, but Milligan tackled him from behind.

Bogart said, "You're only going to hurt yourself, McClellan, so cool it. We have a transport vehicle coming to get you and your friend here."

They walked out into the sunshine. As they waited for the vehicle to arrive, Decker said, "They'd give you up in a minute if the positions were reversed, you understand that, right? Do they even know you kidnapped Davenport?"

McClellan turned to look at him. "What the hell do you know about anything?"

"I know you three bombed a church and an NAACP office."

McClellan sneered. "You don't know jack about shit." He spit on the ground next to Decker's boots.

"If you give them up your time in prison will go down, maybe not by much, but at least it's something. And why should Eastland and Huey get a free pass?"

"Don't know what you're talking about. Fine, upstanding men, both of 'em."

"So you're really willing to take the fall alone?"

"What fall? I came up here with my friend over there to check on my place and found this lady all tied up," he added, indicating Davenport. "I was about to untie her when you boys showed up."

"That's not her story."

"He said, she said. Or *we* said, she said."

"You know that no one is going to buy that bullshit," said Bogart.

Milligan added, "And we have Mary Oliver. She fingered you."

"I don't know what she told you, but it's all crap."

"We recorded her call with you. That's why you came up here."

"Well, that's why we have trials, I guess. To get to the truth. And in Cain, folks will believe me."

"Well, I doubt we'll try this in Cain," said Bogart.

"What we got lawyers for. So I'll post bail, but don't worry, I'll be around for the trial. I'm a highly decorated police chief with strong ties to the community. Not one mark on my record. I'm not a flight risk," he added, with a tiny smile tacked onto his words.

Milligan said, "Gotta hand it to the asshole, he talks a good game."

Decker said, "Despite what you may think, Chief McClellan, we have you dead to rights on the kidnapping. You're going to prison for the rest of your life. Now is your opportunity to ensure that your two buddies get the same treatment. I'm sure the FBI can arrange for you three to go to the same prison. The Three Musketeers in orange jumpsuits. Think about that visual."

The transport vehicle cleared a rise in the land and rumbled to a stop near them.

Bogart said, "Let's go."

He reached out to grip McClellan's arm.

The round impacted McClellan directly in the forehead, tattooing a third eye there. He fell back against Bogart and then dropped to the ground.

Milligan pulled his weapon. Mars grabbed Jamison and Davenport and pushed them to the dirt.

Decker looked at McClellan's body, blood from his head wound pooling around him. Then he launched himself toward the other man, who stood there, shell-shocked.

The second round hit the cuffed man in the chest and blew out between his shoulder blades. He fell back against Decker, who had felt the wake of the bullet as it exited the man's back before slamming into the dirt.

McClellan's buddy slid down to the ground. He had died the second the bullet ripped into his heart.

Two dead men lay on the ground along with six people who were still alive, for now.

The two agents in the transport vehicle had leapt from the front seats and taken cover behind it. "The shots came from over there," one of them called out, pointing to the east.

Bogart called back, "Get us some reinforcements up here. And dial a chopper up and see if they can track whoever it is."

But as Decker lay in the dirt with the dead man draped over him, he already knew that it was too late.

71

Davenport was in a hospital where she would stay overnight to be checked out thoroughly. It seemed that she would make a quick and full recovery, at least physically. The mental and emotional part might take a while.

Jamison and Milligan were there with her now, along with several other FBI agents. They were taking no chances that anything else would happen to her.

McClellan and the other man were in the local morgue.

Their killer had gotten clean away. By the time reinforcements arrived at that remote area of Mississippi, Decker figured he could have walked to Tennessee.

Now he, Bogart, and Mars were sitting around a table in an office at the morgue contemplating the loss of their prime witness.

"Oliver can't tie anything to Huey and Eastland," said Bogart. "She never met with them, never had any contact with them in any way. It all went through McClellan."

"I'm sure that was intentional," said Decker. "Eastland and Huey had a lot more to lose. But they were far smarter and more sophisticated than the late police chief. He was their attack dog, nothing more."

"We're looking into all of his stuff, but his computer was mostly empty and he apparently didn't write anything down. Whatever communication he had with the other two Musketeers must have been face-to-face."

"And it's a long road filled with potholes trying to connect the dots on this," noted Decker. "Particularly for crimes nearly fifty years old."

Mars absently nodded at this comment but said nothing.

Decker said, "They had McClellan and his partner killed, of course. They must have been watching him, or us. McClellan runs out of his office and they follow him up here. Or maybe Eastland and Huey knew about this place. McClellan's dad left it to him. McClellan might have told them he was keeping her here."

Bogart said, "I know that, you know that, but we can't prove it. We recovered the rounds, but we'll never find a weapon to match them to. My guess is that Eastland, with all his work in the defense field, and all his money, hired some pro to do it. And that guy is long gone and living on some island with his earnings. And we don't have enough probable cause to even dig into Eastland's finances to look for a payout. Besides, that guy probably knows every accounting trick in the book. Needle in a haystack that we're not going to find."

"But we did get Lisa back," said Mars.

"And thank God for that," added Bogart.

He looked at Decker, who was nodding in agreement. "And now we have to make sure *everyone* is held accountable."

"I'd love to," said Bogart. "But how? McClellan is dead. Without him we have no evidence against Huey or Eastland."

"There's really only one way," said Decker.

"What?" asked Bogart.

It was Mars who answered. "Roy Mars."

Decker nodded. "He's got all the evidence we need."

"Great, Decker, give me his address and I'll go pick him up," said Bogart sarcastically.

"Maybe we need to have him come to *us*."

"How? We have no way to contact the guy anyway."

"Sure we do."

Mars looked at him. "We do?"

"Just send a reply to the text he sent you, Melvin, when he was pretending to be me."

Mars pulled out his phone. "Damn, I forgot about that."

Bogart was staring at Decker. "Okay, but what's the inducement?"

"We've always had the bait. We've just never employed it properly."

"Oh, thank you for clearing that up," said Bogart dryly. "But for lesser minds, could you fill us in?"

"His wife," said Decker.

"What does my mom have to do with this?" asked Mars.

In answer Decker sat down and wrote out something on a piece of paper and then passed it over to Mars. "Write that in a text to him and let's see what happens," he said.

Bogart came around and read the note over Mars's shoulder. He looked at Decker. "Do you really think this will do it?"

"If that doesn't I'm not sure what else will."

Bogart rubbed his chin nervously and then nodded at Mars. "Go ahead and do it. Like Decker said, I'm not sure what we have to lose at this point."

Mars carefully typed the message onto his phone and his finger wavered over the send button. He looked first at Bogart and next Decker. He said, "He really did love her. He loved her enough to kill her."

"And that's what I'm counting on, Melvin. In fact, it's all that I'm counting on."

Mars pressed the send button and the text flew off.

Bogart drew a deep breath.

"Well, let's hope to hell that this works. Because I don't think we have a Plan B."

72

You've got balls. I'll give you that.

The text came in at two o'clock in the morning three days later. The ping roused Mars, who'd only been half asleep. He rose, read the text twice, and then called Decker and read it to him.

They were now staying at a hotel in D.C. Decker was at Mars's door in less than five minutes.

Mars looked at the fully dressed Decker. "Didn't you even go to sleep?"

"I tried but I never really got there."

"Me either."

Decker looked at the text and then tapped the phone against his hand. "He's intrigued and pissed. But I'd wager more intrigued than pissed."

He typed in a message and held it up for Mars to see.

We can agree on that. So where do we go from here?

Mars nodded and Decker hit the send key.

They waited. And waited.

It was five in the morning before they got a response.

Decker said, "He doesn't seem to sleep either."

The message was terse:

You screw me on this you're dead. And so is Decker. I'll get back to you.

"I like a man who speaks his mind and doesn't dance around the issues," said Decker.

The next night the "get back to you" message came:

Tuscaloosa. Two nights from tonight. Midnight. Just you and Decker. Anybody else within five miles, I'm gone for good.

Tacked onto this was a street address.

Decker closed his eyes and let his mind whir to the correct spot. "That's the location of the NAACP office that was bombed in sixty-eight."

"You think he'll meet us there?"

"I think he's a very careful man."

"He said just you and me."

"And he clearly meant it."

"What about Bogart and the FBI?"

"I'll take Roy at his word. If they're anywhere near, he's gone, Melvin. And the case is over."

"You know, we got Oliver and McClellan. Isn't that enough?"

"Not for me. We've got a prick in Congress wielding incredible power and a billionaire who blew up a bunch of people, including kids. I'm not walking away from that."

"Okay. I'm not either. How do we do this?"

"It won't be easy getting away from Bogart, but it can be done. In fact, it *has* to be done."

"When we get down there he might just kill us. Dude is crazy, Decker. I've seen that. And you've seen that."

"If I had an alternative, Melvin, I'd go for it. But I don't."

"Okay, again, how do we do this?"

"We can't fly or rent a car. That requires a credit card, and Bogart can easily check that."

"What then?"

"I've got enough cash for a bus ride. You up for that?"

Mars looked at him and shook his head. "Buckeye and Longhorn on the same damn bus? How screwed up is that?"

It took two transfers and nearly twenty-four hours to get to Tuscaloosa from Washington. They wended their way through the "toe" of Virginia, passed into Tennessee, and nicked the top of Georgia before bisecting Alabama on a diagonal, zipping through Birmingham. They were scheduled to arrive in Tuscaloosa at seven in the evening.

They had both turned off their phones so that Bogart could not track them that way.

They slept off and on for a good chunk of the trip, two big men in seats that were too small for them.

Decker had brought a bag of food and bottles of water.

They talked, watched the scenery pass, and then talked some more. The buses were pretty full, so they were forced to converse in low voices.

When they finally alighted from their third bus onto the streets of Tuscaloosa, both men stretched out their limbs to the maximum length.

"Reminds me of some trips we took playing football," said Decker.

Mars looked at him funny. "Big-time program like OSU, you guys didn't fly?"

"No, we did. I was talking about high school."

"Yeah, right. Hey, try playing in Texas. We'd drive this far to a game and still be in the frickin' state."

Both of them looked around and then Decker checked his watch. "We got time to kill. How about we find a place to crash and then get some dinner?"

"Sounds good to me. I'm sick of granola bars and trail mix. I want a steak and some potatoes."

"Blame Jamison. She's trying to make a stick out of me."

They found a hotel a few blocks away that took cash, dropped their bags, and went in search of a restaurant.

They found one five minutes later, grabbed a table, and ordered.

Mars gazed out the window. "You ever come down here to play 'Bama?"

"Once. We got our butts kicked."

"We lost to them here, but beat them at home."

The men grew silent.

"You ever miss it?" asked Mars.

"What, football?"

"What do you think?"

"I was not in your league, Melvin."

"Hey, man, don't say that. You made it to the NFL. Better than me."

"Don't go there. We're talking really extenuating circumstances. And I only lasted one play."

Their food came, but before they dug in Mars said, "What was it like?"

Decker was unfolding his napkin. "What was what like?"

"Walking on that field? Seeing, what, eighty thousand people in the stands? Playing with the best in the world?"

Decker noted the serious look on Mars's face and quickly understood how important this was to the man.

"It was pretty incredible, Melvin. When I ran through that tunnel and my cleats hit the turf my heart was pumping so fast I thought I might stroke before we even kicked off. I've never felt that kind of rush before or since. It was like they were all cheering for me, even though I knew they weren't. It . . . it was one of the best damn moments of my life."

Mars grinned, tucked in his napkin, and picked up

551

his knife and fork. "Yeah, I get that, man, I really do." He added wistfully, "Must've really been something."

"You know you would have been one of the best of all time."

Mars shook his head. "You can't know that. I was a tailback, man, one injury away from it all being over. And there are lots of examples of dudes like me coming out after wrecking college ball and then you find out you can't run against the big boys in the NFL. Or you blow out your knee and that split-second difference, that missing burst of speed causes you to lose that little edge on deciding what hole to hit, what cut to make. Then you're gone, man, done, bring on the next piece of meat."

"My money would have been on you being more like Barry Sanders or Emmitt Smith over a one-and-done."

Mars chuckled. "Thanks, Decker, I appreciate the confidence."

"I'm not blowing smoke. I played in the pros. We didn't have one running back on our team that could carry your jockstrap."

Mars stopped cutting up his steak. He was about to say something snarky back until he saw the serious look on Decker's features.

The men's gazes latched onto each other.

Mars said, "Thanks, that does . . . mean a lot to me."

They ate the rest of their meal in silence.

When they were done Decker ordered them two beers. They clinked glasses.

Decker sipped his beer and then set the glass down. He felt nervous and fidgety, his fingers tapping on the tabletop. He wanted to say something, but the words were not forming clearly in his head.

Mars noted his discomfort and said, "Hey, man, you okay?"

Decker took a calming breath, and when he saw Mars's concerned expression the right words finally came. He said, "Whatever goes down tonight, I want you to know that it's been a real privilege getting to know you, Melvin."

Mars seemed to understand how difficult this had been for Decker to get out. He said, grinning, "Hell, I'm just glad you turned on the radio when you did."

They drank their beers and Mars said, "How do you see it going down?"

"Roy is going to show up because we played by his rules and it's just us. But don't think this is all going to be linear and by the book. He's going to throw us some curveballs, it's just how the guy's wired."

"What sort of curveballs?"

"Hell if I know. I played football, not baseball."

73

They walked to the address Roy had given them, arriving there a minute before midnight. The streets were empty, the night chilly but the sky clear. Decker had had Mars turn his phone back on in anticipation of receiving Roy's next communication.

Decker looked behind him. "That's nice."

"What?" said Mars, looking too.

"Where the NAACP office was they built a public library. You know people who read are a lot more tolerant and open-minded than those who don't."

"Great, so let's get everybody in the world a library card."

They waited for about five minutes before Mars's phone buzzed. It was another text from Roy:

Walk directly west for a half mile. There'll be a black Ford parked at the curb. Keys under the front seat. Directions on passenger seat. I've got eyes on you right now. Anyone follows, goodbye.

"And now it begins," said Decker ominously.

"You got your gun?"

Decker nodded. "I just hope I don't have to use it, because that'll mean someone's shooting at us."

They trudged for half a mile due west and arrived at the black Ford parked at the curb. They climbed in. Decker snagged the keys while Mars checked out the directions.

"We drive west on this road and then we're eventually going to get on Route 82 and take it west. Then there're directions from there."

They drove for a while, got on and then off Route 82.

"Looks like we're heading into the boonies," said Decker.

"We're already in the boonies, Decker," retorted Mars. "Look around, there's nothing." He started to look nervous. "You think he's going to ambush us? Kill us?"

"If he wanted to do that he's had ample opportunity, Melvin."

"Yeah, I guess you're right."

"Well, I might not be. Like you said, the dude's a psycho."

"Thanks for the good thoughts."

Decker kept checking the rearview mirror. "He said he had eyes on us, but I don't see anyone back there."

"Maybe he was bluffing."

"He didn't strike me as a bluffer."

Mars looked back too. "They could be driving with their lights off."

"Maybe."

Mars directed him to three more turns, and they finally ended at a tumbledown house set well off the road and that didn't have a neighbor for about a mile.

"Well, this is about as lonely and creepy as it gets," noted Mars as they pulled to a stop in front.

Decker said, "I don't see another car."

A second later from the side of the house a pair of car lights flashed on and then off.

Decker and Mars climbed out of the car.

The car door on the other vehicle opened and there stood Roy Mars.

As he stepped forward into the moonlight they could see he was dressed in faded dungarees, an overcoat, flannel shirt, and work boots. The gun he held in his right hand was large and pointed at them.

Decker stepped forward and said, "I don't think there's a need for that."

"How about the gun in your waistband, Decker? I can see the bulge from here. Even with your big gut."

"It's not as big as it used to be."

"Congratulations. Pull it out muzzle first."

Decker did so and handed it across to Roy.

"Inside," Roy said.

He followed them in.

The room was small and smelled of mildew and rot. Roy stepped past them and turned a knob on a camp lantern that sat on an overturned packing crate. The room was instantly illuminated, the light throwing shadows across the space.

Roy tucked Decker's gun in his pocket and leaned back against the wall. "So, you got the skirt back."

"And how did you hear about Davenport?" asked Decker.

"I didn't. It was a deduction based on the reports of Sheriff Roger McClellan getting blown away at his old man's farm outside Cain. It said nothing of any dead woman. So, you got her back?"

"Yes."

"Mac's dead. So you got what you came for. So why dial me up?"

"There are still two more unaccounted for," said Decker. "That's why."

"You can't expect to get everything you want in life. Doesn't work that way. Just ask Mellow here."

"Then why did you agree to meet with us?" asked Mars.

"Curiosity got the better of me, I guess."

"I think it's more than that," said Decker. "You were once part of the team, maybe the unofficial fourth Musketeer, but then you turned against them."

"Don't know what you're talking about."

In answer Decker took out the page he had earlier torn from the yearbook back at Cain High School.

"You're the fourth from the left, Aaron Callahan."

"What?" exclaimed Mars, staring at the page.

"Roy Mars is actually Aaron Callahan. You've changed, of course, Roy, but it's easy to see that it's you and that you went to Cain High with the Three Musketeers."

"That's good, Decker. How'd you figure that out?"

"We found two sets of initials on the inside of your bedroom closet back in Texas. AC and RB. I ripped those pages out of the class pictures in the yearbook that had the last names beginning with 'C' and 'B.' Didn't recognize anyone with the last name beginning with 'B' as you. But I did with 'C.' So RB must've been the initials for Lucinda's real name."

"Roxanne Barrett." Roy looked at Mars. "That was your mother's real name. But she liked Lucinda better."

"How did you pick Mars as your last name?" asked Decker.

Roy grinned. "Always liked the red planet, even when I was a kid. Seemed cool."

Decker nodded. "You were on the football team with them. Left tackle, which means you guarded Huey's blindside. He was the QB."

"Guy was a mediocre signal caller that we made look good. McClellan was a rabid dog fullback and safety on the D-side. The kind who'd take a bite out of your leg in a pileup. Eastland was the slick scatback. Never went over the middle on pass routes, and on running plays he'd always run out of bounds before he got nailed. Prick didn't like to get hit. A real pussy.

But he was good-looking and smart and came from money and he was obviously going places, so the girls dropped their panties when he showed up anywhere. He and Thurman. But that was because of the old man. He was the big dog in Mississippi. Everybody knew him."

Decker said, "Huey Sr. was an all-around racist. Segregation now and forever, like George Wallace said."

"Hey, back then in Mississippi those were all positives. Maybe they still are in some quarters."

"You grew up with these pricks?" said Mars.

"Well, everyone has to grow up somewhere. But I never ran in their circles. I had the wrong pedigree."

"And you helped them bomb those two places?"

"I told you before, Mellow. I see no need to repeat myself."

Decker said, "And you have the evidence to bury them. Which is why you disappeared after the bombings."

"I chose to leave."

"Why?"

"My reasons. No business of yours."

"Was it the kids? The kids who died in the church?"

"Why do you think I'd care about some colored kids?"

"You said they weren't supposed to be there, that it wasn't part of the plan," said Mars.

"And you ended up marrying a black woman," Decker added.

Roy shrugged but said nothing.

"You can bring these assholes down, Roy. Almost fifty years later. Justice?"

"Why would I care about that? I'm just trying to survive here."

"Eastland's goons killed McClellan. And Huey has already taken steps to throw a monkey wrench in the FBI's investigation."

"None of that surprises me. They were always the brains. McClellan was just the attack dog. It was why he became a cop. I wonder how many skulls old Mac busted when he was wearing the uniform?"

"Plenty," said Decker. "And I would wager most of them were black skulls."

"But why the bombings?" asked Mars. "Like you said, they were going places. Huey had his dad's connections. So why?"

"You hit it on the head, Mellow. Huey Sr. I don't know this for a fact, but I strongly suspect he put them up to it."

"But why would they go along with it? They had to know this might come back to haunt them later."

"They were young punks who thought they were invulnerable. They really saw themselves as like the Three Musketeers, fighting to defend their way of life. Their *white* life. You should've seen them. They always acted so noble, like they were doing God's work or some shit like that. Hell, they could've been living in the 1860s."

"So they were fighting the good fight to keep the South the way God wanted it?" said Mars.

"Something like that. Me, I just wanted the money."

"How *noble* of you," said Mars in disgust.

"Shit, you think this was the only church or NAACP office to be bombed? Hell, in the South in the fifties and sixties, it was like the Middle East. Didn't you ever see the old newsreels? People getting knocked off their feet by fire hoses. Dogs attacking women. Places blowing up. Beatings at the lunch counters. Bodies hanging from trees. Bullets flying."

"I grew up in Texas over thirty years ago with bi-racial parents, so no, I never saw any racism at all," said Mars sarcastically.

Roy smiled and inclined his head. "Anyway, the son always lived to impress the dad. Thurman was going to follow in his footsteps, be a player on the national stage. I'm not speculating here. That's all he talked about in high school. And Eastland was always going to go into business. But he also had a God complex, I guess coming from so much money. He and Huey, knights in shining armor defending their lily-white kingdom. So you had a future politician and a future businessman, match made in heaven. And Mac signed on because, well, as you probably saw, Mac doesn't like people who look different from him."

"And you?" asked Decker. "What was the incentive for you?"

"You're not listening. I already told you. Money! And back then I admit I was a lemming. Just followed the crowd. The Hueys had power. The Eastlands had money. I got to live in that world for a little bit, which was a lot better than my real one. My parents were pretty much sharecroppers. The only toilet I had growing up was the one at school. Most days I went out into the fields and picked my own meals. My parents worked hard, don't get me wrong, but they were never going to have two dimes to rub together."

"So you went along?"

"Hell, yes. They paid me. A shitload of money. More than I'd ever make doing anything else. I was always good with putting stuff together, fixing things. Motors, transmissions, appliances."

"And explosives," added Decker.

"I started making little pipe bombs in high school. Then I moved on to bigger stuff. They got me the materials and I built explosives with a timer."

"And Charles Montgomery ran interference."

"Shit, the local cops knew what was going to happen, but yeah, Chuck did the drunk driving act so they could have a reason to leave the church."

"And the same in Tuscaloosa with the NAACP office?" asked Decker. "Montgomery did his thing to distract so the bomb could be planted?"

"I wasn't there, but I assume so. Huey did tell me

later that the cops were watching that office because there'd been threats."

"And who brought Montgomery in?"

"McClellan and Eastland."

Decker nodded. "He played football with them at Ole Miss."

"Right. But he dropped out of college, got drafted, went to 'Nam, and came back with a lot of problems. He needed money and they had it. I used the same ploy on him when I looked Chuck up to lie about killing us to get Mellow out of prison. Figured a dying guy wouldn't care. And he wanted to take care of his kid. At least that's what Regina told me."

"So what happened?" asked Decker. "Why disappear, change your name, and go on the run?"

Roy didn't answer immediately. "I didn't agree to meet with you so we could play twenty questions."

"Granted, but you *did* agree. Did you have a falling-out?"

"What makes you say that?"

"Because you have something they want. Whatever was in the safe deposit box. They know you're alive, Roy. They're never going to stop looking."

"You think that worries me?"

"I don't know. Why not just give us the evidence and we'll use it to bring them down?"

"And what, you just let me walk off into the sunset?" He shook his head.

Decker said, "It was your leverage against them,

right? They come after you, you'll just turn it over to the authorities."

"Damn straight it was."

"Did Mom know what you did with the bombings?" asked Mars.

"You think she would've married me if she'd known what I'd done?" Roy looked back at Decker. "After the ESPN show aired, I got a letter."

"They threatened you?"

"They threatened everybody. And that's when I found out that Lucinda was dying. She had maybe a few months. I was caught in a real bind."

Decker said, "But you hadn't revealed the evidence against them all these years, Roy. After seeing you on TV, why would they come after you so hard? That might *make* you give up their secrets."

"It was McClellan's doing. He was the one who sent the threats, I'm sure of that. Huey and Eastland would have just sat on it, done nothing. But Roger's not built that way. All those years I know the sonofabitch has been brooding about what I did. He would have seen it as a betrayal. And he doesn't like anyone holding something over his head. He came after me and dragged the other two along, of that I'm certain."

Decker nodded. "After meeting the man I can see how that would be the case. But how did you fund the stuff that Regina Montgomery bought?" he asked. "You couldn't even afford medical care for Lucinda."

"Little safecracking, a few scams, a bit of burglary,

an armed robbery. Took me some time but I got enough cash. Then the dumb bitch went on a shopping spree. I told her to wait till she moved on, but she couldn't wait. Stupid woman. So I had to take care of that little problem."

"And the guy who took your place when you disappeared, Dan Reardon?"

"Don't feel too sorry for him. You know what Reardon was? A pedophile and a murderer. Nobody bothered to look, but he probably has half a dozen kids buried out at his old place."

"And you never told anyone?" said Decker.

"No, I blew his head off instead. Saved everybody a lot of time and money."

"But they know you're alive now, Roy. And they'll come after you and Melvin."

"Well, I'll be a lot harder to find than Mellow."

"And you're okay with that?"

"I'm okay with a lot of things you wouldn't be."

"Even though Lucinda wouldn't have agreed?"

In response Roy held up his phone. "You wrote this text, didn't you? The first one to me. Because I don't see Mellow being that eloquent."

The screen read, *Is this really what Lucinda would have wanted, Roy? It's her son, the only living thing of your wife left. What would Lucinda want you to do?*

"It's a fair question," said Decker.

"Never said it wasn't."

"So, what *would* she want you to do? Not just for

Melvin. But for the others killed. For the little girls who never got to grow up and have their own children."

"Don't try to pull at the heartstrings, I don't have any left."

"And I don't believe that. Because you got Melvin out of prison. You saved his life."

"And yet here you are asking for even more."

"Because the job's not over yet."

"Your job, maybe, not mine."

"We can dance linguistics all night. It's not going to get us anywhere."

The two men stared at each other.

"It would be interesting to see what makes you tick, Decker," said Roy.

"We might be more alike than you think."

"Oh, I think we're very much alike." Roy looked down. "What if I gave you the stuff? Would you really let me walk?"

"If we got the evidence to put Eastland and Huey away, I really wouldn't spend a lot of time looking for you."

"But the FBI might."

"They might. But like you said, you're a hard man to find."

Roy considered this and was about to say something when he froze, and his gaze darted past them. His features hardened.

"You screwed me. You brought the FBI."

The Last Mile

Decker looked behind him and then turned to face Roy. "No, we didn't. Which means it's the other side out there."

74

Roy immediately turned off the lantern, plunging them into darkness.

"Give me my gun," said Decker.

"How do I know it's not the FBI out there and you're just trying to trick me?" countered Roy.

The bullet shattering the window made them all drop flat to the floor.

"Because the FBI usually identifies themselves and doesn't typically open fire into a building with people in it."

The next moment an electronically enhanced voice called out, "We know you're in there, Callahan! Just walk out and bring the stuff with you!"

"Shit," muttered Roy. He slid out Decker's gun and passed it across to him.

"Is there another way out of here?" asked Decker.

"The back door, but I gotta believe they got that covered too."

As if in confirmation of this, a shot blasted in from the rear of the house.

"Okay, that's a no-go," said Decker.

"They've got us pinned down. All they have to do is wait us out."

Decker pulled out his phone.

Roy saw this and shook his head. "That's no good. This is one of the areas on the cellular map that's got no signal. Nobody lives out here. It's why I picked it to meet."

"So we're screwed," said Mars.

"You were screwed the moment that ESPN show aired, Mellow."

"So this is my fault?"

"It's a little late to be apportioning blame," interjected Decker.

He crept to a window and looked out.

"Can't see anything. But those rounds sure sounded like high-powered rifle shots. Like the kind that killed McClellan." He scurried back to the others. "Do they really think you've got the stuff with you?"

"No, but they want me to take them to it."

"Where is it?"

"Not going there. I need leverage right now."

"They're going to kill us, Roy," said Decker.

"They must have followed you here. How else?"

"Nobody followed us."

"Eastland runs an intelligence firm, you dumbass. You don't think he's got ways to watch people?"

Decker turned to Mars. "He might be right."

"I *am* right. I never should've agreed to meet with you two idiots."

"It's not like we wanted to meet with you either," retorted Mars. "You're the one who started all this."

"I asked you this before but never got an answer," said Decker. "You ran and took incriminating evidence with you, Roy, why?"

"You think now's the time to discuss this?"

"I don't think we're going to get another chance."

Roy glanced toward the window as the same voice called out, "You got one minute and then we open fire. And we're packing incendiary rounds."

"Shit," muttered Roy. He looked at Decker. "Okay, you're right. Killing kids wasn't in the plan, not that the Three Musketeers gave a damn. After that I wanted out. But they weren't going to let me. They made that clear."

"What'd you do?"

"I stole the evidence from Huey Sr.'s safe. The old man was proud of what they'd done, but he wasn't stupid enough to let that stuff get out. But I'm a curious guy. I was the one filming their little confessionals, and I'd seen Huey Sr. open his safe a few times, got the combination that way. Figured that's where he'd keep the stuff. When I took it, I left 'em a note telling them what I had and got the hell outta Dodge and left the country."

Mars said dully, "And fell in love with a black woman. Quite ironic."

Roy suddenly looked contrite. "That's the thing about love, you just . . . I mean, you can't control it. I loved your mom and she loved me. From the minute we laid eyes on each other."

"But not me," said Mars. "You never loved me."

"I was *proud* of you, Mellow, for what you did on the football field. But you being black wasn't the reason I could never love you."

"What, then?"

"Every time I looked at you I saw the sonofabitch who hurt the only person I've ever really loved. Not your fault. And I know it sounds effed up and it is, but it was just how I felt." He paused. "Hell, I might as well lay it out for you. All of it. Your father? I lied to you. I never killed him for what he did to your mother."

"What?" exclaimed Mars.

"It wasn't for lack of trying. But he was too rich and too well protected. His goons almost ended up killing me." He pointed to the scar. "They gave me this, along with some other permanent injuries. The prick's still alive down in Colombia living the good life. Makes my blood boil every time I think about it."

Mars said, "Why are you telling me this?"

Now for the first time Roy looked nervous. "Because that's the real reason I framed you for murder, Mellow. Not to protect you. And your mom didn't know I was going to do that. She just thought I was going to disappear. If she'd known my plan to frame you she never would have let me do it. Hell, she would have killed me."

"Why?" asked Mars.

"You really need to ask that question?"

"Yeah, I do."

"Because despite how you were conceived, she loved you more than anything in this world." He paused and added resignedly, "Even more than she loved me."

Mars looked at Roy until the latter lowered his gaze and continued. "Framing you was the only way for me to get back at that asshole for what'd he done. Even though he probably didn't give a shit about you, there still was a part of him in you. And it was the only part I could get to. So I set you up to get back at him."

A long moment of silence went by.

"That's pretty sick, Roy," observed Decker, while Mars just stared at the man he'd thought was his father. "You punished the wrong guy."

Roy shrugged. "Like I told you before, Decker, life ain't perfect and neither am I. I did what I did and I don't have to defend it to you or anybody else."

"Callahan!" called out the electronically enhanced voice. "Your time is running out!"

Decker looked toward the door. "So what do we do about the guys out there?"

"Maybe I got a way out. If I give them what they want."

"And they'll just let us go?"

"Me maybe, but you two are on your own."

"You sonofabitch!" exclaimed Mars. He started toward Roy, but the man pointed his gun at him.

"Don't make me shoot you, Mellow."

"*I'll* shoot you," said Decker.

"No," said Roy. "*I'd* shoot somebody in the back. But I don't think you would. Now, if you'll excuse me, I have to get going."

In the darkness he bumped into Decker on his way to the door. Roy gripped Decker to steady himself. "You *are* losing weight, Decker. For all the good it'll do you."

He let go and called out the window, "I'm coming out. You guys want to know where the stuff is, we can work a deal. But you shoot me, trust me, that stuff will end up where you don't want it to."

"What about the others in there with you?" the voice called out.

Roy didn't even look at the two. "Not my problem," he yelled back.

"You bastard!" roared Mars, but Decker held him back.

"Let him go, Melvin."

"Why? So he gets to live and we die?"

"Don't be such a pussy, Mellow," sneered Roy. "You might get out of this. If not, I'll see you on the other side."

"No you won't," said Mars. "I'll be with Mom. And you know where you'll be."

"I'm coming out." Roy marched out the door holding his gun up.

Decker peered out the window and saw three men race forward, each carrying a rifle and outfitted in cammie gear and body armor. They surrounded Roy.

"Where is it?" one of them said.

Roy looked back at the little house.

"Hey, Mellow, tell your Mom I said—" His voice cracked and tears suddenly filled his eyes. "Tell her that I love her, *Melvin*. Always will, no matter what."

"Oh shit," exclaimed Decker. He grabbed Mars and flung him backward. Mars went sliding across the floor and thudded into the rear wall of the building. Decker raced over and covered him with his big body.

Outside, Roy opened his coat. The packs of Semtex around his waist were rigged to a trigger.

The men surrounding him turned to run.

But it was far too late for that.

Roy Mars hit the trigger.

And the four men simply disappeared.

75

Decker sat looking across at Mars.

They were in a hotel room in Tuscaloosa.

Bogart stood watching both of them and his expression wasn't a happy one.

The house they had been in had partially collapsed when Roy Mars detonated the bomb wrapped around him. Both Decker and Mars had escaped the wreckage without serious injury, but it had been a near thing.

They had driven the truck left behind by the men with rifles to a point where they could make a call. The police had come, and then Bogart had flown in with a team of agents. Decker and Mars had been taken to the local hospital, stayed overnight, and been released to Bogart.

Jamison had flown down with Bogart and was standing next to him. She didn't look any happier than the FBI agent did.

"Never thought to loop me in on this?" he said to Decker.

Decker shrugged. "You were officially off the case,

Ross. I didn't want to get you in trouble, and Roy said to come alone."

"You listen to him and yet you won't listen to me!"

"It seemed like the only way," replied Decker.

"And what about me?" snapped Jamison, hands on hips and a scowl on her face.

"I'm sorry, Alex," was all Decker could manage.

Bogart said, "So Roy's dead and the other guys were blown to smithereens, and we found nothing at the scene tying them to Eastland or Huey."

Mars shook his head. "I still can't believe he just . . . blew himself up."

"He saved us, Melvin. Well, actually he saved you. I don't think he cared if I lived or died."

"But why? After all the shit he put me through? Was it because of my mom?"

"I don't think so. I think it was because of *you*."

"The guy didn't love me. He hated my guts. He framed me for murder. I figured he just took the easy way out."

"I wouldn't call blowing yourself up the easy way out," pointed out Jamison.

"Why would he even come there with a bomb?" asked Mars.

Decker said, "He was a man who hedged his bets. He knew Eastland had a lot of resources. He might have figured we'd get followed somehow."

Bogart said, "Well, whatever the reason, we've got

nothing. Roy was our last hope. And now he's gone. So Eastland and Huey are home free."

"Not yet," said Decker.

They all turned to him.

He eased something from his coat pocket. His arm had been hit by a flying wall stud in the explosion and was still sore. He held up the article.

"Your wallet?" said Bogart.

"Roy's wallet."

"How the hell did you get it?" asked Mars.

"I didn't. He 'accidentally' slipped it into my pocket before he went out and blew himself up."

"Why would he do that?" asked Bogart.

Decker opened the wallet and drew out the only item inside.

"What is that?" asked Jamison. "A credit card?"

"No, a library card."

"A library card?" said Bogart. He looked at Mars. "Was he much of a reader?"

"Never saw him with a book in his life."

"Except the one he would read to you at night," said Decker.

"That's right. How'd you remem—" Mars stopped in midsentence.

"Why a library card?" asked Jamison.

"I think he was leaving us a message." Decker rose. "Shall we?"

★

The drive to the library that now stood where the old NAACP office once had was only ten minutes from the hotel. They drove in Bogart's rental. He pulled in front of the library and parked at the curb. Decker led them inside.

At the front desk sat a middle-aged woman with a stack of books in front of her.

Decker said, "I have a book on reserve." He handed her the library card.

She took it and then checked on the computer in front of her. "I assume this isn't for you?" she said when the correct screen came up.

"No, my nephew. He's just learning to read."

She smiled. "Make a reader early, you make one for life. I'll be right back." She rose and disappeared behind some stacks.

Jamison said, "Are you going to tell us what's going on, Amos?"

"What book did he reserve?" asked Mars.

"The Three Little Pigs," said the librarian, returning into view. "I noticed you checked it out once before," she said to Decker.

"Right. My nephew liked it so much."

"Well, it is a classic. I read it to my grandkids and I still get scared when the Big Bad Wolf comes into the story. And the pictures are really stunning." She handed Decker the book and his library card back.

"Thanks."

They walked out to the car.

"What the hell is all this about?" asked Bogart.

Mars said, "That's the book my da— I mean Roy, I mean Callahan, would read to me."

Decker added, "He really liked the character of the Big Bad Wolf. That's because I think he saw himself in much the same role."

"Wait a minute," said Jamison. "So the three pigs?"

"The Three Musketeers, of course," said Decker. "Except Roy saw them as pigs, not heroes. And he was the Big Bad Wolf who wanted to eat them."

"But the wolf failed," said Bogart.

"In the story he did. Let's see how it turns out in real life."

He sat in the backseat and turned the book over and over in his hands. He flipped through each page but found nothing.

Jamison said, "Decker, look at the top of the spine. It's pulled away from the pages some."

Decker examined this, and tried to get his finger inside the crevice, but his finger was too big.

"Anybody got a light?" he asked.

Bogart handed him a penlight pulled from his jacket.

Decker shone it down in the crevice. "There's something in there."

"Just tear the spine off," said Bogart.

"I don't like to ruin books," Decker said.

"Good God," said Bogart. "Just wait a minute." He went to the trunk of the rental and pulled out his suitcase. "I haven't even checked into the hotel yet," he explained. He pulled out a garment bag and then took out a wire hanger that a suit was hanging on. He handed it through the rear window to Decker. "Here. Try this."

Decker bent the hanger's hook a bit to fit it inside the crevice and then worked it down into the slot. "It's definitely hitting something." He worked away for several minutes until he said, "Okay, it's coming up." He slowly pulled the hanger up until they could see the top of a key.

Jamison had the smallest fingers among them, and she gently reached inside the crevice and eased the key out. It had a chunk of something sticky attached to it.

Decker said, "Roy probably put that glue stuff on the key and slid it down into the spine. That way it wouldn't easily come out."

"What's it a key to?" asked Bogart.

Jamison held it up.

Decker said, "If I had to guess, I'd say it was a safe deposit key."

"Okay, what bank? Tuscaloosa has more than one. If it's even in Tuscaloosa."

Jamison looked out the window. "Well, other things being equal, why don't we try the one right next to the library?"

Bogart gaped and then said, "Sounds like a plan."

They marched into the bank and Bogart's FBI

badge and ID got things hopping. The key had indeed been issued by the bank.

When the necessity of a warrant was mentioned by the bank manager, Bogart said, "I can get one, but it'll mean that some murderers might get away with their crimes."

"But the box holder does have rights," said the bank manager.

Decker held up the grainy picture of Roy Mars. "Is this the guy?"

The manager studied the photo. "Yeah, I think so."

"Well, he won't mind. He's dead."

The bank manager led them into the safe. He inserted the key they had brought and the duplicate one the bank kept. The box was pulled out and the manager left them there to go through the contents.

Decker looked at Mars. "You ready for this?"

"I been ready for this for a long time, Decker."

He opened the box and they stared down at the contents.

Decker slowly pulled one item out. It was a photograph.

Bogart plucked out a letter and started to read it.

Mars took out a map and some pieces of paper with writing on them.

Jamison picked up a DVD. "They didn't have these back in the sixties. Roy—I mean Callahan—must have burned something to it."

It took about an hour to go through all that was in

there, including watching the DVD on a laptop. The content looked to have originally been shot on film and then transferred to the DVD.

When they were finished Decker looked up at the others. They were all staring back at him, stunned. The Big Bad Wolf had finally gotten to the pigs. Decker glanced up at the ceiling. "Thank you, Aaron Callahan, wherever you are."

76

What Callahan had in the way of evidence was so overwhelming that both Eastland and Huey are doing plea deals to avoid the death penalty," said Bogart.

They were in the same conference room at Quantico where they had first taken a look at Melvin Mars's case. They were all present, including Davenport and Milligan. Mars was there too.

"The Three Musketeers apparently wanted to document thoroughly what they were going to do," said Milligan. "Photos of themselves with the bombs. Handwritten letters to each other about what they were planning and more letters after the fact detailing how they did it. Even a film where they bragged about what they had done. They were really proud of it. Maps of the NAACP office and the church. A list of the victims with check marks against their names. And on and on. Unbelievable."

Bogart added, "And all of them in KKK outfits. Even photos of them and Huey Sr. holding nooses and signs with racial slurs on it. How stupid can you get?"

Decker said, "They thought they were untouchable. Huey's father was the man in Mississippi. Eastland's parents were rich. McClellan was the attack dog everybody was scared to death of. And they believed they were doing God's work."

"More like the devil's work," interjected Jamison.

"But he's dead and the other two are heading to prison. Some untouchables," said Bogart.

Mars smiled.

Decker glanced at him. "What?"

"Just thinking of those two pricks in orange jumpsuits mopping floors and living the rest of their lives in an eight-by-ten. Pretty sweet."

Jamison said, "Speaking of, what about Mary Oliver?"

Bogart said, "She cut a deal. But she's still doing considerable jail time."

"Good," said Davenport. "When she knocked on my door I thought nothing of letting her in. Next thing I know some guy grabbed me and held something to my nose. And everything went black. I thought I was dead for sure."

"You would have been," said Bogart. "If we hadn't found you. And you can thank Decker for that."

Davenport smiled warmly at him, but Decker didn't seem to notice.

"What about Melvin?" asked Jamison.

Bogart straightened in his chair. "Melvin, you will not be going back to prison. After this all came out in the news and your role in finding the truth was prominently mentioned, Texas has no interest in trying to send you back to jail."

"But what about his lawsuit for damages?" asked Decker.

"Glad you brought that up," said Bogart. "We had DOJ lawyers get involved. It appears that because you are now quite the hero, Melvin, Texas does not want to be seen as denying you just compensation for what happened to you. Meaning your wrongful incarceration, and then your almost being killed at the prison due to a conspiracy involving some of the guards. Thus they have made an offer that I said I would share with you. Keep in mind that DOJ lawyers told the state to err on the side of extreme generosity, considering how much you could have made playing in the NFL."

Bogart withdrew a slip of folded paper from his pocket and slid it across to Mars. Mars looked down at it for a few long seconds.

"You might as well open it, Melvin," said Decker.

"The suspense is killing me," added Jamison.

Mars slowly unfolded the paper and stared down at the number written there. Under his breath he counted the zeros.

"Holy shit," said Decker, who was looking over his shoulder.

Jamison jumped up to look and nearly collapsed to the floor. "Mother of God."

Mars looked up at Bogart. "I never would have made this much playing in the NFL for twenty years."

"I have to say that the federal government chipped in quite a bit too. And it's all tax-free. A good faith gesture from Uncle Sam. So you get to keep it all."

Decker slapped him on the back. "How does it feel to be stinking rich, *Mellow*?"

Mars grinned and then started laughing. And he couldn't stop. They all joined in, and people walking up and down the halls on serious business stopped and stared at the room, wondering what could be so damn funny.

A week later Decker drove Mars to the airport in Washington. He was wearing new clothes and had two suitcases full of additional outfits, all brand-new and tailored to his imposing physique.

"I really can't believe this is happening to me, Decker."

"Believe it, because when you open your eyes tomorrow it'll all still be there."

"I wish you'd take some of the money. Hell, you earned it. I'd still be in prison but for you."

"Melvin, I suck at money management. I'd probably lose it in a few days."

"Then I'll set aside a chunk in an account for you. I'll invest it. When I was in prison I followed the markets. My degree was in business. I'll do right by you."

"Whatever you want to do, you do. And I appreciate it."

They drove for some minutes in silence as Decker navigated rush-hour traffic.

"So you're heading back to Texas for a bit, and then what?"

"I know the old house is pretty much burned down, but I wanted to see it one more time." He paused. "After that I thought I might head to Alabama."

"Alabama? You mean Tuscaloosa?"

"No. I mean to where the Montgomerys lived."

Decker looked at him curiously. "Okay. And for what reason?"

"I made some calls. Turns out the Howling Cougars need a running backs coach."

"Tommy Montgomery's team?"

Mars nodded. "He lost both his parents. Callahan killed his mother. I sort of feel responsible."

"But you're not."

"But I still want to do it. And I've got the money to help Tommy. I'll set up a trust for him. No reason he should suffer."

"No reason at all. That's very nice of you, Melvin."

"You think I might make a good coach?"

Decker stared at him for a few moments before looking away. He knew Mars simply wanted a little encouragement, that was all. The "old" Decker could have given it with no trouble at all. The words would have just come to him easily. The "new" Decker had to work a lot harder to get there. While his memory had become perfect, much of the rest of his brain, the parts that picked up social cues and emotions and all the little messages that most folks took for granted in understanding, were far from perfect. But when he looked back at Mars a powerful memory took hold of him. It was Melvin Mars, the Longhorns' star running back, trampling over the Buckeyes' Decker on his way to yet another glorious touchdown. That gridiron connection made the jumbled words in his head straighten out into a clear line of thought.

He said, "Let me see. One of the greatest college running backs of all time. Heisman finalist. And a guy who would've made the NFL Hall of Fame first ballot. I wonder what the hell a high school football team sees in *you*."

Mars chuckled embarrassedly. "I knew how to run the ball, Decker. I just don't know if I can teach other people how to do it."

"I think Tommy will be in good hands."

They reached the airport and Decker helped Mars with his bags. The two men faced each other in front of the terminal.

"I guess this is goodbye. At least for now."

Decker said, "For now. But don't disappear on me."

"Come on down to 'Bama and watch the Howling Cougars play. Bring Jamison and Bogart."

"That's a deal."

They looked at each other awkwardly for a moment until Mars gave a bear hug to Decker, which he tentatively returned.

Mars said, "I don't know how I can ever thank you, man. I've never had a better friend, not in my whole life."

"Quite an admission for a Longhorn to make to a Buckeye."

"You know what I mean."

Decker didn't have to hesitate this time. Keeping in his head that memory of their playing against each other he said, "I know what you mean, Melvin. And I feel the same way."

"You never know, we might hook up sometime. I'm starting to like this investigation stuff."

"You're actually good at it."

"You take care of yourself." Mars cracked a smile. "And don't get too skinny."

"Don't lose any sleep over that possibility."

They hugged once more, and then Mars picked up his bags and walked into the airport terminal.

Decker watched him go until the big man disappeared from view.

Then he climbed back into his car but didn't drive off right away.

He turned on the radio. The station was turned to NPR.

He thought back to last New Year's Eve when he had done this same thing. When he had heard a story that had changed his life and so many others'. But most importantly, the life of Melvin Mars.

He glanced once more in the direction of the terminal and dialed up the image of Melvin Mars telling him that he was the best friend he'd ever had.

He suddenly felt like he had when he'd walked onto that grid-iron on opening day. When eighty thousand people were cheering him, Amos Decker, or so it had seemed.

Except for the day he'd married his wife and the day his daughter was born, that experience had been the best he had ever felt in his whole life.

Now that amazing NFL moment had been pushed back to a distant fourth place.

After Melvin Mars being his new best friend.

ACKNOWLEDGMENTS

To Michelle, for doing everything else while I do this!

To Mitch Hoffman, for being a crackerjack editor and now an agent.

To Michael Pietsch, for leading the way so ably.

To Jamie Raab, for being a wonderful advocate.

To Lindsey Rose, Karen Torres, Anthony Goff, Bob Castillo, Michele McGonigle, Andrew Duncan, Christopher Murphy, Dave Epstein, Tracy Dowd, Brian McLendon, Andy Dodds, Matthew Ballast, Lukas Fauset, Deb Futter, Beth deGuzman, Jessica Krueger, Oscar Stern, Michele Karas, Stephanie Sirabian, and everyone at Grand Central Publishing, for all the intense labor.

To Aaron and Arleen Priest, Lucy Childs Baker, Lisa Erbach Vance, Frances Jalet-Miller, John Richmond, and Melissa Edwards, for being the absolute best. Enjoy the new digs!

To Anthony Forbes Watson, Jeremy Trevathan, Trisha Jackson, Katie James, Alex Saunders, Sara Lloyd, Jodie Mullish, Stuart Dwyer, Geoff Duffield, Jonathan Atkins, Anna Bond, Sarah Willcox, Leanne Williams, Sarah

David Baldacci

McLean, Charlotte Williams, and Neil Lang at Pan Macmillan, for making me feel so very special.

To Praveen Naidoo and his team at Pan Macmillan in Australia, for all your hard work.

To Caspian Dennis and Sandy Violette, for being such cool friends.

To Kyf Brewer and Orlagh Cassidy, for your incredible audio performances.

To Steven Maat and the entire Bruna team, for taking such great care of me in Holland.

To Bob Schule, for reading yet another manuscript.

To Roland Ottewell, for a stellar copyediting job.

To auction winner Patricia Bray, I hope you enjoyed your character. Thank you for supporting a wonderful organization.

To Kristen and Natasha, for keeping Columbus Rose on course.

And to Michelle Butler, welcome to the team.

A major young-adult novel from

DAVID BALDACCI

Welcome to Wormwood: a place where curiosity is discouraged and no one has ever left.

Until one girl, Vega Jane, discovers a map that suggests a mysterious world beyond the walls.

A land with possibilities and creatures she has never imagined.

But Vega will be forced to fight to escape. And the price of that freedom may be her life.

Turn the page to read chapter one now

A Place Called Wormwood

I WAS DOZING WHEN I heard the scream. It pierced my head like a morta round, doing terribly befuddling things to my mind, as loud and terrifying as though it were all happening right there and then.

After the sound came the vision: the blue, the colour blue. It was in a mist like a cloud on the ground. It enveloped my mind, pushing out all other thoughts, all memories. When it finally disappeared, my befuddlement cleared as well. Yet I always believed there was something of great importance that had simply not come back to me.

I suddenly sat up straight on my planks atop my tree, the vision along with my sleepiness struck clean from me. At first light, I was almost always up in my tree — a stonking, straight-to-the-sky poplar with a full towering canopy. Twenty short boards nailed to the trunk were my passage up. Eight wide, splintered boards constituted my floor when I got up there. And a stretch of waterproof cloth I had oiled myself draped over branches and tied down tight with scavenged rope represented my roof. But I was not thinking about that, for a scream was ringing in my ears and it wasn't the scream of the blue mist, which apparently existed only in my mind. This scream was coming from down below.

I hurtled to the edge of my planks and looked down to the ground from where I heard the scream once more. This cry was now joined by the baying of attack canines. The sounds shattered what had been a peaceful first light.

Wugmorts did not, as a routine matter, scream at first light or at any other time of the light or night. I scampered down my tree. My booted feet hit the dirt, and I looked first right and then left. It was difficult to tell from where the screams and baying were coming. Amid the trees, sounds bounced and echoed confusedly.

When I saw what was coming at me, I turned and started running as fast as I could. The attack canine had hurtled from out of a stand of trees, its fangs bared and its hindquarters lathered in sweat, a testament to the effort it was employing.

I was fleet of foot for a female Wug, but there was no Wug, male or female, who could outrun an attack canine. Even as I ran, I braced for the impact of its fangs on my skin and bone. But it flashed past me and redoubled its efforts, soon vanishing from my sight. I was not its prey this light.

I glanced to the left and saw between two trees a glimpse of black — a black tunic.

Council was about. The attack canines must have been unleashed by them.

But for what reason? Council, with one exception, was comprised of males, most of them older Wugs, and they kept themselves to themselves. They passed laws and regulations and other edicts that all Wugs must obey, but we all lived in peace and freedom, if not in much luxury.

Now they were out in the forest with canines chasing something. Or maybe some Wug? My next thought was that there had been an escape from Valhall, our prison. But no Wug had ever escaped from Valhall. And even if they had, I doubted members of Council would be out trying to round them up. They had other means to collect bad Wugs.

I kept running, following the baying and the racing footfalls, and soon realized that my path was taking me perilously close to

the Quag. The Quag was an impenetrable barrier that circled Wormwood like a noose. That's all there was in existence: Wormwood and the Quag. No one had ever gone through the Quag because the terrible beasts in there would murder you within slivers. And since there was nothing beyond the Quag, there had never been visitors to Wormwood.

I neared the edge of this most terrible place that Wugs were repeatedly warned from the age of a very young to avoid. I slowed and then stopped a few yards from where the Quag began. My heart was pounding and my lungs bursting, not simply from my running but from being this close to a place that held only death for those stupid enough to stray inside.

The baying had now ceased, as had the sounds of the footfalls. I looked to the left and glimpsed canines and Council members staring into the depths of the Quag. I could not see their faces, but I imagined them to be as full of fear as was mine. Even attack canines wanted no part of the Quag.

I let out one more long breath and that's when a sound to my right reached me. I looked in that direction and in a stunning moment realized that I was seeing someone disappear into the tangled vines and twisted trees that rose up like a barricade around the perimeter of the Quag. And it was a Wug I knew well.

I looked to my left to see if any of Council or the canines had caught sight of this, but it didn't appear they had. I turned back, but the image was now gone. I wondered if I had simply imagined it. No Wug would voluntarily venture into that awful place.

When something touched me on the arm, I nearly screamed.

4

As it was, I just about collapsed to the ground, but the thing, now revealed to be a hand, kept me upright.

"Vega Jane? It is Vega Jane, isn't it?"

I turned to look up into the blunt features of Jurik Krone. He was tall, strong, forty-five sessions old and a fast-rising member of Council.

"I'm Vega Jane," I managed to say.

"What are you doing here?" he asked. His tone was not stern, simply questioning, but there was a certain repressed hostility in his eyes.

"I was in my tree before going to Stacks. I heard a scream and saw the canines. I saw Wugs in black tunics running, so I . . . I ran too."

Krone nodded at this. "Did you see anything else?" he asked. "Other than the black tunics and canines?"

I peered at the spot where I had seen a Wug run into the Quag. "I saw the Quag."

His fingers gripped my shoulder more tightly. "Is that all? Nothing else?"

I tried to keep calm. The image of the Wug's face before he fled into the Quag slammed into me like a spear of skylight. "That's all."

His fingers released and he stepped back. I took him in fully. His black tunic rode well on his broad shoulders and thick arms.

"What were you chasing?" I asked.

"It's Council business, Vega," he replied sharply. "Please be on your way. It is not safe to be this close to the Quag. Head back

5

towards Wormwood. Now. It is for your own good."

He turned and walked off, leaving me breathless and shaking. I took one more look at the Quag and then raced back in the direction of my tree.

I scampered up the boards and settled myself once more on the planks, out of breath and my head filled with the most dreadful thoughts.

~

"WO-WO-WOTCHA, VE-VE-VEGA JANE?"

The voice coming from below belonged to my friend. His name was Daniel Delphia, but to me he was simply Delph. He always called me Vega Jane, as though both names were my given one. Everyone else simply called me Vega, when they bothered to call me anything at all.

"Delph?" I said. "Up here."

I heard him scampering up the short boards. I was very nearly twenty yards up. I was also fourteen sessions old, going on a lot older. I was also female.

Being fourteen and female was frowned on here in Wormwood, the village where we both lived. It's never been clear to me why. But I liked being young. And I liked being female.

I was apparently in the minority on that.

Wormwood was a village full of Wugmorts — Wugs for short. The term *village* suggested a communal spirit that just wasn't present here. I tried to lend a helping hand from time to time, but I picked my causes carefully. Some Wugs had neither trust nor compassion. I tried to avoid them. Sometimes it was

6

hard, because they had a tendency to get in my face.

Delph's head poked over the boards. He was much taller than me, and I was tall for a female, over five feet nine inches. I was still growing, because all the Janes were late bloomers. My grandfather Virgil, it was said, grew four inches more when he was twenty. And forty sessions later came his Event and his height became meaningless because there was nothing left of him.

Delph was about six and a half feet tall with shoulders that spread like the leafy cap of my poplar. He was sixteen sessions old with a long mane of black hair that appeared mostly yellowish white because of the dust he did not bother to wash away. He worked at the Mill, lifting huge sacks of flour, so more dust would just take its place. He had a wide, shallow forehead, full lips, and eyes that were as dark as his hair without the dust. They looked like twin holes in his head. I think it would be fascinating to see what went on in Delph's mind. And, I had to admit, his eyes were beautiful. I sometimes went all willy when he looked at me.

He did not qualify to work at Stacks, where some creativity was required. I have never seen Delph create anything except confusion. His mind came and went like rain bursts. It had done so ever since he was six sessions old. No one knew what had happened to him, or if they did, they never shared it with me. I believed that Delph remembered it. And it had done something to his head. It obviously wasn't an Event, because there would be nothing left of him. But it might be a near peer. And yet sometimes Delph said things that made me believe there was far more going on in his mind than most Wugs thought.

If things were a bit off with Delph inside his head, there was nothing wrong with the outside of him. He was handsome, to be sure. Though he never seemed to notice, I had seen many a female giving him the "look" as he passed by. A snog is what they wanted, I'm sure. But Delph always kept moving. And his broad shoulders and long muscled arms and legs gave him a strength that virtually no other Wug could match.

Delph settled next to me, his legs crossed at bony ankles and dangling over the edge of the splintered boards. There was barely enough space for the two of us here. But Delph liked to come up my tree. He didn't have many other places to go.

I pushed my long, dark straggly hair out of my eyes and focused on a dirt spot on my thin arm. I didn't rub it away because I had lots of dirt spots. And like Delph's Mill dust, what would be the point? My life was full of dirt.

"Delph, did you hear all that?"

He looked at me. "H-hear wh-what?"

"The attack canines and the screaming?"

He looked at me like I was wonky. "Y-you O-OK, Ve-Vega Jane?"

I tried again. "Council was out with attack canines chasing something." I wanted to say chasing *someone*, but I decided to keep that to myself. "They were down near the Quag."

He shivered at the name, as I knew he would.

"Qu-Qu-Qu —" He took a shuddering breath and said simply, "Bad."

I decided to change the subject. "Have you eaten?" I asked

Delph. Hunger was like a painful, festering wound. When you had it, you could think of nothing else.

Delph shook his head no.

I pulled out a small tin box constituting my portable larder that I carried with me. Inside was a wedge of goat's cheese and two boiled eggs, a chunk of fried bread and some salt and pepper I kept in small pewter thumbs of my own making. We used lots of pepper in Wormwood, especially in our broths. Pepper cured lots of ills, like the taste of bad meat and spoiled vegetables. There had also been a sweet pickle, but I had eaten it already.

I handed him the box. It was intended for my first meal, but I was not so big as Delph. He needed lots of wood in his fire, as they said around here. I would eat at some point. I was good at pacing myself. Delph did not pace. Delph just did. I considered it one of his most endearing qualities.

He sprinkled salt and pepper on the eggs, cheese and bread, and then wolfed them down in one elongated swallow. I heard his belly rumble as the foodstuffs dropped into what had been an empty cavern.

"Better?" I asked.

"B-better," he mumbled contentedly. "Thanks, Ve-Vega Jane."

I rubbed sleep from my eyes. I had been told that my eyes were the colour of the sky. But other times, when the clouds covered the heavens, they could look quite silver, as though I were absorbing the colours from above. It was the only change that was ever likely to happen to me.

"Go-going t-t-to see your mum and dad this light?" asked Delph.

I shot him a glance. "Yes."

"Ca-can I c-come t-too?"

"Of course, Delph. We can meet you there after Stacks."

He nodded, mumbled the word *Mill*, rose and scrambled down the short boards to the ground.

I followed him, heading on to Stacks, where I worked making pretty things. In Wormwood, it was a good idea to keep moving.

And so I did.

But I did so in a different way this light. I did so with the image of someone running into the Quag, when that was impossible because it meant death. And so I convinced myself that I had not seen what I thought I had.

Yet not many slivers would pass before I realized that my eyesight had been perfect. And my life in Wormwood, to the extent I had one, would never be the same.

Coming November 2016
The fourth title in the John Puller series

No Man's Land

John Puller's mother disappeared nearly thirty years ago. Despite an intensive search and investigation, she was never seen again. But new allegations have come to light suggesting that Puller's father – now suffering from dementia and living in a VA hospital – may have murdered his wife.

Puller is officially barred from working on the case – and faces a potential court martial if he disobeys orders – but he knows he can't sit this investigation out. When intelligence operative Veronica Knox turns up, Puller realizes that there is far more to this case than he had originally thought. Puller will stop at nothing to discover the truth about what happened to his mother . . . even if it means proving that his father is a killer.

DAVID BALDACCI
The Guilty

When Special Agent Will Robie gets the call to make his first visit home since he was a teenager, it's because his father, the local judge, has been arrested for murdering a man who came before him in court.

The small, remote Bayou town hasn't changed and its residents remember Robie as a wild sports star and girl magnet. He left a lot of hearts broken, and a lot of people angry.

Will and his father, Dan, are estranged, and his mother left years ago. When he visits Dan in jail, he finds that time hasn't healed old wounds. There's too much bad blood between the men, and although Will feels no good will come of staying around, he is persuaded to confront his demons by fellow agent Jessica Reel.

But then another murder changes everything, and stone-cold killer Robie will finally have to come to grips with his toughest assignment of all. His family.

DAVID BALDACCI
Memory Man

His family was murdered.
The hunt for the killer begins.

Amos Decker would forever remember all three of their violent deaths in the most paralyzing shade of blue. It would cut into him at unpredictable moments, like a gutting knife made of colored light. He would never be free from it.

When Amos Decker returned home eighteen months ago to find the bodies of his wife and only daughter, he didn't think he could carry on living. Overwhelmed with grief, he saw his life spiral out of control, losing his job as a detective, his house and his self-respect. But when his former partner in the police, Mary Lancaster, visits to tell him that someone has confessed to the murder of his family, he knows he owes it to his wife and child to seek justice for them.

As Decker comes to terms with the news, tragedy strikes at the local school. Thirteen teenagers are gunned down, and the killer is at large. Following the serious brain injury Amos suffered as a professional footballer, he gained a remarkable gift – and the police believe that this unusual skill will assist in the hunt for the killer.

**Want to find out about the latest
BALDACCI NOVEL before anyone else?**

**Want to meet David at
an event or book signing?**

For all the latest news, signings, events,
extracts and competitions, sign up to the

DAVID BALDACCI
MONTHLY NEWSLETTER

Visit panmacmillan.com/author/davidbaldacci

 /writer.david.baldacci   /davidbaldacci